D0147812

THE BLACK MASK LIBRARY

THE EARLY YEARS (1920–26)

coming soon

THE SHAW YEARS (1926–36)

Blood on the Curb *by Joseph T. Shaw*

Boomerang Dice: The Complete Black Mask Cases of Johnny Hi Gear *by Stewart Sterling*

Dead Evidence: The Complete Black Mask Cases of Harrigan *by Ed Lybeck*

THE LATER YEARS (1936–51)

Dead and Done For: The Complete Black Mask Cases of Cellini Smith *by Robert Reeves*

Let the Dead Alone: The Complete Black Mask Cases of Luther McGavock *by Merle Constiner*

Murder Costs Money: The Complete Black Mask Cases of Rex Sackler *by D.L. Champion*

MURDER COSTS MONEY

The Complete

Cases of Rex Sackler

1939–41

D.L. CHAMPION

introduction by Ed Hulse

illustrations by Peter Kuhlhoff

cover by Rafael de Soto

BLACK MASK
2020

Texts and illustrations © 2020 Steeger Properties, LLC. All rights reserved. Published by Black Mask.

BLACK MASK® is a registered trademark of Steeger Properties, LLC. "Rex Sackler" is a trademark of Steeger Properties, LLC. Authorized and produced under license.

"Introduction" appears here for the first time. Copyright © 2020 by Ed Hulse. All rights reserved.

"Murder Costs Money" originally appeared in the July 1, 1939 issue of *Detective Fiction Weekly* magazine (Vol. 129, No. 3). Copyright © 1939 by The Red Star News Company. Copyright renewed © 1966 and assigned to Steeger Properties, LLC. All rights reserved.

"Death Dresses for Dinner" originally appeared in the December 2, 1939 issue of *Detective Fiction Weekly* magazine (Vol. 133, No. 1). Copyright © 1939 by The Red Star News Company. Copyright renewed © 1967 and assigned to Steeger Properties, LLC. All rights reserved.

"Murder in the Mail" originally appeared in the May 11, 1940 issue of *Detective Fiction Weekly* magazine (Vol. 136, No. 6). Copyright © 1939 by The Red Star News Company. Copyright renewed © 1967 and assigned to Steeger Properties, LLC. All rights reserved.

"Death Stops Payment" originally appeared in the July 1940 issue of *Black Mask* magazine (Vol. 23, No. 3). Copyright © 1940 by Popular Publications, Inc. Copyright renewed © 1967 and assigned to Steeger Properties, LLC. All rights reserved.

"Money to Burn" originally appeared in the October 1940 issue of *Black Mask* magazine (Vol. 23, No. 6). Copyright © 1940 by Popular Publications, Inc. Copyright renewed © 1967 and assigned to Steeger Properties, LLC. All rights reserved.

"Vacation with Pay" originally appeared in the April 1941 issue of *Black Mask* magazine (Vol. 23, No. 12). Copyright © 1941 by Popular Publications, Inc. Copyright renewed © 1968 and assigned to Steeger Properties, LLC. All rights reserved.

"Split Fee" originally appeared in the June 1941 issue of *Black Mask* magazine (Vol. 24, No. 2). Copyright © 1941 by Popular Publications, Inc. Copyright renewed © 1968 and assigned to Steeger Properties, LLC. All rights reserved.

"Pick Up the Marbles!" originally appeared in the October 1941 issue of *Black Mask* magazine (Vol. 24, No. 6). Copyright © 1941 by Popular Publications, Inc. Copyright renewed © 1968 and assigned to Steeger Properties, LLC. All rights reserved.

No part of this book may be reproduced or utilized in any form or by any means, electronic or mechanical, without permission in writing from the publisher.

Visit STEEGERBOOKS.COM for more books like this.

Table of Contents

Introducing the Parsimonious
Prince of Penny-Pinchers

D.L. Champion's Rex Sackler

THE LEGENDARY PULP magazine *Black Mask* created the vogue for hard-boiled crime fiction and was home to many memorable detectives, beginning with Carroll John Daly's Race Williams and including Dashiell Hammett's Sam Spade and the Continental Op, to name just a few. Among the undeservedly forgotten is Rex Sackler, the skinflint shamus who "could squeeze a nickel till the buffalo cried uncle" and whose "affection for money made Abelard's love for Heloise a tawdry and unimportant thing." This greedy gumshoe plied his trade in more than two dozen frequently hilarious novelettes published in *Black Mask* during the 1940s. They are long overdue for reprinting and we all can be grateful to this publisher for undertaking to do so, beginning with this volume.

Sackler's creator was D'Arcy Lyndon Champion (1902–68), an Australian native who emigrated to the United States at an early age and was both a soldier and a sailor before finding his true calling as a fiction writer at the tail end of the Roaring Twenties. His first sales were made to aviation pulps *(Flight, Flying Aces)* and gang pulps *(Gangster Stories, Racketeer Stories, Gun Moll Magazine)* under the pen names Tom Champion and Jack D'Arcy. Using the latter pseudonym he placed yarns in the Macfadden pulp *Ghost Stories* and, beginning in late 1931, the "Thrilling" pulp line edited by Leo Margulies and published by Ned Pines. Champion's first notable series, nine connected novelettes later linked between hard covers as *Alias Mr. Death*, appeared in consecutive 1932 issues of *Thrilling Detective*. These floridly melodramatic tales were bylined to G. Wayman Jones, a Thrilling Group house name. They chronicled the exploits of young playboy James Quincy Gilmore, who adopted the persona of Mr. Death to wreak vengeance on nine members of the Murder Club, a secret society behind the slaying of his father.

Champion's work on this well-received series won him the coveted job of writing novel-length adventures built around the Phantom Detective, a mysterious crime fighter whose eponymous magazine was launched by Pines in February 1933 to compete with Street & Smith's phenomenally successful *Shadow Magazine*, the first single-character pulp. Initially the Phantom yarns, like those featuring Mr. Death, were credited to G. Wayman Jones; after eight issues their authorship was attributed to one Robert Wallace, another house name.

Perhaps weary of cranking out a book-length novel every month, Champion left *The Phantom Detective* in March 1935. Obviously a favorite of Thrilling Group editorial director Margulies, he produced a slew of short stories and novelettes over the next couple years for other Pines-published sheets, including *G-Men*, *Sky Fighters*, *Thrilling Mystery*, *Thrilling Adventures*, and *Popular Detective*. In late 1937 he placed two stories with *Collier's*—the first of his relatively few sales to the slicks.

Champion shortly thereafter cracked such Munsey pulps as *Double Detective* and *Detective Fiction Weekly*, and was welcomed with open arms at Popular Publications' prestigious *Dime Detective,* which had lured away many of *Black Mask's* top contributors (including Raymond Chandler) with higher word rates and more editorial flexibility. For this pulp Champion, using his own name, created Inspector Allhoff, a brilliant but sadistic police detective who became psychologically unbalanced after losing his legs in a friendly-fire incident. The Allhoff series, beginning with "Footprints on a Brain" (July 1938), established Champion as one of the rare pulpsters whose character-delineation skills equalled his ability to invent elaborate plots. It endeared him to editor Kenneth S. White, at whose direction *Dime Detective* had gradually distanced itself from the ultra-hard-boiled style favored by *Black Mask's* legendary Captain Joseph T. Shaw. White was the genre's most vocal proponent of quirky series characters and stories leavened with sardonic humor, and during his tenure Popular's top-selling crime pulp featured generous amounts of both.

("Cap" Shaw's reluctance to deviate from *Black Mask's* well-established formula ultimately atrophied the magazine's circulation and cost him its editorship. His successor, Fanny Ellsworth, made a valiant effort to broaden *Mask's* appeal, but when sales stubbornly refused to rise, publisher Eltinge Warner in 1940 reluctantly sold the sheet to Popular Publications, which immediately installed as its new editor... Ken White.)

Oddly, D.L. Champion's major contribution to the screwball school of detective fiction originally took form in Munsey's *Detective Fiction Weekly.* Rex Sackler and his right-hand man Joey Graham (narrator of the series) were introduced in "Murder Costs Money," lead novelette in the July 1, 1939 issue.

Champion reveals his protagonist's obsession with money in the second sentence: "Sackler had taken his bankbooks and the ledger from the safe and shut himself in the private office to gloat over his riches,"Joey explains. Then the leg man drops a clue about his own predilections: "When the telephone rang I hoped it was someone in search of a drinking companion. It wasn't." A few paragraphs down, conversing by phone with one of the city's ward heelers, he says, "Sackler's given strict orders he's not to be disturbed. He's adding his bank balance. And when Sackler's counting money he can't be disturbed by any crummy politician."

Only 300 words into the saga Champion has established not only the theme but also the tone of the series. We know that Sackler worships money and that Joey is a wise guy who's fond of liquor and doesn't suffer fools gladly. Those basic character traits will never change; indeed, they'll be reinforced in each successive entry.

On the next page the boss is described as having black eyes and a long corvine (like a raven or hawk) nose. Speaking through Joey, Champion adds that "his dark face made him look like a pawnbroker bent over his books." Rex's first words to his assistant upon being interrupted give the reader more insight into Graham: "I pay you fifty bucks a week because of a sledgehammer right and a certain adeptness with a thirty-eight. I expect little from you intellectually. Parenthetically, I may remark, I get it."

Before the first chapter has ended we learn that Sackler was an efficient police detective who left the department three years earlier to become a private dick, reasoning that his "superior intellect" would make him tops in the game and earn him a small fortune. Apparently he has already done quite well and considerably burnished his reputation by the time we meet him in this novelette. A gangster named Benny Green strolls into Rex's office and pays him $10,000 to lay off a case he hasn't been hired to investigate: the murder of notorious Wall Street financier George Lamar, known to be writing a tell-all book expected to name every crooked banker, broker, politician, and racketeer in town. But with Lamar having left behind an estate worth some three million bucks, Sackler smells opportunity. With typical audacity he builds an almost air-tight case against one suspect, then offers to represent the man for a $15,000 fee.

Like many detective-story writers who toiled in the pulps, Champion concocted ingenious plots that generally seemed credible but seldom held up to close scrutiny. Rex Sackler's deductions—justified at considerable length in the last chapter of "Murder Costs Money"—have a basis of roughly 20 percent in fact and 80 percent in guesswork. And his method of exposing one suspect's culpability, while clever enough in concept, wouldn't have passed muster in any court in the land.

Three more installments of the Sackler series graced the pages of *Detective Fiction Weekly* before Champion moved it to Popular Publications, where Ken White elected to feature the character in his second issue of *Black Mask*. "Death Stops Payment" (July 1940) finds Joey in a good mood as the story opens. It's pay day and he knows the boss will reluctantly fork over fifty bucks. ("And Rex Sackler parting with money was as gay and light-hearted as Romeo taking his leave of Juliet.") Arriving in the office, he grins at Sackler and scratches the palm of his outstretched left hand. "Joey," Rex sighs, "you're a money grubber. A beaten slave of Mammon. Your job, to you, is a matter of dollars. Service, you know nothing of. Loyalty is beyond your limited ken. The noble pleasure of sheer altruism is something your material mind cannot grasp."

Needless to say, the leg man invariably shrugs off such hypocritical sermons, coming as they do from a skinflint employer who, in Joey's words, "could smell a nickel before it had left the mint."

As you've probably gathered, it wasn't elaborate displays of ratiocination that made the Sackler series popular. (Which is not to take anything away from the author's ability to present baffling mysteries.) It was the byplay between Rex and Joey, and the increasingly pointed observations made about the former by the latter in his narration. Like, for example, this barb from "Money to Burn" *(Black Mask,* October 1940): "Sackler spent money with all the prodigal abandon of a dying anemic handing out goblets of blood." Champion kept refining the image of his pecunious protagonist. Initially portrayed as merely greedy, Sackler over time evolved into a tightwad of epic proportions. Reading the stories in chronological order, one may well suspect the author spent less time devising cunning murder plots than he did descriptive passages such as this lulu from "Vacation With Pay" *(Black Mask,* April 1941):

[Sackler] rolled his own cigarettes, thus depriving the federal government of six cents in taxes each day. He wore twenty-dollar suits until they literally rotted upon his frame. His hat was a blob of shapeless felt, still stained from the rain that fell during Harding's inauguration. And though he denied it vehemently, I had more than once voiced my suspicion that he laundered his own socks and underwear each night before he went to bed in his six-dollar-a-week room.

Rex Sackler's affection for money was a beautiful thing. His savings, the total of which resembled several telephone numbers laid end to end, were scattered about in scores of Postal Savings Accounts. After 1929, he gambled with no banks.

Joey's loyalty to his boss is the series' most enduring mystery. He seems perpetually amused by Sackler's continual efforts to reclaim the meager salary paid him every Wednesday—efforts that occasionally involve crap games with loaded dice and poker games with marked decks. And he takes muted offense to Rex's constant rebuffs of his pleas for a raise. In the series opener, "Murder Costs Money," Sackler wears "an expression of acute pain" on his face while talking the leg man out of a ten-dollar raise: "Joey... let's be reasonable. In any civilized state, income would be computed on a basis of need. Now, Joey, you're not a cultured animal. You don't buy books, paintings, or go to concerts. You're no epicure and, sartorially, a twenty-two-fifty suit is your idea of big stuff. For one of your simple, elementary tastes, fifty dollars a week is ample. Even munificent."

As the series progresses Sackler contrives ever more wily methods of separating clients from their money—methods that are ethically questionable but which always stop short of flagrant illegality. Notwithstanding their ongoing quarrels over his salary, Joey remains faithful to Rex, despite regularly bestowing upon his boss such uncomplimentary nicknames as "the Shylock of the shamuses" and "the parsimonious prince of penny-pinchers."

Under Ken White's editorship *Black Mask*, like *Dime Detective*, favored recurring characters; it was a rare issue that didn't contain at least three installments of popular series. White published the final pulp exploits of Cap Shaw holdovers such as Erle Stanley Gardner's Ed Jenkins and George Harmon Coxe's Flashgun Casey. He occasionally printed yarns featuring sleuths who were already famous before they graced rough-paper magazines, such as The Saint and Michael Shayne. In addition to Rex Sackler, favorite series characters during White's tenure included Dale Clark's Mike O'Hanna, house dick in a swanky California resort hotel; C.P. Donnell, Jr.'s Walter "Doc" Rennie, psychiatrist-detective and Colonel in the Army Medical Corps; Julius Long's Ben Corbett, two-fisted investigator for ambitious District Attorney Burt Keever; and Merle Constiner's Luther McGavock, chief operative for a Memphis detective agency whose cases frequently took him to sleepy southern hamlets. Of this quartet only O'Hanna logged more *Black Mask* appearances than Sackler, the house dick solving 28 cases to Rex's 26.

In keeping with his relentless adherence to the formula established by Dashiell Hammett, Cap Shaw seldom allowed humor with his homicides. Ken White, by contrast, allowed his contributors more leeway in this regard and often attached punny titles to their stories (i.e., "You're the Crime in My Coffin"). Predictably, Champion's included references to money: "A Corpse Means Cash," "Death for a Dollar" (that one was used twice), "Infernal Revenue," "Killer, Can You Spare a Dime?", and "Money to Burn," to name a few.

The Sackler series drew to a close with the second "Death for a Dollar," published in the January 1950 *Black Mask*. By this time Ken White had vacated the editor's chair, reportedly being replaced by Popular Publications head man Harry Steeger (although no editor was named on the contents page).

Rex and Joey went out on a relatively high note; "Dollar" might have been a little stale by comparison to earlier install- ments, but it still offered more entertainment value than the issue's other stories. Rough-paper magazines were slowly dying off and Champion, like so many of his contemporaries, must have seen the end coming. The venerable *Black Mask* limped along until July 1951, reduced in its latter days to publishing reprints. Popular's *Dime Detective* lasted another two years, also mixing retreads with newly written stories. Its penulti- mate issue, June 1953, featured Champion's final appearance a Popular pulp: "Toast the Poison Princess!", originally published in a 1945 issue of *Detective Tales*.

Murder Costs Money

*The electric chair beckoned, and it was up to Rex
Sackler to decide who should accept its grisly embrace*

1

Strictly the Oil

IT WAS A dull afternoon. Sackler had taken his bankbooks and the ledger from the safe and shut himself in the private office to gloat over his riches. I sat in the reception room grappling with the crossword puzzle in the *Tribune*. When the telephone rang I hoped it was someone in search of a drinking companion. It wasn't.

"Hi," said a hearty voice in my ear. "This is Reynolds. How's my old pal, Joey?"

That was strictly the oil. I wasn't his old pal and he knew it. Reynolds was an old-line politician, a direct descendant of Tweed, who had entirely too much influence both for my liking and that of the new city administration. He'd been in Sackler's hair more than once, too.

"I'm thirsty," I told him. "But you didn't call to find that out."

"Well," he said, "is Sackler there?"

"Yes."

"Put him on, Joey."

"No," I said.

There was a long silence. Then he tried again.

"Listen, pal. I want to talk to Sackler. It's important. Put him on."

"*You* listen," I told him. "Sackler's given strict orders he's not to be disturbed. He's adding his bank balance. And when Sackler's counting money he can't be disturbed by any crummy politician."

"Who's going to pay me my fee now?"
Sackler demanded.

I expected he'd get sore at that. But he didn't. After a pause, he said, "Joey, Lammer's dead."

"Never heard of him."

"Well," said Reynolds, "Sackler has."

There was more silence. I was getting thirstier and more bored.

"I realize," I told him, "that in political circles it is customary to approach a given fact by a wordy and circuitous route. But if you'll come promptly to the point, just this once, I promise never to tell a soul."

"Ha, ha!"

The phoniest laugh I ever heard came over the wire.

"Very good, Joey," he said with that false geniality peculiar to ward leaders. "Now look. You give Sackler this message. Tell him to lay off the Lammer case."

"He's not on it."

"All right, Joey," he said impatiently. "All right. But tell him to lay off anyway. It'll be worth his while. Besides the renewal on his shamus license is due soon. I can sort of help there."

"Is that all?"

"That's all, pal. Be sure to give him the message."

I hung up wondering what he was talking about. I decided to break in on Sackler's privacy and see if he could make it any clearer. I got up, opened the door of the inner office and stood upon the threshold.

REX SACKLER BENT over his desk, a pencil in his hand. Three open bankbooks lay on the blotter before him. A huge ledger was at his right elbow. There was a greedy gleam in his black eyes. His long corvine nose, his dark face made him look like a pawnbroker bent over his books.

"Hey," I said. "Lammer's dead."

Sackler sighed. He put down his pencil, and with the air of a man sorely tried, he looked up.

"Joey," he said wearily, "I pay you fifty bucks a week because of a sledgehammer right and a certain adeptness with a thirty-eight. I expect little from you intellectually. Parenthetically, I may remark, I get it. I do not tell you *why* I want to be alone. That would be beyond the conception of a gregarious extrovert like yourself. I tell you in one-syllable English words that I am not to be disturbed. I expect you to take it on faith. Besides, who *is* Lammer?"

He picked up his pencil again and bent over his books. I winked at myself in the mirror behind the desk and said, "Reynolds said you'd know."

That interested him. He looked up quickly. "Reynolds?"

"Reynolds," I told him. "He said lay off the case if it's offered you. He said you'd have trouble with your license if you didn't."

Now he leaned back in his chair and pushed the books away. There was a frown on his dark brow. He took a package of cigarettes—the ten cent kind—from his pocket and lit one. His ebony eyes glowed thoughtfully.

"Reynolds," he said slowly. "Joey, I smell money."

No one in the world had a better nose for it. Sackler possessed a baffling instinct where a dollar was concerned. He had never loved any woman as he loved those figures in his bankbooks. So if Rex Sackler smelled money now, it was already earmarked with his name. Not that it made any difference to me. I could get more than fifty bucks a week out of him if I put a gun against his chest.

Sackler cocked his head suddenly like a terrier. His thin lips curved into a smile.

"There it is, Joey," he said. "Bring it in."

"Bring what in?" I asked blankly.

"The money. The client. The guy who just came in."

I stared at him. I had heard absolutely nothing but I knew that his unique ears had caught the opening of the outer door. Even after three years association Rex Sackler constantly surprised me.

"All right," he said impatiently. "Bring it in. We're going to get a fee, Joey."

"*We?*" I said sarcastically. Then I went out to the reception room.

When I got there I decided that for once Sackler was wrong. It wasn't a client. It was Benny Green.

"Hi, Benny," I said. "How's the murder business?"

He didn't like that. Benny was the town's number one racketeer. He had never been indicted but every copper on the force knew he'd killed more men than the State Executioner.

"Don't be a wise guy," he said, hardly moving his lips. "Where's Sackler?"

"Inside," I told him. "He's expecting you."

He opened his eyes wide at that but didn't say anything. He walked into the private office. I followed him. I knew Sackler was as surprised to see him as I was. But it was part of the Sackler code never to register astonishment. He crushed out the last millimeter of his cigarette and nodded.

"Hello, Benny."

Benny nodded back. He took an afternoon paper from his pocket.

"Lammer's dead," he announced.

Sackler ran a white well-manicured hand through his thick black hair. "For the love of Pete," he said, "who *is* Lammer?"

Benny laid the afternoon paper on Sackler's desk. Sackler looked down at the front page, sighed and raised his eyes to the ceiling.

"Lammer!" he said to some invisible private deity. "Don't they permit politicians and gangsters in the grade schools? Lammer's dead, they tell me. L-a-m-a-r. It's *Lamar*, you illiterates! Of course I know who *he* is. Even Joey knows."

SACKLER WAS ANNOYED and I grinned. He couldn't tie this on me. After all, I'd only repeated Reynolds' message. Sure, I knew who George Lamar was. And the fact of his death was not surprising. Lamar had taken a fortune out of

Wall Street some years ago. Then, in a sudden frenzy of righteousness and reform had turned upon his former associates.

He had taken a portable typewriter with him and retired to a secluded spot in Long Island. In the days spent acquiring his fortune he had accumulated a great deal of inside stuff. He not only knew the name of every crooked broker, every grafting politician in town; he also knew the dates and places. He had published two books mentioning them.

Those books had wrecked the last administration, had prompted the Securities Exchange Commission to delve into the affairs of a dozen supposed pillars of the community. If Lamar had been killed there were at least half a hundred suspects all supplied with quite reasonable motives.

Sackler looked up from the paper.

"So," he said, "Lamar's servant goes to work this morning and finds the old guy with a bullet in his brain. Did you do it, Benny?"

Benny passed a difficult ten seconds assuming an expression of outraged innocence.

"Me?" he said, wounded to the quick. "Why, I wouldn't do a thing like that, Rex. I ain't no angel. Maybe I done some wrong things in my life. But murder—" He clucked like a shocked old woman. Then he added in his natural voice, "Besides, I got an alibi."

"What do you want me to do?" said Sackler. "Break down the alibi?"

"No, no," said Benny, horrified. "I just dropped in to talk to you private."

As he uttered the last word he glanced significantly at me.

"No," said Sackler. "Joey stays here. Besides being my right arm he makes an invaluable witness in the event of a misunderstanding later on."

Benny thought that over for a minute, sighed and dropped into the chair beside Sackler's desk.

"All right," he said. "Sackler, three years ago you quit the police department. You left a sure pension to go into business for yourself. Why?"

Sackler lit another ten cent cigarette.

"I'll tell you, Benny," he said oratorically. "First, the department was riddled with politics. An efficient copper didn't have a chance. Second, there was a certain envy of my superior intellect. I arrived at the conclusion that I could best serve public interest by working alone. It was my duty to cut loose in order to be able to combat crime more efficiently, to carry on the perennial battle on the side of law and order."

He said this with a completely straight face. I stared at him. Then, Benny said quietly, "Sure. But why did you quit the department?"

Sackler had the grace to grin. "All right," he said. "Dough. I wanted to make dough. Piles and piles of it. Satisfied?"

"Yeah," said Benny. "That's what I figured."

He plunged a hand into the breast pocket of his Klassy-Kut green suit and withdrew a wallet. He opened it. He took out a fist full of bills and laid them on Sackler's desk. I stared, popeyed. I'd never seen so much money in all my life.

Sackler's eyes took on that morbid gleam customary when he contemplated money. He drew his breath in slowly, making a soft sibilant sound. He fingered the bills like a woman handling fine silk. His voice was thick as he spoke. Money always affected him like that.

"What's this, Benny?"

"Ten G's. It's your fee."

RELUCTANTLY SACKLER TOOK his eyes from the money and looked at Benny. "For what, Benny?"

"Lay off the Lamar murder case."

"No one's asked me to take it."

"They will," said Benny. "For that dough you say no. Get it?"

I stood by my own desk staring out the window into the canyon that was lower Broadway. I was cradled in disgust and envy. Here was I, two suits of clothes to my name, drinking cheap blended whiskey while I craved Scotch; collecting a lousy fifty bucks a week. And Sackler, who spent his days sitting at his desk and insulting me, had just had ten grand tossed into his lap. For nothing.

I heard him say in a slow thoughtful voice, "Well, I don't know, Benny."

I swung around, feeling I'd undergone an electric shock. Sackler refusing money? Sackler peering into the mouth of a gift horse? Benny too, stared at him in disbelief.

He said, "And you're getting it for nothing!"

"I know," said Sackler absently. He turned his gaze back to the pile of bills on the desk. I told myself that if Sackler gave that money back I'd never again sneer at people who believed in fairies.

"I'll keep this dough, Benny," continued Sackler, and I breathed again. The world was back to normal now. "But the deal's not closed for forty-eight hours. I reserve the right to return this dough within that time, to act as a free agent."

Bluff, I told myself. He hadn't the slightest idea of returning it. He was merely impressing Benny.

"But," said Benny. "I don't see—"

"We'll do it my way," said Sackler.

Benny sighed again. "All right," he said. "Okay with me."

I could tell from his expression that he had as little doubt as I that Sackler would keep the dough. Benny got out of the chair, nodded an adieu and left the office.

Sackler's swivel chair creaked as he leaned back. He looked as smug as Dewey with a new indictment. He picked the bills up from the desk and waved them at me. Then he put them in a drawer and locked it.

"There," he said with vast satisfaction. "I told you I smelled money."

I drew a deep breath and spoke my mind.

"Sackler," I said, "when I took this job three years ago you implied that regular salary raises would go along with it. I'm still waiting for the first one. Since you've just picked up ten G's with less trouble than the Internal Revenue Bureau, I herewith officially request that an extra ten dollar bill be included in the weekly envelope from here on in."

There was an expression of acute pain on Sackler's face.

"Joey," he said, "let's be reasonable. In any civilized state income would be computed on a basis of need. Now, Joey, you're not a cultured animal. You don't buy books, paintings, or go to concerts. You're no epicure and, sartorially, a twenty-two fifty suit is your idea of big stuff. For one of your simple, elementary tastes, fifty dollars a week is ample. Even munificent."

He watched me anxiously, then added, "You see my point, Joey?"

"I do not," I said firmly. "I see only that the Scotch have been maligned. That, beside you, a pawnbroker is a genial sucker. That—"

I WAS GROPING for another comparison when a tall, well dressed girl walked into the office. Since Benny had left the outer door wide open, she entered without knocking. She was dark and striking. She was clad in a black suit which even my untutored eye recognized as expensive. On her wrist was a bracelet of the kind they offer rewards for.

She glanced from me to Sackler and said, questioningly, "Mr. Sackler?"

Sackler stood up, bowed and admitted his identity. She nodded and sat down in the chair at the side of his desk. She remained there for a silent moment nervously twisting a handkerchief in her hands.

"My name's Jane Winthrop," she announced. "I am—was, rather—George Lamar's secretary."

Sackler shot a swift glance at me and winked. Then he turned to the girl and assumed his professional manner.

"Yes, Miss Winthrop," he said crisply.

"Mr. Sackler," she said earnestly, "I have heard that you are almost infallible." She stopped, wiped her eyes with the handkerchief and swallowed. She continued in a tight dry voice: "I want you to find out who murdered George Lamar."

Sackler looked at her keenly. "Why?" he said.

"Why?" she repeated, and her voice rose to almost hysterical crescendo. "Why?" She stared at him with wide blazing eyes. There was savagery and bitterness in her tone as she continued. "So that the murderer shall be condemned and executed; so that he shall die as his victim died!"

Her blazing tone implied that she was less interested in

justice than in personal revenge. Sackler kept his eyes upon her and nodded thoughtfully. He appeared quite pleased with himself. The girl opened her bag and fumbled in its depths.

"I suppose it's customary to offer you a retainer," she said.

She took a bill from her bag and laid it on the desk. I craned my neck and saw it was a twenty. I stifled a grin. Sackler, having been given ten grand to lay off the case, was now being tendered twenty bucks to take it. That, I was certain, would outrage the fine feeling he had for money. Then, to my surprise, he picked up the twenty and stowed it away in his vest pocket.

"Joey," he said, "get out to the Lamar house right away. See what you can see. Find out what you can. I'll join you there later after I've questioned Miss Winthrop."

I gaped at him. It wasn't like Sackler to put his head in a noose for twenty bucks, for all his love of lucre.

"Well," he said impatiently. "Get going, Joey. The longer you wait the less information'll be left for you to pick up. Now what's the best way to get out there?"

I had recovered somewhat by now. Whatever Sackler did it meant precisely fifty bucks a week to me. No more or no less. If he wanted to doublecross Benny Green or take this girl for a ride, it was strictly his affair.

"The best way to get there?" I said maliciously. "You mean the quickest or the cheapest?"

"Take the subway," he said shortly. "And hurry."

I shrugged my shoulders and jammed my fedora on my head. As I walked info the hall, I could hear Sackler's voice over the transom.

"First," he was saying, "we better come to an understanding about the fee, Miss Winthrop."

2

Ten Pounds of Putty

I DID NOT take the subway for the simple reason that it ran nowhere near Lamar's secluded residence. There were but two means of transportation; car and train. I took the choo-choo.

The house itself was a rambling structure set in the midst of some ten acres of untended garden. The nearest neighbor dwelt a good three miles down the dirt road. Upon my arrival I found a copper on guard in the house. I identified myself, plied him with questions, and recorded the answers in my notebook.

I snooped around the house to see what I could see. During this chore I came upon Ralph Lamar, the dead man's brother who lived with him, and Corley, the dark saturnine man of all work. I duly cross-examined them, carefully noted the answers. Then I retired to the study and put my notes in order.

Fifteen minutes later Rex Sackler drove up in his coupé. Jane Winthrop was with him. I heard him inquiring for me below, then I heard his footsteps on the stairway. He came into the study, closing the door behind him. He sat down in a big leather chair. He seemed vastly pleased with himself.

"Well, Joey," he said, "and what've you got?"

I opened my notebook. "One," I said. "George Lamar was discovered dead at 8:30 this morning. The discovery was made by his man, Corley, who had just returned from a night off in town. Lamar, shot through the head, was slumped on the floor at the side of his chair. A cigar butt was in his mouth. Ashes were spilled on his coat and vest. The Medical Examiner says he was shot while sitting. He fell to the floor after death."

Sackler nodded slowly. "Good work," he said. "What else?"

"Two," I said. "Ralph Lamar, who lives here with his brother, owns a Cadillac roadster. Silas Latham, a truck gardener, who lives three miles down the road told the cops he saw that Cadillac drive past his house a little before midnight. That means a little before the murder. But when confronted with Ralph Lamar's alibi, Latham concedes he was probably mistaken."

"Ralph Lamar's alibi?" said Sackler. "What is it?"

"This is going to kill you," I told him. "Ralph Lamar met two friends in town at six o'clock. He had dinner with them. He remained with them until 4 a.m. Then he checked in at the Mordant Hotel. He returned here at noon today."

"So," said Sackler, "and why is that supposed to kill me?"

"The two friends," I told him slowly, "were Benny Green and Reynolds. They're his alibi."

Sackler frowned. He tapped a forefinger on the arm of his chair. Then he changed the subject abruptly.

"What about this guy Corley? The guy that let me in."

"Three," I said. "Corley's regular night off is Wednesday. However, on Friday morning a friend of his sent him a ticket to the fights. He asked and received permission to take Friday night off. He left on the last train at night. He returned on the first train in the morning to find Lamar dead."

"Well," said Sackler, "there's one alibi that's inconclusive. He could have driven back here, killed the old guy, and driven back to town."

"I thought of that," I told him. "But he doesn't own a car. And he can't drive."

"He told you that?"

"No," I said sarcastically. "I divined it."

He stirred in his chair at that and his eyes flashed. I went on hurriedly before he could speak.

"Four," I said. "Jane Winthrop told the coppers that Lamar was embarking upon another book. He had a brown cardboard envelope filled with documents that proved a number of unpleasant things about a number of people. It was in his desk drawer. It's not there now. The coppers have searched the house without finding it."

"I know," said Sackler. "She told me about that."

I closed the notebook. I sat back and watched Sackler. He was either lost in thought or pretending to be. He stared blankly through half-closed lids at the wall above my shoulder.

"You're not kidding me," I told him. "You're not even warm. You can't break this case in a million years."

He opened his eyes wide and raised his eyebrows.

"Why?" he said. "What's so confusing about it?"

I laughed in his face at that. "Go ahead," I jeered. "Impress me with the mighty Sackler mind. I'll tell you what's confusing about it. Then you can explain it to me."

"Glad to. What's worrying you?"

"Listen," I said, exasperated. "First we have Benny and Reynolds asking you to lay off the case. That argues they were mixed up in it. Those missing papers argue it even more strongly. It's very likely that Lamar's exposé named their names among others. Yet they've got Lamar's own brother as an alibi. Is it probable the dead man's next of kin is going to furnish a lying alibi for them?"

"No," said Sackler.

"All right," I said. "Now we'll consider the angle that Ralph

Lamar killed his brother. He's the only living relative, so he'd get George's dough. But if that's true what are Benny and Reynolds mixed up in it for?"

"What indeed?" said Sackler, grinning.

"And most baffling of all," I went on, "what are you taking the case for? There's a twenty dollar bill on one side and ten grand on the other."

"Wrong," said Sackler. "There's ten grand on one side. Fifteen on the other."

"Fifteen?" I said. "In thousands?"

"In thousands," said Sackler.

I gaped at him. He sighed and reached for one of his ten cent cigarettes.

"YOU'RE A LOUSY detective," said Sackler. "That twenty dollars was a token payment. Did you ever see an ordinary secretary wearing clothes like that? Wearing a bracelet like that? Further, did you notice the tears in her eyes? Did you notice her vehemence when she demanded the killer of Lamar be brought to the chair?"

"I noticed it all," I said. "What of it?"

"It all indicated that Jane Winthrop was more than a secretary to Lamar. He certainly paid her more than a secretary's salary. Her own demeanor demonstrated that she cared for him more than an employee usually cares for an employer."

"True," I said. "But it doesn't indicate that she'll hand over fifteen grand to you."

"No?" said Sackler with a crooked smile. "It convinced me that she was close enough to the dead man to inherit part of the estate."

"Well, and were you right?"

"I was wrong," said Sackler. "She inherits all of it. She paid me twenty dollars cash. I have her note for fourteen thousand nine hundred and eighty dollars. I sent Benny's dough back before I came out here."

"Sackler," I said in hearty disgust, "you're the luckiest guy in all the world."

But he wasn't listening to me. He was staring at the wall again. I lit a cigarette and watched him. I was sore and envious. Once again Sackler was lining his full pockets and I couldn't get a raise out of him with dynamite.

He moved suddenly in his chair and shot a question at me.

"You say Corley got a ticket for the fights. What fights?"

"The Avon Athletic Club. Why?"

Sackler licked his lips slowly. "Reynolds runs that place."

"So what's that got to do with it?"

Sackler stood up. He paced quickly up and down the room. Then he came to an abrupt halt and faced me.

"The trouble is," he announced, "that it's all pure ratiocination. I've got nothing tangible to hang on to. Nothing that will impress the limited mentality of a grand jury. If only I can—"

"Listen," I said. "Are you telling me in your roundabout way, that you know who killed George Lamar?"

"Of course," said Sackler. "But I don't know just how to break the case. I—" He broke off abruptly and snapped his fingers. "Joey," he said crisply. "Get me some putty."

I stared at him. "Putty?"

"Putty," he said.

"Where am I going to get putty?"

"Take my car. Drive to the nearest town. A glazier'll have it. Maybe a plumber. Now get going."

I stood up and walked to the door.

"All right," I said resignedly. "How much do you want?"

"About ten pounds," said Sackler. "The cheapest kind'll do."

I walked down the stairs wondering if the promise of so much money had caused his mind to snap. What in the world was he going to do with ten pounds of *putty?*

3

Wanted—A Client

I RETURNED WITHIN the hour with Sackler's putty. He took it without comment and disappeared in the direction of the garage. I wandered, bored, over the house, failing to find either a drink or companionship. Ralph Lamar paced the floor gloomily in the living room. Corley, taciturn and disgruntled, fussed around in the kitchen. I didn't see Jane Winthrop anywhere about.

I went back upstairs to the study where George Lamar had been slain. I lit a cigarette and stared out the big window into the chaotic garden. It had begun to rain—a fact which increased the depressive atmosphere of both myself and the landscape. I saw Sackler come out of the garage, carefully closing the door behind him. I cursed him more from habit than anything else and reviewed the tangled growth again.

Far off to the south I saw something move. I pushed my nose against the pane and strained my eyes. I made out a slim figure in an old raincoat, the color of the dolorous clouds above. A second glance showed me it was Jane Winthrop. She disappeared for a moment behind the weatherbeaten stones of an old well. Then after a while she emerged again. It seemed to me that there was strange purposefulness in her movements. Though why she should be walking in that wet undergrowth outside was beyond me.

I sighed, turned from the window and began to wonder when

Sackler was returning to town. The door opened suddenly and his head bobbed in.

"We're staying here overnight," he said to my disgust. "I'm driving Corley to the village to pick up some supplies. You better come along."

For want of anything else to do, I went. But before Sackler had gone a hundred yards I began to wish I hadn't.

I sat in the front seat with Sackler. Corley was alone in the rear. He was a short, sallow guy with a dead pan. Since I had met him I had never heard him talk save in answer to a question. He looked like a guy who is perennially sore at the world.

As soon as Sackler got into high, he jammed the accelerator down to the floor. The car shot ahead over the dirt road with all the smooth-flowing motion of a tractor going over the Rockies. He took the first turn without slowing down and we came closer to a telephone pole than I had ever been before.

I stared at him but he kept his eyes on the road. Two miles along the way a huge truck hove into sight. The road was narrow; the truck was wide. Sackler's foot never moved toward the brake. We raced past at a good seventy. I took a deep breath.

"Sackler," I yelled. "Are you crazy? Are you—"

I held my breath again as he passed a truck farmer's wagon in the face of an oncoming car. He got back to his side of the road with an inch to spare. I was pale and scared when we reached the village. I protested volubly and profanely while Corley was buying the supplies. Sackler only grinned at me.

"Some fun," he said, winking grotesquely.

The ride back was only slightly less daredevilish than the trip to town. By now I had almost made my mind up that Sackler had gone nuts. The possession of a note for fifteen thousand dollars had given his nervous system a shock it never could recover from.

Back at the house, I retired again to the study. I had been there some fifteen minutes when Sackler came in.

"Call Headquarters," he instructed. "Get Wolfe. He's in charge of this case. Have him come down here after dinner. Tell him to bring a couple of cops with him. Then call Reynolds and Benny Green. I'd like them on deck when I break this case."

"When you *what?*" I said.

"You heard me," he said. "Tell 'em to be here by eight o'clock."

He slammed the door and left me alone. I shrugged my shoulders and reached for the telephone.

BY EIGHT-THIRTY THEY had all arrived. Corley had served a gloomy dinner, eaten for the most part in complete silence. After the meal everyone scattered as if glad to be rid of the other company. Jane Winthrop, I noted, had hastily donned her raincoat and gone out into the darkness of the garden.

Inspector Wolfe of the Homicide Squad had arrived with two coppers and a red-faced sergeant. Benny Green and Reynolds had driven up a few minutes after dinner. Sackler had retired to the upstairs study. He declined to see anyone until his dinner had thoroughly digested.

I stood alone in the foyer smoking an after-dinner cigarette. I was peering through the window into the wet blackness of the garden beyond. The others were wandering around the big house somewhere, awaiting Sackler's pleasure. But it wasn't Sackler's summons that brought us all together. It was a piercing scream that hung, for a moment, like the tone of a hideous bell throughout the house.

I froze in my tracks at the sheer terror of it. There was deadly silence for a full second, then came the sound of racing footsteps, from all over the house. Ralph Lamar burst into the foyer from the music room at the left. He turned in the direction whence the sound had come, without noticing me behind him. He raced through the curtained doorway that led to the rear of the house.

I was on his heels when he got tangled up with the fringe of the draperies. His coat caught for an instant. He muttered an explosive expletive, jerked himself loose and rushed on. I paused for a moment behind him. Then I dashed along on his heels toward the kitchen.

There were four entrances to the kitchen, and through each doorway the occupants of the house converged. Wolfe and his coppers, Reynolds and Benny, Ralph Lamar and myself from the dual doors to the dining room, Sackler from the back stairway, and Corley from the pantry entrance.

We stood there in a silent, horrified circle staring down at the supine figure of Jane Winthrop. Her face was the color of bleached ashes. From her breast protruded the bone hilt of a sharp kitchen knife. A thin trickle of blood mixed with the water of her rain coat and ran slowly over the floor. Her little fists were clenched tightly in death.

Corley dropped the plate he was holding. His jaw sagged and his face was drained of color.

"Miss Winthrop!" he said.

"Right under my nose," said Wolfe. "And me in charge of Homicide!"

"Who's next?" said Ralph Lamar, and there was fear in his voice.

Rex Sackler stood staring at the corpse. His cheeks were flushed and his brow was wrinkled. He lifted his head, looked around the room, then back at the dead body. His remark was typical.

"Who's going to pay my fee?"

4

Highest Bidder

THEY ALL LOOKED at him as if he had been caught giving a hot foot in a cathedral. But it didn't faze Sackler. When he was worried about money he wasn't conscious of anything else.

Wolfe suddenly remembered his official position. He turned to his sergeant.

"Murphy," he snapped, "call the medical examiner! Get him out here as soon as possible. No one is to leave this house. You, Conners and Lane, stand by the doors. No one gets out. I'll take a look at the body."

He moved toward the inert figure on the floor. Sackler moved forward.

"Let me do it, Inspector," he said.

Without waiting for Wolfe's permission, he knelt at the dead girl's side. He looked at neither the wound nor the knife. Instead he lifted her clenched fists and examined them closely. He forced each palm open. I thought I saw him take something from the dead hand. He shot a swift glance down at his own palm, then put his hand in his pocket.

Wolfe turned to the rest of us.

"All right," he said. "Now where was everyone when that scream was heard?"

Sackler stood up. "You won't find the answer that way, Inspector," he said. "We were scattered all over the house. It's certain there was no eye-witness. At least none that'll talk. Beside, you're going to get stuck for motives, aren't you? Better let me take over."

Their eyes met for a long moment. Wolfe was reluctant to relinquish his authority. But experience had taught him that when Sackler was right he was very, very right.

"All right," he said, then added defensively: "You been here all day. You might've picked up something I don't know about."

"Yeah," said Sackler absently. His brow was corrugated in thought, and that thought, I knew, was very far away. "I want five or ten minutes to think it over."

WE WERE BACK in the sumptuous living room. The corpse of Jane Winthrop lay out in the kitchen beneath a commandeered sheet. The medical examiner and an undertaker were on their way.

They were a silent anxious group. Wolfe and his sergeant sat behind a gleaming mahogany table. The Inspector wore an anxious air. An unsolved murder under the very nose of the chief of the Homicide Squad would be something quite heartening to the editorial writers.

Standing on either side of a huge Spanish fireplace were Benny Green and Reynolds. Neither appeared happy. They constantly exchanged glances as if communicating some unspoken thought. Corley had taken up a position by the sideboard where he stood guard over a gleaming decanter, produced on Wolfe's order.

Ralph Lamar sat by the window staring out into the gloomy garden beyond. As I saw it, he was sitting on the world. The knife in Jane Winthrop's heart had just tossed three million bucks right into his lap.

A heavy meditative sigh broke the heavy silence. I looked up and noted that it had issued from Sackler. He was leaning back in a big armchair smoking an expensive perfecto. Even the fact that he had got it for nothing from Reynolds didn't seem to lift his spirits.

Wolfe spoke impatiently. "Sackler," he said, "you told me a while ago that you knew who murdered Lamar. Do you know, too, who killed the girl?"

Ralph Lamar swung around from his contemplation of the window pane and stared at Sackler. Every other eye was already on him. He stirred uneasily in his chair. He took the perfecto from his lips reluctantly, as if he disliked permitting such expensive tobacco to smolder. There was a worried shadow in his eyes.

He nodded slowly and said, "Sure. I know who killed 'em both. And I know why."

There was utter silence then. Wolfe glanced swiftly at his sergeant, who dropped his beefy hand to his holster. We all waited expectantly for Sackler to speak. But now he was puffing at the cigar again, staring thoughtfully at the floor as if there were weightier things than murder on his mind.

"All right," said Wolfe impatiently. "Speak up, man. Who's the killer? Where's the evidence?"

Sackler sighed and lifted his head. "Listen," he said, and there was dark anxiety in his voice, "who's going to pay my fee?"

"Is money all you think of? We've got two corpses on our hands, and you talk about your fee! Can you pin a murder rap on someone?"

"Sure," said Sackler. "I've already told you that. But be reasonable, Inspector. Jane Winthrop engaged me. We agreed on a certain price. Payable when she inherited the estate. Now she's dead. *She* can't pay me." He glanced from Wolfe to Ralph Lamar. "What about you?" he went on. "You get the estate now. You ought to pay the fee."

Ralph Lamar stared at him for a long time. "All right," he said suddenly. "How much was she going to pay you?"

"Fifteen thousand dollars."

"What!"

"Fifteen thousand dollars," repeated Sackler.

"Ridiculous," said Ralph Lamar. "I won't pay it."

"Absolutely ridiculous," said Wolfe angrily. "I hardly get that in three years."

"You didn't break the case," said Sackler mildly.

"Look here," said Lamar. "There's been murder done. You say you know who did it. That you can prove who did it. All right, go ahead."

Sackler closed his lips tightly and shook his head.

"No," he said stubbornly. "Not till I get my fee."

I WAS BEGINNING to enjoy myself. I hadn't the slightest idea whether or not Sackler had put his finger on the killer. But it was crystal clear that he wasn't going to collect fifteen grand for doing it. I saw Benny Green look quickly at Reynolds. I guessed that all three of us were thinking the same thought: that Sackler had been an awful sucker to return Benny's dough.

Ralph Lamar was furiously angry now. His face was mottled purple. Cords stood out on his brow.

"You mercenary dog!" he roared. "In the face of two killings you haggle. Do you mean you'd turn a murderer loose for fifteen thousand dollars?"

"For fifteen thousand dollars," I said, "he'd open the cages in the Bronx Zoo."

Sackler stirred again in his chair and turned his eyes on me. Then Wolfe got up and saved my being called a nasty name.

"Sackler," he said; his voice shook with rage. I guessed he was still sore at the fact that Sackler had even been promised a fee almost three times the annual salary of a police inspector. "Sackler, you'll talk or spend the rest of your life in jail."

Sackler ran a hand through his hair. He was frowning and worried. *I* knew it was the money rather than any threat of Wolfe's.

"I ought to get paid," he said in an injured tone. "It's only fair—"

"Sackler," shouted Wolfe, "you'll talk here and now or I'll take you in! The D.A.'ll take you before a Grand Jury. You'll talk then or go to jail for contempt. You'll stay there till you purge that contempt by talking. Besides, you're compounding a felony. Now will you talk? Or do I take you back to town in the wagon?"

Sackler sighed heavily. He puffed nervously on his cigar. I grinned broadly. Wolfe had him tied up in a beautiful knot and he knew it. I lit a cigarette and prepared for the edifying spectacle of Mr. Rex Sackler solving a murder case free of charge, gratis, for nothing.

He sat up suddenly in his chair. He jammed the cigar out in a German silver ashtray—an act which surprised me, as the perfecto was but half smoked. His frown was gone now, replaced by an air of assured decision. Uneasily, I recognized the symptoms. The scent of greenbacks was in his nostrils again.

"Lamar," he said, "you flatly refuse to pay me?"

"Flatly," said Ralph Lamar. "For fifteen thousand dollars I can get the entire F.B.I."

"All right," said Sackler bitterly. "You asked for it. I'll talk. Let's begin at the beginning. We start lousy with possible suspects. We know Lamar had documents in this house which revealed several unpleasant facts about a number of people."

"So what?" put in Reynolds. "Not having the documents, we don't know who those people are."

He seemed a little worried to me, but Sackler ignored him. "Now," he went on, "Lamar is found in his library with a bullet in his brain and cigar stub between his lips. What does that indicate?"

"You're answering the questions," said Wolfe grimly. Then he added, "For nothing."

That was twisting the knife in the wound. However, to my surprise, Sackler let it pass.

"All right," he said. "I'm answering 'em. Note this well. Lamar wasn't alarmed when the killer entered his study in the middle of the night. He didn't get up. He didn't move from his chair. He never even took the cigar from his mouth. He wasn't at all surprised when the murderer entered the room."

"That's great," said Wolfe. "But who cares?"

Sackler shot him a malevolent glance. "Lamar *knew* the killer," he went on. "The killer belonged in the house. That's why Lamar wasn't disturbed."

Wolfe's mocking air left him now. Ralph Lamar stared at Sackler with new interest. Reynolds fidgeted slightly while Benny looked bored. Corley retained his dead pan.

"All right," said Wolfe, "go on."

"We all know," resumed Sackler, "that despite apparent evidence to the contrary, Ralph Lamar's car was seen in the neighborhood just before the murder."

"That's ridiculous," said Ralph. "Latham admitted he was probably mistaken."

"He wasn't," said Sackler.

Ralph Lamar's face purpled again.

"What the devil do you mean by that?"

Sackler sighed. "It's all so obvious, I hate to do it," he remarked. "After all, you're the murdered man's brother. His only living kin. What more natural than you should believe his will was made out in your favor? What more natural than you should believe that once your brother was disposed of, you'd come into a cold three million dollars?"

Ralph Lamar was raging angry now. He pounded the window sill with his fist.

"So!" he roared. "And when I found out that my brother's money was left to that girl of his, I killed her, too. Is that it?"

"That's it," said Sackler quietly.

5

Blackmail

THE SILENCE OF the room was broken only by Ralph's stertorous breathing. Corley still did his Sphinx imitation. I saw Benny look at Reynolds and raise quizzical eyebrows. Wolfe's eyes were fixed on Sackler. "Have you any evidence?"

"I can prove he killed the girl," said Sackler. "With that I've offered you enough circumstantial evidence to pin his brother's murder on him too."

"He's mad," said Ralph Lamar more quietly. "Utterly mad, Inspector. He most certainly can't prove I killed anyone. And regarding his circumstantial evidence, what about my alibi? It's foolproof."

"Is it?" said Sackler gently. He turned his head around and faced Benny and Reynolds. "Now, listen, boys," he continued. "I can pin the Winthrop killing on Ralph Lamar here—cold. You have observed that I can build up a very nice case against him for the murder of his brother. Now do you want to reconsider that story of yours about having dinner with him that night?"

Sackler paused. Again I watched Benny and Reynolds exchange significant glances. As they stared at each other, Sackler spoke again.

"It's all very well to help out a pal, boys, when murder's not involved. But if you stick to that alibi story now, the D.A.'ll break his neck to bust it wide open. He'll discredit you on the stand. He'll have his own dicks drag up every item in your lives that'll tend to make you look like perjurers. If there's anything you want to keep under cover, he'll drag it out. Remember, murder is murder. It's still very illegal. Now, do you insist upon sticking to that alibi story?"

Ralph Lamar laughed shortly and confidently as he lit another cigar. Sackler, Wolfe and I looked at Reynolds and Benny, who were still staring at each other. At last it was Reynolds who spoke.

"Well," he said, "since you put it like that, Sackler—all right. After all, a man can't be expected to cover up a murder. We don't want no trouble with the D.A. There are limits to what a guy can do—even for a pal. We didn't have no dinner with Ralph that night. He asked us to cover up for him and we did."

"That's right" said Benny. "Of course we didn't know at the time a killing was involved. We didn't—"

Benny may have finished that sentence but no one heard him. The room was filled with Ralph Lamar's howl of indignant wrath. His face was the color of wet litmus paper. His eyes flamed and his voice was pitched three notes above normal.

"You lying rats!" he yelled. "It's a frame, Inspector. Those two and Sackler are framing me. They're lying. They're—"

"Shut up," said Wolfe sharply. Then, as he spoke to Sackler there was a touch of deference in his tone. "Nice going, Rex. We'll pin him cold on his brother. You say you can also prove he killed the girl?"

Sackler nodded. There was something about his demeanor that puzzled me. By all the rules he should have been in the depths of morose depression. After all, he'd just lost fifteen thousand dollars. Yet he was calm and assured. I even thought

I detected a triumphant gleam in his eye. He raised his hand and pointed toward Ralph Lamar.

"Look at him," he said. "There's a button missing from his coat."

All of us, including Ralph looked at the indicated coat. The second button was missing. The threads stuck out untidily, as if the button had been suddenly wrenched off.

"Well?" said Wolfe.

"That button," said Sackler. "It was in Jane Winthrop's hand. She tore it from his coat when he knifed her."

Something clicked in my brain like a bear trap. Now I saw where Sackler was headed! Now I knew why he wasn't beating his breast about his financial loss. Now I saw a number of things, including the welcome figure of Opportunity hammering at my door.

Ralph Lamar was speaking. His voice wasn't so angry now. Apparently he realized what he was up against. His tone was subdued and fearful.

"It's a frame, Inspector," he said. "Someone tore that button off my coat and planted it. It's a frame, I—"

"Tell it to the death house chaplain," said Wolfe. "You can—"

"Wait a minute," said Sackler. "Perhaps, Mr. Lamar, since you insist you're innocent, you'd like to retain me? Perhaps—"

In another minute I'd've lost the chance of a lifetime. I interrupted him.

"Sackler," I said.

HE JERKED HIS head around in my direction and looked at me inquiringly. "Sackler," I said again, "I've been meaning to speak to you about something for a long time. This seems an opportune moment. I'd like a raise. Say twenty dollars a week. The commodities index, you may have noticed, has risen of late. Things are going up. Roger Babson says that—"

Sackler's eyes were smoldering. But it was Wolfe who cut in on me.

"Do you guys think of nothing but money? First we have Sackler who in the face of two corpses starts screaming about his fee. Now, just as we're about to arrest a murderer, you put in a bid for a raise. Are—"

"Twenty dollars," I said looking steadily at Sackler. "Do I get it?"

Sackler ran a hand through his hair. His quick brain had grasped the situation and he was suffering acutely.

He said, "All right."

I sighed, sat down and lit a cigarette. Ralph Lamar sat down, too. He was deathly pale. I saw that his hand shook as he wiped his brow with a handkerchief. Wolfe clapped Sackler on the back.

"Nice going," he said. "Sergeant, bring Lamar along."

"Wait a minute," said Sackler for the second time. "You still protest your innocence, Lamar?"

"Of course," said Ralph huskily. "I didn't do it. I don't understand. I—"

"What are we wasting time for?" snapped Wolfe. "Sergeant—"

"Wait," said Sackler, holding up an elegant hand. "Maybe you'd like to retain me, Mr. Lamar?"

Ralph looked at him dully. "For what?"

"To prove your innocence."

Ralph's eyes narrowed. "What do you mean?" he said bitterly. "You've just proved me guilty—to your own satisfaction."

"To the satisfaction of any jury," added Wolfe smugly.

"Perhaps I could prove you innocent," said Sackler. "Though of course, not for the same price."

Ralph Lamar stood up. There was a gleam of hope in his eyes.

"Get me out of this," he said eagerly. "I didn't do it. I swear I didn't. Get me out of it. Turn up the real murderer. I'll pay you anything. Anything!"

"Fifteen thousand dollars?" said Sackler.

I had known what was coming, but everyone else in the room gasped. A dawning intelligence came into Ralph Lamar's eyes.

"You mean—" he began.

"I mean the fee is fifteen thousand dollars," said Sackler. "In advance. Results guaranteed."

"Listen," said Wolfe angrily. "Are you making a fool of me, Sackler? Are you making a fool of the law? You've given me enough to burn Lamar twice. We'll take him in."

Sackler ignored him. He was staring at Ralph Lamar.

"Well?" he said. "Are you going along with Wolfe or are you doing business with me?"

Ralph Lamar took a checkbook from his pocket. He filled out a blank with an unsteady hand and gave it to Sackler. Sackler smiled happily. His eyes lit up. He stowed the check away in his wallet like a lapidarian putting the Kohinoor in the safe. Then he turned to Wolfe.

"Inspector," he said, "as the representative of Mr. Ralph Lamar, I have a request to make."

Wolfe roared. "Are you trying to make a monkey out of me, Sackler? First you're on one side, then you're on the other. I've got a case against Ralph Lamar. I'm taking him in."

"If you do," said Sackler, "you'll make a monkey out of yourself with no assistance from me."

Wolfe glanced at him uncertainly. Experience had taught him that Sackler was not often wrong. But the thought of that check in Sackler's pocket had made him sore all over again.

"All right," he said grudgingly. "What is it you want me to do?"

"Have your sergeant here search the house. Thoroughly. Every crack. Every corner."

Wolfe nodded toward the sergeant. "All right, sergeant. Go ahead."

The red-faced copper looked at Sackler. "And what am I looking for?" he asked.

"A brown cardboard folder," said Sackler. "It contains a number of typewritten papers."

Wolfe said, "Are you crazy? We've already turned the house inside out looking for that folder. It wasn't in the house."

"It's here now," said Sackler. There was a long pause as he looked around the room. His gaze came to rest on Corley's dead pan, "Yes," Sackler went on slowly, "it's here now. *Isn't it, Corley?*"

Corley said, "What should I know about it? Lay off me. I ain't got no money for a fee."

"All right," said Sackler, "It'll take a little more time if you won't talk. Search the house, sergeant. When you find that folder handle it carefully. Use your handkerchief. Because the prints on it'll send Corley to the chair. *Won't they, Corley?*"

"Listen," said Corley excitedly, "I—"Then his voice dropped suddenly. He added, "I don't know nothing. See? Nothing."

"Go ahead, sergeant," said Sackler. "When you find that folder, bring it here."

The sergeant clumped out of the room on his flat feet. Wolfe watched him go with doubtful eyes. He turned to Sackler.

"I think you're crazy," he said. "You build up a case against Lamar. Then you tell Corley that *he's* headed for the chair. Corley not only has his alibi. He has no motive."

I was convinced by now that Sackler knew what he was doing. But his air of mystery annoyed me.

"Come on," I said. "You can talk now. You've been paid."

"All right," said Sackler. "Now I'll earn the money. Let's go back to the beginning. Now, Lamar has important documents in his possession, documents he intends to incorporate into a book. These documents, among other things, bear witness to the fact that Benny Green and Reynolds, here, have led evil lives. That much is obvious enough. Aware of this, Benny and Reynolds decide to kill Lamar, to take the incriminating papers."

"That's a lie," said Reynolds, his eyes blazing. "You can't crack my alibi, Sackler. You can't—"

"Shut up!" snapped Wolfe. "Go on, Sackler."

Sackler sighed and inhaled deeply on his cigar. "So," he went on, "they get to Corley. They offer him something—money, I suppose, if he'll kill Lamar for them; if he'll purloin those papers at the same time. They offer, further, to make all the arrangements which will make it appear that Corley could not possibly have been the killer."

Corley was staring at Benny and Reynolds now. There was wild appeal in his eyes. Reynolds was obviously ill at ease and there was a feral snarl on Benny's lips as he glared at Sackler. Knowing his reputation, I dropped my hand to the butt of the automatic in my pocket.

"Now," continued Sackler, "they choose a night that Jane Winthrop will not be here. Reynolds sends Corley a ticket to his own fight club; thus furnishing him with a reason for asking Lamar for the night off. That leaves Ralph to be taken care of. They must get him out of the house, too. Well, the answer to that is easy. Reynolds, a casual acquaintance, asks Ralph to dinner."

"So you're back on *that*," said Wolfe. "A moment ago, you got Benny and Reynolds to admit that Ralph *didn't* have dinner with them."

"I'm representing Ralph Lamar now," Sackler reminded him. "But, to continue. Ralph's dining with them serves a double purpose. It not only gets him out of the house, but it puts his car at their disposal. There is no public conveyance running out here at night. It would have been too risky to hire a car or to have used one of their own. So while Ralph's car is parked outside the restaurant, Corley has been instructed to take it as they eat."

"That's another lie," yelled Benny. "Ralph's car was parked on the corner all the time."

"So," snapped Wolfe. "Ralph Lamar *was* with you!"

"If you'll all shut up," said Sackler wearily, "I'll get on with it. Now, we have Corley in Ralph's car driving back here to the house. He goes up to George Lamar's study where the old guy is working on his book. The documents Benny and Reynolds wanted are right on the desk beside him. The old guy, seeing his visitor is Corley, is mildly surprised to find him back so soon, but he isn't alarmed. He calmly looks up from his desk, his cigar still between his teeth, as Corley plants a bullet in his brain."

"Go on," said Wolfe. He was staring intently at Benny Green. He wore the expression of a hunter getting close to a tiger he has stalked for years.

SACKLER WENT ON. "Now Corley picks up the incriminating papers and begins to think. Why should he give them up to Reynolds and Benny? Keeping them might open up a nice avenue of blackmail and further, it will insure his principals keeping faith with him. After all, Benny and Reynolds have some influence in this town. Corley hasn't. If they decide to throw Corley to the wolves, what can he do about it? So Corley takes Ralph's car back to town, carefully parks it where he found it—and *keeps* the papers."

"All right," said Benny in a hard voice, "then what?"

"Then," said Sackler, "you and Reynolds begin to worry. Neither of you have much faith in Corley's ability as a murderer. You begin to fear that perhaps he left some clue behind him. You also know that if Corley takes the murder rap, he'll sing. Since he's crossed you by keeping those papers, he can substantiate that singing. You discovered, too, that Jane Winthrop was going to ask my help. In order to remove any possibility of the truth being uncovered you come to the only intelligent dick in town and offer him big dough to lay off the case. But there you run up against a man of integrity, and he refuses."

Integrity? That killed me.

"Wait a minute," said Reynolds. "Everything you say is nuts. You forgot something, wise guy."

Sackler raised his eyebrows.

"You forgot that Corley can't drive a car. You forgot that. So how could he take Ralph's car? With no means of transportation how could he get back to the house before morning?"

Sackler laughed aloud. "That was no stroke of genius, Reynolds. As a matter of fact it was the very thing that delivered you into my hands."

"What are you talking about?" asked Wolfe.

"Well," said Sackler, "if Corley really couldn't drive a car, it knocked a wide and jagged hole in my theory. On the other hand, if he could drive a car, and was lying about it, it gave me a bolstering fact that I sorely needed. You see, the conspirators, discovering that Corley never drove around the house, here, that no one here had ever seen him drive, decided to have him deny that he could drive a car at all. They figured no one could ever prove differently. So that would cover up Corley."

"Well?" said Wolfe.

"Well," said Sackler, "after I proved Corley *could* drive a car, I knew I was in."

"You're nuts," said Benny, and I didn't like the expression on his face. "How could you prove a thing like that?"

"I'm a genius," said Sackler modestly. "That's why you tried to keep me off this case. I put a flat square of putty beneath the rubber mat in the rear seat of my car. Put if between the rubber and the floorboard. Then I took Corley for a ride to the village grocery. I drove like a combination of Barney Oldfield and a Saturday night drunk. I scared Corley to death."

"So," said Benny, "what?"

"So," said Sackler. "Corley *can* drive a car. Upon examining that putty when we got back, I found it was very thin at one point, almost worn through. That point was where Corley's right foot had rested on the floor. You see, he was putting on an imaginary brake every time I skimmed a telegraph pole. Now putting on brakes that aren't actually there is a conditioned reflex. But it's a conditioned reflex only in a person who knows how to drive. He's instinctively acquired the brake habit when he sees danger. Do you understand?"

There was another long silence. Grudgingly, I gave Sackler a bow for that putty stunt. But I kept my eyes on Benny. If Sackler was right—and he was a one to three shot in my book right now—there was an excellent chance that Benny Green was going to reach for his shoulder holster.

NOW SACKLER ADDRESSED Corley direct. "You noticed," he said, "that, a few moments ago, your confederates were quite willing to send an innocent man to the chair. The instant they believed I had a case against Ralph Lamar, they lied. They denied dining with him on the night of the murder. Sending Ralph to the chair would have served their purpose well enough. They'll sell anyone down the river, Corley, if it seems expedient at the moment. So, if I were you, I wouldn't rely on them too much. Judicious talking at this point might well save your life."

Corley's dead pan had vanished. He was pale and his mouth was twisted. There was wild animal fear in his gaze as he stared at Benny Green and Reynolds. Reynolds' cheeks were the color of his cigar ash. Wolfe's sergeant came clattering suddenly down the stairs. He was gingerly holding an oblong cardboard folder. He laid it on the table before Sackler.

"Found it," he said. "In the bathroom closet. I'll swear it wasn't there this morning."

"It wasn't," said Sackler.

Ralph Lamar had been staring at Sackler with the admiring awe of a schoolboy.

"If it wasn't here this morning," he said, "how on earth did you know it was here now?"

"That gets us around to the murder of Jane Winthrop," said

Sackler. "After I decided that Corley was holding out those missing documents, the question became: What had he done with them? It seemed unlikely that he'd taken them into town that night, or that he would trust anyone else to keep them for him. Yet they weren't in the house, they weren't in Corley's room."

Quite conscious of the suspense he had created, Sackler paused deliberately, took a cigar from the humidor and lit it. He inhaled deeply before going on.

"That left the grounds. There are ten acres of untended growth surrounding this house. It seemed fairly logical that Corley had hidden his loot there. Jane Winthrop and I worked on that premise. She knew those grounds well. Like a book. It was she who volunteered to search them for those papers."

Now for the first time I saw it all clearly. "And she found them," I said.

"She found them, Joey," said Sackler. "Exactly where, I don't know. No one does, save Corley. She found them and brought them into the house intending to give them to me. Corley saw her. He saw that brown cardboard folder in her hands and he knew the game was up. It would incriminate Benny and Reynolds who, to save their own skins, would turn on him. Furthermore, it undoubtedly bore Corley's fingerprints, although he mightn't have realized that."

"So," I took it up, "he knifed her, snatched the folder and hid it."

"Right" said Sackler. "He rushed upstairs, hid it in the bathroom closet, then came downstairs again at the same time as the rest of us. The thing I found in Jane Winthrop's hand was not a button, but a fragment of brown cardboard that had been torn off the folder when Corley snatched it."

Ralph Lamar sighed heavily. Reynolds collapsed into a Windsor chair. I never took my eyes off Benny Green. I heard Sackler say to Corley, "You'll probably save yourself from burning, Corley, if you'll talk to the Inspector here. If you'll assure him of the apodictic correctness of my theory."

Corley didn't know what that meant any more than I did. But he got the general idea.

"All right," he said, and his words tumbled over each other. "I'll talk, Inspector. It's like Mr. Sackler says, Inspector. I'll sign a confession, I'll tell—"

It was then Benny Green made the move I had been waiting for.

"You'll tell nothing, you rat!"

His automatic came into view a fraction of a second after mine. I fired first and my bullet plowed into Benny's right arm. His smashed through the floor into the cellar below. Then Wolfe's two coppers were in the room. The beefy sergeant was sitting on Benny's chest and Wolfe, himself had a firm grip on Reynolds. Corley, pale and shaken, needed no guard.

"All right," said Wolfe, "we've got two cars outside. I'll take Corley with me. He can talk to a stenographer at Headquarters."

The coppers dragged the trio outside while Sackler accepted the thanks of Ralph Lamar with a magnificent air.

Five minutes later we were in Sackler's sedan headed back to town. We rode a long way in silence, then I took something from my vest pocket and handed it to him.

He looked down at my extended palm and said, "What's that?"

"A button," I told him. "The one you were going to send Ralph Lamar to the chair with."

He grunted. "That was a lousy holdup you pulled on me, Joey," he said. "Where did you get that button?"

"I was behind Ralph when he tangled in a curtain fringe," I told him. "He dropped the button then. I picked it up, intending to return it to him later. Then when I saw you intended to chisel fifteen grand out of him on the strength of it, I put in my own bid."

He said, "It was sheer blackmail."

That was funny to me. "What about yourself?" I said. "Suppose Ralph had refused to pay you. Would you have let him burn?"

"Joey," he said, and there was horrified reproof in his tone, "you don't really think I'd do a thing like that?"

I didn't answer him. But deep down in my heart, I more than half believed he would.

Death Dresses for Dinner

Rex Sackler believes in sharing the wealth, his money is his, and yours is his, too, if he can figure how to get it

1

I Always Lose

IT WAS A miserable day. Rain slapped against the window and ran dispiritedly down the pane. Outside the city was wet and gray. Traffic skidded uncertainly through the streets while pedestrians leaned obliquely into the howling wind that screeched up from the Battery. I sat at my desk, smoked a cigarette and stared out into Madison Avenue. Behind me I heard Rex Sackler sigh heavily. I heard the rustling sound of a deck of shuffled cards. I knew damned well he wanted me to play rummy with him. But I wasn't having any.

There were times when the idea of punching Sackler's nose filled me with enough ecstatic pleasure to arouse the suspicions of Kraft-Ebing. And this was one of those times.

If he thought he was going to suck me into a card game he was very much mistaken. I pretended not to hear his cough. I remained staring out the window simulating intense interest in the American Express truck loading across the way. Then, realizing his gentle hints were getting him precisely nowhere, Sackler made the approach direct.

"Hey, Joey," he said. "How about a fast round of rummy?"

I swung around in my swivel chair and regarded him with an unfriendly eye.

"Sackler," I said, "once a week when you pay my salary your big heart breaks in two. So you spend the other five working days trying to get it back."

*The bullet made a vibrant ping as
it bored neatly through the window*

He raised his eyebrows and tried very hard to look like a misunderstood man.

"Joey," he said reproachfully, "you wound me. Deeply. Constantly you complain that your earnings are too meagre. So I, in my simple way, contrive to throw a little more cash your way. Now how about a little knock rummy? You may pick yourself up five or ten dollars."

"Listen," I said. "At eleven o'clock this morning, I tossed you for a round of beers. At noon I cut the cards with you for lunch. An hour ago I played you checkers for a box of cigars. So far this day's cost me six dollars and eighty cents. I'm through!"

Sackler sighed and reshuffled the cards. "So," he said, "what's six dollars and eighty cents? A pittance."

That from Rex Sackler was funny. If you'll consider how Romeo loved Juliet, how Oedipus loved his mother, how Nathan Hale loved his country; if you'll add all these together, you'll have some rough idea of the affection in which Sackler held green folding money. He didn't overlook the nickels and dimes either.

He'd quit the Police Department, thrown away a certain pension because he'd entertained the idea that he could make a fortune as a private detective. That idea had proved eminently correct. Though how much dough he had actually piled up was a closely kept secret between Heaven and himself.

He bought no stocks or bonds. Industries had been known to crash. He kept very little in banks. Banks had failed before this. Every dime he got his hands on was scattered about in Postal Savings accounts all over the country. Nothing short of a revolution was going to get any cash away from Sackler.

He looked at me over his desk, a mordant gleam in his deep black eyes.

"Joey," he said suddenly, "I'll tell you what I'll do. I'll play a game of Canfield against you. I'll give you fifteen bucks for the deck. You pay me a dollar for each card I get out."

I listened to that. The usual odds in a game of Canfield gave a nice percentage to the banker, and Sackler was offering me something better than the usual odds. I nodded my head.

"Okay," I told him. "Deal 'em out."

HE SHUFFLED THE cards again and began to lay them out upon the desk top. I watched him as he got four cards out almost immediately. As I studied the layout of the deck I felt some misgiving. Then, without raising his eyes from the game, Sackler said, "Joey. Someone in the outer office."

I had heard no one. But Sackler had the ears of an airplane detector. I got up and went out into the reception room. A gaunt man with a tired gray face waited there. He wore the uniform of a police sergeant. I waved him a greeting.

"Hi, Connelly," I said. "What's on your mind?"

"I want to see Rex," he said in a thin worried voice. "Is he in?"

As I led the way back into Sackler's office, I noted with rising horror that he already had eleven cards out. I wondered if I'd been a sucker leaving him alone like that.

"Sergeant Connelly wants to see you," I announced, hoping that Connelly's business would be important enough to get Sackler's mind off the solitaire.

To my disgust he went right on playing as he said, "Sit down, Connelly. What's worrying you?"

Connelly rubbed his hands together and sat down. He was a man well over fifty and he looked much older. His hair was gray and lifeless. His cheeks were an unhealthy white. His eyes, uncertain and restive.

"Rex," he said, and there was a tremor in his voice. "It's about this guy, this chauffeur I brought in for the Noble killing."

Sackler's facile fingers manipulated the cards. I watched him savagely. I was already out eight bucks and from where I stood it looked an even money chance that he was going to run the whole damned deck out.

"Read about it in the paper," said Sackler without looking up. "Nice work, Connelly. You picked him up before the corpse was cold, practically."

"Yeah," said Connelly dully. "But, Rex, I—I—don't believe he done it."

If that next card was the eight of hearts I was cooked. Sackler'd get the whole game out and I'd be in for fifty-two bucks minus fifteen. Thirty-seven dollars. More than half a week's pay. I watched his dexterous fingers reach for the card. I told myself it was a cold twenty to one that it wasn't the eight of hearts. There was absolutely nothing to worry about. There—

Sackler turned the card over and looked up at me. His grin made me think of a vulture in a morgue. I stared down at the eight of hearts in his hand and reached for my wallet.

"Rex," said Connelly again. "I'm telling you I don't believe he done it."

I slapped the money on Sackler's desk.

"Don't bother him," I said bitterly to Connelly. "Can't you see he's busy earning my salary? What the hell does he care who killed old man Noble?"

Sackler shook his head and clucked like an old hen.

"Now, Joey," he said. "No vindictive-ness. After all, what's thirty-seven dollars. A—"

"I know," I told him. "A pittance. But I can remember the howl you sent up when the shoe shine stand short changed you two bits."

"An entirely different thing," said Sackler with dignity. "That was purely a matter of principle."

"Listen," said Connelly. "What's the matter with you guys? Rex, I tell you I got something important."

Sackler scooped up the cards and replaced them in the desk drawer.

"CONNELLY," HE SAID, "if the story in the papers is right, Noble was knifed last night, or early this morning. You, who live nearby, were coming to work when you ran into

Carver, Noble's chauffeur. There was blood on his hands, on his shirt. Back at the house the knife had his fingerprints on it. You have witnesses to testify to the fact that Noble fired him yesterday, that hot words were passed between them. So what do you mean you don't think he did it?"

Connelly blinked his watery eyes. His lips quivered for a moment.

"I'm not *sure* he did it, Rex. I ain't ever sure—any more."

That was true enough. Since they'd burned Georgie Deane at Sing Sing for a murder he'd never done, Connelly had never been sure of anything. Deane was killer enough and he'd deserved what he got. But the specific killing that Connelly had pinned on him had actually been performed by another hood. But that fact hadn't been unearthed until Deane had been lying in Woodlawn for six wormy months.

That episode had changed Connelly from a crack homicide sergeant into a doddering, vacillating old man who was hanging on long enough to rate a pension. In these days, when Connelly handed out a traffic summons he spent the rest of the week wondering if he'd ticketed the right guy.

"Listen," said Sackler. "You got this guy, Carver, cold. What are you worrying about? What are you coming to me for?"

"Well," said Connelly. "I don't believe Carver's really guilty. I figured you might look into the case for me—as a personal favor."

That was a touching and beautiful thought for a dull drab day. The idea that Sackler would ever touch a case for anything except a juicy fee was quaint, unique and entirely original.

"Connelly," said Sackler, "when a forty dollar a week chauffeur is indicted for murder, he's guilty. You need at least ten grand a year to beat a murder rap. Forget it, Connelly. You're a cop. It's your job to bring 'em in. What the D.A., the judge and the jury do is no concern of yours."

Connelly slapped his palm on the desk top. "Rex," he said excitedly, "you can't let an innocent man burn. When he first told me he didn't do it, I—"

"Oh," said Sackler ironically. "So he *told* you he didn't do it. Don't tell me he's a liar as well as a killer."

"There was something honest about him," said Connelly. "Something sincere. I almost believed him then. Later, when I brought him the hamburgers I was sure he didn't do it."

Since the Deane affair, I had always considered Connelly a trifle cracked. I saw no reason to change that opinion now. Even Sackler was baffled. His brow screwed into a frown.

"The hamburgers?" he said bewildered. "The hamburgers, Connelly?"

"I was worrying about him," said Connelly. "They'd been working over him for a confession. He insisted that he'd gone into Noble's study to collect his last week's pay. He found the body with a knife stuck in its heart. He lost his head. He pulled the knife out. Got blood all over him while he was doing it. Then he got panicky, dropped the fingerprinted knife to the floor and beat it. He figured he might be suspected because of the brawl he'd had with Noble the night before."

Sackler pointed at me. "There stands my right arm," he said. "Joey is all brawn. Where Joey's brain should be there is a large hard muscle. Joey has never had a thought in all his twenty-seven years. Joey, in short, is a high grade moron. Yet I'll bet you thirty-seven dollars, Connelly, that Joey can think of a better story than the fairy tale Carver told you. Further, I'll bet he can do it within three minutes. Go ahead, Joey."

That got me sore. I selected an insulting noun. I was searching around for an obscene adjective to go with it before throwing it at Sackler when Connelly spoke again.

"Rex," he said. "Will you please listen to me? You're the only guy smart enough to understand. Inspector Wolfe thinks I'm crazy. Down at headquarters they all think I'm crazy."

I thought he was crazy, too. But the arrant flattery got Sackler. He beamed, bowed, and became more serious.

"All right," he said. "Now what's this about the hamburgers?"

2

A Change of Mind

WHEN THEY FINISHED working on this kid," said Connelly, "I felt kind of sorry for him. I went down to the Greek's and got a couple of hamburgers for him. I brought them into his cell. He took one look at the plate and his face turned green, Rex."

"So," I said. "What does that prove?"

"That he's an epicure," said Sackler. "I've felt that way about the Greek's hamburgers myself."

"Will you stop clowning?" said Connelly. "There's a man's life at stake. He's a vegetarian, Rex. Those hamburgers were rare. Blood was oozing all over the plate. The sight of that blood gave him the horrors. And he wasn't acting, Rex. I'll swear to that. He told me all meat made him sick. Especially rare meat. He never could stand the sight of blood. That was one reason why he lost his head when he found Noble dead. Swore he'd eaten vegetables all his life. When I left him, I checked on that. It's true."

It was still double talk to me. But Sackler seemed to understand what he was talking about. He stroked his chin thoughtfully.

"I see what you mean," he said slowly. "If Carver couldn't stand the sight of rare, bloody meat, he never could have brought himself to knife Noble. Is that it?"

"That's it," said Connelly excitedly. "Maybe he would've shot

Noble. Even clubbed him to death. But no guy who can't stand blood will use a knife."

For a moment I thought Sackler was convinced. Then he said abruptly, "Has he got any dough?"

Connelly shook his head. "No. But you can't let that stand in your way, Rex. You can't let an innocent man die. I've got a little money saved. I—"

"How much?"

"A few hundred. I'll give you that to clear him. I can't let him burn if he's really innocent."

There was desperate appeal in his old eyes as he looked at Sackler. Sackler avoided his gaze as he shook his head.

"No," he said. "It's no good, Connelly. It's too thin. It's quite possible that even a vegetarian who can't stand blood might reach for a knife in a moment of angry passion. If he was sore enough he might forget his sanguinary inhibitions."

Connelly looked at him with despair. "Rex," he said. "You've got to—"

"No," said Sackler with great finality. "Undoubtedly Carver's guilty as hell. I want no part of it."

Connelly stood up. He shook his head wearily and shuffled from the room. His eyes were downcast and I knew that he was thinking of Georgie Deane.

As the door closed behind him, Sackler reached for the cards again.

"Well, Joey," he said. "How about a little game of—"

"Listen," I told him. "I wouldn't play Old Maid with you if you let me stack the cards. I wouldn't bet you a nickel that my own name's Joey Graham. I'd rather try to beat a finance company than you. Socially and financially we're through. And if I knew where to get another job we'd be through profession-ally as well."

Having spoken my vehement piece I turned back to my contemplation of Madison Avenue. I could not forget the fact of my forty-three dollars and eighty cents reposing in Sackler's wallet. I was wracking my brains for a scheme to get it back when Roy Archer came into the office.

He entered breezily without knocking. He was tall, good-looking and wore the assured air of a man who had been born in the upper brackets. He also wore a suit that had cost a cold hundred dollars.

"Mr. Sackler?" he said. "Mr. Rex Sackler?"

Sackler stood up and revealed all his teeth in a welcoming smile. His nostrils quivered slightly and there was a bright glit-ter in his black eyes. Archer gave off an aroma of money, and Sackler's keen nose caught it immediately.

Archer sat down at Sackler's invitation and told us his name. Then he added, "I'm Robert Noble's nephew."

SACKLER LICKED HIS lips and assumed a dreamy expression. Mentally he was transferring a fat fee from Archer's pocket-book into his own Postal Savings account.

"Ah, Mr. Archer," he said. "Very sad about your uncle. Very sad, indeed."

Archer nodded. "A dirty, cold-blooded murder," he said. "That's what I'm here about."

"Well," said Sackler, with the deferential air of a floor walker, "if the police haven't enough evidence against Carver, I'll be glad to offer my services."

"The point is," said Archer, "I don't believe that Carver's guilty."

I raised my eyebrows and wondered if Archer, too, was going to advance the hamburger theory. But he didn't.

"You see, Mr. Sackler," he said, "I just can't bring myself to believe that Carver killed my uncle. Carver's a clean-cut American boy. It's true my uncle had discharged him. Mr. Noble was growing old and querulous. He was a difficult man to get along with. It's true, too, that he and Carver had some words. Still, it's incredible to me that a lad of Carver's type would deliberately murder an old man."

Sackler looked as if he were about to purr.

"So," he said, "you want me to undertake an investigation?"

"Exactly. I spoke to Inspector Wolfe at Headquarters about this but he laughed at me. Said the police had a complete case against Carver and refused to conduct further investigation. Of course, if Carver actually committed the crime, he should be punished. But I want to be sure first. It would be an awful thing if an innocent man went to the chair. I want you to look into the case thoroughly."

"Of course," said Sackler. "I quite agree with you. No price is too great if it saves an innocent man from the chair."

I grimaced mockingly at him. That was indeed a noble sentiment considering what he had just told Connelly. Archer, realizing that Sackler was subtly building up the fee, glanced at him sharply.

"No," he said, "of course not. However, I'm a man of moderate means, Mr. Sackler. Now how much—"

Sackler eyed him appraisingly. "Shall we say five thousand?"

Archer frowned. "Well," he said thoughtfully, "that's a little steep. However—Suppose I give you twenty-five hundred now. Twenty-five hundred more when and if anything comes of the investigation?"

Sackler took a fountain pen from his pocket and tendered it to Archer. He turned his head and winked broadly at me while the check was being written. Archer left the check on the desk, stood up and shook hands.

"I'd suggest you come out to the house as soon as possible," he said.

"Within the hour," said Sackler.

Archer bade him goodbye, nodded to me and left the room. Sackler sat looking down at the green slip of paper in his hand, an ethereal expression on his dark face. I glared at him in frank envy.

"So," I said, "you've changed your mind. Now you're going to clear Carver. I thought you told Connelly he was guilty as hell."

Sackler sighed. He stowed the check away in his wallet with loving care.

"Joey," he said, "what happens to a Communist when someone drops a million dollars into his lap?"

"Well," I said, "I suppose his viewpoint changes and he becomes a Republican."

"Exactly. That, in a sense, is what has happened to me."

"I see," I told him. "When there's no fee in sight, Carver's guilty. But for five grand you're willing to reconsider your opinion and undertake to clear him. Is that it?"

Sackler stood up. "For five grand," he said with wholehearted sincerity, "I'd undertake to clear Judas Iscariot."

He wasn't kidding either.

THE NOBLE ESTATE had existed since the days of the Revolutionary War. It was a vast expanse of wooded land on the South side of Staten Island, flanked by a medium priced real estate development. It was there that Connelly lived.

Sackler and I arrived in the late afternoon and my immediate impression of the house was that it was an ideal spot for some deserving ghost to haunt. It was a huge, gloomy, Colonial structure the inherent melancholy of which was enhanced by the driving rain, by the distant pounding of the surf upon the beach. I found the oppressive atmosphere in no wise lessened when we got inside the house.

We were admitted into a high, dimly lighted hall by a short rotund man with a fat colorless face. He introduced himself as Eben Sweet and volunteered the information that he had been the confidential secretary of Robert Noble. We followed him into a vast drawing room where a cheerless fire smoldered in a brick fireplace.

Four people were seated in that room. Two women and two men. One of the men was Roy Archer.

"Ah, Sackler," he said. "Let me introduce you to the family."

The family consisted of Virginia and Harry Noble, the children of the dead man, and Ruth, Archer's wife. Virginia Noble reclined on a chaise longue by the window, a book resting in her lap. She wore no makeup. Her face was white and haggard. Her eyes were deep, black and morose. She looked as if all the gloomy melancholy of this old house had crystalized itself in her.

Archer's wife was young, pretty and blond, a diametric opposite of Virginia. It seemed to me that as she acknowledged the introductions there was subtle invitation in her smile.

Harry Noble was frankly hostile. He barely nodded to Sackler. Then he took an expensive cigar from his sullen lips and said, "This is a damned fool proceeding. Carver's guilty as hell."

Sackler shrugged his shoulders and said, "Perhaps," noncommittally. Then he followed Archer back into the hall where Sweet was waiting. I tagged along behind.

"Now, Sackler," said Archer, "you're to have free run of the house. Sweet, here, will answer any questions, show you around. Oh, yes, and dinner's at eight. I suppose you'll be staying."

"Sure," I murmured, "it's free, isn't it?"

Sackler glared at me as Archer went back into the living room.

3

I Break the Case—Maybe

SWEET TOOK SACKLER into the room that had been old man Noble's study and I went upstairs to prowl around. I came down some fifteen minutes later with a bundle in my hand and in a high state of excitement. Sweet was still talking to Sackler in the study when I arrived. I carefully held the bundle behind him so he couldn't see it.

"No," Sweet was saying. "None of us saw Mr. Noble that night. He didn't come down for dinner. He was working here in the study. He was still working when we went to bed. As far as I know no one in the house saw him between five in the afternoon and the time he was found dead the following morning."

Sackler grunted. He looked up and noted my frantic pantomime.

"All right, Sweet," he said. "That'll do. I'll send for you if I need you."

Sweet bobbed his round head and left the room. I closed the door behind him.

"Well," said Sackler, "what's the matter with you? Did you find a confession written on the bathroom wall?"

"I found something just as good," I told him. "For once I'm breaking a case instead of you."

He lifted his eyebrows. I flung my bundle on the desk at which he sat.

"Well," he said again. "What's this?"

"A shirt. A dress shirt and a silk handkerchief."

"Very interesting," said Sackler. "Are we going in the laundry business?"

"Wise guy," I said. "Pick 'em up."

He picked up the soiled linen with his thumb and forefinger. Then he saw the blood. There was a jagged red stain on the stiff bosom of the shirt. There were half a dozen little red spots encircling it. The silk handkerchief was marked with crimson as if someone had wiped bloody hands upon it.

"Ah," said Sackler, "and where did you find this?"

"Stuffed in the back of Harry Noble's closet. Underneath a pile of suitcases."

Sackler ran his bony fingers through his thick black hair. "And your theory is that Harry Noble killed his father for the estate?"

"Right. Knowing the old guy had quarreled with Carver he figured the chauffeur'd take the rap."

He considered that for a long time. Then he said, "Joey, it's incredible to me that you could solve a murder case alone and unaided. Frankly, I don't believe it."

I had another card up my sleeve so I didn't get sore.

"It's going to break your heart," I told him. "But I can clinch it. Motive and everything. Here. I found this in Harry Noble's desk."

I handed him the letter. Sackler looked down at it and read aloud:

Gambling debts must be paid. You have one week to pay the eighteen thousand dollars. If you fail we'll take matters into our own hands.

There was no signature.

"See?" I said. "Harry had to have the money. The old man wouldn't give. That Carver brawl was made to order for him. He killed his father. It's cold."

"It's too cold," said Sackler. "Too pat. I don't like it."

That was the trouble with Sackler. Throw something into his lap simple and clean and he didn't like it. It was too easy. He was invariably looking behind the obvious, searching for something intricate so he could take a deeper bow after solving it. I was telling him so when the door opened and Harry Noble walked in.

The moment the knob had turned Sackler with a swift gesture knocked the shirt and handkerchief to the floor behind the desk and thrust the letter in his pocket. He was looking up with an expression of bland inquiry by the time Harry actually got inside the room.

"Now look here, Sackler," Harry said abruptly, "since my cousin's been fool enough to bring you here, all right. I'll give you a day, or so, to look around. But there's one thing I shall insist upon."

Considering the evidence I'd dug up, I hardly thought he was in a position to insist upon anything but Sackler only said politely, "And that is?"

"My sister must be left out of this thing. I won't have you bothering her. She's a manic depressive type. She has recurring spells of melancholy. Pronounced suicidal tendencies. I simply won't have her annoyed."

He spun around abruptly on his heel, left the room and slammed the door behind him. I watched him go, then turned back to Sackler. He was regarding me quizzically.

"Well, Joey," he said. "Can you fit that into your theory?"

"Listen," I said. "I'm not as dumb as you think. His sister, who probably shares the estate with him, undoubtedly knows something about the murder. He's afraid she might crack if you go to work on her. So he tells this manic depressive story to get you to lay off."

He didn't answer me for a long time. Then he pushed his hair back with his hand and said, "Joey, you saw that book Virginia Noble was reading when we were introduced to her."

"Yeah. So what?"

"It was Schopenhauer, Joey. Schopenhauer's essays."

"So? And what does that prove?"

"Among other things, it proves you *are* as dumb as I think, Joey. Now get out of here until dinner time, while I give the problem the attention of a keen intelligence."

DINNER AT THE Nobles was something more than a meal. It was a ceremonial rite. The men, including Sweet, were dressed in tuxedos, while the two women wore evening gowns and the family jewels. The china was Spode and the silver was just that and not plated either.

I was in a little over my head and the atmosphere at the table was hardly conducive to congeniality. Harry Noble and his sister treated Sackler and myself with the same distant politeness they were using on the serving maid. Eben Sweet, who knew his place, hardly spoke at all. Archer and his wife conducted a desultory conversation with Sackler.

As soon as the meal was over I excused myself. I sneaked off to the study, swiped myself a cigar and went into the hall to smoke it. A little later Sackler joined me. I grinned at him.

"Well," I said, "why aren't you having coffee with the gentry in the smoking room?"

"Joey," he said, "you'll never believe it, but I find them duller than you."

I didn't bother answering him. I figured he was still sore because I'd dug up the evidence against Harry Noble. I stood staring out the window into the night. There was no moon and I could hear the rain beating down upon the trees. I began to suspect that the office on Madison Avenue was a far cheerier place than I had thought.

Sackler came over, opened the window and threw his cigar butt out into the garden.

"I'm going back to the study to think," he said. "Better come along, I may need you."

I followed him down the long corridor. Half way to the study we passed a door that stood ajar. A man's voice came faintly from behind it. Sackler put his hand on my wrist as he halted and listened.

The voice—I wasn't sure to whom it belonged—was saying, "Yes, Virginia, there's a lot of truth in that book. Life is a bitter ugly thing. A short space between birth and death. A thing hardly worth living. It—"

Sackler tugged at my sleeve. I followed him down the corridor again. He opened the study door and went in.

Sweet was sitting at the desk, writing a letter. His back was toward the window and a single floor lamp was lit, throwing the light over his shoulder. He stood up as we came in, looking more rotund than ever in his dress clothes.

"Say," said Sackler abruptly, "does everyone dress for dinner in this house? Every night?"

"Oh, yes," said Sweet. "Mr. Noble insisted on it." He frowned and added irritably, "It runs the laundry bills up frightfully. A clean shirt every night on a secretary's salary is rather difficult."

"I suppose it is," said Sackler. He was regarding Sweet with a peculiar expression. "By the way, there's one thing I forgot to ask you this afternoon, Sweet. Tell me, was everyone who is here tonight, present in the house on the night Noble was killed?"

Sweet nodded. "Why, yes. That is, except Mr. Archer. He had dinner with Bishop Winters. It rained so hard he stayed there overnight. Got back here very early in the morning."

Sackler grunted. "Okay," he said. "Now if you'll excuse us—"

Sweet bowed politely, picked up his letter and left the room. Sackler sat down in the chair he had vacated. He lighted a cigarette, shook his head and said, "Joey, I'm afraid they've got me licked this time."

"You'd sooner admit you're licked than admit I'm right," I told him. "Harry Noble's your killer. Only you're too damned stubborn—"

THE SHOT INTERRUPTED me. The report was muffled and distant. The bullet made a vibrant pinging sound as it bored neatly through the glass of the window. It spun past my ear and slapped against the hardwood wall like wet paper.

I looked at the hole it made, then at Sackler's chair. I estimated it had missed his left shoulder by less than six inches. Then I sprang to action.

I jerked my Police Special from my shoulder holster. I raced to the window, flung it open and leaned out over the sill. Behind me I heard Sackler's chair pushed back. He flicked out the light and said, "Get away from that window, you idiot. You can't see anything out there. But you can be seen."

He was so obviously right that I felt like a complete fool as I moved away. Sackler reached over and pulled down the shade before he turned the light back on. He turned a very serious face to me and said, "Well?"

"Rex," I said excitedly, "this clinches it."

"What clinches what?"

"It's got to be Harry Noble. He's missed those clothes, that letter. He figures we've got 'em. So he takes a pot shot at you. It couldn't be anyone else because you've got nothing on anyone else."

He didn't answer for a long moment. He looked at me thoughtfully and his face slowly lit up.

"Joey," he said softly. "You don't know what you've got there. Get me Connelly on the phone. Ask him the precise position of Noble's body when he found it."

I stared at him. That didn't make much sense to me. However I looked up Connelly in the book and made the call. After I concluded the conversation, I reported back to Sackler.

"Body on the floor beside this desk here. Knife in heart. Hilt protruding. Hands in front of chest as if warding off attack. Right leg twisted beneath body. Left leg—"

He waved me to silence. "That'll do, Joey. Now you ask Sweet to assign you to a room. Then go up to bed."

"Bed? My God, it's not half past ten."

"I'm going to call headquarters for a fingerprint man. I've got a few other chores to attend to. Tomorrow morning at seven o'clock I want you to call Inspector Wolfe. Tell him to be here at ten sharp."

"All right," I said. "But why do I have to go to bed?"

"Because you'll be up again at two o'clock. I'll be ready for a mattress myself then. And I'm waking you when I turn in. You'll have to stand guard until morning."

"Guard? What for?"

"Listen," he said testily. "Someone just took a pot shot at me, didn't they? There's a killer loose in this house. What would you do if you found me dead in the morning?"

"I'd take forty-two dollars and eighty cents out of your pants pocket," I told him, "then with a happy heart I'd call the cops."

I got out the door quickly before he could think of an answer to that one.

4

Protector of the Innocent

SACKLER ROUTED ME out of a warm bed at two thirty. For the rest of the night I sat in an arm chair in the upper hall watching the bedroom doors. Nothing happened.

By ten o'clock in the morning, I had Inspector Wolfe on deck and the whole Noble family gathered in the living room. I went back upstairs to Sackler's room. He was fully dressed, standing before the mirror combing his thick black hair.

"They're all waiting for you," I reported. "And the general atmosphere is not friendly."

"Okay," he said. "Go down and keep 'em in order. I'll be there in a minute. I've got to put through a call to Maxie Lord."

Maxie Lord was his personal attorney and I didn't see what he had to do with the matter in hand. However, I kept my mouth shut and went back downstairs.

We waited restlessly in the vast rectangular drawing room for Sackler. It was still raining outside and Virginia Noble sat by the window staring into the wet gray morning. If she really were manic depressive this was a fine morning for it.

Roy Archer and Sweet smoked cigars and chatted aimlessly in a corner. Harry Noble leaned against the mantel-piece and glared angrily around the room. Ruth Archer smiled brightly more from force of habit than anything else, while Wolfe paced up and down the floor registering irritation.

The idea of waiting for Sackler didn't appeal to him. He

didn't care much for Sackler. He envied those postal savings accounts more than I did.

Suddenly he ceased his pacing and came to a Guardsman's halt.

"Where the devil's Sackler?" he snapped at me. "What's he up to, anyway? We already *got* a guy in the can for the Noble killing."

"Of course," said Harry Noble. "The idea of engaging Sackler was absurd, Archer. Carver's the murderer."

Roy Archer looked at his cousin. It seemed to me that there was an expression of gentle mockery on his face.

At that point, Sackler strode in. Judging from the fact that he carried his hat in his hand and his rain coat slung over his arm, he had the case wrapped up, in the bag, and was ready to go home. He tossed the hat and coat on the gleaming mahogany table and bowed to the assembled company like an actor.

Wolfe scowled at him. "Listen, Sackler," he said, "when the police department has a case sewed up why the hell don't you keep your nose out of it?"

"Because," said Sackler piously, "I am a protector of the innocent; a scourge of the evil doer."

That was all very pretty. But if he pinned this killing on Harry Noble—and despite everything he'd said, I was certain he was going to—it had been Joey Graham who had done the scourging this time.

"All right," said Wolfe ungraciously. "If Carver didn't kill old man Noble, who did? If you've got something let's have it. Name a name."

"Sure," said Sackler. He looked around, relishing the fact that he was the cynosure of every eye in the room. The ham in him couldn't resist a taut dramatic pause before he put his finger on the killer. There was a tense atmosphere in the room which touched everyone but me. I lit a cigarette and waited for Sackler to throw the murder in Harry Noble's lap, collect the balance of his fee and go home.

Then to my utter amazement, he said quietly, "Ruth Archer, Inspector. Take her in. Homicide. First degree. I'll sign the complaint."

EVERYONE STARED AT him, goggle-eyed. Myself included. Harry Noble's sullen mouth contorted nervously. Eben Sweet blinked until he resembled a Kewpie doll with the tic. Virginia turned from the window and a flicker of interest crossed her dead pan. Ruth Archer had paled. She appeared frankly terrified. It was her husband who recovered first.

"He's crazy!" he shouted. "A crazy, incompetent money grubber. Inspector, throw him out!"

Wolfe paid no attention to him. The noun may have been accurate enough, but Wolfe knew damned well that Sackler was neither crazy, nor incompetent.

"What's your evidence, Rex?" he asked quietly.

"Eye witness," said Sackler. "Got a secret witness who saw the murder. She took a pot shot at me, too, last night. I saw her do that. And someone else saw her kill Noble."

I blinked at that. If he'd seen the person who had fired through the study window last night, he had defied every known law of optics and light.

"No," said Ruth Archer. "No. It's not true. I didn't kill him."

"Damn you!" roared her husband. "Who's your witness, you liar? Produce your witness!"

"I'll produce him for the D.A. and the grand jury," said Sackler. "I won't risk his life by naming him now. I've given him my word on that. This case is so big that someone tried to kill me. The witness would be in grave peril. Wolfe, take her in. I'll accept the responsibility."

I thought for a moment that Roy Archer was going to throw a fit. His face looked like a bomb about to burst. His breath was coming fast. He swung his head around from Sackler and stared at Sweet. Sweet looked back at him with utter blankness.

"Well," said Wolfe, dubiously. "Are you sure, Rex?"

"Take her in," said Sackler wearily. "I've got an eye witness I tell you. You've only got a circumstantial case against Carver."

Wolfe considered this for a moment. Then he shrugged his shoulders and walked across the room to Ruth Archer. He put his hand on her arm. Her husband went suddenly berserk.

"No!" he shrieked. "No! The fool. The utter damned fool! Can't you see what he's doing? He can't clear Carver, so he's framing my wife in order to collect the balance of his fee!"

Knowing Sackler as I did, that charge wasn't quite as absurd as it sounded. Undoubtedly there were a number of things that Sackler wouldn't do for five thousand dollars. But, off-hand, I couldn't think of one of them.

Sackler met Archer's wild gaze imperturbably. "Take her in, Wolfe," he said again. "And let's get out of here."

"No!" shouted Archer at the top of his voice. "You listen to me, Inspector. There's evidence in this house that's stronger than Sackler's frame-up. Evidence against someone else. Evidence Sackler was too damned dumb to discover himself."

"Click!" said Sackler softly—so softly that only I heard him.

Wolfe, completely bewildered, looked from Archer to Sackler.

"In Harry's closet," went on Archer. "There's a bloodstained dress shirt, a bloody handkerchief. In his desk there's an anonymous letter threatening him with death if he fails to pay a tremendous gambling debt."

Harry Noble gaped. His sister registered puzzled despair. She murmured, "Oh, Harry," in a thick voice. Sackler sighed heavily and it seemed to me there was a lot of relief in that sigh.

Wolfe said to no one in particular, "Is this true?"

"Wait a minute," said Sackler. "If you knew of evidence in the house, Archer, why didn't you give it to the police?"

Archer licked his lips and avoided Harry's gaze.

"It was my own cousin," he said hoarsely. "I couldn't bring myself to send my own flesh and blood to the chair."

"That doesn't make sense," said Sackler. "For sentimental reasons, you won't reveal the evidence yourself. Yet you offer me five thousand dollars to come here and find it."

Wolfe promptly forgot the murder case and thought of the amount of his own salary. His eyes bugged. "My God," he said bitterly. "He's getting five grand for this!"

"Now look here," said Harry Noble. His face was white but his voice was steady. "What's this all about? I never owed a gambling debt in my life. I never—"

"Shut up," said Sackler. "Archer owes me an explanation. I'm waiting to hear it."

Archer bit his lip. "Well," he said, "I— er, I—"

He broke off and looked helplessly around the room.

"Since you're having so much difficulty," said Sackler, "perhaps I'd better explain it for you."

Wolfe stroked his unshaven chin. "Rex," he said, "for the love of God stop playing Mr. Moto. If you've got something to say, say it."

"ALL RIGHT," SAID Sackler. "Roy Archer knew that stuff was in Harry's room because he planted it there himself. He wanted that murder pinned on his cousin. Unfortunately for him, your dumb department gummed it up for him, Wolfe."

Roy Archer threw back his head and laughed. It was a forced and horrible laugh with a touch of hysteria in it.

"I told you he was crazy," he yelled. "He's nuts. Now, he's accusing me of the murder. Well, if I did it why the hell would I go to him, offer him money to find the killer? Boy, that's funny!"

"It's funny as hell," said Sackler. "The fact that I can answer that question is even funnier."

Wolfe stretched his hands out in a pleading gesture.

"Look," he said with the air of a man exercising great restraint. "I'm just a simple copper, Rex. Two years in High School, twenty on the force. Now we got a chauffeur in the can for the Noble murder. Then you proceed to hang it on Mrs. Archer. Next, Archer pins it on Harry Noble. Now you say Archer himself did it. Is this a merry-go-round or a murder case?"

"All right," said Sackler. "I'll begin at the beginning."

"That," I observed, "is the most intelligent remark I've heard this morning."

He ignored me and continued: "First, we have old man Noble stabbed. Roy Archer desires very much that his cousin, Harry, burn for that crime. To this end he plants that bloody shirt, that handkerchief in Harry's room. He also plants that phoney letter to provide Harry with a motive."

"You mean," said Wolfe, "it appears that Harry needs money. The old man won't give. So Harry kills him and inherits the estate."

"That was the general idea," said Sackler. "Archer has the stuff neatly planted for the coppers to find when they arrive. But Fate, Carver, and Connelly wrecked his plans."

As I looked around the room, I reflected that with the exception of Wolfe and Sackler everyone looked guilty as hell. Roy and Ruth Archer were haggard. Harry Noble glared wildly at Sackler and Sweet's face was the color of weather beaten calsomine. Virginia appeared even more horror stricken than usual.

"You see," went on Sackler, "Carver's story was absolutely true. He found the body, touched the knife, got panicky and ran like hell. Only he ran right into Connelly's arms. When Connelly took him in, the homicide squad exercising its customary stupidity decided they had a cold case against Carver and refused to investigate further."

Wolfe muttered something under his breath. Sackler grinned at him and went on.

"So that leaves Archer with a load of planted evidence that no one is going to find. He goes to headquarters. He almost beg 'em to search the house for evidence. But the coppers laugh at him. They've got a guy in the can and a very nice case against him. That's enough for them. The whole thing's thrown right back in Archer's lap. Someone must find that phoney evidence against Harry Noble. Who?"

Sackler looked around the room like Mussolini waiting for his blackshirt mob to yell an answer. I took the cue.

"You," I said.

"Right. When Archer can't get the coppers to help him, he naturally thinks of the best man in the business. So he comes to me."

"Well," I remarked, "you got the commercial in, anyway."

Wolfe's face was screwed up in thought. "That sounds reasonable, Rex," he said slowly. "Can you prove any of it?"

"Of course, he can't," snapped Archer. "How the hell can he prove a thing like that? Besides, what's the motive? Why the devil should I kill my uncle?"

"For eight million dollars," said Sackler. "For the entire Noble estate."

5

Raincoat—Three Years Old

IT WAS AT that point that I became very uncertain as to whether, or not, Sackler actually had something, or was running a terrific bluff. There was a hole in his motive theory big enough to drive an elephant through. Harry Noble put his finger on it first.

"That's utterly absurd," he said. "Roy Archer wasn't in line for the estate. First it comes to me. After my death it goes to my sister, Virginia."

"Sure," said Archer with bitter irony. "Maybe I planned to kill Harry and Virginia, too. Eh, Sackler?"

"Not exactly," said Sackler. "But you planned to *have* them killed."

"What are you talking about?" demanded Wolfe. "Planned to have them killed by who?"

"Well," said Sackler, "he figured on getting a guy named Elliot to kill Harry. Virginia would kill herself."

"He's absolutely mad!" yelled Archer. "I don't even know a guy named Elliot."

"You will," said Sackler grimly. "He's the State Executioner."

Now it began to clear up a little in my mind. Even Wolfe saw it.

"You mean Harry would burn for killing the old man," he said. "So that's one guy out of the way."

"That's one guy out of the way," said Sackler. "Then if Virginia should also die, Archer as next of kin would naturally inherit."

There was hard suspicion in Wolfe's gaze as he kept his eyes on Archer. "All right, Rex," he said. "Keep talking."

"Virginia Noble is a manic depressive with pronounced suicidal tendencies," said Sackler. "Of course, that's something the Homicide Squad would never find out, wouldn't know what it meant if they did. Nevertheless it's so. Now, it's extremely dangerous for a person of that type to be exposed to morbid, or depressing ideas. But Archer's been giving her Schopenhauer to read. He's been telling her about the sordidness, the futility of life. I heard him myself."

"What does that prove?" said Archer very quietly.

"It proves," said Sackler, "that you intended to drive Virginia to suicide. Gradually, of course. It was only a matter of time. So you see, Wolfe, that would remove the two people who stood between Archer and the estate."

Wolfe looked very thoughtful. "Rex," he said. "It sounds swell. You've got me believing it. Almost. But what about Archer's alibi? Connelly's routine examination showed that Archer had dinner with a Bishop that night. He stayed over until morning because of the rain. If we've got to pin a perjury rap on a Bishop to clinch this case, I want no part of it."

Roy Archer smashed his fist down on the table top.

"Of course," he yelled triumphantly. "My alibi! You can't break that down, Sackler. And if I was at the Bishop's how the hell could I have killed my uncle?"

That was something I wanted to know, too. I looked over at Sackler. He retained the air of a man who knows all the answers.

"As a matter of cold fact," he said quietly, "I never said you killed your uncle."

WOLFE JERKED HIS head around and regarded Sackler suspiciously. On more than one occasion Sackler had taken the Homicide Department on a long derisive ride. Wolfe was beginning to think that perhaps it was happening now.

"Sackler," he said suspiciously, "are you trying to kid me? First you accuse Ruth Archer. Then you build up a case against her husband. Just when I'm convinced, you say he didn't do it."

"I hung it on Ruth Archer for an obvious reason," explained Sackler calmly. "I figured that if it appeared she was going to jail, Archer would be forced to mention his own planted evidence against Harry. I wanted to make him admit he knew it was there."

"I can see that," said Wolfe testily. "But now you say Archer's innocent."

Sackler shook his head slowly as if marveling at the dullness of the police department.

"Well," he said with a sigh, "there are a few other items to consider. First, Archer's made-to-order alibi. Second, that pot shot taken at me last night. That puzzled me for a little while. Why should anyone shoot at me?"

"I can think of several good reasons," said Wolfe grimly.

"Really?" said Sackler, grinning. "Well, I could only think of one. And that was, that I wasn't being shot at after all."

Wolfe was getting sore now. Sackler's round-about approach, his apparent paradoxes, were getting under his skin. They were annoying me, too. But I knew Sackler well enough to realize that he was going to produce his murderer in his own sweet, prolix way.

"Eben Sweet was sitting in the same chair that I was occupying three minutes before the shot was fired. He was writing a letter. I'll lay ten to one he was writing a letter that Roy Archer had asked him to write. That shot was fired at Sweet by someone who didn't know that I had taken his place at the study desk."

"That might be right," I said. "There was only one light lit in the study and the window was shut. From outside, your broad back might look like Sweet's fat one."

"Right," said Sackler. "Then comes the question: Why is someone shooting at Sweet? The answer to that can be found in the fact that everyone dresses for dinner in this house."

Wolfe groaned and sat down.

"Gertrude Stein, the great detective," he said bitterly. "What the hell *are* you talking about?"

"So," said Sackler, unruffled, "if some one is shooting at Sweet, it argues that he's somehow mixed up in this thing. Since Archer has an uncrackable alibi, it may even be that Sweet was the killer. And he dresses for dinner."

"Conceded," I said impatiently. "We all admit Sweet dresses for dinner. So what?"

"He wears a clean shirt every night," said Sackler. "He told me so himself. Furthermore, Connelly told me that the position of Noble's body indicated that he had attempted to ward off the knife attack. While doing so he, in all probability, touched his killer's shirt front."

The sweat on Sweet's gray face indicated that Sackler was rapidly approaching the truth.

"In Sweet's laundry bag," said Sackler, "I found two soiled dress shirts. Each of them bore Robert Noble's fingerprints. Which Sweet wore on the night of the murder and which before doesn't matter. For he certainly wore one of them. For he swore he hadn't seen Noble the night he was killed. *Yet each of those shirts bore Noble's fingerprints!*"

Wolfe stood up again. "Now, you're talking my language," he said. "That's real evidence. Fingerprints. And he swore he didn't see the old guy that night, eh?"

But as I saw it Sackler wasn't through yet.

"Motive?" I said.

"Simple," said Sackler. "He was in cahoots with Archer. Archer paid him to kill the old man. Then he decided he'd save the money and the worry of having a living confederate by plugging him as he sat in the study. It's very simple."

One look at Archer and Sweet convinced me that Sackler was absolutely right. Wolfe walked across the room toward them.

"WAIT A MINUTE," said Archer in a high pitched voice. "Maybe you have got something on Sweet. But there's nothing on me that you can prove."

That was true enough. Wolfe looked at Sackler, hoping he had something else up his sleeve.

"Hell," said Sackler easily, "you can beat that out of Sweet in the basement, Wolfe. He's not the sort of guy who can take it. Besides, you can offer him life instead of the chair. Let Archer be the guy that burns."

There was utter silence in the room. Ruth Archer sat down beside Virginia and buried her face in her hands. Harry Noble stared horrified at his cousin. Sweet was a study in abject palsy.

"All right," he said, and his voice was weak and trembling. "I'll tell you. But keep me out of the chair, Inspector. I did it. Noble's accounts were short. He would have discovered I'd been robbing him. Archer told me to kill him. Promised me a quarter of the estate. But if he tried to shoot me, I got a right to talk. Haven't I, Inspector?"

"Come along to headquarters," said Wolfe. "I want to get that down in black and white."

At that moment a very pleasant thought ran through my brain. "Hey, Sackler," I said. "What about the rest of your fee? You don't think Archer's going to give you that other twenty-five hundred now, do you?"

"What do you think I called Maxie Lord for?" said Sackler. "It's a legal debt. I can sue his estate for it if he doesn't give it to me. Do you think I'm a complete sucker?"

"Yes," said Roy Archer.

We all looked across the room at him. He stood with his back against the wall. His face was taut and gray like a steel etching. His eyes blazed with desperate fury. And there was an automatic in his hand.

"Yes," he said again. "I think you're a sucker, Sackler. Especially if you ever expect to collect the rest of that fee from me. I didn't think you'd ever break this case, but I was ready if you did."

He moved his right arm a little as Wolfe took a step toward him. Wolfe stopped dead.

"You were a sucker not to know I'd have a gun ready," went on Archer. "I've got a car in the garage ready to drive out. You haven't got me yet. You never will get me."

I was standing up now but I made no move to get my gun. The garage stood about fifty yards from the window. From where I stood I could see the rain beating down upon the closed doors. I knew it was utterly impossible for Archer to open those doors and keep the gun on us through the window at the same time.

Wolfe glanced at me and shrugged his shoulders. I knew his thought was the same as mine. Archer looked swiftly around the room. Then his gaze fell upon Sackler's hat and rain coat on the table.

He picked up the rain coat and wriggled his left arm into the sleeve, still keeping us covered with the gun. He pulled the right side of the coat over his shoulder, cape fashion so that the threat of the automatic was never obstructed.

At that point, to my utter amazement, Sackler jumped him.

I KNEW THAT Sackler possessed plenty of guts. But he was neither reckless nor insane. And this action was both. Once Archer was out of the room, one of us could have covered him from the front door, another from the window. We had him absolutely cold. And if Wolfe and I had figured that out, it was a cinch that Sackler who thought twice as fast, knew it also. Nevertheless he elected to fling himself across the room in a flying tackle, in the face of Archer's automatic.

I piled up on the two of them and groped for Archer's right wrist. Finally, I got it and wrenched the automatic from his hand. At the same moment Sackler's right hand cracked hard against the point of his jaw. Archer lay very still as Sackler and I came to our feet.

"Are you crazy, Sackler?" said Wolfe. "You damned nearly got a bullet in your head."

Sackler pushed the hollows out of his hat.

"Sure," he said, "and what if he'd started shooting?"

"So," I told him. "There were three of us. We would have shot right back."

"That's what I figured," said Sackler. "And he was wearing my rain coat. You would have shot him right through my coat. You would have ruined it."

He saw the expression of utter incredulity on Wolfe's face and mine.

"My God, man," he said defensively, "that rain coat cost me eighteen-fifty. Besides, I've only worn it three years."

Murder in the Mail

*For once Rex Sackler got so mad that he
worked harder solving a case than trying
to figure who was going to pay him*

1

A Phony Deal

REX SACKLER MADE a cryptic entry in the ledger, closed it and put his dollar fountain pen back in his vest pocket. He sighed deeply.

"The trouble with our business, Joey," he said heavily, "is the unutterable stupidity of the average felon. At times, I am forced to believe that burglars, stick-up artists, and even murderers are illiterate morons who paid scant attention to their teachers in Grammar School."

I stood by the window watching the Madison Avenue traffic and didn't answer him. Sackler, I knew, wasn't in a very happy mood. We hadn't had a case for three weeks. By the same token we hadn't had a fee, either. And there was nothing Rex Sackler regarded with more whole-hearted horror than a static bank account.

"Last week," he went on indignantly, "there were two killings in this town. On one occasion the guy went to the nearest precinct house and confessed. On the other, the damned fool dropped a wallet containing his driver's license and a dozen other items of identification at the scene of the crime."

He uttered an outraged snort and took a sack of tobacco from his pocket. I turned around and grinned as he essayed to roll a cigarette. Invariably he spilled more tobacco into his lap than he got into the paper. But he had been practicing for a week. If the sovereign State of New York slapped a two cent tax on a

*I waited till he was reading
the letter; then I jumped him*

deck of cigarettes and expected to collect anything from Rex
Sackler, the sovereign State was very much mistaken.

Finally, he achieved something twisted and shaped like a
limp rag which he put between his thin lips and lighted. Then
he resumed his squawk.

"If a lot of congenital idiots are going around leaving
visiting cards in the corpse's pocket or having attacks of
conscience which sends them falling over each other to
borrow a pen to sign a confession, the coppers are going to
break every case themselves. No one, Joey, is going to pay
an adequate fee for the use of my keen intellect and your
brawny right arm."

Well, it didn't make any difference to me. I collected my
sixty-five a week whether or not Sackler had any clients to send

monthly statements to. I watched him puff desperately upon the home-made cigarette which refused to draw, then returned to my contemplation of the crawling traffic.

A moment later I heard his chair scrape back across the floor. Sackler got up, crossed the room and stood at my side.

"Joey," he said, and there was an ingratiating oiliness in his tone, "I don't suppose you'd care to bet, odd and even, on the license plates of the cars down there?"

"Absolutely right," I told him. "I wouldn't."

Sackler sighed and puffed hard on his bent cigarette. After paying my salary every Wednesday, he invariably spent the rest of the week trying to win it back from me. He succeeded far more often than not. But this time I wasn't having any.

He cleared his throat and tried again. "Joey," he said, "we'll toss a coin. We—"

"We will *not* toss a coin," I said emphatically.

He gave me a pained look. "Why don't you wait till I've finished?" he said aggrievedly. "I was about to suggest we eat a first class luncheon. I'm sick of the Greek's hamburgers. Today, we'll spread ourselves. We'll go uptown to Tony's and eat the very best. I don't care what it cost."

"You don't care what it cost me."

"Joey," he said, wearing the virtuous expression of an umpire who has just called one wrong, "I am prepared to toss a coin. Should Fate ordain that I pay the check, you may eat the choicest food, drink the rarest wine with no complaint from me. On the other hand—"

"There isn't any other hand," I told him. "I've got exactly forty cents."

Sackler dropped his homemade cigarette to the floor, stepped on it, and helped himself to a Lucky from my desk. Then he said, "Forty cents? You were only paid yesterday."

"I'm getting smart," I told him. "My room and board are paid a week in advance. I've got forty cents for carfare in my pocket. The rest's been properly planked in the bank."

"Oh," said Sackler thoughtfully. Then he brightened again. "We can still toss, Joey, I'll be glad to cash a check for you. I'll—"

"It's a savings account," I told him. "No withdrawals for thirty days."

He looked at me as if he'd caught me stealing a nickel from my blind grandmother's pocketbook. For three years he'd been winning forty per cent of my salary back at various hazards, and now that I'd socked it away where he couldn't get his avid hands on it, his fine feeling for money was outraged.

"Joey," he said, horrified, "I never thought you were a piker!"

He clucked at me, then retired to his desk, a man whose faith in humanity had been bitterly betrayed.

That last remark and his attitude of reproach evoked an ironic laugh from me. Where money was concerned Sackler was a leech from way back. Every dollar he'd made was scattered about in Postal Savings accounts all over the country. And the outlay of any sum exceeding fifty cents caused him acute anguish and profound reflection.

HE WAS GIVING all his attention to the rolling of another cigarette when Nick Lanzatta walked into the office. The physical difference between Lanzetta and Sackler was marked. Sackler was dark, thin and almost foreign appearing. His eyes were black and hard as carbon and he wore a perennial air of anxious brooding. Lanzetta, on the other hand, was plump, blue-eyed, and exuded good-fellowship and well being.

The contrast between their fiscal habits was even more pronounced. Whereas Sackler's fingers constantly ached in their effort to cling to every dime that came into his possession, Nick Lanzetta, gambler and professional wise guy, was a big spender and an easy touch. Nick lived lavishly. A fact which irked the Police Department who had tried often and unsuccessfully to break the gambling syndicate which he headed.

He stood, big, florid, and dressed to kill, looking down at Sackler struggling with his sack of tobacco. A huge diamond flashed on his finger as he moved his hand to the pocket of his fancy vest. He whipped out a cigar and handed it to Sackler.

"Here," he said, "don't smoke that fertilizer. Try one of these."

Sackler took it. He carefully poured the tobacco from the cigarette paper back into the bag, bit off the end of the cigar and lit it. He inhaled happily.

"Hi, Joey," Lanzetta said to me. Then. "Now, Rex, how'd you like to make two hundred dollars?"

Sackler regarded him with interest. "Sure, Nick," he said. "I'm always ready to do business. What's the matter?"

"Some mug blew the door off a safe in my apartment," said Lanzetta. "Took me for a few C's. It ain't the dough, see? But no one's going to put anything over on Nick Lanzetta. I want you to come up and look it over, Rex. There's two hundred in it for you. Besides, I'll give you and Joey your lunch."

That sounded pretty good to me. Of course, I'd never see a dime of that two hundred, but Nick was a gourmet and a wine bibber. If he bought the lunch it would be a damned sight better than I'd get at the Greek's.

But Sackler hesitated for a moment. He regarded the gambler shrewdly over the end of his cigar. "Two hundred bucks," he said slowly. "And I don't have to guarantee any results?"

"For that sort of chicken feed," said Nick, "you don't have to guarantee nothing. Just look things over. That's all. You're the smartest shamus in town, Rex. If you don't find nothing, it's a cinch no one else will. Come on. We'll put the feed bag on first."

Sackler stood up, adjusted his four-year-old fedora jauntily and followed Nick from the office with a springier step than he had used for the past three weeks. I, dutifully, tagged along behind.

AT LANZETTA'S DUPLEX apartment on Central Park West, a Filipino boy served a luncheon that had my palate cheering. Nick didn't spare the wine, either. By the time coffee, cognac and cigars arrived I had begun to feel that perhaps there were worse jobs in town than working for Sackler.

Nick lounged back in his chair, puffing at a perfecto. He glanced down at his wrist watch, then eyed Sackler thoughtfully.

"Rex," he said. "You're a gambling man, aren't you?"

"Only when he deals himself," I put in. "If there's any chance of him losing he doesn't approve of wagering."

Sackler ignored me. He said to Nick, "I thought we came up here to investigate a robbery."

"Plenty of time for that," said Nick. "The safe'll stay there. Me? I believe in relaxing after a meal. Now here's a little game the boys were playing in Lindy's last night."

He thrust a fat hand into his trouser-pocket and produced

a quarter. He slapped it down on the table cloth and held his palm over it.

"We guess the date on this coin," he explained. "The guy that's farthest away pays the other two guys a buck apiece. How's that?"

Sackler whose luck was equalled only by his frugality, nodded his head and said, "Nineteen-twenty-nine."

Nick transferred his gaze to me. "What do you say, Joey."

"Nothing," I said emphatically. "Deal me out. I've exactly forty cents in my pocket."

"Your credit's good," said Nick Lanzetta. "Get in. It's more fun with three."

Sackler looked at me and his eyes gleamed suddenly. "Sure," he said, confident he could take me at anything. "Get in, Joey. Here."

He pulled a wallet out of his pocket and counted out some bills. He pushed them across the table to me. "There," he went on. "There's next week's salary in advance, Joey. Anyways glad to be of service."

I hesitated for a long moment. There always was a big streak of sucker in me. I knew I should lay off, but I figured that unless the law of averages had been suspended, I was due to take Sackler for a large wad. I reached out, picked up the money and said, "Nineteen-twenty-five."

"Okay," said Nick. "I'll take nineteen-twenty-seven."

He lifted his pudgy hand from the quarter. Sackler and I leaned over the table. The date on the coin was nineteen-twenty-six. Sackler frowned and handed each of us a dollar. Nick got up, went to a desk and took a roll of fifty pennies from a drawer.

"All right," he said. "Do you want to flip some, Rex?" He handed the roll of pennies to Sackler. "Go ahead."

We went ahead for forty-five minutes.

At the end of that period I had four dollars left out of next week's pay. But my chagrin at that was almost compensated for by the fact that Sackler was in for two hundred and eighteen bucks. His black eyes blazed angrily. A dark flush burned on his saturnine face. And each time he lost he'd mutter under his breath. It made me feel very happy.

Lanzetta poured a fresh round of cognac and became more expansive with each dollar he stowed away in his pockets. At last, Sackler, flushed and angry, pushed back his chair.

"I'm through," he announced sourly. "Let's investigate this robbery."

"For nothing," I reminded him maliciously. "Not to mention the eighteen bucks you paid for your lunch."

He glowered at me. Nick laughed. "That sort of dough don't mean nothing to us, does it Rex?"

Sackler didn't reply. But I knew the answer to that. That sort of money meant no more to Rex Sackler than his right eye or his government bonds.

He was still muttering profanely to himself as we followed Lanzetta from the dining room. We entered a huge, vast and airy library. Two wide windows formed the entire west wall. Filled bookcases lined the other three sides of the room. That struck me as funny. I knew Nick's favorite reading was the racing form. On the right, standing at the side of a magnificent mahogany desk, was a safe. Its steel door dropped wearily from a single hinge. Part of a metal lock lay splintered on the floor. Papers were scattered on the thick rug before the safe.

Sackler knelt down and looked at the battered steel door. Then he stood up again and grunted.

"When did it happen?" he asked. "And how?"

"Last night," said Nick, "I put about eight hundred bucks in there. That was around ten o'clock. When I got up this morning I found the door blasted off. The dough was gone."

Sackler grunted again. He put his hand on the gleaming desk at the side of the safe. "Nice piece of furniture," he commented. "Must've cost dough."

"Plenty," said Nick proudly. "Picked it up yesterday. It only came in today."

"Oh," said Sackler slowly. "It only came in today, eh?"

Nick nodded. "Just before I went down to your office."

Sackler changed the subject abruptly. "Was that safe opened by you at any time *after* you put the dough away? Before it was blasted open?"

Nick shook his head.

"Who has the combination?"

"No one," said Nick. "No one but me. But it ain't an inside job, Rex. That guy came in the window. Look. He used a glass cutter, took out a hunk of the pane, shoved his hand in and turned the catch."

Sackler and I turned to the window. A neat circular hole had been cut in the pane an inch or so below the lock. As I saw it, Nick's theory was correct and obvious. But Sackler seemed reluctant to accept anything that simple. He stared at the hole in the glass for a long time. Then he lifted the sash higher and peered out over the sill.

"Six stories," he said as he pulled his head in again. "No fire escape. No ledge large enough to hold a man. How could a guy get outside that window to cut it, Nick?"

Nick shrugged eloquent shoulders. "I ain't no dick," he said, and that was undoubtedly the truest statement he had ever made in his dubious career. "Maybe he came down from the roof on a rope. That's the baffling angle, Rex. That's why I called you in. I'm willing to pay two hundred bucks to find out."

THAT CRACK REMINDED Sackler that he was working for nothing. His eyes narrowed and he stared hard at Nick. His lips were tight, his face expressionless.

"What about the servants?" he asked.

"Naw?" said Nick. "Trust 'em with my life. Been with me for years."

"All right. Is it possible someone entered the front door without your knowledge?"

"Naw," said Nick. "I got a chain on it."

He looked down at his wrist watch and I could hear him humming a lilting melody under his breath. Sackler took his tobacco bag from his pocket and proceeded to roll himself a cigarette. As he lit it, he closed one eye. Whether that was to avoid the smoke or to register profound concentration, I didn't know. But I entertained an idea that he was playing the super-sleuth to impress Nick.

To my mind the case was cut and dried. Some second-story man, knowing Nick usually kept a supply of cash on hand, had devised some means of entering the apartment, brewed himself a mess of soup and applied it to the safe door. There wasn't a single mastermind in it. And I said so.

Nick nodded and consulted his watch again. "I guess Joey's right," he said to Sackler. "After all, it's a petty larceny job. There ain't a clue here even Sherlock Holmes could pick up. Besides,

Rex, I don't want to take no more of your time for the lousy kind of dough I'm paying you for this job."

Sackler's cheeks were stained dark red. The fact that he had lost his money was bad enough; the fact that Nick constantly reminded him of it was worse. His eyes were snapping as he met the gambler's gaze.

"Do you want to know who took your dough out of the safe?" he demanded. "Do you want to know who blew the door?"

Nick looked at him wonderingly. "You mean you know?"

"You're damned right I know," exploded Sackler. "You did."

I stared at him in honest amazement. Nick Lanzetta regarded him oddly.

"And how do you figure that?" he asked.

"According to you," said Sackler, "the servants didn't do it. No one could have entered the front door without your knowledge. According to the evidence of my own senses, no one could have come in that window."

"A guy could have come down on a rope," I said. "You've got to admit the window's cut."

"I admit it," said Sackler. "The window is cut. From the inside."

Nick blinked at him as he continued. "Take a look at that glass. There's a slight scratch paralleling the edge of the hole all the way around. It was cut from the inside, and I'll guarantee with your own diamond ring, Nick. You cut it with the edge of a diamond facet. A second edge touched the glass and caused that scratch around the hole. You cut it yourself. And from the *inside*."

"It doesn't make sense," I told him.

"If you want more evidence," said Sackler grimly, "examine

this desk. Nick says it was just delivered. He said, further, that the safe has never been opened since the desk has been here. Yet there's a nick in the elegant mahogany. A freshly made nick at precisely the point where the safe door would strike it if it had been swung carelessly open."

I looked over at Nick. There was a peculiar smile on his thick lips. It held, I thought, something of triumph. But I still didn't know what it was all about.

"So," said Sackler, "as I figure it—and I'll bet you two hundred and eighteen dollars, I'm right—you opened that safe this morning, Nick. Opened it after the desk was delivered. You took your eight hundred bucks out and put it in your pocket. You closed the safe again, souped it up and blew the door off. Then you cut a slice out of the window with that rock of yours, pulled the catch back and opened it."

"And then?" said Nick. He was grinning now.

"Then," said Sackler evenly, "you came downtown and offered me a fee to come up here and tell you this."

It still sounded screwy to me. Nick's expression was bland as he said, "And why the hell would I steal my own dough? Why would I ruin a five hundred dollar safe? Why would I give you two C's to come up here and tell me about it?"

"I don't know," said Sackler. "And if you want me to find out, the fee will be fifteen hundred dollars. Cash in advance."

Nick grinned broadly and raised his eyebrows. "It's not worth it."

"Sackler," I said, "you're crazy. That nick on the desk could've been made by the moving men. Maybe the window was cut by some new kind of glass cutter that causes a different bevel. Why would Nick blow his own safe?"

"Ask him," said Sackler.

Nick's grin grew wider. "Well," he said, "you can't put a guy in the pokey for robbing himself, can you?"

That crack bewildered me more than ever. I had thought Sackler's theory completely screwy and now Nick practically admitted its truth. He consulted his wrist watch again.

"Forget it," he said. "It's petty larceny stuff anyway. Come on. I'll drive you guys back to your office."

But Sackler was so sore he refused to save the nickel carfare. "We'll take the subway," he said shortly as he walked toward the door with me at his heels.

"What's the matter?" I asked him when we got into the elevator. "Afraid Nick'd toss you for five gallons of gas?"

He was so downcast he didn't even swear at me.

2

The Missing Letter

WE RODE BACK downtown in silence. In the office, Sackler threw himself into his swivel chair, wrinkled his brow and gave himself over to deep thought. In my own limited way, I did the same thing.

If it was true that Nick had blasted his own safe, swiped his own eight hundred bucks, why in the name of Heaven had he offered Sackler two hundred bucks to investigate? True, he'd won the dough back on his own little parlor game, but that didn't make it any easier to figure.

Sackler ran his long fingers through his black hair. "Joey," he said, "I don't see it. He *couldn't* have got me up there just to win that eighteen dollars. If that's what he wanted he could have found a million easier suckers in this town than me."

"Oh," I said thoughtfully, giving him the needle, "I don't know."

He glared at me, and I braced myself for a strong dose of literate epithet. Then suddenly his expression changed from rage to a mixture of horror and pain. He clapped a hand to his brow and groaned.

"My God," he said, and there was acute suffering in his tone. "Joey, we're a pair of supreme suckers! It just dawned on me."

"What dawned on you?"

"That game of Nick's. That date guessing game. It was a racket. We couldn't win. He had a cinch."

"I don't see it," I told him. "You tossed more than half the coins yourself. How could Nick frame it?"

"Listen," said Sackler. "Did you notice he guessed last every time? Invariably he waited until we had gone on record with our dates, before he called his own."

"So?"

"So, he couldn't lose. All he had to do was wait until he knew what our dates were. Then he selected a date *between* our two numbers. He couldn't possibly be farthest away. For instance, suppose you said nineteen-thirty. I called nineteen-twenty. All Nick needed to do was call a year within that decade. Say, nineteen-twenty-five. With you and I on either end Nick in the middle, one of *us* had to be farthest away. Now do you see it?"

Now I saw it. "Then the only time he could lose was when we picked dates in consecutive order. Say, twenty-seven and twenty-eight. Then, of course, he had to gamble. He couldn't go in the middle."

"Right," said Sackler. "But that seldom happened. And every other time he had us cold. Us," he concluded bitterly. "Us, the wise guys, taken like a couple of plough-jockeys in town for the Fair."

I thought of next week's salary which I wouldn't collect and began to get sore at Nick Lanzetta. Sackler was a geyser of wrath. His black eyes blazed. He slapped the desk top with the flat of his hand.

He said explosively, "The dirty little tinhorn. That's going to cost him five times what he won. I'll run his syndicate out of business. Larceny! That's what it is. Nothing less. I'll ruin him on Broadway. I'll drive him out of town. I'll—"

The list of dire things due to happen to Nick Lanzetta was

interrupted by the entrance of Denny Lynch. He had come into the office without knocking and stood, now, on the threshold looking at us with his watery blue eyes.

DENNY WAS THE sort of character guys write novels about. Physically, he looked like Maxie Rosenbloom after a steam roller had run over him. In his day, Denny Lynch has been a good second-class middleweight. But his day was long since past. Now he was a punch-drunk wreck who would be living on home relief had not his brother, Bryan, a successful corporation lawyer, taken care of him.

Both his ears were completely cauliflower; his nose was flattened against his face giving the effect of a grotesque mask. His mannerisms and diction were no less peculiar than his appearance.

The circle in which his brother Bryan moved had the bluest blood in town coursing through its arteries. And Denny, after forsaking the fight mob, taking up residence in Bryan's chromium penthouse, had grimly resolved to acquire the culture necessary to his new estate.

To this end Denny purchased a vast number of cheap tomes which treated of such elegant subjects as etiquette, social letter writing and elementary English. To these volumes he applied his addled brains in a futile attempt to impress his brother's society friends in general—the debutantes in particular. For in addition to his other eccentricities, Denny was a wide open sucker for a blonde.

The net result of his efforts had been the acquisition of a vocabulary that would have stunned a professor of English. But Denny, himself, Was firmly convinced that the weird phrases which passed his misshapen lips were choice examples of the conversation of the very best people.

He stood in the doorway bulging out of his Klassy-Kut suit. A ridiculously small Homburg was held in his massive left hand. He bowed formally from the waist in Sackler's direction and said in his stilted idiom, "Gents, I bid you hello."

Sackler nodded to him. I said, "Hello, Denny. Sit down and relieve your rickets."

Denny stepped across the threshold, carefully closing the door behind him. The key was in the lock and he turned it.

"Hey," I said. "What's the idea? Leave that door open, Denny. We—"

I shut up as he dropped his right hand into his coat pocket and withdrew it again holding a blue automatic whose muzzle pointed at Sackler's skull.

"Gents," said Denny very politely, "I hope I will be encountering no trouble here."

For a long moment Sackler and I stared at him in stupefied amazement. Undoubtedly Denny was a screwball. A thousand rights and lefts to his battered face had long since unscrambled his brains. But he had always been harmless.

Sackler recovered first. "Trouble?" he repeated. "You'll encounter it if you don't put up that gun, Denny."

"Leave us not mince no words, Mr. Sackler," said Denny elegantly, with his automatic still aimed at Sackler's temple. "I have come for the letter. I request you give it to me peaceful."

Sackler screwed up his brow. "Letter? What letter?"

"You are very well acquainted with that letter," said Denny, pronouncing each word slowly and distinctly as the book had told him to. "It is the letter written by my brother that must have came in the last mail."

"Denny," I said, "you're screwy. There hasn't been any mail all day."

Sackler was suddenly half out of his chair. "A letter?" he said excitedly. "Written by your brother, Denny? In the last mail? Click, Joey! I've got it."

"Got what?" I asked.

But before he could answer me Denny took a step forward. There was a menacing expression in his crazed blue eyes that I didn't like. I watched him closely, awaiting a chance to jump him, to snatch the automatic from his hand.

He thrust the gun into Sackler's face, and said, "For the last time, Mr. Sackler, will you give me that letter?"

Considering the fact that Sackler was figuratively looking death in the eye, his demeanor was admirable. He grinned up at Denny as if they were the best friends in the world. He used an easy conversational tone as he spoke.

"Now look here, Denny, if I had a letter from your brother, I'd give it to you. But, unfortunately, someone's been here before you. A little while ago—"

Denny Lynch's face wore an even uglier aspect than usual as he cut Sackler short.

"I do not come here to argue," he announced. "If you refuse to give me that letter, I shall search the office and take it with force."

There was a rock-like stubbornness about him. Sackler recognized it, too, and shrugged his shoulders.

"All right, Denny," he said. "Go ahead and search. But be careful of that gun. There's a very strict law against murder in this State."

Sackler threw a swift significant glance at me. But I didn't need it. I already knew what to do. Denny was going to have a tough job going through the office and keeping that gun muzzle on both of us at the same time. The instant the opportunity presented itself, I was scheduled to earn my salary by jumping him. It was one of those occasions when the Joey Graham right arm proved itself as important to the firm as the well press-agented Sackler intellect.

DENNY BEGAN HIS search by pushing Sackler's swivel chair, and Sackler along with it, half way across the room. He pulled out the top drawer of the desk and emptied its contents on the big green desk blotter. His right hand kept the automatic's muzzle wavering between Sackler and myself, while he sorted through a pile of old letters with his left.

Fortunately, Denny did not have the eyes of a lynx. He picked up each letter carefully and held it within six inches of his nose in order to read the writing. I waited, tensed, until he reached for the third epistle. Then, at the instant his attention was riveted on the letter, I sprang across the room.

I swung at his jaw with my right, and clutched at his wrist with my left. A bullet burned past my ear and hammered its way into the ceiling as Denny staggered backwards. He would have fallen had it not been for the bulldog grip I had on his right wrist.

But he wasn't done yet. He cracked me on the temple with a nasty jab. He jerked the wrist I held hard. I clung on with everything I had. I smashed him again on the jaw with every ounce of strength in my right arm. But he only shook his head and jabbed me back again.

I realized apprehensively that Denny Lynch had been taking it professionally for years. Since I dared not release his gun hand, the brawl was developing into a one handed slugging match. My right against Denny's left. When I hit him it was as if I was battering a brick wall; when he hit me it hurt like hell. I was getting very discouraged when Sackler came to the rescue.

He prodded Denny in the stomach with the muzzle of a thirty-eight.

"All right," he said. "Break it up. Drop that automatic, Denny."

Denny dropped his gun. I let go his wrist and stepped back, panting.

I wiped some blood from the side of my cheek where Denny's signet ring had scraped off the skin. Sackler poked Denny hard in the ribs with the muzzle of his thirty-eight. He jerked his head in the direction of the swivel chair.

"Sit down," he said. "Sit down, Denny, and do some talking."

Denny sat down. He bit his lower lip and appeared very worried. However, he remembered his social position and the elegant language it demanded.

"I will thank you to leave me get out of here," he said. "I apologize for the intrusion."

"If you don't talk," said Sackler grimly, "I'll leave you get out of here in charge of a police sergeant. And *he* won't leave you get out of where he takes you for at least twenty years."

Denny looked up and blinked. His battered face was pale and his fingers moved nervously in his lap. He was scared now and when he spoke he reverted to his natural Tenth Avenue dialect.

"Now listen," he said. "You ain't got nothin' on me. I ain't done nothin'. You gotta let me go. See? I didn't mean no harm."

"Let's see," said Sackler thoughtfully. "First, the chances are you have no permit for that automatic. That's ten years, maximum. Attempted robbery with a deadly weapon is at least fifteen more. And if your car is parked downstairs, it's already exceeded the twenty-minute limit. That'll be ten dollars or ten days. It adds up to quite a lot, Denny."

Denny wasn't particularly quick witted. But Sackler's meaning poured through his cauliflower ears into his addled intelligence rapidly enough. He became panicky. He pounded the arm of the chair with his massive fists.

"No!" he yelled and his voice broke just this side of hysteria. "No! Don't get the coppers. I got trouble enough. I got—"

"You'll have more trouble," said Sackler, "if you don't tell me what it's all about."

Denny swallowed something in his throat. He peered at Sackler through half closed lids like an animal at bay.

"Lemme think," he muttered. "Leave me alone for just a minute and lemme think."

Sackler sat down on the edge of the desk and let him think. Denny's brow was screwed up like corrugated iron. His little blank eyes stared at the far wall. His teeth were sunk far into his lower lip. Cerebration was a difficult endeavor for Denny Lynch and he showed it. At last he raised his head and nodded.

"ALL RIGHT," HE said. "I'll talk." He paused for a moment and his hands clutched the arm of the chair. He appeared to be laboring under great emotional stress. "It's my brother. Bryan. He's dead."

Sackler's eyes lit up. Bryan Lynch had made a lot of money

in the past five years. If there was a case here, there would be money in it.

"Dead?" said Sackler. "When? How?"

"I find him half an hour ago," said Denny. "With a gun in his hand and his brains blown out. In the sound-proof study at the penthouse. Gee, it was awful. Gee—"

He broke off, shuddered, and put his hand over his eyes. Sackler regarded him shrewdly and unsympathetically.

"What's all this about a letter?" he asked sharply.

Denny breathed hard and spoke earnestly. "There was a letter he sent to you about a half hour before I found him. The elevator boy who mailed it told me about it."

"So," said Sackler, "why the devil did you come in here with a gun and try to get it?"

There was a long silence before Denny replied. His face was screwed up so painfully, that I figured he was thinking again.

"Well," he said at last, "I'll tell you. I kinda thought maybe that letter would name the name of the guy who drove my brother to suicide. I was going out and get the guy myself."

Sackler looked as credulous as a Frenchman being told of Hitler's pacific intentions.

"For the moment," he said, "we'll let that go. Do the coppers know Bryan Lynch is dead?"

Denny nodded again. "I told the elevator boy to call 'em just before I came up here."

Sackler tapped his gun muzzle thoughtfully against the palm of his left hand. Then he looked up suddenly and shot a question at him.

"What's Nick Lanzetta got to do with this?"

I looked over at him in surprise while Denny was frankly

bewildered. He blinked and said, "Nothing. Nick ain't got nothing to do with it. Why?"

"You know Nick, don't you?"

"Sure, I know him. But I ain't seen him for over six months. I don't mix with that mob no more."

Denny's surprise at that question seemed so honest that I believed him. Besides, I couldn't see what Nick had to do with it myself and I said so.

Sackler gave me the special look he reserved for those times when he found me unutterably dumb.

"He took the letter, didn't he?"

"What letter?" I said. "And when did he take it?"

Sackler sighed wearily. "You're a very bright shamus," he said in a tone which implied I wasn't at all. "Somehow, Nick knew that letter was due here in the twelve-thirty mail. So he blew the door off his own safe in order to give us a case to solve during the lunch hour."

I recalled, suddenly, Nick's constant interest in his wrist watch while we had been with him.

"You mean," I said, "that he deliberately sucked us out of the office? That letter from Bryan Lynch came while we were out. And Nick had someone come down here with a skeleton key, maybe, and swiped it?"

"Just that," said Sackler. "Moreover," he added bitterly, "he made us pay a couple of hundred dollars for the privilege of having our mail stolen."

"Well," I said, "and what are you going to do about it?"

Sackler got up off the desk and dropped the thirty-eight into his coat pocket.

"I'm going to work on a case," he said. "The case of Bryan

Lynch's death. Lanzetta's mixed up in it somewhere and I owe him some trouble."

Denny, the threat of Sackler's gun removed, stood up and licked his lips nervously.

"There ain't no call for you to bother yourself, Mr. Sackler," he said. "Bryan killed himself all right. Lanzetta ain't got nothing to do with it. Besides—"

"You shut up," said Sackler, "and do as you're told. I'm still holding twenty years over your head, Denny."

He put on his hat, took Denny's arm and walked toward the door.

"What do I do?" I asked. "Tag along."

"No," said Sackler, turning. "The cops must have the corpse out of the house by now. You go down to headquarters, Joey. See Inspector Wolfe and the Medical Examiner. See what you can pick up. I'll be over in Lynch's penthouse when you're through."

"Wait a minute," I said, "you're forgetting something vital."

"What?"

"Who's your client? Suppose you break this screwy case, who's going to pay your fee?"

"I hope it's Nick Lanzetta," said Sackler. "But I don't really know. However, don't worry about it, Joey. I'll find someone to pay the fee, I'm pretty good at that."

On that score there certainly was no room for argument.

3

The Round-Up

I SPENT ABOUT a half hour down at Headquarters interviewing the Medical Examiner and Inspector Wolfe of Homicide, who didn't appear very happy as he heard Sackler was working on the case. Then I came thundering uptown again in the subway to the Lynch apartment at Park and Seventy-sixth Street.

As I got out of the elevator on the top floor, I saw a uniformed employee of the building enter the door of the Lynch penthouse. I followed him inside. I walked through a huge foyer into a living room. There, in a wide modernistic chair sat Denny Lynch. His elbows were on his knees and his chin was propped up on his hands. He stared blankly at the floor. He did not look up as I passed him. Evidently the death of his brother had thrust his addled wits still further across the line of insanity.

A big door, four inches thick stood open further down the hall. I looked across the threshold to see the attendant standing respectfully before Sackler. The room held a big desk and a number of bookcases. This, I realized, was the sound-proof study where Bryan Lynch had met his death.

Sackler nodded to me as I entered. I noticed that he was holding a long piece of twisted wire in his hand.

"Close the door, Joey," he said. Then, when I had done it, he addressed the man before him.

"Now, Luke," he said, "you mailed a letter early this morning.

A letter addressed to a Mr. Rex Sackler on Madison Avenue. Is that right?"

Luke nodded. "That's right, sir."

"Did Mr. Bryan Lynch give you that letter personally?"

"No, sir. I found it in the hall outside."

Sackler frowned. "What hall?" he asked. "Out there by the elevators?"

"No, sir. In the hall outside the service entrance."

Sackler toyed thoughtfully with the wire in his hand. "Where is that hall?" he said. "Show it to me."

Luke walked across the room. Now, I saw, for the first time, a second door on the far side of the study, almost directly opposite the one I had entered. Luke opened it to reveal a narrow corridor beyond. He stepped across the corridor and opened still another door which led to a hallway outside the apartment.

"It was here," he said to Sackler. "I was walking down this hall when I saw the letter on the floor. I figured someone had dropped it. See, there's two more penthouses with service entrances opening on to this hall, here. Anyways, I mailed it, and remembered the address on it so's I could find out who dropped it."

Sackler grunted. "The motive being to collect a tip, eh?"

Luke grinned but didn't answer. Sackler closed the outside door, crossed the inside corridor and returned to the study.

"Now Luke," said Sackler. "You spoke to at least two people about that letter. Who were they?"

Luke looked surprised. "That's right," he said. "I did. I told Mr. Denny Lynch and the lady with him, when they came in around ten o'clock this morning. I—"

"Wait a minute," said Sackler sharply. "Did you get your tip?"

"Why, no," said Luke. "As soon as I told them about it, they ran into the elevator and went upstairs. I went out to get a cup of coffee. When I came back I found out Mr. Bryan Lynch was dead. That his brother and the lady had left the house after telling the elevator boy on duty to call the police."

"Did you tell the police about that letter?"

"No, sir."

"Why not?"

Luke shrugged his shoulders. "They didn't ask me."

Sackler drew a deep breath. "Luke," he said. "You're a smart boy and you've been a lot of help. When I get my fee for this case, I'll see that you get a nice cash present."

Luke grinned, thanked him and made his exit. I watched Sackler as he went into a meditative hop.

"What fee?" I asked. "You haven't even got a client yet."

He looked up and smiled faintly. "I'm beginning to think I have, Joey," he said. "Now what did you find down at Headquarters?"

"The first thing I discovered," I told him, "was that Wolfe and the rest of the Homicide Squad wish to hell you'd go back to your office and leave the case to them."

Sackler's smile grew broader. "What else?"

"They kind of figure it was suicide," I told him. "Except for one thing that's a little screwy."

Sackler lifted his eyebrows.

"The Medical Examiner's report," I went on, "finds that Bryan Lynch suffered from malnutrition for some time before his death. They figure he didn't drink any water for a couple of days, too."

FOR A LONG moment, Sackler's expression was one of

deep thought. Then his eyes lit up and his smile was so ethereal that I knew he was thinking of money. He held up the twisted wire which was still in his hand.

"Do you know what this is?"

I squinted at it. "It looks as if it had been a wire coat hanger once. Someone's twisted it out of shape."

"Joey," said Sackler, "perhaps I've been wrong all these years. Maybe you have a mind, after all."

I let that pass. "There's one more item of my report," I said. "You may be interested in knowing that the coppers want Denny Lynch for questioning. They'll probably be up here after a while."

"Denny," said Sackler thoughtfully. "Bring him in, Joey."

I went back into the living room. Denny hadn't moved an inch. He still sat in the big chair, chin propped on his arms, staring like a brooding madman at the pattern on the rug.

I spoke to him twice before he answered. Then he followed me, docilely enough, into Sackler's presence. Sackler looked at him sternly and said, "Denny, the cops are combing the town for that girl. If they find her, they'll give her the works."

I blinked at him. I didn't know what girl what cops were going to give what works. But rather to my surprise Denny seemed to know what it was all about.

His throat moved convulsively. "They wouldn't do that, would they, Mr. Sackler?" he said. "She didn't do nothing. She ain't got nothing to do with it. Besides the coppers wouldn't slug a dame, would they?"

Sackler's ironic laugh indicated that every copper on the force slugged a couple of dames before breakfast just for the hell of it.

"Look here, Denny," he said. "I'm in this case half way, I may as well get in completely. There's just a chance I can get a good lawyer to protect that girl for you. You like her, don't you?"

"Sure," said Denny, twisting his fingers nervously. "I like her a lot, Mr. Sackler."

Sackler snatched up a pencil and piece of paper from the desk. "What's her name, Denny? What's her address?"

Denny mumbled a name and address which Sackler scribbled down on the paper.

"Now, Denny," said Sackler, "you wait outside in the living room. I'll start telephoning right away."

Denny shuffled out of the room. I watched him go with some perplexity. There was something wrong with Denny. And by that I mean something wronger than usual. He had completely forgotten his elegant and phoney diction. He seemed scared, and then again he seemed just plain dopey. Perhaps it was that he was as scared as any guy too dumb to get scared can get.

Sackler handed me the paper with the name and address on it.

"Audrey Murray," he said. "Upper West End Avenue."

"So," I said, "and what do I do? Make a date with her?"

"Correct, Joey. Take Denny with you. Get that girl. Then take them both over to Nick Lanzetta's apartment. Hold the three of them there, at the point of a gun, if necessary, until I get there."

I stared at him. "We'll lose our license," I said. "If that's not kidnapping, it's so close a jury'd never know the difference. What's Nick going to say when I bring Denny and a strange woman to his apartment and hold them there?"

"She's no stranger to Nick," said Sackler. "As a matter of fact she knows him quite well."

I twisted up my face and stared at him. "And how do you know that?"

He grinned broadly. "I'm a professional detective," he said. "I detected it, Joey."

"Listen," I said, irritated, "you're always accusing me of being dumb. But you're always holding out on me. Maybe if I had all the facts of a case I could figure it as easily as you."

He didn't like that. The grin disappeared from his face. Any deficit in his Postal Savings Accounts or intimation that the Sackler brain wasn't on a par with Einstein's invariably ruffled his temper.

He took a folded green slip of paper from his pocket and handed it to me. I opened it up and looked at it. It was a check on the Federated Bank. Across its face were written the words: *No. You damned fool. I want to talk to you.*

"So," I said. "What?"

"I found that in the wastebasket in the living room," said Sackler.

Again I asked, "So what?"

"So," said Sackler in his best sneer, "now you have all the facts in the case that I have. Do you want to take it over? Or shall I stick around for a little while?"

I screwed up my brow and considered. For the life of me I couldn't figure any fresh angle on Bryan Lynch's death, Nick's blasted safe, and Denny's odd conduct.

"All right," I said at last. "You stick around. But I bet you haven't figured out who's going to pay the fee."

I made that crack to needle him. But it didn't work. "The hell

I haven't, Joey," he said. "That was the first problem I worked out."

"I hope you're right," I told him. "Or else we'll be sharing a room up the river for kidnapping."

I left him in the study, picked up Denny and took him uptown to Audrey Murray's apartment.

I HAD A big easy chair pushed up against the door of Nick Lanzetta's living-room. I lounged back in it and balanced an automatic upon my knee. From the other side of the room, three pairs of eyes regarded me with frank hostility.

Denny Lynch perched his huge body on the edge of a wide sofa. His massive hands were clenched into fists which moved slowly in front of him as if he were preparing to charge an imaginary opponent. The expression in his eyes was not as blank as usual. He stared at me as if he was looking for an opening, a chance to slug me and snatch my gun.

Audrey Murray, red haired, gorgeous and possessed, paced the floor like a caged tigress. She watched me through smoldering black eyes. She was tall, lithe and very beautiful. It occurred to me it would be equally dangerous to incur either her hatred or her love.

Nick, quite accustomed to extra-legal dilemmas, was the calmest of the trio. He stood, one arm on the mantle-piece, smoking a cigar. His gaze was shrewd and calculating and there was a tiny frown upon his brow. He looked down at his wrist watch and sighed.

"Joey," he said. "I'm already late for an appointment. Let's get down to business."

"I'm actively engaged in my business right now," I told him.

"I'm Rex Sackler's assistant. Remember? He told me to hold you three here until he arrived. Maybe I'm not doing it very subtly. But I'm doing it."

Denny took his eyes off me and appealed anxiously to Lanzetta.

"Nick," he said. "This ain't legal, is it? It goes against the laws of the State?"

Audrey Murray ceased her pacing, fixed me with burning eyes and said savagely, "It's against every law in the book. He came up to my apartment with a gun and dragged me here. It's kidnapping. It's a life rap." She turned to Nick and there was thick contempt in her tone. "And you let him get away with it! I thought you were supposed to be a hard guy."

"Hell," said Nick reasonably. "Even Joe Louis can't lick an automatic."

I had left the front door off the latch, now it was with relief I heard it open. I stood up, jerked the chair away from the door, and opened it.

"Now," I announced, "if you want to squawk, you can squawk to the boss, himself."

Sackler came into the room. His face seemed darker and thinner than usual. There was dark brooding in his black eyes. Nick, Denny and the girl all began to talk at once. Sackler closed the door, put his back against it and regarded them coolly.

Audrey Murray's voice, more strident, more dominant than the others, filled the room.

"Listen, you smart shamus," she said bitterly. "Who the hell do you think you are? You can't get away with this. You'll lose your license. You'll get ten years in Dannemora."

Sackler raised his eyebrows. "On the contrary," he said evenly. "You will."

I noticed the girl exchange a swift glance with Nick. "For what?" said Nick. "You got nothing on her."

Denny stood up. He punched his open left palm with his right fist. As he spoke there was something in his voice which was either baffled rage or fear. I wasn't certain.

"Ain't I suffered enough?" he demanded in a high cracked tone. "Ain't it enough that the finest brother I ever had is taken from me. Ain't that enough without having to sit here and look a gun in the eye?"

"Sit down," said Sackler without sympathy.

There was an authority in his words which Denny backed away from. Nick, flushed and angry now, deserted the mantelpiece and walked across the room. He stood before Sackler and spoke his piece vehemently.

"Say," he said belligerently. "I got enough influence in this town to get my rights. Anyway, I guess Headquarters wouldn't have its heart broken if you lost your license. You've held three people against their will. It's a violation of our constitutional rights. It'll break you, Sackler."

THAT, I REALIZED, was true enough. If Sackler didn't have anything to pin on these three and make it stick, I was going to be out of a job. For that matter, so was Sackler.

Sackler took his tobacco bag from his pocket and rolled a cigarette with steady fingers.

"When the D.A. gets an open-and-shut murder case handed to him on a plate, Nick, you'll find he's rather inclined to overlook the civil rights of the killer."

Denny moved even closer to the edge of the sofa. "Murder?" he said with a hissing intake of breath.

"What do you mean?" asked Audrey Murray in a low tense voice.

Nick Lanzetta watched Sackler through narrowed, appraising eyes. "A murder case?" he said quietly. "Who's been murdered?"

Sackler sighed heavily. "If you'll all sit down and shut up," he said. "I'll tell you who killed Bryan Lynch. Morever, I'll tell you how. And why."

There was utter silence for a moment, then Audrey Murray said, "Bryan Lynch murdered? You're crazy."

"The evening papers called it suicide," said Nick quietly.

Denny put his head in his hands and rocked back and forth like a lamenting woman.

Sackler sighed again. "You people don't seem to appreciate the fact that I'm giving you a scoop," he said. "I'm giving you the story of the Bryan Lynch murder before I give it to the police. All right, if you don't want to hear it…."

Nick Lanzetta put out his cigar with a studied gesture. "All right, Sackler," he said. "Go ahead and talk."

"Bryan Lynch was murdered," said Sackler. "Shot down after being held prisoner for several days."

Denny took his head from his hands and stared wildly about the room. Nick Lanzetta laughed without mirth.

"That doesn't make sense to me," he said. "If Bryan Lynch was found in his own apartment how could he have been held prisoner. Besides, according to the evening papers, the coppers seem to believe it was suicide."

"It wasn't," said Sackler. "And Bryan Lynch *was* held prisoner in his own apartment."

"You can't prove that," flared Audrey Murray.

"I can make a beautiful try," said Sackler. "Consider this. The Medical Examiner reports that Bryan Lynch suffered from malnutrition and lack of water for some days before he died. Now, in my book there never was a suicide who starved himself to death. Since Bryan Lynch was a wealthy man there was no reason for him reaching the verge of starvation. That argues he was a prisoner. Since the kitchen in his penthouse contained plenty of food, it argues, further that he was a prisoner in a specific room of the apartment. To be exact he was confined in his own soundproof study."

Nick Lanzetta tried to look amused. He wasn't very successful.

"It still sounds screwy," he said. "Why should he be locked in his own study?"

"With the exception of Joey, here," said Sackler, "every person in this room knows the answer to that, Nick."

Well, he was twenty per cent right anyway. *I* didn't have any idea.

"However," went on Sackler, "Bryan wrote a letter to me, telling me of the spot he was in, asking for help."

"Sure," said the girl with heavy irony. "So he's locked in the study yet he gets out to mail a letter."

4

Frame Upon Frame

SACKLER CLUCKED AT her in mild reproof. "You know better than that," he said. "That letter was found in the hall outside the service entrance of the penthouse. Found and mailed by Luke the elevator relief man."

"Listen," said Denny, his brow screwed up in painful and anxious thought. "If my brother was locked in that room, how could the letter get out there in the hall?"

"That's been worrying you all day. Hasn't it, Denny?" said Sackler. "Well, I'll relieve your mind on that score. There was a coat hanger in the study—a wire coat hanger. Bryan pulled it apart, untwisted it until he had a single long piece of wire. Using that he pushed the letter underneath the study door on the service entrance side, pushed it across the narrow corridor and underneath the outer door leading to the hall outside the apartment. He gambled that someone would find it and mail it."

"So what?" said Nick. "What's that got to do with me?"

"A great deal," said Sackler. "You have that letter now."

Denny jerked his eyes from Sackler and stared at Nick. "You?" he said. "How did you get it? What—"

"It was a very interesting letter," went on Sackler, interrupting him. "It undoubtedly told me who was holding Bryan prisoner. It's also quite likely that it stated his captor had threatened his life. You knew about that letter, Nick. You wanted it very badly. Badly enough to blast your own safe open to provide an excuse for getting me out of the office while your confederate, probably Miss Murray, entered my office with a skeleton key right after the mail had arrived."

"Wait a minute," said Denny. "She ain't no con—confederate of Nick's."

Sackler paid no attention to him. Nick looked up and said, "How could I have possibly known about the letter?"

"The elevator boy told two people about that letter," answered Sackler. "Denny and the lady who was with him. Now, certainly, Denny had no reason to tell you about it, Nick. So that left the lady. She told you. Didn't you, Miss Murray?"

The girl lighted a cigarette and blew smoke through her long nostrils.

"Supposing this theory is all true," she said. "What in hell would either Nick or I want with that damned letter?"

By now, I was completely convinced by Sackler's manner that he had all the facts at his finger tips. His cat and mouse manner of circumlocution was annoying me.

"Will you get to the point?" I asked him. "Who was holding Bryan prisoner and why?"

"I thought even you could figure that, Joey," he said. "It was Denny. It had to be Denny."

Denny stood up and beat his fists together. He opened his mouth as if to speak when Nick snapped, "Sit down and shut up, you fool!"

"Listen," I said patiently, "why did it *have* to be Denny?"

"One," said Sackler, "Denny's interest in obtaining the letter. Two, the fact that since Denny lived with his brother it would be almost impossible for Bryan to be held without Denny's knowledge. Three, the matter of Bryan's letter being addressed to me. Under normal circumstances, Bryan would have sent his message to the police. Sending it to a private detective indicated Bryan wanted help without trouble or publicity. He had no desire to get Denny into a serious jam. Four, that blank check Denny slipped under the door for Bryan to fill out, bore the notation: *No. You damned fool. I want to talk to you.* Hardly the sort of message one would send to a resolute gangster. But quite the tone to take with a punch drunk relative."

I looked over at Denny. His head was in his hands again and he was swaying back and forth uttering low inarticulate sounds.

"All right," I said. "So Denny's got his brother locked up in the study. I suppose the motive is financial, considering that check. But why does Denny have to go to those lengths to get dough from Bryan? Bryan always gave him enough."

"Not always," said Sackler. "Consider. What's the weakest link in Denny's quite fragile character?"

I looked across the room at Audrey Murray. Something clicked at the back of my brain.

"Dames," I said.

"Inelegant," said Sackler, "but nevertheless correct. Dames is the answer. Suppose some girl told Denny she'd go away with him, maybe marry him if he settled a large sum of money on her. Suppose Denny asked his brother for that money. Suppose Bryan laughed and told him to go to hell."

Denny's voice came thick and plaintive through his hands.

"He should of give it to me. Fifty grand meant nothing to him. When I had it I would of give it to him."

Sackler lifted expressive eyebrows. "Fifty grand? A lot of dough, Joey. Worth a great deal of hard work, eh, Miss Murray? Picture it, Joey. Miss Murray using all her charms to get Denny to force Bryan to hand over fifty grand. She wields so much influence over him that, at last, he imprisons his brother in that sound proof study and tries to starve it out of him. But Bryan isn't having any."

"It sounds nice," I admitted. "But I still don't see why they killed him. I don't see where Nick and his interest in that letter fits in."

SACKLER CAST HIS gaze around the room. There was an expression of assured mockery upon his dark face. Denny wept softly into his gnarled fingers. The girl stared defiantly at Sackler, hatred in her flashing eyes. Nick Lanzetta was pale and his fat cheeks were shadowed with anxiety.

"This morning," went on Sackler, "Denny and his girl friend arrived at the Lynch apartment house for another try at Bryan. Downstairs, Luke, the elevator boy, looking for his tip, told them about the letter he had found addressed to me, told them he had already mailed it.

"That put both of them in a panic. They knew that the letter undoubtedly exposed the whole scheme. Audrey Murray realized it meant the end of the fifty grand she wanted. Denny was scared to death that it meant he would go to jail."

"So," I said, "they rush upstairs to see if Bryan's loose."

"They do," said Sackler. "They find he isn't. They demand to know how he got that letter out. Bryan laughs at them. He threatens them. There is a fight. In the brawl, either Denny or Audrey Murray killed Bryan."

The girl said tensely. "I didn't do it. I never carried a gun in my life. Denny tried to scare him with the gun. Bryan tried to grab it. Denny shot him."

"He should of give me the money," sobbed Denny. "I didn't mean to kill him. He was the best brother a guy ever had."

His shoulders moved convulsively. He wept like a child into his hands.

"Now," said Sackler. "Denny wanted that letter badly. Without it he'd face a first degree murder rap. But his girl friend has other ideas. She fixes the gun in Bryan's hand so that the cops will, perhaps, believe it's suicide. Then she runs up to see Nick. If she and Nick get possession of that letter, if Denny escapes a murder rap, they can clean up a fortune."

I didn't quite see how and I said so.

"Because," said Sackler, "if Bryan is a suicide, Denny gets his money and Nick and the girl have a letter which may well send Denny to the chair. Denny would be blackmailed for the rest of his life."

There was a long silence. Sackler took his tobacco bag from his pocket, then noting the box of Nick's cigars on the table, thought better of it. He was lighting the cigar when Nick Lanzetta spoke.

"All right, Sackler," he said. "What are you waiting for? You've just cleaned up a murder case. In addition to your evidence, you now have a confession. So, will you take Denny along with you and get the hell out of here?"

Sackler's grin reminded me of a wolf bidding good morning to a fat ewe.

"Oh, no, Nick," he said softly. "It's not as simple as that."

At that moment Denny ran amok. His punch-dazed mind, at last, cracked completely. He stood up. Tears ran down his ugly face.

"Why did he have to die?" he cried in a shrieking, insane

tremolo. "Why didn't he give me the money? He was the best brother a guy ever had. He was—"

He swung his head around until he faced Audrey Murray. The girl flinched before the threat she saw in his eyes. Denny's face contorted to a grotesque mask of madness.

"You!" he yelled. "You made me do it. You killed him as much as me. You—you—"

He sprang across the room, his fists moving. His left smashed against the girl's jaw. His right belted her twice as she was falling. I charged across the room toward him. Then, I heard Sackler say, "Look out, Joey. He's got a gun."

I pulled up short. Denny had jerked a big thirty-eight from his pocket. I stood stock still for a moment, wondering if I dare draw my own automatic. Then Denny solved that problem for me.

He lifted the thirty-eight and held the muzzle against his temple. The shot cracked out and reverberated back from the walls. Denny swayed for a moment. His knees buckled and he fell to the floor for the last count he would ever take.

Over by the mantel-piece Nick Lanzetta stared down at the unconscious figure of the girl, at the gory corpse of Denny. He was as haggard as is possible for a man with a fat face. Sackler regarded Denny with thoughtful mien. His left eye was closed and his tongue was between his teeth.

"Nick," he said suddenly. "Hand me that gun. Denny's gun."

Nick glanced at him, startled. "Why?" he said. "I thought you ain't supposed to touch nothing until the cops get here."

"Damn you," roared Sackler in his best quarter deck manner. "I'm running things here. Hand me that gun!"

NICK WAS TOO shaken to argue. With obvious distaste he bent over Denny's corpse. I watched him closely, my hand on the butt of my automatic. It didn't seem the brightest thing in the world, just then, to permit Nick Lanzetta to possess a gun. But he didn't try anything. He took the thirty-eight from Denny's inert fingers and handed it to Sackler.

Sackler indicated a smoking stand at his right. "Put it down there, Nick."

Nick dropped the weapon on the taboret and stood back. Sackler took a deep breath and said, "Now let's discuss the fee."

I stared at him. If Sackler could find a fee in this case, I was willing to concede that he was half as intelligent as he thought he was. Nick ran his fingers through his hair and regarded Sackler.

"Hell," he said. "I ain't got nothing to do with this case. You don't expect me to pay your fee. Do you?"

"Yes," said Sackler. "The price I quoted you, I believe, was fifteen hundred."

"Are you crazy?" asked Nick Lanzetta. "You quoted me no price at all."

"Yes, I did," said Sackler. "You will recall this morning when I told you that you'd blasted your own safe. I told you then, that if you wanted me to tell you why you did it, the fee would be fifteen hundred dollars. All right, Nick. I've told you why you did it."

"You're still crazy," said Nick again and I quite agreed with him now. "You won't get a dime from me. You got your case cleaned up. You got your killer. You ain't got anything on me. Or Audrey."

"No?" said Sackler. "First you're both accessories after the fact of murder. You both had knowledge of the crime which you concealed for your purposes. They hand out quite a number of years for that. Second, this business of attempting to extort money from Bryan Lynch comes under the heading of conspiracy. I'm certain Miss Murray will implicate you in that when they question her downtown."

Nick nodded. "I get it," he said.

Personally, I didn't. True, Sackler was money mad. But in his own way he was honest. I could no more imagine Sackler making a deal with a criminal to escape the law than I could imagine him voluntarily buying anyone a drink.

"All right," said Nick. "So I give you fifteen hundred dollars and you keep your mouth shut. You don't implicate Audrey and myself. Is that it?"

Sackler looked shocked.

"Oh no," he said. "Nothing like that, Nick. I'll do my best to see that you and Audrey serve a maximum sentence."

"Then," said Nick, "why in the name of Hell should I give you dough."

"Because if you do your maximum sentence will merely be a jail term. If you don't, you'll burn. You can't miss."

Nick blinked at him. "For what?"

"Murder," said Sackler. "First degree murder of Denny Lynch. Your prints are on the gun that killed him. When he was shot, Joey happened to be looking out the window. But I saw you do it."

Nick uttered a howl.

"Sackler! You wouldn't do it. You can't do it! Denny killed himself. We all saw him do it. Didn't we, Joey? Didn't we?"

I kept my mouth shut.

"You can't do it!" said Nick again. "It's blackmail. That's what it is."

"Oh no, it isn't," said Sackler. "Nothing as crude as that. All I ask you to do is to join Joey and me in a little game. It's a game the boys were playing down in Lindy's last night. You just have to guess the date on a coin. Here, I'll show you." He took a handful of pennies from his pocket. Nick licked his lips nervously.

"You mean," he said at last, "that if I play that damned game with you, you'll tell the cops that Denny bumped himself."

"Absolutely," said Sackler. "You and Joey and I are going to play. But I always go last, Nick. Remember that. I guess after you two. Joey, I'll cut you in for ten percent of the winnings."

I thought that over. "Twenty," I said.

Sackler looked pained.

"Twenty," I said. "Or else I wasn't looking out the window when Denny died."

"It's extortion," said Sackler, gloomily. "But all right."

He tossed a penny, slapped his hand over it as it fell on the table. "We'll make it ten dollars a throw," he said. "You go first, Nick."

Nick Lanzetta shuddered. He looked down at Denny's cooling corpse. He looked over at the unconscious figure of the girl. He sighed the sigh of a man who is thoroughly beaten, and knows it. "All right," he said, reaching for his wallet, "Nineteen-thirty-four."

Death Stops Payment

Anything to make a couple of grand—or even a plugged nickel. That was Rex Sackler's code of life—and death. For he was equally quick to euchre lucre from the living or cash out of a corpse.

1

After All—What's Money?

I ARRIVED AT THE office at ten minutes past nine and received a surly good-morning from Sackler. He glowered at a story of the national debt in the *Tribune* and I sat down, lit a cigarette and grinned at him. His dyspeptic mood was no stunning surprise to me.

This was Wednesday—pay day. And Rex Sackler parting with money was as gay and light-hearted as Romeo taking his leave of Juliet.

I took the cigarette from my mouth and coughed politely. He lifted his head from the paper and stared at me with his dark sullen eyes. With nice delicacy, I scratched the palm of my left hand with the index finger of my right. Sackler folded the *Tribune* with great deliberation and sighed the sigh of a sorely tried man.

"Joey," he said, "you're a money grubber. A beaten slave of Mammon. Your job, to you, is a matter of dollars. Service, you know nothing of. Loyalty is beyond your limited ken. The noble pleasure of sheer altruism is something your material mind cannot grasp."

That, coming from Rex Sackler, was uproarious. He had quit the police department because of his theory that a man of his talents could make a fortune as a private detective. To the regret of several people, he had been right. Not only was he competent but he could smell a nickel before it had left the

mint. He possessed all the business instincts of a Scotsman, an Armenian trader and a bank vault. He made money hand over fist. He disgorged it with the reluctance of a slot machine.

I put out my cigarette and stood up. "I'm strictly a strong-arm guy," I told him. "However, I *can* grasp the simple fact that you owe me some sixty-five slugs for last week's wages. Do I collect?"

Sackler shook his head and this time his sigh came from the soles of his feet. He put his hand inside his breast pocket and withdrew his wallet as if it had an anchor attached. He counted out some bills with the meticulous care of a near-sighted croupier and laid them on the desk.

I put the money in my pocket. I said, very politely: "Now just what plans have you formulated for taking this away from me?"

He looked at me reproachfully. "Joey," he said, "your misconstruction of my motives is incredible. Merely because I sometimes gamble with you for pastime, you appear to believe I really care about winning. Crass, Joey. And gauche. After all, what's money?"

I picked that cue up fast. "Money," I said, "is what you've got socked in every Postal Savings account in the city because you think banks are a wild gamble. Money is what you'd sell your grandmother to the Arab slave-dealers for. Money is what you reluctantly pay me every week, then devise schemes for winning back. Money—"

He wasn't listening to me. He had taken a pair of dice from his pocket and was caressing them in his hand. There was a little click as he spun them over the desk blotter. I watched them come to rest, revealing a pair of deuces. Then I suddenly caught myself and walked to the window.

"Oh, no," I said. "You can put those right back in your pocket. You're not getting a nickel out of me this week, even if you offer a dime for it."

I stood at the window showing him my back and contemplating the thrumming Madison Avenue traffic. I still heard the gentle click of the dice behind me and the gambling corpuscles in my veins throbbed nervously. Resolutely, I stared through the glass.

I turned only when I heard the door of the outer office slam. Sackler lifted his head like a hyena scenting prey. He adjusted his cuffs and cleared his throat, preparatory to the onslaught on the client's pocketbook. Inspector Wolfe of the Headquarters Squad strode into the room.

Sackler's phoney smile of welcome faded. He reached for the dice again and said ungraciously: "Oh, it's you."

"It sure is," said Wolfe with loud affability. "And how's business, Rex? How's every little thing with the sharpest shamus in town?"

That speech coming from Wolfe was far, far phonier than Sackler's smile had been. As a general rule Wolfe and Sackler go along like Martin Dies and a liberal thought. Sackler believed Wolfe a pompous incompetent, which he was; while Wolfe's heart dripped envy every time he compared Sackler's income with his own.

"Rex," said Wolfe, "I'd like to ask you a question. To settle a little discussion we were having downtown. Exactly why did you quit the department to go in business on your own hook?"

Sackler took a package of ten-cent cigarettes from his pocket and lighted one. Carefully, he replaced the burnt match in its book. When he answered he did not speak the truth.

"Public service," he said virtuously. "With my talent it stands to reason I can accomplish more civic good than under the orders of a block-headed police commissioner."

"Exactly," boomed Wolfe. "That's just what I said. Now how about lending us a hand on the Capek case?"

Sackler blinked at him. I leaned forward in my chair and said maliciously: "Free, Inspector?"

"Well," said Wolfe as if he were the Chamber of Commerce and I was looking over the factory site, "we're all working for the public good together. After all, what's money?"

THIS MAGNIFICENT INDIFFERENCE to money on the part of all hands was beginning to overwhelm me. But in spite of all this idealistic chatter, I knew damned well Sackler wouldn't stir out of his chair to solve a tabloid cross-word puzzle until someone slapped a large bill on the desktop.

He was staring unpleasantly at Wolfe. He resented the trap into which the inspector had led him. He took a deep breath and proceeded to squirm out of it.

"Wolfe," he said with a fine air of regret, "I'd like to help you. But it wouldn't be fair to my other clients. You see, if they pay high rates for my services it isn't right for me to work for nothing. It would offend them."

Wolfe grunted skeptically. "Well," he said slowly, "I sort of thought of that myself. So I got together with some of the boys and raised a little purse for you."

Sackler's eyes gleamed. "A purse? How much?"

"A couple of hundred."

Sackler looked insulted. The gleam went from his eyes faster than it had come in. I knew quite well he wasn't going to let that two hundred get away from him. But he was going to indulge in some very fancy haggling first.

"That's not much money, Wolfe," he said. "Make it five."

"My God," said Wolfe. "Ten coppers put together don't make as much money as you do in a year, Rex. Besides, we're gambling with you. We'll give you the two hundred free and clear. We ask no guarantees. Even if someone else breaks the Capek case you can keep the dough."

That didn't sound so bad. This Capek case was no cinch. Capek was a very odd character. With all the dough he'd piled up I suppose he had a right to be. He'd come to this country, a ragged immigrant boy, about fifty years ago. He'd rolled up his sleeves and gone to work—hard and successfully. Today, he controlled a dozen corporations and half a dozen banks. He was a strong, square-jawed character who possessed a great deal of pride and no friends. Hardly any acquaintances, save for a young guy named Rawson, who had once been his secretary and was now his partner.

Capek had been missing for about two weeks. His household on Long Island and the police suspected kidnaping, although no ransom demand had yet been received. Anyway, it made a good newspaper story and the whole police department was going nuts looking for Capek.

As Wolfe's unprecedented visit attested, they hadn't had much success.

Sackler was looking at Wolfe and there was a shrewd glitter in his eye. I knew quite well what he was thinking. As Sackler's fees went, two hundred bucks was no fortune. But this was an opportunity to get it for nothing. I knew, moreover, that he was going to accept the deal ultimately, but first he was going to break his neck to have Wolfe raise the ante.

"Three hundred," he said, "and it's a deal."

Wolfe drummed angrily on the desk with his fingers. He got very little more than three hundred a month. Sackler yawned elaborately and picked up the dice again.

The telephone jangled suddenly. I picked it up. It was for

Wolfe. I handed him the phone and he talked rapidly into the receiver, listened for a moment and hung up. He turned to Sackler, a wide grin on his face, and all the false affability had vanished from his voice as he spoke.

"Wise guy," he jeered. "Just a shrewd business genius. Well, you just haggled yourself out of two hundred bucks, my friend. They've found Capek."

Sackler dropped the dice and jerked his head up angrily. "Where?"

"In the caretaker's lodge on his own estate. And dead. Apparently a suicide." But Wolfe wasn't interested in Capek anymore. He reverted to the subject nearest his heart. "But you, you could have had two hundred bucks just for sitting at your desk until that phone call came in. You wouldn't have had to move a muscle of a brain cell."

He walked to the doorway, grinning triumphantly, and added: "And it's breaking your chiseling marble heart."

The door slammed behind him and he was gone.

WHETHER OR NOT there were any cracks in Sackler's cardiac region, I didn't know. But I was very happy about it all. It wasn't every day I was granted the privilege of seeing Sackler lose money.

He looked up suddenly, saw my grin and rolled the dice again. Double six came up.

"What do you say, Joey? Just one roll. For a buck."

I hesitated. Sackler had been rolling craps with a fair degree of regularity this morning. Besides, if the law of averages hadn't been suspended, I was due. I took a dollar from my pocket and laid it on the desk.

"Just once," I said. "One fast roll. That's all. Win, lose or draw."

"Sure, Joey. Just one."

Twenty minutes later when the outer door slammed for the second time that day, I was out precisely thirty-three bucks. Sackler snatched up the dice as our caller entered the room.

He was tall, well built, about thirty-five and exceedingly well dressed. He gave out a strong aroma of ready cash and Sackler came to point like a bird dog. I sat down sulkily at my desk and wondered why the hell I'd ever got in that crap game. In four years I'd never won a dime from Rex Sackler at anything.

The stranger nodded his head and said briskly: "Mr. Sackler?"

Sackler admitted his identity.

"I'm Rawson. Harold Rawson."

Sackler's face lit up. Wolfe's two hundred was water under the dam now.

"Rawson," he said quickly. "Karl Capek's partner?"

"Not anymore," said Rawson briefly.

"Ah," said Sackler like a doctor at the death bed, "that suicide. Very unfortunate. Very—"

"It wasn't suicide," snapped Rawson.

Sackler's eyes opened wide. It was neither surprise nor shock, I knew. It was wholehearted satisfaction that here, indeed, was a fee.

"You're sure of that?"

"Positive," said Rawson. "I have information which precludes all suicidal possibilities."

"Ah," said Sackler again, "and you want me to find out—"

"I want you to find out who killed him."

Sackler rubbed his hands together and gazed dreamily at his client.

"The fee," he murmured, "will be twenty-five hundred dollars. In advance. Make the check out to cash, please."

Rawson sat down. He took a fountain pen and a check book from his pocket. He said, "Quite satisfactory," and proceeded to write. Sackler watched him happily. Then Rawson spoke again.

"I'm a little short of cash, Sackler. Been out of town on business. Just got back to find this awful tragedy. Can you let me have fifty in cash if I make the check out for that much additional?"

"Of course," said Sackler, always willing to exchange fifty for twenty-five hundred. "Glad to oblige."

He counted out five tens and picked up the check. "Now," he said, "first, what is this information you have that makes you so sure Capek was murdered?"

Rawson stood up. There was a hard coldness in his eyes. "I shall tell you that tonight," he said. "Can you be at the Capek mansion tonight, at nine o'clock?"

"Yes."

"All right," said Rawson. He turned and walked to the door. He paused on the threshold and for a moment his brusque businesslike air dropped from him.

"Karl Capek was a great man," he said, and there was a peculiar huskiness to his voice. "He was my best, my only friend. And by God, I will avenge him!"

He swung around on his heel and marched into the corridor.

Sackler held the check in his hand as if it were a diamond he'd just picked up in the gutter, which it more or less was.

I stood over by the window bathed in envy. Here Sackler

had just had twenty-five hundred dollars dropped into his avaricious lap while I was out thirty-three bucks of last week's salary. If there was any justice in the world it never seemed to get around to this office.

"Joey, my lad," said Sackler, "run over to the bank with this check. Get it cashed right away."

That was Sackler all over. Whenever he got a check he rushed it over to the bank, cashed it and sank it in one of his Postal Savings accounts. Nothing short of the revolution was going to get a nickel out of him.

I sighed, put on my hat and coat, and went out into the street.

I RETURNED HALF an hour later. I was grinning happily from ear to ear. There was a soothing, gloating sensation in my heart that almost made me forget about my thirty-three bucks. Sackler looked up as I approached his desk.

"Ah," he said, "get to the bank all right?"

"And had a very pleasant trip," I told him. "Here."

I groped in my pocket and laid Rawson's check down on the desk before him. He looked at it, then looked at me.

"Well," he said testily, "where's the cash?"

I smiled at him sweetly. "There isn't any cash."

"What the devil are you talking about, Joey? What do you mean there—"

"There isn't enough cash anyway. Insufficient funds."

He looked for all the world as if someone had slugged him over the head with a mallet.

"My God, Joey, you don't mean—"

"I mean that Harold Rawson, who's probably worth several hundred thousand times as much dough as you are, has given you a bum check. Moreover, you've been taken for fifty bucks in cash. I might add, I think it very, very funny."

"My God," said Sackler in an anguished tone, "twenty-five hundred and fifty bucks. I've been taken for twenty-five hundred and fifty bucks. I'm a ruined man. I—"

"Do we still keep that appointment at Capek's joint?" I asked him.

"You're damn right we do," he said explosively. "I'm going to see that Rawson. He can't do this to me. Good heavens, twenty-five hundred and fifty bucks is one hell of a lot of dough, Joey."

"You're actually out only fifty," I pointed out. "That's all you gave him in cash."

He paid no attention to me. He buried his face in his hands and muttered over and over again: "Twenty-five hundred and fifty bucks, my God!"

In my book he was still out only fifty but in his present distrait condition all the arithmetic in the world wasn't going to convince him.

2

You Can't Get Cash From a Corpse

IT WAS A raw blustery night as we drove through Long Island on the Grand Central Parkway. Sackler had recovered somewhat from his fiscal grief. He had arrived at the conclusion that it was a ghastly and horrible mistake, but nevertheless, a mistake. Considering Rawson's position, his wealth, the fact that he was Karl Capek's partner, I was reluctantly inclined to agree with him.

But I wasn't so optimistic about my thirty-three bucks as Sackler was about his twenty-five hundred and fifty. All afternoon, I'd been racking my brains for some cinch bet which would enable me to win it back, without success. Now, as I heard Sackler humming gayly at my side in the car, I tried another tack.

"Hey," I said, "I'll make a deal with you."

Sackler kept on humming.

"If Rawson makes good for you on that check, how about giving me back that dough I lost at dice?"

The melody died on his lips. "Why, Joey," he said reproachfully, "they're two entirely different things. Yours was a gambling debt. I couldn't insult you by offering to return it."

I sighed and said: "No, I hardly thought you could."

We made the rest of the trip in silence. Some twenty miles out I turned through an elaborate pair of wrought-iron gates and drove through the heavily wooded estate of Karl Capek. The wind blew cold from the Sound and the sky was starless. It was a cold cheerless night that fitted in well with my own mood.

I brought the car to a halt underneath a high Colonial portico. A moment later Sackler pressed the doorbell. After another moment the door was opened by a liveried butler.

The first thing I heard was Wolfe's familiar voice. We found him in the living-room, a glass of brandy in his hand, a cigar in his mouth, holding forth on his police adventures to a politely bored audience. We were introduced all around and informed that Rawson hadn't arrived yet, although he was expected soon.

Without delay we went into our usual routine. Sackler demanded he be assigned a room in which to mastermind. I whipped out my notebook and proceeded to do the rounds, picking up bits of information I thought might be useful. Since Sackler was actually starting to work before he had negotiated about the check, I became more certain that he wasn't really worried much about it.

I snooped around the house for a good hour. I questioned Wolfe, the servants and everybody else. I went out into the windy night and personally examined the caretaker's lodge where they'd found Capek's body.

I CAME BACK cold as hell, commandeered a pint of brandy from the butler's pantry and went up to the second-floor study which had been assigned to Sackler. I took out my notebook and sat down.

Sackler was having one hell of a time with a humidor of cigars he had found. His pocket was stuffed and he was rolling one around lusciously in his mouth. Since they were free the taste, I presume, was much improved.

"All right," he said. "What have we got?"

"Not Rawson," I told him. "He phoned a little while ago. He'll be another half-hour. Business held him up."

"What else?"

"First, those guys downstairs. That watery-eyed young blond guy is a relative of Capek's. Name of Crosher. Only living relative as far as anyone knows. He's been here for a month. He's broke and was trying to get some dough from the old guy. Came from Chi. Never seen his cousin before. In fact, he only just found out he *was* Capek's cousin. He's in direct line for the estate."

I thought maybe I had something there. But as I glanced quickly at Sackler he seemed more interested in his cigar.

"Next, the Union League Club stuffed shirt in the wing collar is Granville S. Colby, of whom you may have heard."

"Often," said Sackler. "Lawyer. Old family. Blue-blood stock. Stiff-necked. Don't like him."

"Then there's that guy Benjamin. He's the skinny one with the thin face. Another lawyer. Colby's assistant. They've both been here for a little over a month. Colby's supposed to be resting. Doctor's orders. But he was handling some legal stuff for Capek and Rawson. Was doing it out here."

Sackler looked up. "Notice anything funny about that Benjamin?"

"Yeah. Face seems familiar. Can't quite place it. Maybe I've seen him somewhere around in court. Why?"

"Keep talking," said Sackler. "What about Capek?"

"There's a caretaker's lodge out there in the forest," I told him. "They don't use it anymore. It was all boarded up. That's where they found Capek. A revolver was in his hand and his brains were on the floor. There was a portable typewriter there with a suicide note in it. Capek's fingerprints were on the keys. The doc said he's been dead three days."

"He was missing two weeks," said Sackler. "What was he doing the rest of the time? Contemplating suicide?"

"You think you're kidding," I told him, "but you're dead on. That's exactly what he said in the suicide note."

For the first time, Sackler appeared interested. "What's exactly what he said in the note?"

"I got it from Wolfe. He didn't have a copy of it with him. Gave it to me from memory. Something about being tired of life, retiring to the lodge alone to think things over. Deciding finally to die. Wolfe seems to think it's on the level. Thinks Rawson's crazy for asking him to come out here tonight."

"Don't bother me with Wolfe's opinions. Anything else?"

"Well, there was the faucets."

"The faucets? What about the faucets?"

"The ones in the lodge. They were smashed. There was a stove lid on the floor. I guess that's what had been used. There was one faucet over the kitchen sink, another in a washroom just off the kitchen."

Sackler frowned. "And they were smashed?"

"They'd been battered about a hell of a lot. But that might have happened a long while ago."

Thoughtfully, he crushed his cigar out in a silver ash tray. I took a cigarette from behind my ear and lit it. A moment later Sackler sniffed and said: "That's a fancy brand for you, isn't it? What is it, Egyptian?"

"Right," I told him. "And from the exalted case of Granville S. Colby."

Sackler grunted. "Must cost a lot of dough."

"The way he smokes them it does. He's a chain smoker. Lights one from the butt of the last."

Sackler stood up. "Well," he said, "since there's nothing more to do until Rawson gets here, I guess I'll go downstairs and bum one from him. Come along, Joey."

I FOLLOWED HIM down the winding staircase. In the living-room Wolfe was still holding forth to Crosher and Benjamin. They didn't appear very interested. Colby's eardrums must have revolted already. Sackler and I found him alone in the library on the other side of the foyer, with a half-smoked Egyptian cigarette in his hand.

Sackler, who wouldn't hesitate to ask the President for a match, put the bite on Colby for a smoke. Colby patted his pockets, looked up and said coldly: "My cigarette case is in my overcoat pocket. It's hanging in the hall closet."

I took that to mean why in hell didn't Sackler buy his own butts but that spendthrift said casually, "Don't get up. I'll find it," and walked out into the hall.

I followed along aimlessly; then I turned into the living-room just in time to catch Wolfe's recital of the time he raided the murderer's nest single-handed. Just then there came the sound of a wounded banshee and the cook ran into the living-room, her mouth wide open and her larynx vibrating like an off-key harp.

Sackler and Colby came racing into the room. We got the cook into a chair and poured a slug of brandy into her. At that she became coherent enough to shriek: "The garage! Mr. Rawson! For heaven's sake—"

There was more to it than that but we didn't wait to hear. I was in the lead with Sackler and Wolfe on my heels. We rushed out into the bitter night, across the sweeping back lawn to the garage. The door was open and the light was turned on. There was a car inside, its headlights aglow.

At the wheel slumped Rawson. There was a gun in his hand and an ugly hole in his head. He was as dead as hope in Poland. Wolfe, Sackler and I did some routine looking around and found nothing.

Behind us, young Crosher said: "My God, this is awful. There's a murderer in this house."

"Maybe," said Colby's deep bass, "it wasn't murder."

Wolfe seized on that. "My idea, too," he said, his voice thickened by the brandy he'd been drinking. "Rawson worshiped Capek. Brooded about his death. Killed himself."

"The only virtue in that theory," said Sackler, "is its convenience. Everybody commits suicide so the coppers can go home. Otherwise it stinks."

Wolfe turned on him angrily. "Maybe you got a theory, wise guy."

"Maybe," said Sackler. "Has anyone been outside the house tonight?"

"I have," I reminded him.

"I don't suspect you, Joey," he said magnanimously. "Anyone else?"

Individually, everyone denied having left the house since dinner time. We trooped back to the Capek mansion. Wolfe went to the telephone to call headquarters. Colby used his best courtroom persuasion on the cook, assuring her it would be quite safe for her to sleep in her quarters above the garage.

Sackler, registering heavy thought, retired again to the second-floor study. I trailed along behind him.

Sackler sat down at the desk and rested his head in his hands. There was utter despair on his face. It was hardly customary for Sackler to take violent death so seriously and I commented upon it.

He looked up at me. "Joey," he said, and his voice was drenched in gloom, "don't you see what this does to my check? It may never be good now."

I hadn't thought of that, but now that I did I brightened considerably. It would be an edifying spectacle to see Rex Sackler solve a case free.

He looked up again and now there was an odd light in his eyes. He slapped his fist on the desk.

"Joey," he said, "I think I've got something. Go and see that Benjamin guy. Ask him what a writ of replevin is."

That didn't sound very sensible to me. But I went downstairs and did it. I came back and reported: "He says he's a little rusty on it but he believes it's something like a habeas corpus."

"Good," said Sackler. "I thought so."

I needled him by deliberately misunderstanding. "You mean you think it's like habeas corpus, too?"

"No, you idiot. I mean that guy's not a law clerk at all. He's Benny Bagel. I've been trying to place him all night. But now I'm certain."

"Bagel?" I said. "Benny Bagel? Sounds vaguely familiar, but it still doesn't click."

"Forger," said Sackler, and there was a little tremor of excitement in his tone. "Indicted twice. Never convicted. I've seen his picture in the tabloids. Considered the best guy in the field."

"What's he doing here as Colby's law clerk?"

"It'll take me all night to figure that," said Sackler. "But at last I'm beginning to see the light. Hey, get me the phone number of that bank Rawson's check was drawn on. I want to call them early in the morning. Tell Wolfe he better stay over tonight, too. Then get the hell out of my sight and let me think."

I LET HIM think for the rest of the night. In the morning, Wolfe, sticking stubbornly to his double suicide theory, was anxious to get back to town. Sackler insisted he stay. I saw little of either Sackler or Colby before lunch. When neither of them appeared then I went up to the study to find Sackler still sitting at the desk.

"Well," I said, "what have you got?"

He drew a deep breath. "Plenty," he said. "Do you realize, Joey, that Capek never made a will, never owned a driving license, that Rawson held his complete power-of-attorney in every deal?"

"So," I said, "what? Maybe Rawson killed him, then got the horrors about it and killed himself."

Sackler snorted. "That sounds like a Wolfe theory," he said. "You get to the phone, Joey. Call Postal Union. Tell them to send me their most trusted messenger. And tell him to hurry. Then tell Wolfe I'll be right down to solve his case for him."

"Free?" I asked maliciously. But to my surprise even the mention of his lost dough didn't get a rise out of him. He smiled benignly.

"By the way," I said as I went to the door, "where's Colby? I thought he was with you."

"Somewhere around," said Sackler vaguely. "Hurry with that messenger, will you?"

3

Madman's Millions

IT WAS TWO thirty in the afternoon and Wolfe was getting impatient. He paced the broad living-room floor, scowling at Sackler, who sat at his ease before the fire and smoked a cigar he'd cadged from Crosher. Crosher stood by the window twining his fingers about each other like nervous snakes.

Benny Bagel, the forger law clerk, avidly conned a stack of old-fashioned stereopticon views. At last Wolfe stopped his pacing. He came to a guardsman's halt in front of Sackler and spoke his vehement piece.

"Damn it, Sackler. Last night you said you'd have something this morning. This morning's gone. So's half the afternoon. Capek was a suicide. Quite obviously he was something of a wack and he killed himself. Can you improve on that theory?"

"Infinitely," said Sackler.

"Well, go ahead."

"I'm waiting for my messenger boy," said Sackler. "I can't do a thing until he arrives."

"My God," said Wolfe, "what the hell can a messenger boy have to do with the death of Karl Capek?"

"Nothing," said Sackler. "But he may have a great deal to do with the solution."

The doorbell jangled then. Benny turned to answer it but Sackler stayed him with a gesture. He strode out into the foyer and admitted a Postal Union boy. He spoke to him earnestly for a moment and in a tone so low I couldn't hear him.

I admit I tried.

THERE WAS AN expression of relief on his face when he returned to the living-room. He drew a Windsor chair up to a table and sat facing us all.

"Now," he said with a business-like air, "how do you figure this Capek case, Wolfe?"

Wolfe glared at him. If he'd told him how he figured the Capek case once, he'd told him a dozen times. Now he lifted his voice and told it again—loud.

"Capek was an eccentric. A nut, as I figure it. His typewritten note gave that away. He went out to that unused lodge to think things over. After a few days of brooding, he killed himself. It's obvious, isn't it?"

"No," said Sackler. "And what about Rawson?"

"Rawson was devoted to the old guy. Capek gave him everything he had. He was so broken up at Capek's death that he killed himself, too."

"That," remarked Sackler to me, "is typical modern police work. When you can't solve a killing you call it suicide in a loud authoritative voice, then go back to a nice warm station-house and finish reading the comic papers."

There was confidence in his manner. As a matter of fact he seemed so assured I began to think he'd cooked up some way to save his twenty-five hundred dollars.

"All right," said Wolfe, annoyed. "I've told you. Now you tell me. What did happen to Capek?"

"What was the first official police theory?" asked Sackler.

"Two weeks ago when Capek was first reported missing?"

"Kidnaping. But we exploded that."

"Ah," said Sackler gently, "did you? This may be incredible to you, Inspector, but you were right the first time."

"Hooey," said Wolfe. "Who the hell would kidnap a guy and hold him prisoner on his own estate?"

"A very bright guy indeed," said Sackler. "The coppers never looked for him there, did they?"

"There were no ransom notes, were there? What the hell sort of a kidnaping would it be without any ransom notes?"

"An extremely unusual one," said Sackler.

I watched Sackler closely. This talking in circles wasn't like him at all. When he had a case broken he usually threw it in everyone's face abruptly and without waste of words. But now his eyes kept straying to the big clock on the mantelpiece and his manner was that of a man who is just trying to use up time.

I LOOKED AROUND the room. Our old pal, Benny, now stood a graven image by the fireplace. Crosher had turned his back to the window and stared at Sackler. I reflected that had I killed Capek and Rawson, I would have made a point of appearing less apprehensive than Crosher.

Wolfe's face was ruddier than usual. Sackler invariably irritated him and today's circumlocution was angering him even more than was customary.

"Sackler," he said, "will you stop horsing around? If you've any evidence, present it."

"All right," said Sackler. "Let's begin with the kidnaping premise. There's a guy, a certain guy who knows Capek. He's in a jam—a financial jam. He needs dough badly. So he takes

Capek down to that boarded-up lodge and demands a juicy check. Capek won't give it to him. So he kills him."

That was too much even for me. Wolfe was just two points this side of apoplexy.

"That's the screwiest thing I ever heard," he yelled. "What good is Capek to him dead if he needs dough?"

"None whatever," said Sackler, "but the killer didn't know that at the time." He paused for a long moment, then he glanced over at the fireplace and added: "Did he, Benny?"

Benny Bagel almost fell over the fire tools. His face was suddenly pale. His eyes opened wide and his jaw dropped so quickly I expected it to bounce off his chest. Wolfe noted his expression and some of his doubt left him.

"What's he got to do with it?"

Sackler turned to Crosher, who viewed the proceedings blankly.

"You see," he said, "there's your police department for you. Benny's a forger. He's served two raps and is considered by his pals the top man in the business. Right, Benny?"

Benny had recovered somewhat by now. "I'm afraid you're making a mistake," he said politely. "I've been in law or law school all my life. You're confusing me with some criminal."

"Of course," said Wolfe hopefully. "Of course."

"Sure," said Sackler. "Did you see him register when I threw it in his face? He's Benny Bagel. You've got his fingerprints downtown, Wolfe. You've got his Bertillons and everything else. In a very short while you're going to have him in person."

Wolfe looked from Benny, who appeared very uncomfortable, to Sackler, who didn't.

"What's it all about?" he asked. "Are you saying this guy killed him?"

"Accessory," said Sackler. "After and during the fact of murder."

"Well, for the love of God," roared Wolfe, "Who did the actual killing?"

Sackler looked at the clock again before answering. It was two minutes to three.

"First," said Sackler, "let me tell you why and how."

"For heaven's sake," snapped Wolfe, "tell me something."

"This certain guy I mentioned a little while ago—let's call him Smith. Well, he was in trouble. So he took Capek out to that caretaker's lodge and proceeded to put the bite on him. He demanded that Capek write a letter asking for a hell of a lot of ransom. A note which would be delivered to Rawson, who, being quite fond of the old guy, would undoubtedly pay. Colby was named as the intermediary."

"Colby," said Wolfe suddenly. "Where the devil is he?"

"Don't bother about him," said Sackler. "We don't need him until later."

Benny Bagel screwed up his brow and shot a puzzled glance at Sackler. Wolfe banged the table impatiently with his fist and said: "All right. Get on with it."

"Well," went on Sackler, "Capek wouldn't sign. This guy Smith got pretty sore about it. He knew Capek was a pretty stubborn guy. Torture, ordinary physical torture, was rather out of this Smith's line. So he hit on what he thought was a brilliant idea. He thought of a torture which was bloodless, horrible and very effective."

BY THIS TIME Sackler had me as bewildered as anyone in the room. Usually, I could follow his reasoning at least halfway.

But for a guy who apparently had nothing to work on he was delivering one hell of a lot of detail.

"So," said Wolfe, "what was this unusual torture?"

"Water," said Sackler, "or rather, lack of it."

Benny Bagel uttered a little sigh and sat down. I said: "Now how can you figure a thing like that?"

"It's not too hard, Joey. First those smashed faucets. If they'd been smashed in rage or blind fury, it's quite probable that something else, the furniture, the light bulbs, would also have been wrecked. But it was only the water faucets. Smashed by a man who is dying of thirst, who turns on the tap to get nothing but emptiness for perhaps the hundredth time. Then he did go nuts. He took the stove lid and crashed it down on the taps."

I thought that over and conceded to myself there might be something in it. Wolfe scratched his graying head in silence. Crosher opened his mouth for the first time.

"It's impossible," he said. "What about the medical examiner? He would have noticed dehydration. If Cousin Karl had been on the verge of death from thirst, the medical examiner couldn't have failed to notice it."

"Right," said Wolfe emphatically. "Absolutely right. You're screwy, Rex."

"You all forget," said Sackler, "that Capek was in that lodge for fourteen days. He had been dead three when he was found. Suppose he'd been deprived of water for a week. That's enough to drive a man mad. But after he was mad there was no point in dealing with him. This Smith decided to kill him then. But he waited some four days before he did so. During those four days he gave Capek water and food. He did that so that the medical examiner wouldn't know just what had happened."

"If this Smith guy was so smart," I said, "couldn't he figure Capek might go nuts from lack of water?"

Sackler shook his head. "No. He thought Capek would give in to his demands before then. Besides, when Capek proved adamant, Smith got himself another idea. He figured out how to get the money even after Capek was dead."

Wolfe shook his head and shrugged his shoulders. "Rex," he said, "it won't do. First, Capek had one hell of a lot of money. It seems reasonable to me that he'd be quite willing to surrender any amount of it to save his life, particularly if he was going mad for water."

"Besides," said Crosher, "how could he obtain a signed ransom note if Cousin Karl was dead?"

"I'll answer the second question first," said Sackler. "That's where Benny Bagel came in. Faced with Capek's point-blank refusal, our friend Smith cooked up a second idea. He decided, since Capek was going nuts, he'd have to kill him anyway. So he brought in Benny here."

"Why?" said Wolfe.

"My God," said Sackler wearily, "are you that stupid? I told you Benny is a forger. The best in the business. Benny was going to sign Capek's name to the note."

"All right, then," snapped Wolfe. "So why didn't he?"

"Because," said Sackler slowly, "they couldn't find anything to copy."

"Couldn't find what to copy?" shouted Wolfe impatiently. "Rex, what the devil are you talking about?"

"To forge a signature, you must have an original to copy from. It's a prime rule of the profession, isn't it, Benny?"

"Listen," said Benny Bagel in a low hoarse voice, "I want to see a lawyer. Where's Colby?"

"Well why couldn't they find a signature of Capek's to copy from? There must be plenty of them around the house somewhere," Wolfe stated.

"That," said Sackler, "is where you're wrong. There's not a single signature of Karl Capek in existence."

Wolfe and Crosher gaped at him. But at this point something lit up in my brain.

"You mean he couldn't write?"

"I'm glad someone got it at last," said Sackler. "Capek couldn't write. He was a proud man, a strong character and a man whose success had made him ashamed of his lack of education. Capek couldn't write and there was only one person in all the world who shared his secret. That was Rawson."

WOLFE WAS HALF convinced. His brow was corrugated, his eyes shaded with deep thought. "How can you arrive at that conclusion, Rex?"

"Consider the circumstances. Capek never held a driver's license. He never made a will. All his business, even his income-tax returns, was handled through Rawson's power-of-attorney. In Capek's desk I found a hundred documents, all in the same handwriting. That handwriting was Rawson's. Consider again. Capek had no friends, no acquaintances, save Rawson. We know he came here from Middle Europe as a lad of seven. We know he never went to school. We know, further, that he was generous with his money. He'd made munificent endowments and donations, yet he wouldn't spend any of it to save his life."

"You mean," I said, "that he died rather than admit he couldn't write?"

"That's my theory," said Sackler. "Of all the statements I'm making this afternoon, that one will always have to remain a theory. But nothing else fits. It's quite logical. It was Capek's secret. No one knew it. He intended no one ever should. He wouldn't admit it to Smith until thirst had driven him mad, probably too mad to know what the hell was going on. So Smith called in his forger and killed him."

"Then," I said, "he killed his own scheme because he couldn't find any signature of Capek's to copy."

"True," said Sackler, "but he did salvage a little from the wreck, didn't he, Benny?"

Benny stared at Sackler in horror but he didn't answer.

"Seeing all was lost," continued Sackler, "our pal, Smith, embarked on a new plan. After Capek's body and phony suicide note which Smith had typed with the dead man's fingers, Smith was told by Rawson that Capek couldn't write. Told today, in fact. That fact, once known, was dangerous. So Smith planned to murder Rawson, too. The afternoon before he killed him, he had Benny here forge his name to a check for a hundred thousand dollars. That cleaned out Rawson's bank account."

I might have known that Sackler would find out why he hadn't got his twenty-five hundred and fifty bucks. Undoubtedly, he'd checked on that before anything else.

"Wait a minute," croaked Benny Bagel, "you can't prove that."

Sackler smiled at him benignly. "The hell I can't," he said. "I called the bank. The last check that was presented was for something in excess of a hundred grand. That check is down at Wolfe's fingerprint bureau right now."

"So what?" said Benny. "There'll be a dozen sets of prints on it by now."

"True," said Sackler. "One of those sets will be yours, and what is equally important, none of them will be Rawson's. Even you can't forge a check with gloves on, Benny. And it'll be conclusive proof of forgery if Rawson—the supposed maker of the check—hasn't left his own fingerprint on it."

"Well," said Wolfe grudgingly, "at last we've got some evidence instead of theory."

Crosher coughed nervously. "Who is this Smith?" he said suddenly. "Why have you deliberately concealed the name of the killer? Who is it?"

Wolfe spun around on his heel. He had been so engaged in trying to figure how Sackler could be wrong, he'd completely overlooked the minor fact of the killer's identity.

"Of course," he snapped. "Who did it? Who's the mastermind? Who was working with Benny, here?"

Sackler suddenly looked acutely uncomfortable. He stared at the clock. I followed his gaze and noted it was exactly twelve minutes past three.

"Well," said Wolfe again. "Who is it? Is this whole thing a fairy story or do you know who it was?"

Sackler appeared more upset than he had a moment ago. In inverse ratio, Benny seemed to perk up a bit.

"Well," said Sackler with obvious reluctance, "maybe it was Crosher, here. It's quite possible that—"

Crosher's mouth twisted suddenly. His eyes shone like pale blue ice. He took a step forward toward Sackler and his voice trembled as he spoke.

"Damn you!" he screamed. "Are you accusing me of killing my own flesh and blood? Are you saying that—"

"Pay no attention to him," said Benny, and there was relief in his tone. "He knows nothing. It's all wild guesswork. He can't check anything he says. He—"

The doorbell sounded imperiously. Sackler took a deep breath. He lifted his head to heaven and said fervently: "Thank God! Joey, open the door!"

4

Blood From a Turnip

I WENT OUT, opened the door and returned with the Postal Union boy Sackler had sent out three-quarters of an hour before. I led him into the living-room. He stood before Sackler, thrust his hand into his hip pocket and pulled out a thick roll of bills.

The boy began to count aloud. I was seized with a sudden cold suspicion that Sackler had somehow contrived to get his twenty-five hundred bucks after all. I remembered, abruptly and without satisfaction, that I still hadn't retrieved my thirty-three.

Wolfe gaped at the mounting money on the desk. Envy, frank and hostile, was in his gaze.

"Great God," he said, "is this a murder case or a private business deal?"

Sackler didn't answer him. He was gazing at the stack of bills with an ethereal light in his eyes. The Postal Union lad laid a final fifty on top of the pile, announced: "Twenty-five hundred and fifty. That's right, isn't it?"

That, as I knew too well, was absolutely right. To the penny. Sackler took a worn leather change purse from his pocket and handed the boy a dime. He was impervious to the look of scorn he received in exchange. The messenger left the room and Sackler stood up, stowing the bills away in his pocket like a hophead who has just come upon a mountain of cocaine.

He walked into the foyer and called back over his shoulder: "Hey, Joey."

I went along, not having the slightest idea what he wanted. I could almost feel Wolfe's outraged glare on my back.

"Joey," said Sackler in a whisper, "within the next three minutes sneak out of the room on some pretext. Go upstairs to the attic. The third door on the right at the head of the stairway. There's a transom there. Half open. Throw this over it into the room."

He handed me a sealed envelope. There was something small, hard and heavy inside it. I put it in my pocket without asking questions. By the time I returned to the living-room, I began to have vague visions of getting back my thirty-three bucks.

"Do you mind telling me," said Wolfe, restraining his wrath with a noticeable effort, "what the hell is going on here? Damn it, Rex, in the name of the law, I demand to know who your murderer is. You're obstructing justice."

Sackler nodded frantically to me. I murmured something about going to the bathroom and slid out of the room. I raced upstairs to the attic. I stood for a moment before the door Sackler had designated, listening. Then I tossed the envelope over the transom. I heard the metallic click as it hit the floor within; then I heard a sigh and a shuffling footstep. I scooted back down the stairs.

When I got back to the living-room, Wolfe was pounding the table savagely. His voice roared against the tapestried walls and reverberated back again. He threatened Sackler with decades of imprisonment for obstructing justice. He accused him of being an accessory after the fact of murder for withholding evidence. Sackler sat there in uncomfortable silence till he saw me. Then he brightened.

"All right, Joey?" he shouted above the noise of Wolfe's voice.

I nodded my head. "Shut up, Inspector," said Sackler. "I'll give you your killer."

Wolfe shut up for a moment, breathless. He inhaled quickly and said: "Who is it?"

"Colby," said Sackler. "Granville S. Colby. Embezzler of his clients' trust funds. Murderer. Kidnaper and a consorter with a forger. There's your man."

"Colby!" yelled Wolfe. "Where is he? He was here this morning. Search the house. My God, perhaps he got away. Perhaps he—"

The shot sounded through the house like a fragment of thunder. Benny sat up in his chair. Wolfe froze where he stood and Crosher looked more afraid than ever. Sackler stood up. He pointed at the clock.

"The time," he yelled. "Note the time. I want witnesses. It's exactly three twenty-eight. Look!"

We all looked at the clock.

"Come on," yelled Wolfe. "Let's investigate that shot. It was upstairs."

I caught Sackler's eye. "It seemed to me to come from the attic," I said.

Wolfe grabbed Benny before he raced up the stairs. He was taking no chances on losing one of his prisoners. The rest of us followed him to the attic.

THERE WAS A smell of cordite coming over the transom through which I had thrown Sackler's envelope. Wolfe tried the door. It had a mortised lock which had been secured. He handed Benny over to me, and smashed his broad shoulder against the door. At the second thrust, the lock gave.

The five of us catapulted into the room. "My God," said Wolfe. "I bet you were right, Rex. Look at that!"

I didn't have to look. I knew quite well what was there on the floor. It was Colby. Colby with a revolver in his hand, a bullet in his brain. A trickle of blood stained the dusty boards at our feet. Crumpled and lying across the room was the envelope I had brought upstairs a moment before.

Wolfe looked at the body closely, then turned around and examined the door.

"Say," he said. "There's no key here. If he locked himself in here where's the key? Say, don't tell me this isn't a suicide either."

Rex Sackler heaved a profound sigh.

"This one's a suicide," he said. "I personally guarantee it."

Wolfe went pounding down the stairs again to the telephone. Crosher, Sackler and I followed leisurely. I was holding on to Benny's arm and I could feel him trembling. We arrived on the ground floor as Wolfe completed his call to headquarters.

"Rex," he said, "there's still some things I don't understand. First about Rawson. Are you sure Colby killed him, too?"

"That's the first thing I was sure of," said Sackler. "That's what started my whole train of thought. Once I decided Colby had killed Rawson, it was easy to figure the rest."

"But how, Rex? How?"

Wolfe was almost respectful now.

"Colby was a chain smoker. Do you remember? He'd light one butt from the end of the other. Last night when I asked him for a cigarette he patted his coat pockets and told me his case was in his overcoat. It was. I got it out myself."

"So?"

"Yet Colby swore he wasn't out of the house last night. A chain smoker like that doesn't keep butts in his overcoat so he's got to go out to the hall closet every time he wants a smoke. But if he went outside, he would put them *in* his overcoat. That's just what Colby did. He undoubtedly lit a cigarette after he killed Rawson and he hadn't finished smoking it when I borrowed one from him."

"Borrowed," I said. "Very funny."

But Sackler was so pleased with himself he didn't even glare at me. However, I didn't much care. Sackler's play was over. I still had a little something up my sleeve.

"Well," asked Wolfe, "why the hell didn't he get Benny out of here when the job was done?"

"He didn't know Rawson had called me in. He didn't expect the police to question the suicide theory. But the servants may have mentioned Benny and it'd look funny if he wasn't on the spot since he'd been staying here for three weeks as Colby's clerk. You see how simple they made it? Living here in Capek's house, holding him a prisoner on his own estate, who'd ever suspect them?"

"And the dough?" said Wolfe. "What about the dough that boy brought you?"

"Oh, that," said Sackler, as if he'd never given it a second thought. "Just a little personal matter."

I DROVE THE coupé for a good five miles before I opened up. Then I said, very casually: "It'd be a good idea if you got rid of that key before we got back to town. Wolfe might start thinking and figure out the whole deal."

Sackler raised his eyebrows. "Deal?" he said. "Key?"

"Key," I said. "Deal. Maybe I'm not quite as dumb as you think I am."

He looked at me for a long time. Then he put his hand in his pocket and took out a key. He said: "I imagine it's safe to throw this out the window here."

I said that I guessed it was. He flung it into the ditch.

I drove another five miles. Then I said: "There's a couple of minor items I'd like to discuss with you."

He nodded a trifle grimly. "I was afraid of that, Joey."

"First," I said, "I'd like a bonus."

"A bonus, Joey? How much?"

"Thirty-three bucks," I told him. "Cash money."

For once he was very quiet at the mention of money. Finally he said, in the tone of a man suffering great physical pain: "I think that can be arranged, Joey."

"Good," I said. "Then there's the matter of a ten-dollar-a-week raise."

Now he looked like a man with the black cholera. "Joey," he exclaimed. "That's over five hundred a year. That's a lot of money, my boy."

"It's only one-fifth of twenty-five hundred," I told him.

There was another long silence. Then, "Suppose, Joey, I didn't see my way clear to letting you have it?"

I made a clucking sound with my tongue and shook my head sadly.

"It's my conscience," I told him. "My damnable conscience. It's driving me to perform my civic duty. To tell Headquarters how you told Colby what you'd figured before you told Wolfe. How you explained to Colby how you'd figured he must be in a bad financial jam in order to have murdered Capek. How you pointed out that his peculations were bound to come out when you had him pinched for murder."

"Yes, Joey," said Sackler weakly. "Anything else?"

"Why, yes," I said. "It occurs to me that you offered him an easy out. Instead of being pilloried in the press, instead of bearing the sneers of his upper-crust friends, you offered to let him commit suicide. For a consideration."

"A consideration, Joey?"

"Twenty-five hundred and fifty dollars," I said. "Of course, you couldn't let him kill himself before the check was cashed. It wouldn't have been legal. That's why you called our attention to the time when we heard the shot that killed Colby. Your check was in the bank by then."

I looked at him and observed with vast satisfaction that for the first time in our joint careers I had him on the run.

"To insure his not dying before you cashed the check you locked him in the attic and gave him a gun with no ammunition. Moreover, you referred to him as Smith so that Wolfe wouldn't arrest Colby, at once, thus wrecking your deal. Then when you had the dough in your pocket you sent me up with a bullet, all as per private and strictly extralegal agreement with Colby."

"Joey," he said, "you figured all that out yourself?"

"I did, indeed," I said. "And my reward will be five hundred and twenty dollars spread over the coming year, plus thirty-three bucks in cash—now."

He sighed heavily. He thrust his hand into his pocket and

took out some bills. He handed them over to me, then delivered a speech which, coming from Rex Sackler, has always seemed a classic to me.

"Joey," he said reproachfully, "sometimes I think there is nothing you wouldn't do for money."

Money to Burn

In which that cash-crazy and congenital money-grubber, Rex Sackler, finds himself in the ghastly predicament of having to accept the smaller of two fees, then sit calmly by while his assistant lights his cigarette with a thousand-dollar bill.

1

The Midas Touch

I SAT AT my bare desk and looked idly out the window at the Madison Avenue traffic below. Business had been so bad lately that I was actually beginning to like my job. Clients or no clients Sackler had to lay my salary on the line each Wednesday, a procedure which caused him all the anguish of Gethsemane.

Behind me he rustled the morning paper, angrily threw it to the floor. I looked around to see him running a hand through his thick black hair.

"Joey," he said in an agonized tone, "this *can't* go on. Not a single client in five weeks. I see a black future before me, Joey. I see myself in rags, dwelling in the gutter. Without shelter, without food. And for this I sacrificed a certain pension with the police department." Here he sighed a sigh that sounded like the wings of a bat in a melancholy cave. "Ah, well, I never had the gift of making money."

I eyed him without sympathy, "My heart bleeds for you," I told him. "You and the Vanderbilts and the Whitneys. If Hitler knew how much gold and silver you've got stored away, he'd invade you."

He stared at me reproachfully. "Joey, you should know better than that. Maybe it seems to you that my fees are high. But so are taxes. Besides I live well. I spend a great deal of money."

A man who laughs easily would have gone into hysterics at

"Manny probably wants to be alone with his dead," Sackler said.

that. Sackler spent money with all the prodigal abandon of a dying anaemic handing out goblets of blood. He had God knows how many thousand dollars scattered around in postal-savings accounts throughout the country. Banks, he often announced gravely, had been known to fail. He rolled his own to avoid the State cigarette tax. He bought a suit at least every two years, and repaired his own shoes with some patented rubbery substance he'd seen advertised in the *Police Gazette*. Compared to Rex Sackler, J.P. Morgan was a financial Red.

The gangster just sat there staring at the crescent sunburn on the drowned girl's arm.

He bent over in his swivel chair and retrieved the crumpled newspaper from the floor.

"Look," he said, "crime goes on. Why don't we get our share of it? Here's a bank holdup. Thirty thousand dollars. If the insurance company would call on me instead of their own flatfeet they might get somewhere. Then there's this Judson kidnaping. A rumored sixty-thousand-dollar ransom. Hell, I'd break that case for a tenth of that."

"According to what I read and hear," I told him, "Old man Judson doesn't want it broken. He's obeying the kidnaper's instructions. He won't even let the coppers touch it. He wants to pay the dough and get his daughter Amy back alive. Why not? He can afford it."

"I wouldn't pay it," said Sackler emphatically. "Compounding a felony, that's what it is."

I studied him curiously. If it had been *his* daughter, I was quite certain he wouldn't pay. But whether because of the felony angle or the awful idea of parting with so much cash I didn't know.

He dragged another sigh out of the bottom of his being and went on.

"Here's Benny Langer dead. A suicide. That's no good. No one ever pays to find out who killed a gangster. Oh, well, sometimes, I wish I'd been more frugal with my money."

"The only way to accomplish that," I told him, "is to stop eating."

He ignored that. He took his bag of tobacco from his pocket, some cigarette papers from the desk drawer. He proceeded to roll a smoke with all the deft agility of an elephant knitting a pair of socks. Then suddenly he flung the twisted white cylinder into the waste-basket, got up, and helped himself to a tailor-made from my desk.

He lit it over my protest and looked at me with a shrewd gleam in his eye. I knew what that look presaged. I got up hastily and walked to the window.

"No," I said firmly. "Whatever it is, I won't do it. Flatly and finally, *no.* Besides I have no money."

"Now, Joey," he said, "don't be a piker. After all, with no business, active minds like ours must pass the time somehow. This is a simple little game. For very small stakes."

I folded my hands behind my back and assumed my best adamantine expression.

"No," I said firmly. "Once a week you pay me. You devote the other six days to trying to win my salary back again. Four times this week I've tossed you for lunch. I've lost three. Knock-rummy has stuck me for six dollars and eighteen cents. You've odded and evened me out of another two dollars, and twice I've had to buy you cigars. I'm through. I wouldn't play bingo with you at a church festival."

"I've got a new game, Joey. It's fascinating. You can hardly lose. I'll bet you two smackers we don't get a case within the next half-hour. If we do you get half the fee minus the two bucks—"

"No! No!" I roared.

At that moment I heard the door of the outer office open. Sackler heard it, too. He sprang back to his own desk, seated himself and played with some old letters, thus giving the impression of a very busy man. I walked into the anteroom and conducted Pete Wells into Sackler's presence. Sackler looked up, recognized the visitor and groaned in disgust.

"God," he said, "it's you. I thought ft might be a client."

Pete Wells sat down in the chair near Sackler's desk. "You're right, Rex," he said. "I *am* a client."

SACKLER LIFTED HIS eyebrows. I registered a tithe of surprise, too. Wells was in the private-detective racket himself. He was less than half as good as Sackler and made twenty times less money. His big and usually unsaleable asset was his utter integrity. If ever there was an honest shamus it was Peter Wells. All the dough buried under Fort Knox couldn't tempt him to touch a case that gave off the slightest odor of halibut. Sackler, of course, wasn't so particular, a fact to which his bank account attested.

"Good Lord," said Sackler, "the shamus business is so lousy that we've got to be each other's clients."

"What do you care?" asked Wells, "as long as there's money in it."

I thought I detected a trace of bitterness in his tone. Sackler's dark eyes took on the unholy gleam which was natural to them when cash was under discussion.

"Money?" he said. "How much?"

"*I* usually ask what the case is first," said Wells pointedly.

"Sure," said Sackler. "And look at you. In a lousy two-by-four office. No assistant. Living in a cheap slum in Brooklyn. I'll bet you haven't a grand in the bank. Me? I get the dough settled first. I've already arranged an annuity. I've got more money salted away than you'll ever hear of, Pete. I've got—"

"Well, well," I said, "I thought you were headed for the gutter. In rags. No food, no shelter. I thought—"

Sackler had the grace to flush. "Oh, that," he said hastily. "Figure of speech, Joey. Figure of speech. That's all. Now, Pete, what is this case?"

I retired to my own desk grinning happily. It wasn't often I scored over Sackler and I wanted to gloat.

Pete Wells cleared his throat. "You've read of the Benny Langer suicide?"

Sackler's heavy eyebrows lifted in surprise. "You don't want me to solve a suicide, do you? Besides, you can't possibly have a client who gives a damn about a little rat like Benny?"

Pete Wells lit his pipe with slow deliberation. "No," he said at last, "I don't want you to solve it, Sackler. There's nothing to solve. It was a suicide—cold—according to the police. I am prepared to offer you a fee for *not* finding Benny's killer, provided he *was* killed."

"How much?"

"Fifteen hundred dollars."

Sackler, a difficult man to surprise, gasped. I stared goggle-eyed at Wells. Yellow envy crept into my heart. Here was Sackler being offered fifteen hundred bucks to keep his nose out of a suicide case that he'd had no intention of investigating in the first place.

"Wells," I said, "are you crazy? Sackler's not on the case. Anyway, why the hell should anyone work on an admitted suicide? What's he supposed to solve? Whether Benny's ended up in Heaven or Hell?"

"You keep out of this, Joey," snapped Sackler.

I knew what he was figuring. If Pete Wells *was* crazy, Sackler wanted that fifteen hundred before the wagon carted him off to the loony-bin.

"I'm not at liberty to give you much information," said Wells. "You're getting a fat fee for nothing. I shouldn't imagine you'd be interested in anything else. Will you take the fifteen hundred dollars to keep Benny Langer a suicide?"

"Will he?" I said. "Did Dewey wish he'd got the nomination? Will Bernarr Macfadden eat spinach? Will a duck enter a natatorium? Will a—"

Sackler turned blazing black eyes on me. "Will you shut up, Joey?" he roared. He turned back to Wells. For a long time they looked at each other. Wells, blond, big, with a fat honest face. Sackler, dark-jowled, black-haired, with shrewd calculating eyes that could look through the leather of anyone's wallet and count the money.

"Pete," said Sackler at last, "I don't know that I can do it."

My brain reeled at that. Sackler offered fifteen hundred dollars for nothing and haggling about it!

"I must be getting deaf," I said politely. "I thought you said you didn't know if you could do it."

Sackler paid no attention to me. Wells shifted uncomfortably in his chair. Then he spoke with grave earnestness.

"Rex, what have you got to lose? You boast you're only in this business for money. All right, I'm offering it to you. Free—gratis—clear."

Normally any one of those words would have appealed to Sackler, but he still shook his head.

"I'll tell you what I'll do," he said at last. "Give me the money. I still retain freedom to act as I see fit. If I don't do it your way you get your money back. Satisfactory?"

Wells nodded reluctantly. "If that's the best you can do, I suppose it has to be. All right. Here."

He reached for his wallet, withdrew it and took out a check. As he did so both Sackler and I saw a photograph of an exceedingly pretty girl pasted in the driver's license compartment of his pocketbook. Knowing Pete Wells, I lifted my eyebrows. Sackler appeared too engrossed in the check to pay much attention to anything else.

Pete Wells handed Sackler the check. He said: "You understand the terms?"

Sackler picked up the oblong piece of paper and his black eyes glowed. "Sure. If Benny Langer wasn't a suicide, if he was killed, if I turn up the murderer, you get this dough back. If none of these contingencies come to pass, I keep it. Right?"

"Right," said Pete Wells. He walked from the room with the air of a troubled man.

SACKLER STOWED THE check in his wallet like the custodian of the crown jewels locking them up for the night. I watched him, torn between envy at his damnable luck and utter astonishment at two other items.

"You explain it to *me*," I said not without bitterness. "Two major miracles in five minutes. First, instead of snapping up fifteen hundred bucks which drop into your lucky lap, you proceed to make terms about it. Second, why in the name of Heaven is an honest shamus like Pete Wells paying out cash to cover someone up."

Sackler proceeded to roll a cigarette. More tobacco dropped onto his knees than into the paper. He clucked like an old hen as he noted the waste. After he had lighted the twisted, drooping thing in his lips he answered me.

"That second problem you mentioned, Joey, has been bothering me, too. The first is easy enough."

"Not to me. I never expected to see you playing dentist to a gift horse."

He puffed on his cigarette like a vacuum cleaner. It still wouldn't draw. He sighed, crushed it out in the ashtray and leaned forward in my direction. This time I was too fast for him. I snatched up my package of tailor-mades and stowed them away in my pocket. He looked at me reproachfully. When he spoke he was loftily patronizing.

"It stands to reason, Joey, that if Pete Wells offers me a fee to lay off the case, someone is going to offer me a fee to take it. Perhaps the second fee will be larger. Elementary."

He was so obviously right I felt sick. It was bad enough to watch him pocket Wells' check while I sat here getting no more than my meager weekly salary. But the thought of him getting even more was too much.

"But," he went on, "Wells is a straight guy, too straight for his own good. He wouldn't cover up his own grandmother. I'll have to figure that angle."

He leaned back in his chair and frowned at the opposite wall. When he engaged in these mental gymnastics, I never quite knew if he actually *was* thinking or merely trying to impress me. At the moment I didn't care. I was too sorry for myself. For the first time in my life I had restrained my gambling instinct and it had cost me precisely seven hundred and forty-eight dollars. I stared at the wall along with Sackler and brooded.

THE PAIR OF us sat like a couple of crystal-gazers for some twenty minutes. Then the outer door opened abruptly, slammed angrily, and hasty footsteps came into the room. I stopped brooding and looked up.

Our visitor was dressed in a suit that cost more than Sackler's entire wardrobe. His shirt was custom made and his tie was a silken symphony. His face was hard and handsome, the eyes gray and ruthless. His lips were full, red and, at the moment, twisted. I stood up, bowed to him, and announced to Sackler, who still stared at the wall like a hypnotist: "Mr. Manuel Campeau to see you."

Sackler lifted his head. "Go away, Manny," he said. "I am a respectable private detective. I can not jeopardize my business consorting with murderers."

I braced myself against the desk and flexed my muscles. That was a dangerous remark to make to Manny Campeau and the strong-arm department of this outfit was all mine.

Wrath boiled up into Manny's gray eyes, lighting them like sun behind a cloud. His mouth became more twisted than before. He took a step forward toward Sackler. So did I.

Manny stopped suddenly and his right hand which had been edging toward his coat pocket fell to his side again. I breathed with relief and shot a glance of annoyance at Sackler. It was all very well for him to go around insulting tough guys but I was the sucker who had to take the bumps.

"I'm leaving that crack go," said Manny, "because I want you to do a job for me."

"Yes," said Sackler disinterestedly, then added his routine question, "How much?"

"Five G's," said Manuel Campeau. "Cash."

Sackler's bored air fell away almost audibly. He sat upright in his chair. His greedy black eyes shone like ebony. His facial expression reminded me of a very hungry man about to eat. Manny thrust his hand into his hip pocket and withdrew a slim roll of bills. He tossed them on the desk. They spread, revealing their denomination. They were thousands.

I felt as happy as Leo Durocher losing a ball game. Never since the days of Midas had there been anything like it. Money dropped into Sackler's lap like golden rain. I thought of my own depressed wages and uttered a groan.

"This is what they call a contingency fee," said Manny. "No results. No dough."

Sackler picked up the bills. His fingers toyed with them like snakes scratching their bellies on rubble. I turned my head around. I could bear the sight of Sackler and all that money no longer.

"Now listen," said Manny. "A pal of mine got knocked off. I want the killer turned up. I want to know his name. If you can't give it to me within a week, I want that dough back."

The last two words alarmed Sackler. Hastily he stowed the bills away in his pocket.

"Consider the case solved, Manny," he said. "Who's the guy that was killed?"

"Langer. Benny Langer."

Sackler drew a deep breath. He exchanged a swift glance with me.

"Langer," he said slowly. "The papers and the coppers call that a suicide, Manny."

"It wasn't."

"How do you know?"

"Look," said Manny, "you're the shamus. I ain't. I know Benny Langer never killed himself. Why would he, with all that—" He broke off abruptly and seemed to get sore. "Hell, don't ask me questions. You find out yourself. That's what you're getting paid for. I guarantee you Benny didn't knock himself off. From there on in you're on your own. Will you take the job?"

Would he take it? My God, with five grand in his desk he'd undertake to find out who killed Cock Robin!

"Sure, I'll take it," said Sackler quietly. "Let's get it straight now. You guarantee me Benny Langer didn't kill himself. You want me to turn up the murderer within a week. If I don't you get this dough back. If I do, I keep it."

"Right. Put the dough in your pocket. Keep it there. Don't spend a dime of it. Don't bank it. Hold it for a week. Then either give it to me back or do what you like with it."

"You've hired a detective," said Sackler.

"One thing more. When you find the guy who knocked off Benny, don't start calling a copper until you've told me his name. I want first chance at the rat."

Sackler thought this over for a long time. "All right," he said at last. "I give you my word I won't inform the police before I've told you."

"All right," said Manny. "I just bought a bungalow at Lake Witherton. Here's the address." He scribbled on Sackler's desk-pad. "Get in touch with me there."

He spun around on a highly polished heel and strode toward the door.

AT THE THRESHOLD, Sackler's voice stopped him. "Hey, Manny! Did you happen to mention to anyone that you were going to see me about this?"

Manny Campeau registered high indignation. "Am I a sucker?" he demanded. "Am I a punk? Am I a smalltime loud-mouth?"

"You answer *me*," said Sackler. "Did you tell anyone?"

"No," snapped Manny. "Certainly I didn't tell anyone. I ain't a fool "

With an aggrieved air he slammed the door behind him.

Sackler looked across the room at me and grinned.

"All right," I said bitterly. "Go ahead and gloat. You're shot with luck. I shall pray each night that you don't turn up Langer's killer. Beside the regular deities, I shall pray to Mohammed, Buddha, and Confucious. I'm taking no chances. If you have to turn that dough back, if you get out of this without making a dime, I'll be as happy as an imbecile who thinks he's Napoleon."

Sackler's grin grew broader. "Ah, Joey," he said, "you miss the important aspect of the situation. It's a dream case. I can't lose."

"Can't lose?"

"Of course not. If I turn up Langer's murderer, I get Manny's five grand. If I fail, I get Pete Wells fifteen hundred. It's a perfect set-up, Joey. We *can't* lose."

My spirits sank. I had forgotten Wells. Now that I remembered him I forgot my financial woes for a moment.

"How do you figure it?" I asked. "An honest, straight-shooting guy like Wells offers cash to cover up a guy. A racketeering crook like Manny Campeau pays five grand to have the killer turned up. It's screwy, Rex."

"Sure it's screwy. But we can't expect a juvenile crossword puzzle for the kind of dough we're getting for this."

"We?" I echoed miserably. "You mean you. Fifteen hundred slugs if you lose. Five grand if you win. I suppose you'll try for the larger amount first?"

Sackler sighed heavily and ran a hand through his dark hair. He shook his head with grave concern and when he spoke there was anxious worry in his tone.

"If there was only some way, Joey," he said plaintively, "some way whereby I could keep *both* those fees—"

I stared at him in such speechless indignation that the epithet I thought of wouldn't come out of my throat.

2

The Girl in the Snapshot

A HASTY EXAMINATION of the newspapers told us that Benny Langer had been found dead in a cheap hotel room on Fourteenth Street, where he had registered under a phoney name. A gun was in his hand and a bullet in his brain when the screaming chambermaid had found him. A call to Inspector Wolfe at headquarters verified this but added no detail.

Wolfe had laughed when he answered my questions. "It looked like suicide, Joey," he said. "But what the hell does Rex care? When a punk like Benny gets knocked off the department doesn't care very much why or how. One less lug to bother about, that's all."

Anyway, obeying Sackler's instructions I got the address of Benny's furnished apartment in Brooklyn, and we started for the subway. As usual Sackler outfumbled me and I was stuck for the nickels.

In life Benny Langer had masked himself in respectability. A two-room flat in Columbia Heights had been his home. There, among the Brooklyn bourgeoisie, his nefarious criminal enterprises had remained unsuspected. Sackler opened the door with a master key, and we rolled up our sleeves and went to work. I went through the living-room and kitchen like a fine-tooth comb, while Sackler took the bedroom.

A half-hour later, I lounged in an arm chair after turning up a net of nothing, when Sackler emerged from the bedroom with a glass in one hand and a half-bottle of brandy in the other. He poured himself a stiff slug of the corpse's liquor as he spoke.

"Find anything?"

"Not a thing. Did you?"

Sackler drained the glass, carefully recorked the bottle and put it in his pocket. With his customary freehandedness he did not even offer me a drink.

"I got these," he said, taking something out of his pocket. "What do you think?"

I took two snapshots and a bundle of letters from his hand and glanced through them. The photographs were of a very pretty girl who was oddly familiar to me. The letters, I judged were from the same person. With one deviation, they ran the gamut of the usual brief, taut and illicit love affair. Those dated earliest avowed love and passion. Later, a note of caution appeared. The last letter was frankly panicky. *He*, wrote the girl, would kill her if he ever found out. They must not see each other again. The epistle concluded with an injunction to destroy all letters, an instruction which Benny had obviously disobeyed.

I looked up to see Sackler pouring himself a second drink. I stared at him steadily. He met my eyes and read my register correctly.

"Oh, all right," he said, "all right. I suppose you want a slug of this. Get yourself a glass."

I got myself a glass, filled it and said: "These letters, now. I suppose you figure some guy killed Benny over the girl?"

Sackler shook his head. "No, Joey, it's too damned simple. Besides, that wouldn't explain Wells' interest. He's hardly the type for a love-nest murder."

He certainly wasn't, I reflected as I drank the brandy. Sackler paced around the living-room aimlessly, apparently lost in thought. Then he came to a guardsman's halt before the open writing-desk. He pounced on a scratch-pad that I had seen half an hour ago.

"What's this?"

I glanced over his shoulder. Figures had been scrawled over the paper.

"Probably Benny figuring the month's budget," I told him. "Why?"

"Look at it closely, Joey."

I looked at it closely. The figure *60* was at the top of the sheet. Directly beneath was the number *33.33 1/3*. The two numbers had been laboriously multiplied. The result at the bottom of the page was, accurately enough, *20.00*. I looked up at Sackler again and shrugged.

"So?"

"So," said Sackler, "what does that indicate?"

"Probably, that Benny Langer was arithmetically illiterate. Too dumb to realize that you can get a third of sixty by dividing by three. He didn't have to do all that multiplication by thirty-three and a third."

"Sound, as far as it goes," said Sackler. "Anything else?"

"Nothing," I said, "and would you please stop putting that bottle back in your pocket?"

I poured myself another drink as Sackler put the scratch-pad, the photographs and the letters on the table. As I sipped the brandy, he pawed over the desk-papers like a vulture.

"Look," I said, annoyed. "I've been all through those papers. There's nothing there."

He held up an envelope and said: "Yes? What's this?"

I looked at it. There were two columns of scribbling on its back. "All right," I said. "I'll be straight-man. What is it?"

"It's a list," he said slowly. "A list of banks. If you'll notice there are just sixty of them listed."

"So what?"

"I don't know myself yet. But the germ of an idea is crawling through my brain."

SACKLER, WHOSE EARS were those of a lynx heard the door open. Watching his face I knew something was wrong. I spun around facing the same direction as he did. Framed in the doorway was a girl, a striking and attractive girl whose hand was tipped with blood red nails. The most interesting fact from my own point of view was that, at the moment, her slim fingers were wrapped around the butt of an automatic.

Sackler, whose, disregard for danger affecting my person had always been magnificent said: "Take her, Joey. Get that gun."

"If you do, Joey, you'll wind up in Woodlawn," said the brunette in the doorway. "Don't you get in an uproar, either, Mr. Sackler. I've only come for what belongs to me."

She came into the room. She looked around shrewdly over the top of her gun. Sackler urged me to the attack with his eyes, but I had no desire at the moment to die gallantly.

Her smoldering eyes saw the papers Sackler had put on the table-top. She moved toward it, swept up the letters and the photograph. She clutched them grimly in her hand and backed toward the doorway.

"This is all I want," she said. "I'd advise you not to follow me too quickly. I'm one hell of a good shot."

She slammed the door and her footsteps sounded diminuendo on the stairs outside. I reached for my thirty-eight and started after her when—"Wait a minute," said Sackler. "We don't need her, Joey. Do you know who she was?"

"Sure. She was the girl who was in the snapshots she swiped."

Sackler nodded. "True, Joey. Did you ever see her photograph anywhere else?"

I felt sure I had, but it took two minutes heavy thought before I said suddenly: "Sure, I remember now. Pete Wells had her picture in his wallet. I saw it when he took out the check."

Sackler nodded again. "And how do you figure that?"

"It's funny," I told him, "that Pete Wells and Benny should be pally with the same girl."

"It's even funnier than that," said Sackler. "If I'm right, Pete Wells, Benny and Manny Campeau are *all* pally with the same girl. Despite his denial, it's obvious Manny told someone he was bringing his case to me. Quite probably he told a girl, a girl he figured he could trust. The girl, whose picture was in Wells' wallet, repeated the news to Pete. Evidently she was scared of something. Maybe the finding of those letters she just swiped."

"And Pete liked her well enough to invest dough to keep you out of the case, eh?"

"Obviously, Joey."

"It sounds screwy to me."

He headed toward the door and I followed him. In the street, I asked: "Now what?"

"I think we'll go out to Manny's beach bungalow. I'd like to see Manny."

"About what? He wouldn't be offering you five grand if he knew any of the answers himself."

Sackler didn't answer.

I bought myself an evening paper to read in the subway. The front page was solid on the Judson kidnaping. The ransom had been paid, but the missing heiress had not yet put in an appearance. Sackler read the black headlines over my shoulder.

"Joey," he said suddenly, "that reminds me. When you get a chance call Wolfe at headquarters again. Tell him I may have something for him on the Judson case. Get whatever details you can from him. Who the intermediary was, how the money was paid and so forth."

I stared at him blankly. "My God," I said, "we're finding out who killed Benny Langer. Remember? We're not on the Judson kidnaping case."

Sackler pulled another sigh out of his boots. "Maybe we are, Joey," he said very thoughtfully. "Maybe we are."

WE WENT BACK to the office first and I telephoned Inspector Wolfe. Then I reported to Sackler who stood dolefully rattling the silver in his pocket. Even the jingle of the coins didn't appear to cheer him up.

"Well," he said, "and what did Wolfe have to say?"

"First and emphatically," I told him, "he said that if you're going to help the department on the Judson thing, O.K. On the other hand, if you're going to use his information for your own fee-collecting ends, he'll have your scalp and your license."

Sackler grunted. He liked Wolfe only a little less than Wolfe liked him. "What about the ransom money?"

"Delivered," I told him, "as ordered. In thousand-dollar bills. Sixty of them."

"Thousand-dollar bills? Hell, that doesn't make sense. Why

the devil would a snatcher want big bills? It's tough enough to pass small ones after the serial numbers've been taken. Big ones are impossible."

"Ask the kidnaper. I wouldn't know."

"Who handled the dough? Who was the intermediary?"

"Guy called Graves. Works for Judson. Lives out in Bayside. Collects rents and stuff for Judson out there. And Wolfe says you're to leave Graves alone. Strict orders from Judson. He doesn't want anyone monkeying with the case until he gets his daughter back. And he's got enough political influence to get what he wants."

Sackler apparently wasn't listening to me. He rubbed his hand over his forehead and muttered: "Big bills. Big bills."

After he said that some twelve times, I got tired of it and went back to the evening paper.

TWO HOURS LATER we drove up to Manny Campeau's summer bungalow, situated in a beautiful secluded spot right at the edge of the lake. An expanse of clean white beach formed Manny's front porch. A wall of pine trees barricaded the north side of the property and a vast expanse of scrubby brush lay to the south.

We banged on the front door to discover that the house was empty. At Sackler's suggestion we strolled down to the beach in the sun, assuming that Manny had probably gone swimming.

A hundred yards or so from the house stood an ancient ramshackle boathouse. As we passed its open door, Sackler stopped suddenly and sniffed.

"Joey," he said, "what do you smell?"

"Bananas," I told him. "Someone's been eating bananas."

"Wrong again, Joey. It's banana oil. Probably nail polish. There's a high percentage of the stuff in that. Let's take a look."

We entered the boathouse. It was damp and run down. Through a crescent-shaped hole in the roof a spot of sunlight entered reluctantly. Sackler looked up at the roof, then down and his sharp eyes surveyed the floor. Suddenly he bent over. When he straightened up again he had a half-empty bottle of nail polish in his hand.

I was about to ask him what that indicated, if anything, when, I suddenly saw through the open doorway, the figure of Manny, in a bathing suit, about a hundred yards down the beach.

Manny," I said. "There he is. Down there. He just found something, too."

Sackler joined me in the doorway. We saw Manny in the distance bending over something he had apparently pulled out of the water.

"My God," said Sackler, "if that's what I think it is— Come on, Joey."

He broke into a run and I followed him down the sandy beach. Manny looked up and saw us when we had covered half the distance. He looked at us morosely as we halted panting before him, staring down at the bloated body at his feet.

"Drowned," said Manny and there was a break in his voice. "She's drowned. I warned her about the currents. Oh, God, she wouldn't listen. That's Ruth Pixley, Rex. Gee, I never liked any dame like I liked her. She was my girl, Rex."

I looked down at the corpse and reflected, as I studied her features, that in all probability she had also been Pete Wells' girl and Benny Langer's, too. For less than three hours ago Ruth had thrust a revolver under my nose and swiped her own letters back from Benny's joint.

I glanced inquiringly at Sackler, but he gave no hint of ever having seen the girl before. He knelt down on the beach and examined the body.

"Drowned is right," he said. He lifted her left arm and frowned. "That's funny. Look, Joey. Sunburn."

On her left forearm was a faint curved blotch of sunburn.

"You'll note," said Sackler, "that she's burned nowhere else. Just that one patch. That's all."

"She was swimming nearly all day," said Manny. "I just found her washed up on the beach. Probably lay here for hours with her arm exposed to the sun. Oh, why didn't she listen to me? Why didn't she?"

Sackler stood up and there was on odd light in his eyes. "Manny," he said, "I feel for you. You must want to be alone with your grief. We'll go back to town. I'll send a doctor out to sign a death certificate. I'll get in touch with you tomorrow."

We walked slowly up the beach toward the car leaving Manny Campeau alone with his dead.

3

The Sudden Sickness of Sackler

I ARRIVED AT the office a few minutes before nine the following morning. Rather to my surprise, Sackler was already there. He was barking into the mouthpiece of the phone as I came in.

"It's the Judson case, I tell you, Wolfe.... Yes. I want a good sergeant and half a dozen men.... Yes. I'll have it wrapped up and in the bag for you by noon if I get those men.... Yes. Meet me at Graves' house at noon.... Graves. The guy who was the intermediary in the Judson case.... All right then."

He hung up and met my inquiring gaze.

"You don't mean to say you've solved the Judson case?" I said.

"I've figured it," he said. "The evidence is a little weak though."

"What about Benny? That's what you're getting paid for."

"Oh, that. That's simple enough, Joey."

"Well, who did it?"

He didn't answer me directly. Instead he said: "Did it occur to you, Joey, that Benny Langer was registered at a strange hotel under a phoney name for one single purpose? Did it occur to you that only a limited number of people could have known he was there? One of those people must have killed him."

I asked him what the hell he meant, but he fell into one of his brooding silences and didn't speak until Sergeant Conners arrived from headquarters. He took the policeman out into the anteroom and talked to him out of my hearing. I was burning with curiosity but wouldn't give him the satisfaction of showing it.

When Conners left he dragged me down to the car and we drove out to this guy Graves' house in Bayside.

Graves was tall and thin. His face was long and his hands far too beautiful for a man. He was sitting at a desk in his study when his ancient and ugly secretary ushered us in. There were a couple of ledgers on the desk, and at his right hand was a pile of bills. The top one I noted was a five-hundred. Unless Sackler was slipping badly, he noticed it too.

Sackler announced our identity and Graves went even paler than he had been when we came in.

"If it's about the kidnaping," he said, "I'm afraid I can tell you nothing. I'm under Mr. Judson's strict orders. I mustn't discuss the case with anyone. After his daughter is returned he'll do all the talking that's necessary."

"That's not a very broad statement," said Sackler cryptically. "Tell me this. Did you personally deliver the ransom money?"

Graves nodded. "Since the papers already have that story, I can admit that much."

"Where did you deliver it?"

Graves shook his head. "I can't answer that."

Sackler looked at him for a long silent moment. "Maybe, I can," he said quietly.

Nobody said anything for some time. Then Sackler jerked his head in the direction of the cash on the desk.

"What's all that?" he asked. "You seem pretty careless with all that money?"

Graves smiled faintly. "I hope you don't think I've held out any of the ransom, Mr. Sackler. No, those are collections from

Mr. Judson's properties. I pick them up three times a week and my secretary banks the money."

"It's a lot of cash for rentals," said Sackler.

Graves nodded. "There are some fly-by-night businesses in the Judson properties out here. They pay cash and weekly. We don't want them to move out on us suddenly."

"Gambling?" said Sackler with a raised eyebrow.

"I don't inquire too closely," said Graves. "My job is to collect from the tenants and I might say they pay one hell of a high rental."

Sackler grunted. "So old Judson despite his church connections is landlord to a gambling syndicate. Judging from the amount of dough you've got there, he's more than just landlord. He's a silent partner."

Graves shrugged. "It's still none of my business."

He picked up the money and put it in the drawer. "Careless of me to leave it lying around. I usually keep it in the drawer until Flora, that's my secretary, goes to lunch at twelve thirty. She banks it then in a special account held in my name for Mr. Judson."

SACKLER WALKED OVER to the window and stared thoughtfully into the garden beyond. The door opened and Flora, the secretary came in.

She had a lot of prominent teeth, a leathery complexion and the sort of a face they cast for cruel stepmothers in Hollywood.

She talked a little shop to Graves, then he told her: "These two gentlemen are detectives, Flora."

She looked up at me and showed all her teeth. "We-ell," she said, "that must be exciting." She moved closer until her arm was touching mine. "You must tell me about your thrilling adventures sometime."

I agreed hastily and moved away. There never was any law of averages in my love life. Inevitably the same type of dames go for me. Flora grinned at me again and, followed by my sigh of relief, left the room.

Sackler came back from the window and sat down next to Graves. "Graves," he said, "I want you to tell me everything you know about the Judson kidnaping. Where you delivered the money and everything else."

"I'm sorry. But I've already told you—"

"All right," said Sackler as he stood up. He said brusquely to me: "Joey, you'll use Graves' phone. You'll call Manny Campeau. Pete Wells. and Inspector Wolfe. Have 'em come here right away. Insist upon it. You, Graves, let me have a quiet room I can do some thinking in."

Graves was on his feet protesting loudly.

"You can't bring the police here," he said. "Mr. Judson'll get sore as hell. You can't bring—"

"The hell I can't," said Sackler. "Joey, get on that phone. Now Graves, will you take me to a room or shall I commandeer one myself."

I picked up the phone. Graves, completely licked by Sackler's domineering air, sighed heavily and conducted him from the room.

INSPECTOR WOLFE'S PRIME and most obvious characteristic was his muscular larynx. Running it a close second was his impatience. At the moment he trod the rug in Graves' living-room and demonstrated them both.

"Sackler," he roared, "I don't stand for any of your stalling. On my own responsibility I've let you have a sergeant and six coppers from headquarters. I've got to have results. You told me you'd solved the Judson kidnaping. Well, have you, or haven't you?"

Sackler sighed, opened a silver cigarette box, found it empty and reached for his bag of makings.

"I've solved it," he said wearily. "But I'd have a much tighter case if I could have a little more time. I—"

"Time!" bellowed Wolfe. "This is a big case. If you've got the answers, I want them now. At once. If not I'll withdraw my six coppers."

From my vantage position behind Sackler's chair, I regarded the occupants of the room over his shoulders. Manny Campeau sat in an arm chair smoking a cigar. His poker face, I thought, was a trifle too apparent. Flora, Graves' secretary stood by the mantelpiece, smiled coquettishly at me. I hastily averted my gaze.

Pete Wells and Graves relaxed side by side on a divan. Graves smoked a cigarette calmly enough but it seemed to me there was a tightness about his mouth that had not been there before. Wells made no effort to conceal his nervousness. Wolfe glared at Sackler over a cigar whose end looked as if it had been mistaken for chewing gum by an irritated lion. He opened his mouth wide and cleared his throat.

"All right," said Sackler hastily, holding his hands up like an umbrella against the torrent of Wolfe's words. "All right, I'll tell you all about it. But don't blame me if the D.A. squawks because you have a frail case."

"Tell me who pulled the Judson job. I'll get my own confession."

Sackler took a pin from his lapel, inserted it into the final millimeter of his cigarette and almost committed arson on the tip of his nose as he puffed at it.

"The key to the case," he announced, "was the Pixley girl. Ruth Pixley."

Manny glanced at Sackler through narrowed lids. Wolfe chewed his cigar for a moment and snapped: "You mean she snatched the Judson girl?"

"No," said Sackler, "but she found her body."

"Body?" yelled Wolfe. "You mean the girl's dead?"

"Let me tell this my own way," said Sackler. "This Pixley was quite a two-timer. It seems she once made Pete Wells fall for her, she was living with Manny, and to pass a dull moment she also had an affair with Benny Langer."

Pete Wells and Manny sprang out of their chairs. "That's a lie," they said in chorus, then stopped, staring at each other.

"Oh, no it isn't," said Sackler. "When Pixley discovered Benny had been killed she began to worry. True, the coppers had called it a suicide, which would preclude any further investigation, but Manny let it slip to her that he was going to commission me to find Benny's murderer. That made Pixley panicky that I'd find the letters she'd sent to Benny."

Pete Wells and Manny Campeau stopped looking at each other and looked at Sackler. Wolfe took his cigar from his mouth and said: "I ain't interested in the morals of Manny's women. Tell me about Judson."

Sackler ignored him. "Pixley was deathly afraid Manny would find out about her affair with Benny. Hearing I was about to take the case she went to Wells, appealed to him to stop me. She even went so far as to tell Wells she killed Benny, didn't she, Pete?"

"She's dead," said Pete Wells savagely. "Can't you let her rest in peace?"

"No," said Sackler. "Not with a fee involved."

You're crazy," said Manny. "She didn't kill Benny. She didn't even know he—" He broke off and bit his lip.

"Didn't even know she was in that hotel room, eh Manny?" said Sackler. "However, I didn't say she killed Benny. She merely told Pete that. After all you can't tell one lover you're afraid of a second lover finding out that you've just had an affair with a third lover."

"My God," said Wolfe. "Who cares about all this pornography? Tell me about Judson. Pixley's dead. Benny's dead. And I don't care. I *do* care about the Judson girl."

"Well," said Sackler, "Pixley recovered her letters anyway. Manny never heard about her escapade with Benny. But he killed her anyway, didn't you Manny?"

MANNY LICKED HIS lips and glared at Sackler. "She was drowned," he said. "No one can prove she wasn't drowned. Anyways, if you admit I didn't know about her and Benny, why should I kill her?"

"I'm glad you asked that, Manny." Sackler leaned forward over the table and fixed Manny with his dark piercing eyes. "Because she found the Judson girl's body, Manny. Because she stumbled over the corpse of Judson's daughter. You didn't want to kill her Manny. You rather liked her. But after taking all afternoon to think it over, you figured you had to do it. You couldn't gamble on her knowing you'd done the Judson snatch."

Wolfe suddenly looked like a man who has come into a

million dollars. "You mean he snatched Amy Judson, Rex? Give me the evidence!"

"He's nuts," said Manny. "He ain't got no evidence. He ain't got no case."

"If you can explain one thing," said Sackler, "I'll concede I have no case. You said Ruth Pixley had been swimming all afternoon. Only one part of her body was sunburned. A little crescent patch on her right forearm. How do you explain that?"

"She must've got drowned, washed up on the beach and had her arm twisted around somehow so it got burned, that's all."

"The only hole in that," said Sackler, "is that corpses don't sunburn. Nothing dead burns. It rots."

Something clicked in my mind at that. I came galloping into the conversation. "The shack," I said, "that boathouse. There was a hole in the roof. A crescent-shaped hole. She must've been lying in there while she was alive."

"That's the answer," said Sackler. "It's ridiculous to suppose that she would go to sleep or lie down in that dank shack. If she lay there long enough to get sunburned through that hole, she must have been unconscious. Manny didn't want to kill her if he could avoid it. He slugged her, put her in the boat-house till he thought things over. When he could find no other solution, he dragged her out and drowned her."

Manny's lips were white and his face was pale. Pete Wells glared at him and there was murder in his gaze. I moved forward in the room and took up a position between them.

Wolfe turned appealingly to Sackler. "But what about Amy Judson?" he asked. "For God's sake tell me about that girl, Rex."

Sackler rolled another cigarette. "From what I observed at Benny Langer's apartment, I was convinced that Manny and

Benny were in on that Judson affair. That's the reason I went out to Manny's beach place. There was a bottle of nail polish in that boathouse. Polish of a different color than the Pixley girl would have worn. She was a blonde. From that I figured Manny had kept the Judson girl in the boathouse until he got around to killing her."

"He's absolutely nuts," said Manny Campeau. "He can't pin that rap on me just because he seen a bottle of nail polish."

"How did you know he killed the Judson girl?" asked Wolfe.

"Because," said Sackler, "he killed Ruth Pixley. He liked her. He certainly had not found out about her affair with Benny. So why should he kill her? Only because something drastic had occurred. As, for instance, her discovery of Judson's body. Probably in the brush to the east of the house."

Manny took a deep breath, preparatory, I suppose to announcing once again that Sackler was nuts. The ringing of the telephone stopped him. Sackler nodded to Wolfe.

"Take it," he said. "It's probably your six coppers that I've had searching Manny's property. I think you'll discover they've found Amy Judson's corpse."

I watched Sackler closely as Wolfe went to the phone. He seemed quite sure of himself, although he still hadn't announced the murderer of Benny Langer, an item for which he had already been paid five grand.

Wolfe hung up the receiver, turned triumphantly to Sackler. "You're right," he roared. "Absolutely right. They found Amy Judson's body on Manny's property. Moreover the polish on her nails checks with the bottle you gave the sergeant."

He turned to Manny, who stood, braced, watching him. "You've got no case." Manny said desperately. "A bottle of nail polish. What's that? A sunburned arm. A body found near my house. What do they all add up to in a grand-jury room? Sackler's private opinion ain't evidence."

Wolfe frowned. It didn't need Frank Murphy to see that legally the case was as strong as the Latvian army. Manny glanced from Wolfe to Sackler, observed their hesitancy and pressed his advantage.

"Besides," he said, more assured, "I want my dough back. I want my fee. I give it to you to find out who killed Benny. You ain't done it. Gimme back my dough."

"You've got that mixed up," said Sackler. "It's Pete Wells who gets his money back. He paid me a contingent fee *not* to solve that killing, when he believed Ruth Pixley had committed it. But I solved it anyway. He gets his dough back. You don't, Manny."

AS USUAL SACKLER was very cool about exchanging fifteen hundred dollars for five grand. He took from his pocket two sheets of paper. One of them bore Benny's laborious arithmetical figures. The other, the list of metropolitan banks. Wolfe took them from his hand and looked them over inquiringly.

"You'll note," said Sackler, "that Benny in his circuitous way, has figured out how much one third of sixty is. The ransom in the Judson case was exactly sixty thousand dollars. If my figuring was right it appeared that someone had offered Benny thirty-three and a third percent of the ransom money. Benny, an illiterate, had worked it out the hard way to see how much dough he was getting."

Graves screwed up his brow and said: "That's pretty slim isn't it, Mr. Sackler?"

"Wait," said Sackler. "On that second sheet of paper is a list of banks. Sixty of them. Do you get it Wolfe?"

Wolfe screwed up his brow and tried to think. "Sixty grand," he muttered. "Sixty banks. Sixty—"

"Sixty," repeated Sackler. "Sixty banks. Sixty grand. And the ransom demand was for big bills. Thousand-dollar bills. Now do you get it?"

Wolfe evidently didn't. I did and I said so. "Benny was going to change those bills. Change one at each bank he had listed. He knew the serial numbers of the original bills would be registered. But since those numbers wouldn't be released until Amy Judson was returned, he figured it was safe to cash 'em in right away. There'd be no record of the smaller bills he received in exchange."

Sackler nodded. "Obvious," he said. "So obvious even Joey understands it."

Manny laughed aloud. "So what?" he demanded. "I still say he ain't got no evidence. The D.A.'d throw him out of the office. Besides, I want my dough back. I paid you to find out who knocked off Benny. You ain't done it."

Wolfe chewed his cigar glumly. Sackler was handing him a pretty handful of logical theory but he was rather short on tangible evidence.

"With a fee involved, Manny," said Sackler, "I rarely fail. You wanted the killer of Benny. I give him to you."

Manny's eyes narrowed, became hot and menacing. "Who?" he said tensely. "Who knocked off Benny?"

Sackler waved an airy hand in Graves' direction. "Graves," he said. "Didn't you, Graves?"

"Graves?" said Manny in astonishment.

"My God!" said Wolfe. "What's Graves got to do with it?"
Graves didn't answer. His lips were tightly closed.

"Look," said Sackler, "Benny's hiding out in a hotel room for the specific purpose of receiving the Judson ransom. Now there were only three people in the world who knew he was there under his assumed name. They were old man Judson, his intermediary, and Benny's confederate, Manny. The confederate certainly didn't kill him, since he was offering me a stiff fee to find out who did."

"Old man Judson certainly didn't," said Wolfe, looking at Graves who stood frozen and pale, "and that leaves the intermediary."

"That leaves the intermediary," said Sackler slowly. "Graves is no fool. He had specific instructions from Judson to do nothing to jeopardize his daughter's safety. Nevertheless when Benny shoved a gun in his back, told him that he would be forced to accompany Benny to those sixty banks to change the bills, Graves knew the answer to that."

"You mean," said Wolfe, "Graves realized that he would be killed when Benny was through with him. Benny couldn't risk a guy living who could identify him. With Graves and Amy Judson dead, the ransom bills exchanged, the scheme was foolproof."

"Exactly," said Sackler. "Graves realizing that got in a brawl with Benny, somehow managed to get his gun during the struggle. He killed Benny. He was scared to report it because Judson would be furious figuring the kidnapers would be revenged upon his daughter. Graves would lose his job and his patron. So he merely left the money behind him and kept his mouth shut."

MANNY WAS GLARING at Graves. He edged toward him and I dropped my hand to the butt of the gun in my pocket. I judged from his obvious wrath that Sackler was dead right once again, that Graves had inadvertently wrecked Manny's fool-proof kidnap scheme.

Despite all the light Sackler had thrown around, Wolfe still looked uncomfortable.

"It sounds good, Rex," he said, "but it ain't much of a case. Haven't you any direct evidence? Haven't you—"

"He's got nothing," said Manny. "Nothing. I don't believe Graves killed Benny. I want my dough back."

"Of course," said Graves uncertainly. "Of course, I never killed him. He was alive when I left him."

Graves and Manny exchanged glances. In this moment they were solid allies. Wolfe looked appealingly at Sackler who for once was at a loss.

"He can't prove nothing," yelled Manny again. "I want my dough back! Now!"

Suddenly Sackler lifted his head. The shadow slipped from his eyes and the old familiar gleam of gloating triumph was there. He clapped his hands together excitedly.

"Good Lord," he said happily, "what a fool I am. I've been so damn busy figuring the hard parts I missed what was under my nose. It's a cinch, Wolfe. Sure I can prove it."

Wolfe grinned from ear to ear. Manny and Graves looked vaguely apprehensive.

"You want your money back, eh, Manny," said Sackler. "That's very interesting. Get your handcuffs out, Inspector. Here's your case. I can—"

He stopped suddenly. The lilt had gone from his tone. The

shadow had crawled back into his eyes and there was stark consternation in his face. His head slumped down on his chest and he covered his eyes with his hands.

"Oh my God," he groaned and there was genuine anguish in his voice. "My God, my God!"

"Rex," said Wolfe anxiously, "what's the matter? Are you ill? What's the matter with him, Joey?"

I didn't have the slightest idea. His cheeks were pale and hollow groans were emanating from his larynx. He looked up suddenly and banged his fists together.

"I'm a fool," he muttered in a tortured voice. "A damned idiotic fool. Oh, my God. My God!"

"Sackler," said Wolfe sharply. "Will you pull yourself together for a moment. You were going to give us proof. Remember?"

Sackler ran his hands through his hair and looked as if he were about to embark upon an epileptic fit. Then he said abruptly: "Inspector, hold these people here for a few minutes. I must have a private conference with Joey."

"With Joey?" echoed Wolfe. "What for?"

"I want to ask his advice."

I nearly fell on my face at that. Sackler's opinion of my mentality was as low as French morale. But he gave Wolfe no opportunity to ask any more questions.

He stood up, grabbed my arm and led me from the room. On the threshold, he said to Wolfe over his shoulder: "Just a few minutes, Inspector. Don't let anyone leave."

4

Money to Burn

HE DRAGGED ME upstairs to the guestroom, closed the door, and said with terrible earnestness: "Joey, I've never felt so utterly low in all my life."

Concerned, I said: "Are you ill? Shall I get a doctor?"

He glared at me. "No, you fool. It's not my health. I only wish it were."

I eyed him shrewdly, said: "Money?"

He groaned again. "How could I have been such a fool. It was so damned obvious."

"What was?"

"That five grand Manny gave me. It's the ransom money, Joey! I just thought of it. He's paid me with the Judson ransom money!"

I considered that. True, it had been under our noses all the time, but even so it seemed a matter for rejoicing rather than sorrow.

"Then you're in," I told him. "That proves your case against Manny. If he gave you the ransom money, you've got him cold. You *can* prove the case."

"Sure, I can prove the case," he said bitterly. "That's what I thought of downstairs. But what about me? That's marked money. I can't keep it. I can't spend it. I prove the case and lose the fee. Oh, my God!"

In that moment I knew what the poets meant by ecstasy.

Happiness flooded my heart like a rising river. I watched the grin that spread over my face in the mirror opposite and it was a beautiful thing to behold.

"So," I said and the lilt in my voice was music on a spring morning. "So, you've got to give Pete back his check, and your fee from Manny is worthless. Spend a dime of it and you're in the can. You'll have to give it back to Judson. You've solved two murders. Free, gratis, for nothing! Ah, Mr. Sackler, I was not born in vain."

I threw back my head and howled with laughter. This was the biggest moment of my life and I was enjoying it to the full.

Sackler glared at me and I wouldn't have been surprised to see him foam at the mouth.

"All right," he snarled. "Laugh. Laugh you dim-witted fool. I'm not licked yet. I've thought my way out of other tough spots."

I obeyed his injunction and kept on laughing as he paced the floor, his brow wrinkled in thought. With five grand involved there wasn't a brain cell loafing. Sackler was giving it every ounce of mentality he had.

Suddenly he came to a halt. There was a glint in his eye, half maniacal, half of hope.

He grabbed my arm and said tensely: "Joey, what time is it?"

I consulted my watch. "Twelve twenty. Why?"

"You know that dame downstairs? Graves' secretary?"

"Flora?"

"That's her name. She likes you, Joey."

"That's very interesting," I told him in a tone which implied it wasn't.

"Joey, I want you to go down to the study. Get her out of there. Take her out in the garden."

I eyed him suspiciously. "For what?"

"Make a date with her. Offer to take her to dinner tonight."

"Oh, no. Not me. I want no part of her."

"Joey," he said and there was desperation in his voice. "Joey, you've got to. I'll give you five dollars."

I shook my head. "There's an ugly word for men like you," I said in falsetto.

"Damn you!" he shrieked, beside himself. "Will you stop clowning. This is terrifically important. Go down there. Date her up quickly. I'll give you seven dollars."

I DIDN'T KNOW exactly what he had in the back of his slippery brain, but I knew he was a desperate man and I appraised the situation accordingly.

"Twenty bucks," I said. "Give me twenty bucks and I'll do it. And with her face I'm losing money on the deal."

"Joey," he said, anguished. "This is robbery. I'll give you twelve."

"Twenty," I said, quite sure of my ground now. "Twenty. Not a penny less."

His moan of agony would have touched a lesser man, but I stood firm. He peeled twenty dollars off his roll and handed it to me like a man submitting to the amputation of his right arm.

"All right," he said. "I can't afford to dicker. But hurry, Joey. Hurry."

I stuffed the twenty in my pocket and tripped reluctantly down the stairs. I thrust my head through the door of the study and asked Flora if I could see her in the garden for a moment. She gave me all her teeth, slid out from her desk and grabbed my arm as if she feared I'd change my mind.

I went outside with her, sat down beneath an apple tree and asked her if she'd have dinner with me. Parenthetically. I asked *myself* why wasn't this Heddy Lamarr.

It seemed she would have dinner with me. In fact I was given the rather ghastly impression that she'd have anything with me that I desired. I stalled around for about fifteen minutes then decided Sackler had had his twenty dollars' worth.

"Well," I said at last. "I'd better get back to work."

"Oh, so must I," she giggled. "I'm late now. I'm supposed to go to the bank at twelve thirty."

I took her back to the study, then returned to the living-room.

SACKLER HAD ALREADY arrived. He was sitting at the table. Wolfe watched him inquiringly. Manny and Graves were sullen.

"Well," said Wolfe sarcastically, "have you digested Joey's advice? Are you ready to give me enough evidence now."

"Here it is," said Sackler. He put his hand in his pocket and withdrew a thousand-dollar bill. "Part of the Judson ransom money. I just called Judson's bank and checked on the serial number."

"Where did you get it?"

"From Manny. You've heard him bellyaching that he wanted his fee back from me. Well, here it is. He gave me that bill to find Benny Langer's murderer. It's ransom money and it'll burn him."

Manny uttered a howl of rage. "Where's the rest of it? Where's the other four grand?"

Sackler stared him down. "A grand you gave me, Manny. That's all."

"It's a lie," screamed Manny. "Inspector, watch him. He's putting something over. He's—"

"Shut up," said Wolfe. "One bill will burn you as easily as ten. Besides what the hell would Sackler hold out hot money for? He couldn't spend it."

He walked across the room and put his hand on Manny's arm. Then he glanced quickly from Graves to Sackler.

"What about this guy?" he asked. "Do I take him in on suspicion of killing Benny?"

"Sure," said Sackler, "I'm sure some iron-clad evidence will turn up."

"Now wait a minute," said Graves, alarmed, "I—"

The ringing of the telephone interrupted him. Sackler smiled happily. "Probably for you, Inspector," he said.

Wolfe snatched up the receiver. He spoke rapidly into the mouthpiece, hung up and turned a grim face to Graves.

"So," he said, "Rex was dead right all the time. After you killed Benny you just couldn't help appropriating a little of that sixty grand for yourself, could you? Come along, Graves."

"Me?" echoed Graves. "I took no money. What are you talking about?"

"They're holding your secretary at the bank. She tried to deposit three of the ransom bills in your account. Probably thought you'd get away with it, since they knew you were working for Judson. Didn't think they'd bother checking on *your* money, did you?"

"My God," said Graves. "I had nothing to do with the kidnaping. I swear—"

"No one said you did," said Wolfe. "You'll be charged with

murdering Benny and pinching three grand of the ransom money afterwards. It's a cinch Benny never let you take that dough while he was alive. Come on, both of you."

He took the pair of them from the room, Graves silent and shaken, Manny shrieking imprecation at Sackler.

I WAS WRAPPED in a mood of bitter brooding on the way home in the car. Sackler sat at my side, humming a little tune under his breath. After six miles I could keep silent no longer.

"You're a pretty wise guy, aren't you?" I said acidly. "I know what you did."

"What *I* did?" he said with Fauntleroy innocence. "Why, what ever do you mean, Joey?"

You know damned well what I mean. While I had that apparition, Flora, in the garden, you went into Graves' study. You took his collections out of the drawer and substituted those ransom thousand-dollar bills. All except one. You had to hold out one to hang the snatch on Manny. You put the good cash in your pocket, and let Flora take the G-notes to the bank in order to clinch the case against Graves. It's a low lousy frame-up and I think I'll tell the D.A."

"You can't," he said smugly. "You're an accomplice."

"An accomplice?"

"Sure. You got the girl outside so I could do it. You're in it as much as I am."

I gave him my nastiest look. "So, I'm an accomplice. I get a lousy twenty-dollar bill and you make four grand net."

"No," he said dolefully. "Three grand. There was only a little more than three G's in Graves' drawer so I could only switch three of the ransom bills."

"And one you gave to Wolfe to hang Manny with. So you've got one left. What are you going to do with it?"

"Joey," he said, "you've been squawking about money. So I'm going to split a fee with you. Here, I'm giving it to you."

He thrust a thousand dollar note in the outer breast pocket of my coat. He grinned happily. He was giving away absolutely nothing and he knew it. I couldn't spend it. I couldn't bank it. All I could do was take it home, frame it and hang it on the wall. Sackler smirked at my side.

I put my foot on the brake and stopped the car. I reached for a cigarette and put it in my mouth. Sackler eyed me inquiringly.

"What are you going to do?" he wanted to know.

"I'm going to do something I've always wanted to do. Incidentally, I'm going to break your miserly heart."

I took a book of matches and the thousand-dollar bill from my pockets. I struck a match and touched the flame to the bank note. I applied the burning bill to the end of the cigarette.

Sackler shuddered. "Joey," he said. "Good God!"

I puffed away, taking a good light from the thousand-dollar bill. Sackler clapped his hands over his eyes, uttered a sickly moan. From the expression of his face, you would have thought he had caught me beating out his mother's brains with a crucifix....

Vacation With Pay

Sackler was the master money-grubber of all time and kale cascaded into his lap like Democratic votes into a Tammany ballot box. When he and his runner-up in the nickel-pinching marathon decided to take a hoarder's holiday across the border in Mexico it was only to be expected they'd do all right for themselves—murder notwithstanding—and we don't mean PESOS!

1

Nothing to Lose

SACKLER WATCHED THE gas gauge anxiously. He ran his fingers through his black hair and made a clucking sound with his tongue.

"We're not getting the mileage I figured, Joey. This trip is going to cost more than I expected."

"Everything costs more than you expect," I told him. "What do you expect from a load four years old? It's going to eat a lot of oil, too. Why didn't you buy a new car?"

He looked at me reproachfully. He thought silently of the cost of a new car and a shudder ran through his frame. He embarked upon a long speech calling attention to the virtues of the jalopy I was driving much in the manner of Jack Benny upholding his creaking Maxwell.

I stopped listening to him as I drove the car through the sun-baked streets of Laredo. In the distance the waters of the Rio Grande ran muddily to the Gulf. I halted the car some three blocks on this side of the International Bridge.

Sackler stopped talking and looked at me apprehensively. "My God, Joey," he said. "Don't tell me we need oil again? Don't tell me—"

"Pesos," I said. "We need pesos."

"Pesos?" he said and looked at me blankly. I sighed. For an intelligent guy he could be very dumb about money matters when it suited him.

*Stirred by the ghastly sight, Sackler
yelled, "Shoot them, Joey!"*

"Pesos," I repeated firmly. "We are about to cross into Mexico, a foreign country. The natives will want pesos when we buy. Not dollars. In New York the landlord wouldn't let you pay your rent in Bulgarian levs, would he? Well, in Mexico they'll expect to be paid in pesos. Since I assume that even you will have to spend *some* money we'll have to exchange dollars. Look. There."

His gaze followed my outstretched finger. At the edge of the street was a small square building with wide open doors. A sign outside read: *4.80 to the dollar.*

Sackler's expression of concern grew. "We should have looked up the current rate of exchange, Joey. Maybe we can get better than 4.80 somewhere else. Maybe—"

"Listen," I told him. "There's nothing but the bridge in front of us. Get some pesos. A few anyway. We can get more at a bank on the other side."

"Look, Joey," he said, and there was something in his voice which aroused my suspicions, "let's do it this way. You get the first twenty bucks' worth and we'll use it for joint expenses. I'll get the next twenty and so on. It'll save trouble."

I eyed him closely. Entering a financial deal with Sackler was something like getting into a poker game with Shylock and Richard Whitney. But after turning it over in my mind and finding no apparent loopholes, I sighed, got out of the car, and bought twenty bucks worth of pesos at 4.80.

Three minutes later we drove over the bridge into Nuevo Laredo, Mexico, and Rex Sackler had officially embarked upon the first vacation he had ever taken in his life.

Don't infer from that that he was one of the busy guys who doesn't dare leave his desk. On the contrary, the private detective business underwent long periods in which it seemed every citizen in the country had turned honest, devoted himself to a life of virtue and probity.

The prime reason that Sackler had never taken a holiday was found in the I.C.C. chart containing the railroad rates, and the horrifying fact that gasoline cost money. Sackler's idea of Utopia was a place in which everything was free. Realizing that this millennium would not be achieved in his lifetime, he devoted himself to the next best thing—that is, living as cheaply as possible.

He rolled his own cigarettes, thus depriving the federal government of six cents in taxes each day. He wore twenty-dollar suits until they literally rotted upon his frame. His hat was a blob of shapeless felt, still stained from the rain that fell during Harding's inauguration. And though he denied it vehemently, I had more than once voiced my suspicion that he laundered his own socks and underwear each night before he went to bed in his six-dollar a week room.

Rex Sackler's affection for money was a beautiful thing. His savings, the total of which resembled several telephone numbers laid end to end, were scattered about in scores of Postal Savings Accounts. After 1929, he gambled with no banks.

However, of late, business had been even worse than usual and the idea of sitting back and living on his capital gnawed at his breast like that Spartan fox. Eventually he decided that if he couldn't make any money he could at least spend less. A Mexican vacation was the answer.

From government reports, from returned tourists, Sackler had learned that living conditions south of the border were cheaper by a hundred per cent than they were in New York. He had calculated it all very carefully and come to the conclusion that the pair of us could live for a couple of months in Mexico City for as much money as we'd use up in three weeks in the city. Now we were on our way.

FROM NUEVO LAREDO to Monterrey is a hundred and seventy miles of straight flat narrow road. Desert and scrub lie to the left and right. The heat is fearful and the tourist's first impression is that he should never have left that air-conditioned hotel in San Antonio. This, coupled with the fact that the one item in Mexico which costs more dough than it does in the States is gasoline, had reduced Sackler to a glum and brooding silence.

The dusk was turning to night as we approached the outskirts of Monterrey. We were speeding through a badly lighted narrow street, lined with open air fruit and vegetable stalls, when Sackler suddenly half rose in his seat, uttered a shout of "Stop!"

I put my foot on the brake and brought the car to the curb.

Sackler jumped out onto the sidewalk and disappeared into a building through a door upon which was painted in English: *Tourists! Exchange your dollars! 4.99 to the dollar.*

I grinned to myself. Only Sackler could have seen a sign like that two hundred yards ahead while we were traveling at a rate of fifty miles an hour. A moment later he emerged with a roll of bank notes in his hand. He wore the smile of a Cheshire cat who has just dined very well on a pair of canaries prepared by the Stork Club chef.

"So," I said as he got into the car, "we pick up an extra nineteen centavos on each buck, eh?"

He turned to me and lifted his eyebrows. "We, Joey?"

"Why not? I change the first twenty, you change the second. Wasn't that the agreement?"

"Not entirely," said Sackler suavely. "It's all a matter of pesos, you see. You got 4.80 for your twenty. Let's see now. That's a total of 96 pesos, isn't it? You contributed 96 pesos, so I shall contribute 96. The odd 3 pesos, 80 centavos, because of the more favorable exchange, naturally belongs to me."

I opened my mouth to tell him what I thought of him when the guides came down upon us.

They gather, I discovered later, on the outskirts of the larger cities waiting for a tourist's car. Then they descend like vultures for an assault on the sucker's pocketbook. They surrounded us now, hurling broken English at us, offering us everything from a guided tour of the cathedral to a box of reefers and the address of the most magnificent bagnio in town.

Sackler waved them away with an elegant gesture of his hand. With the net result of their crowding closer about the car, deluging us beneath a barrage of dialect.

"Listen," I said, "maybe we ought to hire one of these guys. I don't know how to get to a hotel. I can't even drive through the town. Don't know the roads."

Sackler set his lips primly and looked at me. "There are times, Joey," he said, "when you talk a little like J.P. Morgan. Do you think we own a gold mine? We're here on a strict budget. These guys are going to cost money. Drive on."

I put the car in gear and raced the motor hoping the noise would frighten the babbling natives off the running board. It didn't. The car, Mexicans festooned about it, moved slowly forward.

A taxi chugged precipitately around the corner in front of me, came to an abrupt halt. A short swarthy individual stepped out, paid the driver and placed himself directly in front of our car. He stood there, like a traffic cop, with upraised hand. Perforce, I stopped.

He strode jauntily toward the car. The babbling of the guides ceased as they watched him. He turned a baleful gaze upon them, opened his mouth and uttered ten terrible Spanish words that I didn't understand. The guides, apparently, did. They jumped down from the running board and scattered in all directions. The swarthy man, showing a set of gleaming teeth, approached us.

"I am Miguel," he said in better English than you hear in Brooklyn. "I shall guide you to food and lodging for the night. You shall be guests of—"

"Go away," said Sackler wearily. "We have no money."

"Money," said Miguel, with magnificent contempt. "And what is money?"

THAT WAS A very neat question to put to Sackler, but before he could answer that it was his life's blood, Miguel continued, "You are the guests of our country. I shall guide you free, gratis, for nothing. Your lodging will be without charge. You are guests. I, Miguel, shall supply the host."

He hoisted himself up on the running board and made a sweeping gesture with his arm. "To the left. Turn here to the left."

I glanced inquiringly at Sackler who shrugged. "Go ahead, Joey. It's free, isn't it? What've we got to lose?"

I put the car into gear again and off we went, Miguel giving me loquacious directions from the running board. In a few moments, we had left the firm concrete of the Pan-American highway and the tires were rolling over a hard dirt road. The dusk disappeared and the night came down. I turned on the bright lights.

"We go to Ramos Arizpe," said Miguel. "There our host awaits us. Up and around the mountain and we are there."

I glanced rather uneasily at Sackler. We'd been traveling for over twenty minutes over a dark and completely unfamiliar road. I thought of several tales I'd heard of kidnapings by Mexican bandits. Sackler, however, looked out at the moonlit terrain and hummed softly to himself. The fact that the night's lodging was to be free overcame any other emotion within him.

"There," said Miguel, pointing suddenly. "Our destination. Look!"

I looked. On the side of the mountain, a few hundred yards to our right stood a magnificent hacienda, painted silver by the full and glowing moon. Light streamed from its windows. Through the first floor window, I saw plainly the figures of two men, heads bent over a table as if engaged in a game of chess or checkers.

"Ah," said Sackler, "we've arrived, eh?"

"Not yet," said Miguel. "The road winds around the mountain. Though less than three hundred yards as the crow flies it is four more miles by the road. By the way, it is well to drive here with dimmed lights."

He reached into the car, turned the dimmer two or three times before he became satisfied with the adjustment.

A little over ten minutes later I pulled the car up in the fragrant courtyard of the hacienda. Sackler, still gloating over the hotel bill he was saving, continued to hum as we disembarked. I remained suspicious. My hand was on the butt of my gun as Miguel escorted us through a tree-filled patio into a huge oblong living-room.

Two men sat by the window bent over a half finished chess game. As we entered one of them sprang to his feet. He looked rather like a decorated barrel. His chest was wide and round above the beginning of a pot belly. He wore a row of clattering medals that almost encircled him. He grinned widely showing all his teeth, bowed, and announced: "I am the General Gonzales. I welcome the great Señor Sackler and Señor Graham to my abode."

He waved Miguel out of the room and approached us with an outstretched hand. Behind him, the second guy, obviously drunk, picked up a chessman and moved it diagonally across the board. He looked up at the general, laughed and said something in Spanish. The general turned from us with blackening brow. He spoke loud and rapidly. The second man bowed his head, muttered, *"Si, señor. Si, si,"* got up and left the room.

Sackler at last forgot how much dough he was saving and became suspicious.

"So you know who we are," he said. "I take it you had us brought here deliberately."

The general beamed. "Of course, of course. When I heard from a friend of mine in the consulate that Rex Sackler had procured a *tourista* card, I said to myself, Gonzales, there is the man you want, there is the man you must have."

Sackler's eyes lit up. He accepted a cigar from the general and sat down.

"Ah," he said, "a case, perhaps."

"Ah," said the general, "a case, indeed."

SACKLER LICKED HIS thin lips and a dreamy expression came over his face. I knew he was thinking of money, that mentally he was deciding how much the general was good for.

"Now, first," said the general, "there is—"

Sackler held up a restraining hand. "First," he said, "there is the matter of the fee."

The general made a gesture much the same as Miguel had a little while ago under similar circumstances. "Money," he said with vast contempt, "and what is money? It is nothing."

Sackler looked pained. As if he had heard someone cheering Roosevelt in the Union League Club. The general watched him and read him as easily as did I.

"I mean, of course," he said, "that money is of so little importance to me that I am willing to pay any fee you ask."

The glint came back into Sackler's eyes. "Shall we say three thousand?"

The general lifted his eyebrows. "Pesos?"

"Dollars."

Now the general looked like a man who regretted his hasty speech about the relative unimportance of money. His eyes met Sackler's, and seeing no financial mercy there, he swallowed hard and nodded his head.

"Dollars," he said. "If you promise to accept the assignment."

If he promised. I couldn't imagine anything Sackler wouldn't promise for half the money.

Sackler nodded happily. "I'll take it," he said. "But, of course, I can't guarantee results."

The general bowed and his medals tinkled. "In you, señor, I have infinite faith. I have heard of you. One of your ability can not fail."

A guy who thought less of himself than Sackler might have become suspicious when it was laid on that thickly. But not Sackler. He took it well in stride, much as Toscanini would if you implied he knew something about music.

The general lit a cigar, sprawled out in a huge chair, and sighed heavily.

"My most famous Spanish ancestor was named Paco Gonzales. He first came to this country with Cortez. He was killed during one of the first battles with the Aztecs. Some time before he died, Cortez as a token of his esteem, had presented him with a crucifix. An invaluable crucifix of gold, rubies and untold precious stones. This cross was buried with my ancestor."

He sighed again and stared broodingly at the far wall. Sackler, without invitation stood up, crossed to the sideboard and poured himself some brandy. Since the general made no objection, I followed suit.

"A couple of centuries ago, another of my ancestors, having heard of the crucifix, dug it up. In turn, it was stolen from him. As the years have passed it has turned up from time to time, then disappeared again. The federal government has claimed it for the National Museum. But, rightfully, it belongs to me."

Sackler exchanged a glance with me. On the face of it, the case was impossible.

"And," said Sackler, "I suppose you want me to find it again. Is that it?"

The general shook his head. "But, no. It has been found. I merely want you to pick it up for me. To deliver it to me here when you're driving back to the United States."

Sackler regarded him suspiciously. A moment ago the case had been too hard. Now it was by far too easy.

"You see," went on the general, "there is a man in Mexico City who has it. I have paid him well. Now he wants to get it to me. We don't trust the mail in this country. I need a trusted messenger to bring it to me."

Sackler ran his long fingers through his black hair. "Why?" he asked, looking at the teeth of a gift horse for the first time in his life. "Why should you pay me the fantastic sum of three thousand dollars merely to act as a messenger boy. Certainly you must know someone you can trust. Certainly you could get your errand performed for one per cent of what you're offering me."

The general smiled and shook his head. "You do not understand our country, señor. It is not like the United States. Word has leaked out that the crucifix has been recovered. I have a number of personal enemies. Besides, the government is watching, too. They claim the jewel. It is unsafe for me or anyone connected with me to bring it from Mexico City. That is why I offer the task to you. It is simple enough. At precisely noon next Friday, you will go to room 618 of the Monte Carlo hotel. You will enter without knocking. My man will expect you. He will hand the crucifix over to you. In your possession it is safe. International conditions being what they are, no one would dare bother an American citizen. You will bring it to me when you drive north again. Do you agree?"

2

Death of a Chess Player

THE GENERAL WAITED as Sackler regarded him a long time. I regarded Sackler with unabashed envy. Money fell in his cap like Democratic votes in a Southern ballot box. I still struggled along on the meager salary which broke his heart to pay me.

"All right," said Sackler at last. "I'll do it. It is customary for me to collect my fee in advance."

"Fair enough," said the general. "I shall pay you three thousand American dollars in pesos. I—" He held up his hand to stem the tide of Sackler's protest. "Don't forget you will need pesos in Mexico and the exchange I give you will be the official rate, better than you can get at any money changer's. On the other hand, I keep American currency here. On the way back I shall redeem the pesos into dollars for you."

Sackler considered this. He said: "Suppose, the exchange drops?"

The general shrugged. "Naturally, you take that chance. On the other hand there is a strong movement in Mexico to stabilize the currency. The chances are strong that the peso will become more valuable in the next few days."

Sackler licked his lips and looked harried. Within him, I knew, an old struggle was taking place. His avid desire for more money was grappling with the awful fear that perhaps he might lose some. After a silent moment, the former won.

"All right," he said. "What *is* the current exchange rate?"

The general stood up, crossed the room to a telephone. He picked up the receiver and spoke rapid Spanish into the receiver. He hung up and said: "We shall know in a moment, señor. The telephone operator at Ramon Arizpe is getting in touch with Mexico City."

He poured himself a drink and grinned at us. "A fine girl, that operator. Studied in your country. Speaks English like an American." A frown crossed his dark brow and he sighed. "Unfortunately, she is unapproachable romantically. But not financially. I keep her loyal to my interests with money. Women are very avaricious, señor."

Sackler looked bored. Only his own avarice was of any interest to him. A moment later, the phone trilled and the general answered it.

"The rate," he told us, "is five pesos, one centavo to the dollar. Three thousand dollars is fifteen thousand and thirty pesos. I shall have the money ready before you depart in the morning. Now, perhaps you would like to be shown to your quarters?"

Alone in our room, I said to Sackler: "It sounds screwy to me. Why should he hand out all that dough for a messenger boy's job? Besides, that tale about the crucifix sounds very phoney. So phoney that I guess it must be true. No one would invent such an incredible yarn."

Sackler glanced at me and there was a faraway look in his eyes.

"Maybe, Joey," he said slowly, "it's meant to sound phoney. Maybe it's meant to sound so fantastic that no one will believe it."

I blinked at him. I wondered aloud if he was being cryptic

to impress me or if he actually meant anything. But he didn't answer me. He lay down on the bed and stared at the ceiling with thoughtful black eyes.

WE LEFT AT dawn. I steered the car carefully down the winding mountain road as the sun came up out of the Atlantic Ocean behind us. Overhead the sky was clouded with buzzards. Sackler looked up and shuddered.

"I don't like those things, Joey. They give me the horrors."

I grinned at him. "Considering you've been emulating one professionally all your life," I told him, "I don't believe it." I reached for my gun with my right hand. "I think I'll take a pot shot at one anyway. It'll sort of be like shooting you."

Sackler's hand came down upon my wrist.

"No," he said. "Are you crazy? There's a fifty-peso fine in this country for shooting those birds. Do you want to toss money in the gutter? They're the garbage collectors of Mexico. Without them these sewerless towns would be filled with decaying offal. Those birds are protected."

I shrugged my shoulders and put my gun away. Sackler still stared at the buzzards.

"Odd," he said after a while. "You don't usually see them so far from a town. There's no garbage to eat out here."

He stared at the swooping black fowl as I drove another half mile. Then, "Joey," he said suddenly. "Stop the car."

I pulled up on the deserted mountain road and asked why. Sackler stared down into a gully covered with shrubbery upon which the gliding buzzards descended, then disappeared in the foliage.

"Joey," he said, "would you play tennis with an armless man? Would you play football with the lame?"

I didn't quite see where this was leading. "No," I said. "I wouldn't take a blind dame to the movies either. Why?"

"Well," said Sackler, "why would Gonzales play chess with a guy who didn't know how to play—with a guy who moves his castle diagonally across the board?"

"You mean that guy last night?"

"I mean that guy last night. The guy Gonzales bawled out in Spanish and sent out of the room after he moved that piece."

He got out of the car and motioned for me to follow him. I put on the emergency and got out, too.

"Where are we going?"

"Down there, Joey. To see what it is that so interests those buzzards."

"I think you're being overly suspicious," I told him. "It's probably some dead animal. What do you expect to find?"

"I wouldn't be overwhelmingly surprised, Joey, if we found the body of a guy who knew how to play chess."

Doubting, I followed him down the mountain side into the gully. We fought our way through the shrubbery with the whirring of powerful wings in our ears as the birds, frightened at the sound of our approach, took to the air again. I pushed aside a branch that had slapped my face, took another step forward and stood transfixed with horror.

"Rex," I yelled. "Good God, look!"

Sackler came up at my side and stared over my shoulder. Before us on the gully floor lay some forty per cent of a man. The clothes had been stripped neatly from his body. Before our eyes his flesh was being stripped as neatly from his bones. Half his skull was already exposed and half a dozen vultures dined placidly on what was left of his face. One ancient bird waddled obscenely up and down his torso snapping here and there like a dowager parading before a tray of hors d'oeuvre. Overhead wings whirred as other fowl prepared to land for their breakfast.

Sackler was so stirred by the ghastly sight that he forgot the fifty-peso fine. "Shoot them, Joey," he yelled. "My God, I'll—"

My own gun blasted twice. The rest of the birds moved their wings and fled at the sounds of the shot. I turned to see Sackler staring at the body, his hand in the pocket of his top coat. There was a peculiar expression on his face.

"Joey," he said. "My gun. It's gone."

"Gone?" I said. "Perhaps, it's in the car."

Sackler shook his head. "It's gone," he said positively. "The chess player's dead and my gun's gone. Let's get back to the car."

We went back to the car and got in. The buzzards, I observed, were coming down again.

"You're sure that was the chess player?" I asked. "How do you figure that out?"

SACKLER'S EYES NARROWED. "When we were four miles from the house Gonzales was playing chess with some guy. We saw him in the window. While we traveled that four miles around the mountain, Gonzales killed him."

"Who was that other guy, then? The drunk he was playing with when we got there."

Sackler shrugged. "Some henchman of his, I guess. Some guy that couldn't play chess. You see, Gonzales knew we'd probably seen him at the window. To allay any possible suspicion he wanted to be still playing when we arrived."

"How did he know we were coming at that moment?"

"The lights. You remember how Miguel leaned over and played with the dimmer? When he told you bright lights were no good on this road?"

I remembered it, said so, and scratched my head. "And now we, or rather you're collecting three grand for practically nothing and he rolled you for your gun. How do you figure it?"

Sackler shook his head. "I don't, Joey. It's all so screwy, so suspicious, I wouldn't be surprised if he tried to get this dough back from me somehow. But, by God, he won't do it. We'll fight him tooth and nail, Joey. We'll save this fee with everything we've got."

I eyed him with distaste. The fee, of course, was all his. But when it came to fighting for it, tooth and nail, I noted he cut me in for a good fifty per cent.

I turned right on the Pan-American Highway. While Sackler frowned and stared thoughtfully at the tropical landscape, I speeded south toward Mexico City.

AT PRECISELY TEN minutes to twelve on Friday Sackler and I entered the elevator of the Monte Carlo Hotel on Calle Uruguay in Mexico City. We stood for a moment before the door of suite 618 and Sackler unleashed a sigh that came from the bottom of his being.

"Joey," he said, "I sense trouble."

"From your morbid attitude," I told him, "it must be financial."

He nodded. "That, too, I'm afraid. Well, here goes."

He turned the doorknob silently and entered the room. I followed on his heels.

We found ourselves in the empty living-room of a typically

cheap hotel. Two broad windows formed the eastern wall and directly opposite us was a door which led, undoubtedly, to the bedroom. We looked around and upon the table top saw the same object simultaneously.

"My God," I said, taking a step toward it, "that's your gun, Rex. Your automatic."

I stretched my hand forth to pick it up when Sackler's voice stopped me.

"Don't touch it. Don't touch it, you fool!"

I didn't touch it. I turned and looked at him in surprise.

"Why not?"

"Keep your prints off it. God knows it's probably got mine on it already."

He ran his hand through his hair and looked like a man with the weight of the world on his shoulders. He uttered the name of the Deity five times in descending scale.

"So," I said, "What are you worried about? You got your rod back, didn't you? You save the price of a new one, don't you? You're in money again."

He looked at me like a schoolmaster glaring at the class dunce.

"Joey," he said bitterly, "you are a cretin. You are an unutterable idiot."

"You've told me that often enough before. Have you some new reason for repeating it."

"Joey," he said, "what do you think is in that other room? In the bedroom, there?"

"Beds," I said brightly. "Plus, from what I've learned of Mexico, a pair of chamber pots. Have I left anything out?"

"Yes," said Sackler. "The corpse."

"Corpse?"

"Of course, you lunatic. Can't you see it's a frame? Here's my gun, which was stolen from me. Obviously, for one reason. The reason you'll undoubtedly find dead in the bedroom."

"Good God," I said. "Then let's take a look and see if you're right. If you are, let's take a powder—fast."

I moved toward the bedroom door. I had my hand on the knob and was looking back over my shoulder toward Sackler when I saw the revolver come through the other door jamb. Before I could get my own gun, a brown hand came into the room, clasped around the gun butt. This was followed by a Sam-Browned policeman, with a gay little mustache, even white teeth and a menacing look in his eyes.

"Buenos tardes, señores," he said. "I am Genarro of the police."

I stood frozen, staring at him, wondering if I dared make a move for my gun. The icy glint in Genarro's eyes convinced me I couldn't. Sackler's face was gray. His deep, black eyes were shadowed with worry. Genarro took a step into the room and closed the door behind him.

"I just disarm the señores," he said simply and proceeded to do so.

He put my gun on the table next to Sackler's. Then he said amiably: "If you two señores will precede me with your hands up, we will see what is in the bedroom."

We put up our hands. I opened the bedroom door and stepped inside, Sackler close behind me. It took a single glance to inform me that Sackler had been catastrophically right. A man lay on the bed. There was a jagged hole in his head and blood stained the counterpane. Genarro nodded his head.

"Ah," he said. "It is as I expected."

"It's as I expected, too," said Sackler. "Now look here, you, let me explain."

3

The Stomach-Pump Talks

GENARRO LIT A cigarette with one hand, sat down in a chair with his gun balanced on his knee and said most politely: "But, of course, señor, I shall listen to anything you want to say."

I took a deep breath and started to talk. I didn't want to gamble on Sackler's talent for antagonizing people. I told Genarro, breathlessly, of the general, of the crucifix, and of how we were hired to pick it up. When I finished Genarro was smiling more politely than ever. I noted, however, that the cold glint remained in his eye.

"You see," said Sackler with a sigh, "he doesn't believe it. I told you the story was deliberately fantastic. So ridiculous no one we told it to would believe us. Well, Genarro, what are you going to do with us?"

Genarro stood up and shrugged beautifully. "To the police headquarters we will go. Then it is out of my hands. However, señores, there is no need for worry."

I grasped at that straw. "You mean," I asked excitedly, "that the coppers know something about this? They know it's a frame? They only want us for evidence?"

Genarro shook his head. "What I meant, señor, was merely that in Mexico we are civilized. There is no capital punishment here."

"A very joyful thought," said Sackler bitterly. "We shall rot in a verminous cell for the rest of our lives, Joey."

He was, at the moment, more despondent, more utterly beaten than I had ever seen him. There wasn't any fight in him. Nor, for that matter, in me. The frame was perfect. Sackler's gun had undoubtedly killed the guy on the bed. Our weird tale about Gonzales' crucifix was going to be greeted with as much credulity as a release from the German Propaganda Bureau.

"Now," said Genarro, "there is one thing more before we go to the headquarters. You, Señor Sackler, are carrying several thousand pesos. You have no more use for them. Will you hand them over to me, *por favor.*"

Sackler's eyes flashed. A sudden flush colored his cheeks. He looked like a retired war horse who has heard the bugle for the first time in years. His dejected defeat of a moment ago had absolutely disappeared.

"Give *you* the money?" he roared indignantly. "Why, by God, I—"

As he howled epithet at Genarro he moved slidingly to the policeman's left. Genarro, in order to keep him covered swung his gun and body around with Sackler's movement. That left me, on the right, clear of the revolver muzzle for a moment. Sackler flashed me a commanding glance and nodded his head decisively. I took a deep breath and moved in.

I SPRANG ACROSS the room, my right hand outstretched and aimed for Genarro's right wrist. He turned around as he sensed my coming. But my fingers landed where I wanted them. They closed over his wrist. A moment later I was locked in embrace with him, holding on to his gun hand with all my strength.

Sackler raced from the room, returned a moment later with

the gun Genarro had taken from me. He jabbed it, none too gently in the policeman's ribs.

"Drop that gun, my little friend," he murmured triumphantly. "Put him on the bed and sit on him, Joey, while I think."

Genarro's weapon clattered to the floor. I put an armlock oh him, flung him onto the bed beside the corpse. Obeying Sackler literally, I sat on him.

Sackler paced up and down the floor and ran his fingers through his hair. He did this in complete silence for some ten minutes. Beneath my posterior Genarro was getting restive.

"Listen," I said, "will you kindly master-mind something rapidly. After all, I can't sit on this copper all day."

For one of the few times in our career, Sackler and I were in perfect accord. "For a fact, Joey," he said anxiously, "you can't."

He stopped pacing, drew a deep breath and said: "There are two things we must have. Information and the guy who brought that gun down from Monterrey."

"Out of eighteen hundred thousand people in Mexico City," I said, "how are you going to find him?"

"It's simple enough," said Sackler. "The guy who brought that gun of mine and in all probability fired it, too, must have flown. It's the only way he would have got here before we did. We can check names at the airport. The information I believe we can get from Calkins. Remember him, Joey? The kid that used to be on the *Post* in New York? Well, I understand he's down here now. Working for A.P. We did him a favor once."

I shrugged my shoulders. "What good can he do us?"

"I'll handle him. You handcuff that comic opera cop to the steam pipe. Then go out to the airport. Check everyone who flew down from Monterrey during the past two days. I'll get in touch with Calkins. Get going now."

I got up from Genarro's chest and took his handcuffs from his pocket. He cursed me in lovely liquid Spanish as I made him fast to the steampipe. Sackler was already at the telephone when I left the room for the airport.

I RETURNED TO the hotel to find Sackler sitting between a wiry dark little man and a peculiar metal gadget that looked like a bicycle pump designed by Salvador Dali. I blinked and said: "What happens here? Is this Calkins?"

Sackler shook his head. "This is Señor Meana, Joey."

The "señor" stood up, bowed and shook my hand. Sackler ignored my look of inquiry at the metal gadget and asked what I'd brought back from the airport. I took a piece of paper from my pocket and proceeded to read the list.

"Arrived from Monterrey today," I told him, "a guy called Ruiz, his wife and daughter, and a government mine paymaster. Yesterday, there was an American, Sutherland. Sort of a promoter as far as I could find out. And a Mexican colonel. Name of Gomez. Raoul Gomez."

Sackler and Meana exchanged glances. Meana bit his lip and nodded his head slowly. Sackler lit a cigarette and looked up at me. "Did it occur to you to find out where these people went when they left the airport?"

"It did. This Ruiz—"

"Damn Ruiz. What about Gomez?"

"Gomez, I found out from the hack drivers, went to the Geneve Hotel. But how do you know—?"

"Shut up, Joey," said Sackler without bitterness. He got up

and went into the bedroom. He returned a moment later with a suitcase. He opened it and put his bicycle pump inside. Meana watched him approvingly. I was frankly baffled.

"What the hell is that thing?" I asked. "And what are you going to do with it?"

Sackler put his hat on and grinned. "You've drunk enough cheap gin to know what it is, Joey. Now come on, señor."

He held the door open and Meana walked out into the hall. Sackler followed with the suitcase. I dragged along in the rear, wondering silently what the hell it was all about.

Colonel Raoul Gomez was tall for a Mexican. He wore horn-rimmed glasses and the darkness of his skin indicated he was a good sixty per cent Indian. The three of us entered his presence in a luxuriously furnished suite. Meana bowed to him and unleashed two paragraphs of Spanish. Whereupon, the colonel grinned, bowed and shook Sackler's hand as if he were a long-lost friend. He pantomimed us into the room, waved us into chairs, chattering all the while.

He went to a well-stocked sideboard and poured four brandies and soda. As we sipped the drinks Meana and the colonel pursued an unintelligible conversation. Once Meana turned to Sackler and said in English: "He says he is very happy to see you. Will you start the interview now?"

Sackler nodded gravely. "Sure. Tell the louse anything you like."

Meana continued his talk with Gomez. I turned an inquiring eye upon Sackler. He deigned to explain.

"Meana's telling him we're American newspapermen interviewing him about the Mexican Army."

"So where's that going to get us?"

Sackler didn't answer me. He put his glass down on the table with a bang. Gomez sprang to his feet and reached for it. Sackler waved him back into his chair. Meana jabbered some more Spanish. Gomez smiled and said: *"Gracias. Muchos gracias, señor."* Which were the first words of the dialogue I had understood.

Sackler collected all the glasses and went to the sideboard. I followed him. "Now what?" I asked. "What's he thanking you for?"

"Very polite fellow," said Sackler blandly. "Meana merely told him I'd fix the drinks while he goes on with the interview."

I took my glass back to my chair still in a state of complete bewilderment. Meana conducted the supposed interview for another ten minutes. Then Sackler said suddenly: "O.K. Now we'll give it to him."

Meana nodded. "What shall I tell him first?"

Sackler lit a Mexican cigarette, inhaled gratefully, probably remembering they had cost only a nickel for twenty.

"Tell him," he said, "that I know his boss is Gonzales. Tell him that I'm Sackler, the guy Gonzales played for a sucker. Tell him in Mexican idiom that now I've got all the answers."

MEANA RATTLED AWAY at the translation. As he spoke all the beaming geniality left Gomez' face. His dark eyes glowered at Sackler. I watched the holster at his side and kept my hand on my own gun. Gomez exploded loudly in Spanish and Meana translated.

"He says he hasn't any idea what you're talking about."

"I'll enlighten him," said Sackler. "Tell him I've found out his boss Gonzales is a notorious revolutionist. Tell him further that the dead guy in the Monte Carlo hotel was a copper who was working on evidence to convict Gonzales of treason. Gonzales had him killed. The inference is obvious. This copper had dug up some evidence. But instead of turning it over to his superiors he decided to blackmail Gonzales with it. That's why he was killed."

Meana put that into Spanish. Gomez glowered at Sackler. He said a lot of words, two of which I recognized as oaths.

"He says you're crazy," Meana told Sackler.

"Sure," said Sackler. "I'm crazy as Einstein. When Gonzales got word of the blackmail he decided to knock off this copper. He didn't want to do it himself, he didn't want any of his men to do it. For the simple reason that they'd be the first suspected. He wanted cast-iron alibis for all his gang when the copper was knocked off. So he tried to hire a killer—a chess-playing killer."

Gomez received this information in complete silence. I observed that the flap on his holster was buttoned. That fact would give me plenty of time if he translated the expression in his eyes to action.

"Tell him," said Sackler, "though now I enter the realm of pure conjecture, I'm certain I'm right because no other explanation will fit. Gonzales made an error hiring his killer. Once he'd told the thug what to do the guy became greedy. He knew Gonzales would have to pay his price or else he could inform the federal authorities what was going on. He demanded an exorbitant sum. Gonzales pretended to be considering it. Actually he was searching for a fall guy. He got me."

Meana told him. Gomez spat Spanish like hail.

"Deleting the profanity," said Meana, "he says merely that you are a damned liar."

"Sure," said Sackler easily. "Sure. Gonzales heard from his connections in the States that I'd applied for a *tourista* card, that I was coming to Mexico. He knew when I crossed the border and sent his man to pick me up at Monterrey. That man, Miguel, signaled Gonzales with our headlights as we were coming up the mountain. Gonzales wasted no time. He killed his own potential killer immediately."

Sackler committed the prodigal act of lighting one cigarette off the end of the other as Meana translated. Meana turned back to Sackler and announced: "He says he will call the police."

Sackler grinned. "I'll give him ten to one he won't. But to get on with it. Gonzales knew we'd probably seen him playing chess through the window as we came up the mountain, that we'd be expecting to find a second man with him. To allay any possible suspicion on my part, he called in one of his servants and sat him down at the chess board. The guy was drunk and overplayed the hand after we arrived. He took upon himself to move a piece. To move a rook diagonally instead of in a straight line. That was the first thing that got me wondering."

After Meana had unloaded this on Gomez, Sackler continued.

"Gonzales rolled me for my gun and sent Gomez, here, down on a plane. He had instructions to kill the blackmailing copper a little while before my arrival, to leave my gun in the room so the ballistics expert could easily pin the murder on me. He gave me a weird cock and bull story about a crucifix so that the coppers would never believe me when I told them the truth. Moreover, he told this Genarro who was to make the pinch that he could roll me for my pesos for his end in the deal. God knows what sort of a rap they would have pinned on me in a court-room."

WHILE MEANA WAS relaying all this Gomez suddenly started in his chair. He clapped a hand to his paunchy stomach. He said something in groaning Spanish and stood up. Sackler watched him keenly.

"What did he say?"

Meana smiled. "He says he's sick. He must go to the bath-room."

Sackler nodded. "O.K. You go with him, Joey. Don't leave him alone."

I accompanied the moaning Gomez into the lavatory. I remained there unhappily while he attended to a very private function. Then I escorted him back. Gomez sank into his chair. His face was sallow and screwed up with pain. He moaned again and spoke.

"He says," said Meana. "he is very sick. Very, very sick."

"Good," said Sackler. "Tell him he's going to die."

Judging from the expression of terror on Gomez' face, Meana told him so in no uncertain words.

"He states," said Meana a moment later, "that this is a civilized country. There are courts of law. You can prove nothing you have said. Why are you doing this to him? Also, what are you doing?"

"Tell him I poisoned his drink. Tell him, moreover, that I concede I can prove nothing. That's why I want his confession."

Meana spoke. Gomez uttered a terrible howl and raised his hands in supplication to heaven. Sackler got up and opened the suitcase. He took out the thing that looked like a bicycle pump.

"Inform him," said Sackler, "that this strange device is a stomach-pump. If he confesses the truth of all I have said, I shall use it on him. If not, he can die in that chair."

Before Meana completed the interpreting, Gomez got up with a loud cry.

"Excusado!" he yelled. *"Excusado!"*

He rushed off toward the bathroom. I, holding my breath, dutifully followed. Sackler and Meana came along behind us. Gomez proceeded to vomit and perform several other functions at the same time. Sackler to my indignation, closed the door leaving Gomez and myself inside.

"I can't bear watching him, Joey," he said. "We can talk just as well through the panel."

After some three minutes of writhing agony, Gomez dropped to his knees upon the floor. He pounded on the door with his fists. He said something that sounded like a prayer.

I heard Meana's voice through the door. "He asks for mercy," he told Sackler. "He says spare his life. Use the stomach pump. He'll admit everything. "

I heard Sackler's long drawn sigh of relief through the panel. The door opened. Meana, I noted had a typewritten sheet of paper in his hand. He helped Gomez to a chair where the colonel signed with trembling fingers. Sackler calmly packed the stomach-pump back in the suitcase. Gomez watched him and raised a howl that could've been heard in South America.

"Oh, that," said Sackler. "Tell him he doesn't need this. I only gave him an old-fashioned Mickey Finn. He'll get over it before he's been in jail one day. Take him away, señor."

Meana dragged the shaken Gomez to the door. He bowed gravely to Sackler.

"The Secret Service is grateful to you, señor. For a long time we have searched for evidence against this man and General Gonzales."

"O.K.," said Sackler. "But don't forget your promise. You're not to arrest Gonzales for three days."

"I shall not forget," said Meana with dignity as he left the room.

4

Gonzales Pays Up

I STOOD STARING at Sackler when we were alone. "Now," I said, "will you condescend to tell me what it was all about? How did you figure what you figured?" Sackler assumed his expression of superiority. "Simple enough, Joey, after I had the facts. I got most of them from Calkins, who in turn called a pal of his, Meana, connected with the Mexican Secret Service. Once I had the identifications clear, those of the dead cop and Gomez, and the knowledge that Gonzales was a revolutionist, it was simple enough. Inductive reasoning, we call it."

"Why don't you want Gonzales pinched for three days?"

"I have business with him, Joey. Financial business. You know I never trusted him from that first night."

"Why? Because of that chess business."

"Well, no. It was because he gave me the fee I asked. He didn't haggle, Joey. Never trust a man who doesn't haggle."

We checked in the Monterrey hotel a little after five o'clock in the evening. I headed at once for the shower and was rather surprised when Sackler asked me for the keys to the car and went out. He returned a couple of hours later, volunteering no information as to where he had been.

After dinner, he went directly to bed. I hung around the bar, drank a few tequilas and began to feel a craving for feminine companionship. There were a lot of women in the bar but there weren't six syllables of English among them. Then an idea struck me.

Gonzales had told us that the telephone operator at Ramon Arizpe spoke English. He had also implied that she was attractive. I went outside, climbed in the car.

I arrived at the telephone exchange fifteen minutes before she went off duty. I made a pretty speech with the net result of my finding myself, a half-hour later, sitting across from her at a cafe table. She was small and dark with full red lips and deep calculating eyes. She ordered the most expensive drink in the house and said, dreamily, "I love to go out with the Americans. They have so much money. Already today a rich American has spent a number of pesos on me. The Americans are so generous."

I sipped my drink and began to wonder what I'd let myself in for.

"What business are you in that makes you rich?" she asked.

"I'm a private detective," I told her.

She lifted her plucked eyebrows. "That is funny. Veree funny."

"What's funny?"

"That other gentlemen who was so good to me was a detective, too. He bought me champagne and gave me many pesos. A very generous gentleman. His name was Sackler. Maybe you know him, yes?"

I gripped the sides of my chair to prevent my falling on my face on the floor. Sackler a generous gentleman? Sackler buying champagne for dames and handing out many pesos? The world teetered uncertainly on its foundations.

Then in place of wonder came suspicion. I leaned across the table. "Baby," I said, "I'll buy you champagne, too. Keep right on drinking and never mind the expense."

GENERAL GONZALES STARED at us as if we were a couple of his ancestors' ghosts who had broken the tomb and dropped in to pass the time of day. His smile was weak as we entered his huge living-room.

Sackler took a small cardboard box from his pocket and handed it to the general. Gonzales stared at it.

"And what is this?"

"Your ancestors' crucifix," said Sackler with a tinge of malice in his voice.

Gonzales swallowed something in his throat. "Oh, of course," he said.

He opened it slowly. He withdrew an iron crucifix set with imitation jewels.

"But this," he said. "This is not it. This is an ordinary cross that can be picked up in any store for a peso or two. It is not the priceless Gonzales crucifix."

"No?" said Sackler. "You'll recall, General, that the federal government wanted your cross for the National Museum? If you don't want it, I'll turn it over to them."

The general stared at Sackler for a long, long time. Then he sighed heavily.

"I see what you mean, señor," he said. "It is as I have heard about you. Señor Sackler is interested in his fee. Nothing more. If I accept this crucifix, you will have no further dealings with the government authorities. Is that it?"

Sackler did not answer him directly. "I have come here to exchange the pesos you gave me for dollars. Do I get them?"

Gonzales bowed graciously. "You get them," he said. "I shall ascertain the current exchange rate."

He went to the telephone and poured Spanish into the

mouthpiece. Sackler grinned happily at his back. Gonzales hung up the receiver, turned around and announced: "We shall know in a moment. The operator will call me back,"

I stood up and faced Sackler. The loud pounding in my ears was Opportunity hammering like hell at my door.

"Rex," I said. "While we're waiting there's something I'd like to take up with you."

He was so pleased with himself he failed to catch the note in my voice.

"I think it only fair," I went on. "That, because of my invaluable assistance on this case, I receive a bonus, of, let us say, five hundred dollars."

Sackler lifted his head and looked as amazed as Willkie on election night.

"*Your* invaluable assistance? And what in the name of God did you do?"

"Well," I said modestly, "I had a lot of trouble with this case. I laid out my own dough buying champagne for a girl, which, incidentally, was the second time she'd had champagne that day. I had to listen to a lot of drunken babble in which she told me—"

Sackler shot an agonized look at Gonzales, who frowned out the window, paying no attention to me.

"You mean," said Sackler and there was pain in his voice, "you mean that you'd be louse enough to—"

"I would be louse enough."

"One hundred dollars, Joey."

"Five," I said, as the telephone rang.

Gonzales got up to answer it and Sackler looked from the telephone to me. My face was merciless rock.

"Five," he said and his voice was projected from Gethsemane.

Gonzales put down the phone. "You are lucky, señor," he said. "And for that matter so is my country. The peso is getting firmer. It is quoted at only three to the dollar. Just a moment, señor."

He left the room. Sackler took a roll of pesos from his pocket and counted them out. He did not meet my eye. A moment later Gonzales returned.

"Fifteen thousand pesos," said Sackler handing them over. "At three to a dollar that makes five thousand. Right?"

Gonzales counted out five thousand dollars in American money. Sackler put it moodily in his pocket.

Gonzales slapped him on the back. "After all, señor, we are business men, are we not? Even though this crucifix you have brought me should turn out not to be the right one, it does not matter. I consider I have paid your fee because you did not go to the government, thus permitting those stupid politicos to mix into our business."

Sackler glanced at him fishily and we headed for the door. The general waved us farewell. *"Adios, señores. Hasta la vista!"*

We were halfway down the mountainside when I said: "My money. I'd feel better if I got it now."

Sackler counted five hundred dollars from his roll and handed it to me with all the enthusiasm of Bethlehem Steel, obeying an order of the Labor Relations Board.

"Joey," he said reproachfully, "you got that girl drunk. She told you I'd paid her to tell Gonzales the peso was at three to one."

"I did."

"Joey," he said like a disappointed warden to a trusty who has accidentally dropped a file, "you blackmailed me out of that five hundred. You are devoid of morals."

A car sped past us. It was painted brown and filled with soldiers.

"*I'm* devoid of morals," I said. "Look. There go the boys to arrest Gonzales. And you deliberately gave him the impression he was in the clear with that mumbo-jumbo of the cheap crucifix."

"But, Joey, he was a criminal."

I gave him a cockeyed look. "You mean that if he'd been an honest man you wouldn't have pulled that exchange gag?"

"Joey," he said primly, "money is nothing when honesty is at stake."

I stared at him for a moment. I choked back my answer because I knew that, at the moment, he really believed it. Noble rationalization is a failing of the moneyed class. Hell, the *Wall Street Journal* runs editorials like that every day.

Split Fee

When the No. 1 money-grubber of all time contracted to solve a bank mulcting and murder, all he really had on his mind was heaping more kale on his already full-to-bursting Postal Savings account. But the way Sackler squeezed a fat fee from a svelte and streamlined sinner, even his mooching Man Friday felt compelled to yell "Foul!"

1

A Fool for a Fee

IT WAS A long car, maroon and rakish. Its lines were those of a clipper ship and its engine would have driven a liner. It aroused my acquisitive instinct every time I looked at it. For three weeks now, I'd been ogling it every morning on the way to the office and today I realized I wanted it more than I wanted anything for years.

Unfortunately there was a plate glass window and a matter of twenty-three hundred dollars between me and the automobile. I stood before the window, my nose almost pressed against the glass, and did some rapid mental arithmetic.

A third down would run to almost eight hundred bucks. The rest strung out over twenty months would be something like eighty dollars a month. Well, by cutting down here and there I could manage the installments. It was the first payment that had me worried.

I sighed, walked down Madison Avenue toward the office, engaged in more fiscal calculations than the president of the Reichsbank. By the time I reached the elevator I thought I had come upon a solution. Actually, I was a victim of wishful thinking and should have known better. I strode into the office, into Rex Sackler's presence with a jaunty step and a hopeful gleam in my eye.

Sackler sat, dark and brooding, at his desk. His hands supported his chin and the desk blotter supported his elbow.

"You are to drink, my friend," I told him, "three of those drinks."

He looked up as I came in and took a book of matches from his vest pocket.

"Ah, good morning, Joey," he said. "Do you happen to have a cigarette? Carelessly, I forgot—"

I sighed and reached for my pack. "I know," I told him, "you forgot to buy a bag of roll-your-own this morning. Moreover, you will forget all day as long as you can chisel butts from me. Here."

He extracted a cigarette from the package with long slim fingers. He lighted it, inhaled deeply, and replaced the matches in his pocket.

"Thank you, Joey," he said. "Perhaps, if you have a second package, I can keep these until—"

I snatched them from his hand, put them back in my pocket and underwent my first misgivings about my down payment. I came immediately to the point.

"Rex," I said, "I want you to do me a favor."

He inhaled luxuriously, enjoying the fact that the cigarette was free even more than he did the tobacco.

"Of course, Joey," he said expansively. "Anything at all. From my wealth of experience, from my lucidly functioning brain, any advice I can offer you is—"

"I don't want advice," I said shortly. "I want money."

Sackler took the cigarette from his mouth and stared at me like an archdeacon who has overheard an urchin discussing the facts of life.

"Money?" he said as if he were repeating some blood curdling blasphemy. "Did you say money, Joey?"

"I said money. However, I don't expect you to *give* it to me."

That didn't reassure him much. He still stared at me, alert, like a deer ready to break and run.

"All I'm asking you to do is one of two things. Either advance me eight hundred dollars on my salary, collecting, say, thirty a week, or else—"

I got no further. Sackler's eyes were open wide. There was horror on his face. He said in an incredulous tone: "Eight hundred dollars, Joey. Good God, eight hundred dollars!"

"Why not?" I said, hope leaking from me. "You've got it hidden away in Postal Savings. You're not using it. You may as well lend it to me. If you don't want to do that, endorse a note for me. A note for eight hundred dollars."

Sackler shuddered perceptibly. He leaned back in his chair and closed his eyes. I lit a cigarette, and sat down morosely at my own desk. I had been, I realized now, a damned and unutterable fool. I had been trapped by my own desires. In any sane moment I would have known that Rex Sackler wouldn't lend anyone eight hundred bucks in cash with the Kohinoor diamond offered as security.

SACKLER'S AFFECTION FOR money made Abelard's love for Heloise a tawdry and unimportant thing. Despite the fact of his commanding enormous fees, he lived like an indigent immigrant. He bought a suit only after his bare knees came peeping through the threadbare material. His hat was a blob of shapeless felt that I'm certain some doting uncle had awarded him on the day of his grammar school graduation. His shoes were odd lot three dollar bargains. But there was nothing shabby nor cheap about his bank account.

He had piled money into Postal Savings accounts scattered about the country. Banks had failed before this and Rex Sackler was taking no chances. He rolled his own cigarettes when he wasn't bumming mine rather than pay a nine cent tax. His heart held a crack wider than the Liberty Bell every time he was compelled to pay me my weekly salary. To compensate for this he devoted the other five working days trying to get it back. Gambling—at which he rarely lost—wheedling, and borrowing quarters which he invariably forgot to repay were his customary tactics.

This was the guy who I had figured in a moment of incredible insanity would endorse my note for eight hundred bucks. Once again I thought of that job in the salesroom window, contrasted it with my own '37 Ford coupé, and sighed audibly.

Across the room, Sackler, having smoked my tailor-made down to its final millimeter, was using a pin to hold it to his lips for one more drag. He had recovered from his initial horror by now and was gazing at me with hypocritical benignity.

"Now, Joey," he said, "of course, if you stop to think you'll realize I can't do as you ask. Of course, the money itself means absolutely nothing to me."

"Nor," I said bitterly, "does your right eye."

He ignored that. "The lending, the borrowing of money," he went on, "wrecks friendships, Joey. It is something that should never be done. Why did you say you wanted this money?"

"I didn't say. But I wanted a car. A new car."

He shook his head like an admonitory school teacher and clucked like an old hen.

"A car, Joey. How foolish. Your old car is good enough. Now why not let me save part of your salary each week. Then when we have a thousand dollars or so, we'll buy you a bond."

"I don't want a bond. I want a car."

"But a bond, Joey, is something—"

"I'd look damned funny," I said angrily, "driving a dame out to Westchester in a brand new bond, wouldn't I?"

"Now, Joey—"

"Shut up," I said. "Leave me alone with my poverty and sorrow."

I stood up and walked across the room to the window where I gloomily regarded the Madison Avenue traffic. There were times when being Rex Sackler's assistant was very trying. I brooded at the window imagining what hogsheads of champagne, what platoons of women, what Lucius Beebe wardrobes I could indulge myself in if I had Sackler's money. I was enjoying something of a masochistic good time when the girl came in the office.

She was a tall girl with blue-black hair, draped about a face, thin and ending in a pointed chin. Her eyes were black as Sackler's and attractive in a hard way as polished steel is attractive. She walked across the room and sat down in the chair I drew up for her. She measured Sackler with her gaze, said interrogatively, "Mr. Sackler?"

Sackler admitted his identity and eyed her speculatively. She was well dressed and there was a ring on her finger which sparkled like a great deal of money. Sackler, I knew, was drinking in these details. The girl met his gaze steadily and said in an even contralto: "Am I correct in believing that the relations between a private detective and his client are completely confidential?"

"Legally," said Sackler, "perhaps not. Actually, in my case, they are as confidential as those between a priest and a sinner, a doctor and his patient. There is no difference."

"There is a slight difference," I corrected him. "In this office the fee is collected in advance."

Sackler glared at me and I felt a little better. The girl lifted her eyebrows, shrugged her shoulders with a worldly air.

"I expected as much," she said. "I came prepared for that. First, Mr. Sackler, my name is Agnes Magruder. I am employed as a secretary at the Federated Loan Company."

SACKLER'S EYEBROWS LIFTED a full inch. Knowing him as I did I read his mind. He was mentally figuring how she could afford her clothes on a secretary's salary. Her next remark made me wonder if she read him as accurately as I.

"I am ready to pay you a fee here and now. First, I want your word that whatever I tell you is secret, whether or not you agree to help me."

Sackler's eyes glinted. If the fee was big enough he would undertake to keep Hitler's death a secret from the Associated Press. Oratorically, he made himself quite clear on that point.

"Very well," she said opening her bag. "I shall give you five hundred dollars in cash with the promise of a thousand more if you can do what I ask."

She laid a roll of bills on the desk. Sackler picked them up and fingered them like a mother running her fingers through her baby's hair. He stowed them away in his wallet and said: "Command us, madam."

I noted that once he had the dough stowed away, he cut me in.

The Magruder girl cleared her throat and lit a cigarette with slim fingers that trembled slightly.

"The vice-president of Federated was murdered this afternoon," she announced. "His name was Wallace Kates. I'm afraid suspicion will point at me."

"Why?" said Sackler.

She blew two streams of smoke from her nostrils and shook her head. "I see no point in answering that. If the police find out so will you. If not, why should I stick my neck out?"

"All right," said Sackler. "Give me the details. Tell me what we're supposed to do."

"When I came back from lunch today, I went into Mr. Kates' office. He was in his chair, his face on his desk. There was a bullet hole in his head and five thousand dollars missing from the safe."

"So," said Sackler, "you reported the murder, then came here?"

"I did not report the murder."

Sackler frowned. Five hundred bucks in his pocket and a pledge of secrecy was one thing. Trouble with the coppers was another.

"You see," said Agnes Magruder. "I wanted no part of it. I closed the office door, got my things and came here at once. I intend hiding out at a small hotel. In the meantime, I engage you to look after my interests, to find out who killed Kates."

Sackler blinked. If the coppers were looking for Magruder in the matter of the Kates killing, the girl was asking him, with magnificent calm, to compound a felony. True, he had five hundred slugs in his pocket, but that wouldn't do him a great deal of good if they lifted his shamus' license.

"Well," said Magruder, after a long pause, "do you take the case? I remind you that there's another thousand involved if you solve it."

Sackler closed his eyes and suffered. For all either of us knew the bland Miss Magruder may well have blown Wallace Kates' brains out herself. In Sackler's mind he weighed fifteen hundred bucks against one hell of a lot of potential trouble. He opened his eyes again and said sharply: "All right. What hotel are you hiding out in?"

"You'll keep your mouth shut?"

Sackler swallowed something in his throat. "I'll keep my mouth shut."

"All right. I'm at the Regal Hotel in Harlem. I'll register under the name of Grey. Call me when you get something."

She ran a powder puff over her nose and walked to the door. Sackler's gaze followed her, rather resentfully.

"You know," he said, "if you really did kill this guy Kates, I'm in one hell of a jam."

She turned on the threshold and regarded him coolly. "True," she said. "So am I."

Her heels clattered down the tile of the corridor outside and her footfalls died away.

I LOOKED OVER at Sackler and grinned. He tapped his forefinger thoughtfully on the desk top. He raised his eyes, caught my smile and said, annoyed: "Why the simian grimace, Joey?"

"Your neck," I told him, "is protruding like Mount Rainier. Your reluctance to surrender five hundred bucks cash may have you covering up a killer."

"Ridiculous," said Sackler. "That girl's no murderess."

"Why not?"

"Her face. Was it the face of a killer?"

I unleashed a long incredulous whistle. Sackler, the skeptic, reading character from faces! It was utterly amazing what money would do to his normally lucid mind. I told him so.

He didn't pursue the conversation. Instead he said: "Joey, call the coppers. See what they've got on that Kates' killing."

I picked up the phone, put through the call and got Inspector Wolfe on the wire. We had a long, and on his part, profane, conversation. I cradled the phone, turned to Sackler happily.

"Well, Joey, what did they say?"

"They said, among other things, that you were a meddling, larcenous phoney. They said that you were a damned nuisance, a burdensome cross on the police department's back. They wanted to know how the hell you knew about Kates' death when they only got the call three minutes ago. They wanted to know, further—"

"I don't care what they wanted to know," roared Sackler. "Tell me what *I* want to know. What have they got on Kates?"

"That'll interest you, too. Kates was murdered all right. And it seems that some ten grand is missing from the safe in his office. What do you think of Magruder's face now?"

His groan was music to my ears.

"The way I figure it," I told him gayly, "is that Magruder knocked him off, helped herself to the dough and by now is halfway to Pittsburgh."

"Ridiculous," he snapped, but there was anxiety in his tone. "If that were true why should she come here and hand me a fee?"

I shrugged my shoulders. "I don't know the answer to that. But I know another question. If she's merely a secretary at Federated Loan, where in hell did she get that five hundred? Where's she going to get the other grand she promised you?"

"Oh, that," said Sackler. "I figured that right away."

"How?"

"It's obvious. She was Kates' secretary. She wears clothes that cost too much for her salary. She owns a ring that cost a thousand bucks. She is also worried that she may be suspected of Kates' murder. Add them up, Joey."

"You mean—"

"I mean that it's apparent she was more than Kates' secretary, that she spent more time with him in his bedroom than in his office. It's quite possible they quarreled recently, had some disagreement which is known to witnesses. That would account for her concern that she may be accused of the murder."

"Well," I said reluctantly, "maybe."

2

The Careful Client

THE OUTER OFFICE door was flung violently open. A short man of about thirty-five, hatless and agitated, burst into the room. "Sackler," he said breathlessly. "Which one of you is Rex Sackler?"

I pointed across the room. The little man sat down, took off his glasses and polished them with his handkerchief. Then he made the most tactless approach I had ever heard a potential client deliver.

"Mr. Sackler," he said. "I want you to know I don't have much money."

Sackler appeared about as interested as W.C. Fields was in a glass of water.

"My name," went on the little man, "is Cummings. I work for Federated Loan. My salary is eighty dollars a week."

Sackler exchanged a swift glance with me. His interest revived.

"Now," went on Cummings, "a young lady also works for Federated Loan. She has disappeared. I want her found."

"Her name?" said Sackler.

"Magruder. Agnes Magruder."

"Ah," said Sackler, "and how much did you expect to pay for my services?"

Cummings cleared his throat. He took a piece of paper from his pocket and unfolded it. I craned my neck and looking over his shoulder noted that it was filled with single spaced type-writing.

"Well," he said, "I've heard you're an expensive man, Mr. Sackler. I've heard, too, that you like immediate payment. Unfortunately, I'm not in a position to pay cash. Here, however, I've drawn up a lien on my salary, promising to pay you fifty per cent for six months if you'll help me."

Sackler and I both did some rapid calculating. Sackler, of course, had the answer first.

"One thousand and forty dollars," he said. "You offer me that if I find Agnes Magruder for you, is that it?"

Cummings nodded. "Of course I would expect you to find her. I'm not prepared to pay that fee if you get no results."

"I accept those terms," said Sackler quickly. "Will you kindly sign that paper?"

Cummings scrawled his signature at the bottom of the type-written sheet and handed the paper to Sackler who scrutinized it carefully. I watched him in envious disgust. Money fell into his lap like bombs on London. While I still grappled with the problem of the down payment on the car, Sackler was offered a thousand dollars to find the whereabouts of a girl who had, five minutes before, told him her address. He grinned at me gleefully as he stowed the paper away in his pocket.

"Now," he said to Cummings, "can you tell me what your interest is in the matter?"

Cummings shook his head. "That's not necessary. Just find the girl. She disappeared suddenly, probably because she was upset at the death of her boss."

"What boss?"

"A fellow called Kates. Officer of Federated Loan. Killed

himself this afternoon. Was some ten thousand dollars short in his accounts."

Sackler raised his eyebrows. "Killed *himself?*"

"Undoubtedly. The accountants were due in. He'd evidently been using the firm's money, so he blew his brains out. Make that clear to Miss Magruder when you find her."

Sackler drew a deep sigh. "Mr. Cummings," he said, "you will go into the outer office with my assistant. You will tell him all the pertinent facts. Give him the names of Miss Magruder's friends, the addresses of places which she usually frequents. Take him outside, Joey, and get the facts."

I took him outside with all the enthusiasm of a Pole en route to a concentration camp. I knew quite well that Sackler was merely attempting to give the impression that he was earning his fee. He knew damned well that the Magruder girl was at the Regal Hotel without eliciting any information from Cummings.

However, I asked a lot of routine questions, jotted down the answers and dismissed our client. I came back into the private office to find Sackler, a ledger open before him, conducting involved calculations with a pencil. He looked up as I came in.

"Joey," he said, "business isn't so bad. We should show a profit this year."

"We?" I said bitterly and sat down at my desk.

Sackler closed the book. "You, my strong-armed friend," he said, "labor under the impression that I'm simply picking money off trees in this case. I, possessing an imagination, believe there is more to it than meets the eye."

"Sure," I said with heavy irony, "A dame takes it on the lam because she thinks she may be held in a murder. She offers you a fee to cover her up. Then it develops that the murder was a suicide and some other brainless idiot offers you a grand to find her when you are one of the two guys in New York who knows where she is. Hell, I could've told him for a sawbuck."

"Your prices are too cheap, Joey. Now get on your hat and coat and run over to Federated Loan."

"For what? Am I supposed to find another member of the staff who's looking for a shamus with a checkbook in his hand?"

Sackler shook his head. "Find out what you can about that Kates business. Find out what the cops have. Get me all the information."

I PUT ON my hat and coat none too happily. The coppers weren't going to appreciate the fact of Mr. Rex Sackler's assistant nosing around the case. They were going to be downright insulting and I stood an excellent chance of being tossed out on the seat of my two-year-old pants.

I told Sackler as much as I went out the door. But he was so engrossed in his damned ledger he didn't even lift his head. On the way across town to Federated Loan, I noted that the maroon car was still in the window.

Federated Loan was one of those great-hearted institutions which maintain a hundred branch offices scattered across the country and devote half their incredible profits to advertising how simple it all is to borrow a couple of hundred dollars. They make no mention of the fact that the interest runs to something just under forty per cent a year.

Their main metropolitan office was some eight blocks from Sackler's. It was rather on the ornate side, with dozens of small cubicles where clients signed their salaries away, in addition to a magnificently furnished group of executive offices. The first thing I saw upon my entrance was the police department in the person of Inspector Wolfe.

Wolfe regarded me with all the cordiality of Henry Ford greeting an emissary of the C.I.O.

"Well, what do *you* want?" he roared. "What's that ghoul Sackler doing in this case? Go back and tell him to prepare to return the fees he's already collected. We already got the guy that done it."

I made a mental note of the fact that Wolfe believed it a murder. Apparently the police didn't hold with Cummings' suicide theory.

"All right," I said. "Who?"

"Abe Weldon."

The name stirred some vague memory in my brain. Wolfe, observing my frown, went on.

"You probably wouldn't know him. He was before your time. He was up the river until about six months ago. Served a twenty-year rap for manslaughter. Should've got life."

"Motive?" I asked. "Or aren't you talking."

"I'm talking," he said, "and loud. I'm talking to everyone including the press. I'm talking before Sackler can tell his client he figured it all out and collected more dough. I broke this case myself. Sackler's going to get no bow and no cash this time."

"If you think either of those facts enrages me," I told him, "you're crazy. Go ahead, tell me about Abe Weldon. I sort of remember the name now."

"Well," said Wolfe proudly, "I remember the guy the minute I lay eyes on him. He's been out of the can six months. Before he was sent away the only honest trade he ever knew was plumbing. Yet we find him here drawing ten grand a year, mark you, as an officer of the company. Besides, he had a big raise coming up."

"So what?"

"So it's a gag of some kind. He must have got this job on forged references or something. He gets in here. Then he knocks off this Kates."

"Why?"

"Dough. There's fifteen grand missing from Kates' cash. Kates was in charge of all the dough. You know, for loans, and what dough had been paid in during the day. There's fifteen grand missing. He put Kates' own gun in the dead man's hand to make it look like suicide. But there wasn't even a powder burn."

I raised my eyebrows but kept my mouth shut. The girl had said there was five grand missing. Cummings had lifted the ante to ten. Now Wolfe said fifteen.

"And," I said, "has this Weldon guy confessed?"

"Not yet," said Wolfe slowly. "The boys are working on him now. But, hell, there's no doubt about it. It's plain as the nose on Sackler's face. I'm hanging around to see Fredericks, the president of this outfit. I've found out he employed Weldon personally. The only link missing is the forged references he must've used. That'll clinch the case."

"Where is this guy, Weldon? Can I see him?"

"Go ahead. He's in that office over there."

I LEFT WOLFE to his pacing and entered an office whose door bore the legend: *Assistant Cashier.* The first thing I saw was a ring of blue uniformed backs standing around a chair.

They were all talking at once, loudly and authoritatively to a little squat guy with defiant eyes who sat in the center of them. Abe Weldon wasn't talking.

The office door opened behind me. I turned to see Wolfe entering with a wide, pompous individual, with gray hair and black-ribboned glasses. He pushed through the cordon of coppers. He put his hand on Weldon's shoulder and said angrily: "What's the meaning of this outrage? Is this a third degree in my own office?"

The coppers looked at him, bewildered and then at Wolfe.

"Now, Mr. Fredericks," said Wolfe. "You won't take that attitude when you know who this man is."

"Who he is? He's Weldon. My assistant cashier."

"He's an ex-con," said Wolfe. "I spotted him the minute I lay eyes on him."

"So," said Fredericks, "what?"

"Well," said Wolfe. "It's obvious. He gets a job here with forged papers. He knocks off this Kates. He steals the money."

"Ridiculous," said Fredericks. "I vouch for this man. Whole-heartedly."

"You don't understand," said Wolfe. "He's an ex-con. He served time."

"Of course, he did," said Fredericks. "I was well aware of that fact when I hired him."

The coppers stared at him as if he had announced he was in the habit of hiring rattlesnakes.

"You policemen," said Fredericks patronizingly, "have an entirely wrong attitude. I make it a matter of policy to give employment to men who have been unfortunate enough to spend some time in jail."

"But, good God," said Wolfe, "you don't have to make them assistant cashiers."

"The more responsibility, the more chance of their making decent citizens out of themselves. Listen to me. Have you ever thought what it meant to a man to spend several years in jail? Never even seeing a woman, never enjoying the simple comforts which the lowest specimen of humanity needs. Have you ever considered the ghastly brutality of locking men away in solitary confinement? Have you?"

That was one hell of a question to ask a group of coppers but there was something so compelling, so sincere in Fredericks tone that no one gave him a short answer.

"Well," said Wolfe, "no matter how you figure it, Mr. Fredericks, I'm taking Weldon downtown with me."

"I don't suppose I can prevent you," said Fredericks. "But I can assure you, Weldon, I'll have my lawyer down there immediately. Don't worry for a minute, old fellow."

Weldon gave him an odd look. "I won't," he said and he certainly sounded as if he wasn't.

Wolfe's coppers escorted Weldon out the door. Fredericks' eye fell on me.

"Who are you?" he asked. "A plainclothesman?"

I told him who I was.

"Ah," he said. "Rex Sackler. I've heard of him. Is he working on this case?"

"In a way."

Fredericks cleared his throat. "Well, if he finds out anything I wish he'd let me know immediately. If not during office hours, here is my home address and phone number."

He took an engraved card from his wallet and handed it to

me. I said goodbye and left the office.

On the way back, I stood and watched the maroon car again. Then on sheer hunch, I went a block out of my way and got an application blank for a loan from the personal loan department of a big bank.

3

Sackler Signs Up

I RETURNED TO the office, told Sackler everything I'd found out and gave him Fredericks' card. Where upon he banished me to the outer office and gave himself over to profound thought.

I hadn't left the house the following morning when he phoned.

"Joey," he said. "You can go to work. I want you to get in touch with Fredericks. Tell him I want to see him at his home tonight. That I'm bringing some people with me. Then round up that Magruder girl, Cummings, and get in touch with Wolfe."

"Wolfe? What'll I tell him?"

"Tell him that Weldon's not guilty. Tell him if he doesn't want to make an idiot of himself to bring Weldon to Fredericks' house tonight."

I hung up, shrugging my shoulders. What he had in the back of his head, I didn't know. But I was very much afraid that he was going to make some more money.

Martin Fredericks had the sort of apartment which you'd expect of a guy who collects thirty-six per cent interest on his money. It was a penthouse on upper Fifth Avenue with a living-room larger than Sackler's bank account and a view of Central Park through the biggest piece of plate glass I had ever seen save in a department store window.

A butler in the best Surrey and Hollywood tradition opened the door for us and conducted us into the drawing-room. Fredericks came forward to greet us as I, casting my eyes about the room, took inventory.

The Magruder girl sat on a divan near the window. She was wearing a low-cut gown which revealed a pair of startling shoulders. Her legs were crossed and shapely. She regarded Sackler with dark and smoldering eyes that held little trust in them.

Seated beside her and watching her with a hopeless sort of admiration was Cummings. Somehow he seemed smaller than ever, more ineffectual, as Inspector Wolfe, pacing back and forth, towered over him. On the far side of the room sat a stranger. He was gray-haired and well dressed. His eyes were the color of his hair and remarkably alert. He looked like the average business man's conception of the average business man.

Fredericks introduced him to us as Ralph Daley. It seemed he was a minority stockholder in Federated Loan. It seemed, moreover, that he was quite annoyed at the fact of a murder having been committed on its premises.

"It is an outrage," he said to the room at large. "Bad enough that Fredericks, here, exercises some hypnotic influence over the other stockholders who keep him in power, bad enough he runs the company as if he were running a carnival. Now, he has a dead man on the premises. It's going to give us a great deal of unfavorable publicity."

"Come, come, Daley," said Fredericks amiably. "You've been making that same speech about my administration for years. I show a profit, don't I?"

"At our rates who wouldn't? The point is, you don't show enough."

By now Wolfe had ceased his pacing. He had come to a guardsman's halt and stood staring across the room at Sackler. The expression in his eyes was not one of amity and friendship.

"The point is," he said, shaking a thick forefinger beneath Sackler's nose, "Why has this little gathering been called this evening? I've got the killer tied up and in the can and if you're trying to spring him for a fee, Rex, I'll make damned certain you don't. This is my case and I've broken it."

Sackler raised his eyebrows and looked at him coolly. "I'll lay you three to one you haven't," he said. "How much of that do you want?"

Wolfe opened his mouth to answer, then closed it again. I knew that precisely the same thought that was in my mind was in his. If Rex Sackler was offering a reckless three to one on anything, taking him would hardly come under the heading of shrewd financial practice.

"Well," said Wolfe, covering up quickly. "If you've got something, what is it?"

"First," said Sackler, "where is Weldon?"

"Coming. Due here any minute. But if he's innocent, what do you want him for?"

SACKLER DIDN'T ANSWER him. The butler came back into the room with a circular tray filled with cocktail glasses. He put the tray down on a small revolving table, and, with the greatest formality, transferred them one by one to a silver salver. He repeated this process until everyone had a drink.

I noted that Cummings took his glass without lifting his gaze from the Magruder girl. She, in turn, remained staring with some apprehension at Sackler. I raised my glass and took a deep swallow. Only my early training in manners prevented me from immediately spitting it out again on Fredericks' expensive rug.

It was without doubt the vilest alcoholic concoction I had ever tasted. On snap judgment I decided it had been made of equal parts sulphuric acid and manure. I glanced over in Sackler's direction. His glass was half empty and the expression on his face indicated that for once he was not enjoying something that had cost him nothing.

Even Wolfe whose palate was as discriminating as that of a goat drank his cocktail down as if it were a dose of hemlock. There was an atmosphere of relief in the room as the butler collected the empty glasses, returned them to the tray and carried them out of the room.

"All right," said Wolfe, wiping his lips with a handkerchief, "let's get down to business. What is it you have to say, Sackler?"

"I'm waiting for Weldon," said Sackler. "I—"

He broke off as the door bell sounded through the apartment. A moment later, the butler reappeared, escorting a blue uniformed copper who, in turn, escorted Abe Weldon. The copper saluted Wolfe who acknowledged the gesture curtly.

"All right, Kelly," he said. "Sit down over there and keep a steady eye on your prisoner."

"You've got nothing on me," said Weldon angrily. "I demand bail. I—"

"Shut up," snapped Wolfe irritably.

Fredericks crossed the room and put his hand on Weldon's shoulder. "Take it easy," he said gently. "We'll get you out of this all right."

Sackler, I noted, was staring distastefully across the room. I followed his gaze to see the butler emerging from the pantry bearing another tray of cocktails. Just as he set the tray down upon the revolving table, a telephone rang somewhere in the house. He hastened away, leaving the execrable drinks.

I stood by the taboret, wondered how he managed to hold his job with such poor bartending qualifications. I bent down, idly spun the table around. I glanced up to see Fredericks regarding me oddly.

A moment later the butler returned, gave Fredericks some inconsequential message and stooped to pick up the first drink. Fredericks crossed the room, took it from his hand and smelled it.

"Terrible!" he snapped. "This is without a doubt the most awful stuff I've ever sniffed. For God's sake, take them back, pour them down the sink. Make some more. Properly this time."

The butler, without changing his expression, picked up the tray and left the room. I exchanged a glance with Sackler. If Fredericks had swallowed his first drink without protest, this second round must be nothing less than a Mickey Finn.

Sackler was staring thoughtfully at Weldon. There was a deep frown on his brow. He looked up, met my eye, and said: "Joey, come here."

I put my ear in his face.

"Go out to the kitchen," he said. "Pull your gun on the butler. Order him to drink three of those drinks. Hurry."

I stared at him. "Is this a gag? It's not very funny."

He gave me his nastiest look. "I'm not in the habit of clowning with the hired help. Do as you're told."

I SHRUGGED MY shoulders. If Sackler was going suddenly nuts, he certainly had enough dough stashed away to pay for a very exclusive asylum. I went into the kitchen.

The butler stood by the sink with his tray of glasses. I came up behind him and touched him gently on the temple with my revolver. He turned around. He also turned green.

"You are to drink, my friend," I told him, "three of those drinks. Here." I picked up a glass and handed it to him. He looked from me to the mixture and back again. His eyes were frightened brown blobs of dirty ice. His lips trembled.

"Come, come," I said. "I know they're lousy! But I drank one and so can you."

He took a deep breath. He smacked my gun aside with his left hand and started a roundhouse right with the other. I ducked easily and slugged him on the side of the head with the barrel of the revolver. He went down to the floor like a tired bag of potatoes.

I put the gun back in my pocket and ran four puzzled fingers through my hair. Sackler's mad instructions hadn't covered this contingency. I couldn't very well leave a butler lying unconscious on the floor to go back and join in polite conversation.

I decided it would be better to get him out of the way while I consulted Sackler. I picked him up by his collar, dragged him across the room to a broom closet. I deposited him inside and locked the door. I put the key in my pocket.

I stopped by the sink and picked up one of the drinks. It was pretty awful but there was alcohol in it. I adjusted my tie and went back to the living-room.

Sackler stood to one side talking to Cummings. The others were grouped about silently. Wolfe's frown was indicative of his impatience. I took up my position some few feet away from Sackler so that I could get his ear as soon as Cummings moved away. I listened to the conversation. Sackler was talking.

To my complete amazement he seemed to be regaling Cummings with an involved and none too funny story about a traveling salesman. He finished it to no gale of laughter and Cummings went back to his position on the left side of the Magruder girl. I went up to Sackler and told him *sotto voce* what I had done.

He stunned me by offering the first words of commendation I had heard him utter in years.

"Fine, Joey, fine. That's just what I wanted. You're improving every day."

Across the room, Wolfe stood up. "Is he improving enough to tell me why the hell I'm here tonight. If you haven't told me what this is all about in five minutes, Sackler, I'm taking Weldon back to the can."

"Sit down, Inspector," said Sackler. "I'm prepared to tell you anything you may have a desire to know right now."

Daley cleared his throat like a bolt of thunder. "Damned silly," he said. "Thing never should have happened. Wouldn't have, if I'd been in charge. Fredericks, you should be thrown out of Federated. You and all your gang. I could move in there, throw out all your incompetent staff, get in new blood, and make a fortune for the stockholders."

Fredericks shrugged his shoulders. Sackler remained strangely silent.

"Well," said Wolfe. "Get going, Rex."

Sackler ran his fingers through his hair and his expression

wasn't one of happiness. He sighed heavily. There was a shadow in his eyes. Then suddenly he snapped his fingers.

"First," he said, "I would like to speak to you and Mr. Fredericks, Inspector. In another room, please."

Fredericks got up "Certainly. We can use my study."

He led the way, Sackler behind him. Wolfe followed surlily and I brought up the rear.

SACKLER CLOSED THE study door and the three of us looked at him. Fredericks inquiringly, Wolfe annoyed, myself frankly suspicious. Sackler helped himself to a cigar from the humidor on Fredericks' desk and lighted it.

"Now, Mr. Fredericks," he said, "the solution of Kates' death is at hand. Its clearing up requires a small act on your part."

Fredericks blinked. "My part?"

Sackler nodded. "You as president of Federated Loan are empowered to sign contracts for the corporation, aren't you?"

"Yes, but—"

"Very well," said Sackler, "if you will give Cummings a contract for the same job he holds now at the same salary for a period of, say, six months, I'll hand over the killer to Inspector Wolfe."

Wolfe stared at him through narrowed eyes. "I've got the killer," he said doggedly. "It's Abe Weldon. I don't know what you've got up your crooked sleeve, Sackler, but—"

Sackler held up his hand. "It's not Weldon," he said.

Fredericks toyed nervously with his watch chain. "Then who is it?" he asked. "And in any event, what can the solution of the murder have to do with a contract for Cummings?"

"Cummings is our witness. He's worried about his job. He

figures if he cleans up this thing he's entitled to some sort of reward from the company. His idea of that reward is a contract."

Something in the back of my brain began to function. I sensed that maybe something was going to come my way any minute, now. But first I had to figure all the angles. I screwed up my brow and submerged myself in deep thought.

"Listen," said Wolfe, "you mean Cummings is an eyewitness? You mean he actually seen Weldon do it? You don't need to give him a contract, Mr. Fredericks. I can make that guy talk. He's no pro like Abe Weldon."

Sackler shook his head patiently as if he were correcting an impulsive child.

"Weldon had nothing to do with it, Inspector. Now, Fredericks, will you write Cummings a contract? Here and now?"

"If Weldon didn't do it," said Wolfe angrily, "and you know who did, you'd better tell me. I represent the law here. You're nothing but a money-grubbing shamus who—"

"Who," finished Sackler, "knows the name of the person who killed Wallace Kates. Fredericks, do I get that contract?"

"Why, of course," said Fredericks and there was a note of anxiety in his tone. "Of course, you do. But first will you tell us the name of the killer."

"You promise me the contract no matter what the inspector may advise?"

"I promise."

"Very well. Kates was murdered by his mistress. Agnes Magruder."

"You can prove this?"

"I can prove it," said Sackler. "Write me out a contract."

Fredericks shrugged his shoulders. He took a sheet of paper

from the desk and proceeded to write with his fountain pen. Wolfe took a step forward in Sackler's direction and said, belligerently: "How can you prove it?"

Sackler didn't answer. He was craning his neck over Fredericks' shoulder, reading as the other wrote. There was an expression on his face that indicated he was taking an internal bow. I kept right on thinking, trying to fit the fact of his calling Magruder a murderess into the problem I was grappling with.

WOLFE, BECOMING MORE furious as Sackler ignored him, pounded the desk with a heavy fist.

"I'm the law," he roared again. "Stop treating me as if I was the visiting scout master. Sackler, I asked you can you prove Magruder did it."

"With Cummings' aid, I can," said Sackler. "You observed him talking to me a little while ago? He told me everything. He told me Magruder did it. He told me what his evidence was. It's all tied up and in the bag."

I lit a cigarette and actually managed to get the package back into my pocket before Sackler put the bite on me for one. Now, I was positive that he was telling a Gargantuan lie. Cummings, quite obviously, was utterly screwy about the Magruder girl. He had never taken his eyes off her all night and he'd been willing to go into hock for half his salary in order to find out where she was hiding. If, after these things, he was willing to sell her down the river, I was Doctor Watson. Moreover, I had eavesdropped on at least half the conversation Cummings had had with Sackler and during that time, at least, not a word had been said about the murder.

Fredericks blotted the paper and held it out to Sackler.

"Of course," he said, "we'll have this typed and fixed up more formally tomorrow. However, I know a little law and I'm sure you'll find it binding. And I must say it's a load off my mind. Cummings is certainly entitled to it."

"All right," said Sackler, "Sign it. I'll have Cummings sign it later."

He handed the sheet of paper back to Fredericks who reached for his pen. In that instant a blinding light flooded my brain. There was a terrific din in my ears as I became aware of opportunity hammering like hell at my door. I whipped my loan co-maker's statement from my pocket and took a step forward.

"Just a minute, Mr. Fredericks," I said. "Suppose we call Cummings in now and have him sign."

Fredericks shrugged. "Why not?"

Sackler looked at me like a starving Pole at a Storm Trooper. He spoke in a voice of jagged ice.

"Suppose, Joey, you let me handle this?"

I slapped the co-maker's statement down on the desk before him. I took his fountain pen from his vest pocket and thrust it in his hand.

"All right," I said. "You handle it. But, in the meantime, would you mind signing this for me?"

He looked at the note. He frowned and his breath came quickly.

"This is the money for that damned car. I told you I'd have nothing to do with it."

"Circumstances have changed," I told him. "Everyone else is signing papers, why not you? I can get Cummings in and you can all sign together. I think—"

Sackler looked across the room at Wolfe, transferred his gaze to Fredericks. He opened his mouth and uttered an obscene noun. I grinned happily. He scrawled his name at the bottom of the statement. He turned to Fredericks and said: "All right, sign that contract. My assistant here is afflicted with a mercenary sense of humor."

Fredericks signed the contract. Wolfe said with bad grace: "All right, give me what you've got and I'll let Weldon go, take in the dame."

"We will go back to the living-room," said Sackler. "Then I shall begin at the beginning and once more do the police department's job for them, Inspector."

"You get enough dough for it," snapped Wolfe as we trooped out of the study.

4

Poison for One

IN THE LIVING-ROOM Daley was impatiently pacing up and down the floor. The Magruder girl smoked a cigarette silently and gazed abstractedly at the far wall. Cummings, still at her side, kept his eyes upon her like a dutiful dog. The copper and Abe Weldon sat handcuffed congenially together. They chatted quite amiably about hockey. Apparently no one had yet missed the butler.

"Now," said Sackler, taking up his position in the center of the room, "if I may have some attention I will solve the Kates killing to your satisfaction. I—"

"Look here," said Wolfe, "you don't have to make a speech, Rex. Give me the fundamentals and I'll take her in. Cummings can tell his story to the D.A. later."

His words fell like a bombshell on Magruder's ears. She stood up and stared at Sackler like an enraged cat.

"Take *her* in!" she cried. "You mean you're trying to pin this thing on me? You mean—"

"Shut up," said Wolfe. "We got you dead to rights. Ain't we, Rex? Cummings' testimony'll—"

"Cummings!" she shrieked.

Cummings stood up. "I don't understand," he said, "I—"

"I understand," said Magruder. "Somehow Mr. Sackler's discovered a method to make more money by framing me. Somehow I'm going to get a good chance to sacrifice myself for his bank account."

It was amazing, I reflected, how Sackler's reputation got around. For all I knew, at the moment, she was right. I knew he was doing something devious and lousy, but precisely what I hadn't been able to figure. He seemed calm enough before the girl's outburst.

"A half-hour's silence," he said, "and I assure all my clients they will be well satisfied. Now, will you all sit down?"

They all sat down, more or less quietly. I heard Daley mumbling to himself something about Fredericks' inefficiency being responsible for the whole thing.

"Now," said Sackler, "let's go back to my first connection with this case. Miss Magruder came to my office, told me a murder had been done, a murder that might well point in her direction. She intended to hide while I solved that murder for her. She reported further that there was five thousand dollars missing from Kates' accounts."

"Five?" said Daley. "I thought it was fifteen."

"Wait," said Sackler. "A few moments later, Cummings came into the office. He said that Kates was a suicide. The motive he offered was the fact that there was ten thousand dollars gone from his safe and the accountants were due in any day."

"It was fifteen thousand," said Daley stubbornly.

"It was fifteen altogether," said Sackler blandly. "Five that Magruder took, ten that Cummings took. Add them up. It makes a fifteen thousand dollar shortage."

I expected another outburst from Magruder at that. But it didn't come. She stared at Sackler through half closed eyes. Cummings looked fearful.

"What do you mean they took the money?" demanded Daley. "You mean they stole it. Our employees stole it. That's because of the slipshod way the place is run. The whole staff should be thrown out. It—"

"Let me go on," said Sackler. "Magruder, here, first discovered Kates' body. She became panicky. She had been Kates' girl friend for years and there must have been a number of people who knew it. She was a logical suspect. However, she took five grand out of Kates' office when she left. Probably for two reasons. First, she could use it with her boy friend gone. Second, it might make the killing look like robbery which might turn suspicion away from her. Is that right, Miss Magruder?"

"I'm not talking," said Miss Magruder.

SACKLER SHRUGGED AS if it were of no moment. "We come to Cummings," he went on. "If you've observed Cummings tonight, you'll note that he's crazy about that girl. I knew it as soon as I heard what he wanted from me. He told me that Kates had killed himself because he was ten thousand dollars shy. That he wanted me to find the Magruder girl for him. It's easily explained. He saw Kates' corpse after the girl. He assumed at once that Magruder had done the murder. He knew of her relationship with Kates. Fumblingly he tried to cover her up. He rearranged the corpse, took Kates' gun from his desk and attempted to make it look like a suicide He stole the ten grand to make Kates look like a defaulter. Didn't you, Cummings?"

Cummings ran a trembling hand over his face. "I—I didn't steal the money," he said. "You can't accuse me of that. I hid it. I hid it in the office. In the washroom. That's not stealing."

I watched Sackler closely. He was smirking like a cat who has just swallowed a particularly succulent canary. He was quite sure of himself. Wolfe sat forward in his chair.

"What the devil are you talking about? How could this girl discover the body if she committed the crime?"

"Easy, Inspector. The mind can't assimilate too many things at once."

Wolfe, being none too certain of the meaning of "assimilate," growled and sat back again. Fredericks stood up, rang the bell on the wall and said: "I think we'll all feel better for a drink."

I exchanged a swift glance with Sackler. In another moment, the butler's disappearance was going to be noticed. Sackler, however, took it in stride.

"You'll wait some time for your servant, Fredericks. He's locked up in the pantry."

"What do you mean? I—"

"Damn it all," snarled Wolfe. "What the hell's going on here? Now, you've got the butler in it. I suppose he committed a murder."

"He damned nearly did," said Sackler. "Fortunately, I stopped him."

Wolfe ran his hand through his hair. "All right," he said with heavy irony. "Take your time. I ain't got to be anywhere until nine tomorrow morning."

Sackler thanked him elaborately. "When we first arrived here tonight," he said, "you will all remember we were served cocktails? I don't know how many of you are frequent drinkers but it certainly took no connoisseur to realize that those drinks were the vilest ever to pass a palate. That fact indicated two others."

"What were those?" Abe Weldon asked in a whisper.

"First, that Fredericks must know damned little about drinking and that his butler couldn't have had a great deal of experience butling."

"I am a patient man," said Daley as his finger drummed on the chair arm indicating he wasn't, "but what has all this to do with murder and how is the butler involved?"

"One member of our little gathering missed the first drink," said Sackler. "Weldon hadn't arrived yet. After Weldon arrived a second tray of drinks was brought in. Before they could be served, our butler was called away to answer the telephone. When he returned, Fredericks, here, walked over to the table, picked up one drink, smelled it and howled that it was terrible. He sent his man back to mix some more. Why?"

"Why what?" said Wolfe.

"Why should a guy who drank that first cocktail without protest, squawk like Escoffier sniffing a Mickey Finn about the second? Good God, it couldn't have been any worse than the first."

"All right," I said, since he appeared to be waiting for a straight man, "why?"

"Because," he said, italicizing every word, *"because while the butler was at the telephone, you, Joey, idly twirled the revolving table that held the drinks."*

WE ALL STARED at him. For a moment I thought perhaps his mind had cracked under the diurnal strain of counting each dollar he had stowed away in his Postal Savings accounts.

Daley spoke first. "Suppose you make it clearer, Mr. Sackler."

Sackler smiled quietly. "Being a professional detective," he said with a snide glance at Wolfe, "my mind went immediately into action. I came upon a hypothesis at once. Suppose, I reasoned, one of those drinks were poisoned? Suppose the revolving of the table by Joey when the butler was out of the room disarranged the location of the glasses so that the butler no longer knew *which* glass contained the poison? That would explain Fredericks' sending him back to mix another batch."

"See here," said Fredericks angrily, "are you—?"

"You're nuts," Wolfe cut in. "How can you have the gall to base anything on a theory like that without making any attempt to check up on it?"

"I've checked," said Sackler. "That's why the butler is locked in the pantry."

A light dawned on me. "That's why you sent me in to order the flunkey to drink three drinks while I held a gun at his head?"

"That's why," said Sackler. "No matter how bad a cocktail tastes a man will drink it with a gun at his temple. Your butler, Fredericks, wouldn't drink even under those circumstances. Why not? Because he knew one of those drinks was poisoned. He jumped Joey and Joey was compelled to slug him and lock him up."

"Ridiculous," said Fredericks. "Utterly ridiculous. Where are those cocktails?"

"They're locked up, too," said Sackler. "They'll remain locked up until a police department chemist can get at them."

"Damn it," snapped Wolfe, "even if you're right which I hope you're not, I don't see what you're driving at."

"Listen," said Abe Weldon and there was a dangerous note in his voice, "who was it that monkey was trying to poison?"

"I'll give you one guess," said Sackler.

Weldon lit a cigarette and looked at Fredericks who did not meet his eye.

"As a matter of fact," went on Sackler, "only one guess is

necessary. Quite obviously there was no poison in that first round of drinks. We all drank one. There was poison in the second round. And there was only one guy here for the second round who was not here for the first round. That was the man at whom the poison was aimed."

"Me," said Weldon very calmly.

"You," said Sackler.

"Why," said Wolfe, "would a lousy flunkey want to kill Weldon?"

Sackler sighed. "Did it ever occur to you to suspect the man who gave Weldon his job?"

"You are a very smart guy," said Weldon, with his eyes still watching Fredericks.

"Why," asked Sackler, "would a guy give a crook like Weldon such a good job with the promise of a raise?"

"Why not?" said Wolfe "There's plenty of dopes give ex-cons jobs."

"True. But they don't make such an impassioned speech about it. From what Joey told me, Fredericks spoke quite feelingly of prison life. The lack of women, of society, et cetera. It occurred to me that he spoke from experience. And if that were true, it followed that perhaps Weldon knew of that experience. That Weldon had blackmailed himself into his job because he had known Fredericks in the can."

"That's a lie," snapped Fredericks. "You can't prove—"

"Of course, I can," said Sackler. "You never should have given Joey your business card. As soon as I figured out the possibilities, I had the prints on it checked. I can quote your record, Fredericks, from 1910 to here."

"Wait a minute," said Wolfe, "granting all you say is true,

what the hell has it got to do with Wallace Kates being killed?"

"I figure it this way," said Sackler. "Kates knew Fredericks' record, knew he was milking the company. Kates blackmailed him for cash. Then along came Abe Weldon and demanded a job. Fredericks gave it to him. Weldon apparently was satisfied with his salary. Kates was the big drain on Fredericks. Fredericks decided to kill him. He knew that Weldon would suspect him, so he told Weldon about it before he did it. Promised Weldon a raise in salary to keep his mouth shut."

"Then," I said, "when Weldon was pinched, Fredericks was afraid he'd talk, so he decided to poison him here."

"That's it," said Sackler. "And there's your case, Inspector. You can take it away."

WOLFE STOOD UP, frowning unhappily. "I don't know," he muttered, "it sounds good. But can we prove it? It seems long on theory to me, but damned short on evidence."

"You've got a witness," said Sackler. "A prime, Grade A witness."

"Who?"

"Weldon. Analyze those drinks. Show Weldon that one was poisoned. I think he'll talk."

Weldon glared at Fredericks. "You're damned right I'll talk," he said.

"You can begin right now," said Wolfe as he jerked Fredericks to his feet, nodded to the copper and the four of them went into the study.

Daley got up and wrung Sackler's hand. "Magnificent, sir. Magnificent. At last Federated can be properly run. I'll fire every member of the staff. Clean 'em all out and start afresh."

"Except Cummings," said Sackler. "He's got a contract. Signed by Fredericks for the corporation."

He crossed the room and handed the contract to an astounded Cummings.

Daley grunted. "Well, I guess one holdover won't hurt. "

Sackler ignored him. "Miss Magruder," he said. "You'll probably have some trouble with the police about that money you took. That's no fault of mine. You owe me a thousand dollars. I cleared you and found Kates' killer."

"You'll have my check in the morning," she said. "I keep my word."

Sackler nodded and turned to Cummings. "You," he said, "have a six-months' contract. Fifty per cent of your salary accrues to me. Correct?"

Cummings shook Sackler's hand fervently. "Of course it does, and I'm very, very grateful."

Why the hell he was grateful about paying all that dough escaped me.

Sackler gazed broodingly through the windshield as I drove the car downtown. With the maroon car almost mine I felt very lighthearted.

"So," I said, "that was why you made Fredericks sign a contract? You knew when you pinned a murder on him he'd lose his job. You knew that mug Daley would fire Cummings. You knew you'd never collect. So you told a filthy lie to get Cummings a contract. You have no ethics."

He blinked at me. "I have no ethics?" he said, outraged. "You miserable hound, Joey. You knew I was lying, and you were prepared to call in Cummings and ruin the whole deal in order to coerce me into signing that note."

"Well," I said happily, "maybe neither of us have any ethics."

Then I thought of something that caused me to undergo an odd queasy sensation at the pit of my stomach.

"And besides," I shouted angrily, "in the future will you kindly let me in on your plans? Those drinks, I drank one of them in the kitchen. My God and one of them was poisoned. My God—"

Sackler seemed amused.

"You drank one, eh, Joey? Let's see, there were eight drinks there. That made it seven to one against your death. Seven to one against my having been blackmailed into endorsing that damned note. Well, Joey, that's the first time you ever won a bet from me."

"All right," I said angrily. "You can laugh. But from here on you can worry a little more about my health."

"Why, Joey?"

"That note runs a year. If I die or lose my job during that time, you're liable for the loan. Think that over."

I felt him shudder. "A year, Joey? Good God!" He was silent for a moment, then he said hopefully: "But you're a healthy specimen, Joey. Strong as a horse. In the pink, eh?"

"Superficially," I told him darkly. "However, there's a horrible hereditary cardiac condition in our family. My father went out like a candle. And only last week my Uncle Lou was sitting talking to me just as I'm talking to you right now. He keeled over in the middle of a sentence. Out like a light."

"Joey," said Sackler anxiously. "But surely not you. You're husky as an ox. Joey, how do you feel?"

"Terrible," I told him happily. "Awful. There's a flutter in my chest."

I glanced at him from the corner of my eye. He looked for all the world like an Italian General watching the arrival of an Australian tank corps.

Pick Up the Marbles!

Rex Sackler, unchallenged world's champion penny-pincher, howled with anguish when his client told him he wanted to rid himself of a $3,000,000 inheritance. But—anything for a fee. And then, when the loathsome assignment was finished and he was counting the take, Sackler nearly found himself taking the count instead. That ungrateful pup, Joey—his own assistant—had pulled a fast one that nicked the master money-grubber for 20 (twenty) per cent!

1

Too Much Money

SACKLER'S HAND REACHED for the ten of diamonds with a gesture which reminded me of a cormorant's dive. He turned the trick over, flung his cards on the desk top and said with oily satisfaction: "That's cards, spades and two points, Joey. You can't win."

I withdrew my wallet and took out two dollars with no enthusiasm whatever. I said bitterly: "I never win. Barnum would've loved me. I'm the great American sucker. Have you an old Brooklyn Bridge you want to get rid of?"

Sackler clucked like a dowager hen. "Let us keep our tempers," he said with episcopal suavity. "Let us remain good losers. Let us—"

"Let us stop gambling," I interrupted, "I haven't drawn a full week's pay in five years. You combine the luck of a four-leaf clover with Shylock's soul. I'm through. Forever."

Sackler riffled the cards with his long white fingers. He eyed me speculatively. He knew quite well I had eight bucks in cash left. He was going to feel quite cheated until he got it.

"One fast one, Joey," he said cajolingly. "Just one more."

I stood up and said "No," with finality.

Sackler's eyes narrowed. He looked at me long and thoughtfully. He drew a deep breath. "Joey," he said, "I'll tell you what."

"You need tell me nothing," I told him. "Except the address of the nearest safe deposit vault in which to sink my eight bucks. I am not interested in any complicated wager. I do not care to take a sporting chance. This week I intend to spend my food money for food."

"One more hand of casino," said Sackler. "Your eight bucks against twenty per cent of the next fee. And I'm a golden hearted fool to offer that price."

My emphatic refusal froze on my lips as I performed some rapid mental arithmetic. Sackler's average fee ran to some-

"Get out, you blundering idiot!" roared Blandship.

thing higher than a thousand dollars. Twenty per cent of that was well above two hundred. Two hundred to eight was a very sweet price. For the first time since I had known him I had the edge.

"I am putty," I said sitting down again. "Deal."

He dealt and the miracle for which I had waited five years happened. At the end of the fourth deal I found myself in the amazed possession of cards, two aces, and little casino. I beamed at him and felt like the century plant in the year of its bloom.

"Twenty per cent," I said, "of the next fee. And thank you."

Sackler blinked. He wasn't used to losing, especially to me. He picked up the cards again with a sigh that came from the very bottom of his being. He looked like a man who had lost everything but honor and retained not very much of that.

"One more," he said. "You've got to give me a chance to win my money back."

"*Your* money?" I said. "I've been keeping you in cigarettes and carfare for years. Every Wednesday you pay me, then spend the rest of the week devising schemes to win the money back. With damnable success, too. I—"

I was interrupted by the opening and closing of the outer office door. Sackler and I exchanged a swift glance. He ran his long fingers through his black hair, adjusted his tie and donned his professional mien. I walked over to the door and opened it.

Our visitor was tall and thin. He wore a black derby, a neatly creased black suit, a black shirt, and a pair of brilliant black shoes. His face was gaunt and cadaverous, his eyes gloomy. He gave the impression of a man clad in a shroud. He advanced into the room slowly and said in a tone of marked melancholy: "Mr. Sackler? Mr. Rex Sackler?"

Sackler inclined his head and admitted his identity. The stranger sat down.

"My name is Tony Marsden," he announced sadly. "I am in trouble."

Sackler's eyes lit up. He was very partial to people in trouble, especially if he sensed they would permit him to use their bank accounts to pull them out.

Marsden's eye wandered morosely around the room. They came to rest on a pile of junk at the edge of Sackler's desk. Sackler who threw nothing away save verbiage had been cleaning out a drawer containing the accumulation of several years. Cigar bands, ancient letters and a hotel key that he had never returned formed a pyramid by the telephone.

Marsden lifted his eyebrows suddenly. He picked up the

hotel key turned it over and read aloud the name on the tag. "The Ralton," he said musingly. "Damned bad service there. No wonder they went broke in '33."

Sackler said, "Yes," impatiently, then went into his professional spiel. "Mr. Marsden, we specialize in extricating clients from trouble. We are very good at it." He paused to let this sink in, then came to the point like a setter. "That's why we command such ample fees, eh, Joey?"

I NODDED MY head enthusiastically. As a general rule the only moment I ever glimpsed a fee was during that swift period of transition between the client's check book and Sackler's eager fingers. Mr. Marsden, however, was different. I had twenty per cent of Mr. Marsden and for once I wasn't going to resent the Sackler take.

"Indeed," I said, "we have a marvelous record. Ninety-seven per cent perfect."

"Ninety-seven point four," corrected Sackler who was lying, too. "Now, Mr. Marsden, tell me exactly what is your trouble?"

I watched Marsden closely and hoped it was nothing less than murder with two millionaires involved and money absolutely no object. My heart sank as I heard him say gloomily: "My brother-in-law is a sadistic brute."

Sackler scratched his left ear. "Do you want me to psychoanalyze him, Mr. Marsden?"

Marsden shook his head wearily. "It's my sister. He treats her very badly. And now for the past week I've been unable to get in touch with her. I am refused admittance to the house. I am constantly told on the telephone that she is not in. I need to consult her about a piece of property we jointly own. Though that, at the moment, is unimportant. Frankly, I'm worried about her. God knows if he's holding her incommunicado, has injured her, or what."

Spiritually, I beat my head against the wall. If there was more than two hundred slugs gross in this I was going to be a very lucky man. Sackler glanced across the room at me and grinned. He knew quite well what was going on in my mind.

"What is it you want us to do, Mr. Marsden?"

"Simply reassure me that my sister is all right. You are somehow to get inside the house, speak to her. I hesitate to call the police just in case that nothing is really wrong. But I must know. I must know at once. Today."

"The address?"

Marsden gave him an address so far in the Bronx that it might as well have been Yonkers.

"You'd better take your assistant," he added. "Symington, my brother-in-law is a dangerous man on occasion. You may have some trouble." He consulted his watch. "It is now one fifteen. Can you get up there say, by three? I'd like to know as soon as possible."

"We'll leave before two," said Sackler, "provided we accept the assignment."

Marsden's eyebrows lifted. "You mean you won't accept it?"

"There is," said Sackler, averting his eyes coldly, "the matter of the fee."

For a moment I hoped wildly that Marsden would offer something so ridiculously low that Sackler would turn him down. Then I'd have a whack at the next customer. From where I stood it hardly seemed to me that it was worth more than fifty bucks to take a short jaunt to the Bronx checking on the welfare of Marsden's sister.

Marsden took a checkbook from his pocket. "Shall we say two hundred dollars?"

My groan was in inverse ratio to Sackler's beam. Two hundred dollars was first-rate pay for the job as far as Sackler was concerned. However it was far beneath his average fee and my twenty per cent was a lousy forty bucks.

Marsden handed Sackler the check and a card. "You will get in touch with me at this address as soon as possible. And thank you."

Sackler stood up and bowed him out of the room. "Thank you," he said exaggeratedly. "We will call you later this after-noon."

Marsden walked gloomily from the room. Sackler turned on me, an unholy glint in his dark eyes. "Twenty per cent, Joey. Forty bucks. A nice little piece of change, eh?"

"Terrific," I said. "You're one lucky-guy. The rope'll break when they get you on the gallows. That's the lowest fee you've had this year. I get twenty per cent of the cheapest client that ever came into the office. Don't talk to me. Leave me alone with my sorrow."

He made a clucking sound of phoney sympathy and reached up for his four-year-old hat. I raised an eyebrow.

"Where are you going?"

"The bank, Joey. I see this check is drawn on the Agricultural Trust down the street. They know me there. They'll cash it for me. I don't like the idea of banks holding any money of mine. I'll be back immediately with your cut."

He strode out of the room, slamming the door behind him.

WHEN REX SACKLER stated that he didn't like the

idea of banks holding his money he epitomized his own character. Sackler's adoration of a dollar bill was a beautiful thing to behold. The rustle of a Federal Reserve note was a sweet summer zephyr to his ears, the jingle of a pair of quarters in his pocket was a heart-warming symphony.

He liked hoarding money as much as he disliked disgorging it. His wealth was scattered across the country in a score of Postal Savings Accounts. In 1929 a number of banks had failed and if Wall Street had forgotten it, Rex Sackler most certainly hadn't.

He lived in a cheap furnished room and bought two twenty dollar suits every three years. His shapeless fedora was stained by the rain that had fallen at Hoover's inauguration and his shoes were the best that four dollars and eighty cents could possibly buy—wholesale.

Withal, he was the luckiest guy who ever dealt a card or rolled a pair of dice. He was an artist at squeezing the last possible penny out of a client and on those occasions where he had had to fight to save his fee he had shown an ingenuity worthy of the German General Staff. His shrewdness, in short, was equaled only by his cheapness.

He paid me a salary each week, then devoted the other five days endeavoring to win it back again. He rolled his own cigarettes, thus saving the tax money. He came down with ague and chills regularly on March fifteenth of each year. Beyond that, and the fact that he detested dogs and children, he was a thoroughly beautiful character.

Sackler returned from the bank wearing the expression of a cat who has just swallowed a particularly succulent canary. He hung up his hat, sat down at the desk and cleared his throat.

"Joey," he said in his most benign tone, "let's have a heart to heart talk."

"Oh, no," I said hastily, "If you think you can talk me out of that forty bucks, you're crazy. Save your oily words for the Collector of Internal Revenue."

Sackler shook his head and clucked again. "Joey," he said, "you misjudge me. I haven't the slightest idea of trying to get back the money you so fairly won. I am about to shower coals of fire upon your head."

"At how much a shovelful?"

Sackler sighed and tried very hard to achieve the register of a man who is sorely put upon.

"Joey," he said, "you are constantly berating me. By implication, and at times by profane direct statement you make it appear that I am, shall I say, frugal."

"Frugal? You are one cheap thus and thus."

"Joey!" There was hurt reproach in his voice. "You misunderstand me. I possess an intelligent regard for money. I also have your welfare at heart."

"You certainly take good care that I don't die from gout."

"Joey, I am about to offer you more than words. I am about to demonstrate, substantially, that I am not the money grabber you think I am."

"Put up," I said, "or—"

"I owe you," said. Sackler, "twenty per cent of that last fee. Correct?"

"Eminently."

"I have decided to give you one hundred per cent."

I blinked at him. Sackler giving away money was roughly parallel with Churchill surrendering the British fleet.

"Perhaps," I said, "my ears are going back on me. I'd swear I heard you say you were giving me a hundred per cent of the Marsden fee instead of the twenty you owe me."

Sackler beamed like the Sunday school teacher bestowing the Bible Class prizes.

"You heard me correctly, Joey. One hundred per cent. Of course, if I present you with the full fee, you disavow all further claim to the debt."

That should have warned me. But I'm the sort of sucker who is always blinded by an immediate prospect.

"Of course," I said. "When do I get this dough?"

"Forthwith," said Sackler. "At this moment. Here you are, Joey."

HE TOOK HIS wallet from his pocket and extracted the check Marsden had given him. I snatched it from him before he could change his mind. I turned it over, noted Sackler's endorsement on the back and two rubber stamped words that sent rage coursing through my veins.

"No account!" I screamed. "It's rubber. Marsden's a phoney. He hasn't any dough in that bank."

Sackler looked like a bookmaker after the favorite has run a bad fourth. Hypocritical commiseration spread itself like butter over his face.

"The breaks, Joey," he said. "That's the way it is. It just so happens that the fee you had a piece of turned out badly. Well, it all evens up over a year."

I employed a prepositional phrase which mentioned part of a pig's anatomy. Then I calmed down a little and tried to prod him.

"I'm only out forty bucks," I said. "You're out the rest. So what are you beaming about?"

He shrugged. "Why not? I'd be very angry, Joey, had I done the work and the check had bounced. Since I found out about the check first, I do nothing. I'm just even."

"Then," I told him, "this doesn't constitute a fee at all. I insist that—"

"The door," said Sackler, who had the ears of an airplane detector. "Someone just came in."

I went into the outer office. There I beheld a guy wearing a set of good gray tweeds that I was never going to afford while working for Sackler. He was bald, with a round red face that bespoke good living. There was a single pearl in his tie and a ruby on his finger that resembled a stop light. He looked like a guy who was born on a blanket of hundred dollar bills. This, I reflected gloomily, was the client I *wasn't* going to get a piece of.

"My name is Beresford," he said in a slow mid-western drawl. "Mr. Sackler has been highly recommended to me. May I see him?"

I towed him into the inner office. Sackler eyed him as he approached and his nostrils dilated. He was smelling money as surely as a bloodhound smells a convict's heel print.

"Mr. Sackler," said Beresford without preamble. "I have a most delicate task for you. I am willing to pay any sum within reason if you accomplish it."

Sackler's eyes gleamed. They sized up Beresford like a crooked dealer on a gambling ship. Beresford lit a cigar which filled the office with expensive fragrance, inhaled deeply and continued.

"I have a friend," he said, "Cyrus R. Blanship. Perhaps you've heard of him."

Sackler, whose mind was built on the order of Dun & Bradstreet, nodded. "Coal," he said. "West Virginia. Probably worth three million."

"Precisely. He intends leaving most of those three million to me when he dies."

The expression on Sackler's face at that moment was positively sickening. He looked as if he was restraining himself, by great effort, from bending low and running his tongue across Beresford's foot. Instead, he said, oleaginously: "Really? Most interesting."

Beresford nodded glumly. "Those three million are what I want to see you about."

"Anything," said Sackler. "Anything at all I can do."

I tried, for a moment to conceive of something he wouldn't do with three million slugs involved. Imagination tottered.

"You see," said Beresford, "I want pressure brought to bear on Blanship to change his will."

"To *change* his will?" echoed Sackler, as if he were on the verge of sending for the wagon. "You mean you don't want the money?"

"I certainly do not," said Beresford with emphasis.

SACKLER AND I exchanged glances. Here indeed was something foreign to the philosophy of both of us. Beresford cleared his throat and continued.

"I earn a comfortable income. I have a wife and two children. I dare say I am a happy man. I'm a mining engineer who clears some fifteen thousand a year. That's enough for my needs. I crave neither power nor limitless wealth. I may be hopelessly old-fashioned but I believe too much money brings unhappiness."

Sackler nodded in lying agreement. Beresford lighted another expensive cigar and went on.

"I had a friend once who inherited a lot of money. It broke up his home, sent him cruising around with a mob of playboys and finally the responsibility of his possessions drove him to drink and the sanitarium."

"I see your point perfectly," said Sackler blandly. "Too much money, at times, can be an evil thing."

I blinked at that one. It was something like Genghis Khan toasting the Golden Rule with a cup of his victim's blood. Beresford exhaled a cloud of smoke worth at least twelve cents toward the ceiling. I refrained from lighting a cigarette in the hope that he might pass the Habanas around at any moment.

"Well," said Beresford, "I'm glad you understand. There are money-grubbing men who wouldn't."

Sackler took a hypocrite's bow and said: "What is it you want me to do about it, Mr. Beresford?"

"I want you to see Blanship. I want you to talk him into changing his will. Originally, he had willed all his money to the Foundation for Anthropological Research. A year or so ago he changed it in my favor. I'd like to see the Foundation get the money."

I thought that one over very carefully. It sounded more than a little screwy. Although I knew Sackler hated my butting in when he was smearing a client, I came clattering headlong into the conversation.

"Well," I said, "if you feel that way about it, why can't you take the dough when the old guy dies and hand it over to the Foundation yourself?"

Sackler glared at me and I knew he'd thought of that, too. I knew, moreover, the reason he hadn't mentioned it was because there would be no fee in it for him if Beresford acted on that particular piece of advice.

"A fair enough question," said Beresford, "but it is more complicated than that. First, there are three living relatives of Blanship's—all rather remote but nevertheless kin. The will now allows them some five thousand apiece to insure against their contesting the will. Two of these relatives are very good friends of my wife. They would be extremely bitter about it. The fact of my giving the cash to the Foundation would not allay that bitterness. Then, there is my wife to be considered."

Sackler nodded. He picked this one up fast.

"You mean," he said, "that your wife, of course, being a woman would never condone your giving all that dough away?"

"Exactly. She knows nothing of the will. She is a good woman. A devoutly religious woman, yet I'm certain she'd never forgive me if she knew I had handed a fortune over to a non-profit making institution. I'm not a particularly ambitious man. I have enough to keep me comfortably for the rest of my life. I don't want the responsibility of the Blanship fortune. I don't want any part of it. Perhaps that seems strange to you?"

Strange to Sackler? It was as baffling as an eclipse of the sun to a retarded Australian aborigine. Manfully, however, he remembered that this was a client with, probably, a very juicy fee tucked away in his vest pocket. He lied with the glib finesse of Goebbels' third assistant.

"Not at all," he said heartily. "I see your point of view. You have a family, you have children. You want to pursue the even tenor of your life. You don't want your kids to become moneyed idlers. You want them to work their way to the top, the rightful heritage of every American."

That certainly was laying it on with a trowel. For a moment, I thought Beresford would see it. On the contrary, he agreed with what to me was eagerness.

"Precisely," he said. "You'll accept the assignment?"

"Of course," murmured Sackler, "there is the minor matter of the fee."

"One thousand dollars if the will is changed. Satisfactory?"

Sackler sighed like an amorous cat. "Satisfactory," he said. "Quite."

"There is this point," said Beresford. "Blanship believes he owes me a great debt. Years ago I pulled him out of a mine sump. It was simple enough but he has the impression that I saved his life. I have argued with him about the legacy. He imputes my motive to a natural modesty which makes him even more determined to leave me the money. It is of no use to tell him you represent me. That will make him more bull-headed than ever."

Sackler didn't like that. It made the assignment seem more difficult. And now there was a matter of a thousand dollars at stake.

"I can't just walk in," he protested, "and offer advice as a complete stranger."

"Of course not," said Beresford. "I have already arranged that. I have been in touch with the Anthropological Foundation. Naturally, they want the money. They see eye to eye with me on this. As a matter of fact I have already promised them in writing the entire estate if it should be left to me. I told them I was engaging you. It is quite all right with them if you act as their agent. You will speak to Blanship, ostensibly on their behalf.

Sackler smiled dreamily. A thousand silver dollars were clinking in his mind.

"I accept, Mr. Beresford," he announced. "I shall see Blanship immediately."

Beresford stood up. "If you will let me know the result of your efforts, phoning me at my home some time this evening, I shall send the check out at once."

They bowed punctiliously to each other. Beresford handed Sackler a Habana from his vest pocket, completely ignoring me. He walked from the room followed by Rex Sackler's most benign and unctuous grin. I lit a cigarette and told Sackler what sort of a lucky guy he was. The Hays office would have swooned at my diction.

2

You Can't Take It With You

BLANSHIP'S HOUSE WAS isolated in a neglected Long Island estate. The grass grew long and weeds towered high upon what once had been a magnificent expanse of lawn. I pulled the car up beneath a Colonial portico, and with Sackler behind me, punched the doorbell.

After a full minute's wait the door opened a trifle and the first thing I saw was the automatic. A hand thrust it through the door-jamb into the pit of my stomach. There was a thirty-eight of my own in a shoulder holster but it seemed very far away at that particular moment.

Sackler, looking over my shoulder, murmured with magnificent calm: "Take him, Joey."

I turned my head and glared at him. "What do you want to do? Roll my corpse?"

He didn't answer. The door opened wide now and the man who held the weapon stood framed on the threshold. He was a blond of medium height and effeminate features. His lips were fuller and redder than they should have been and his eyes were blue and cold like the Arctic Sea.

He said icily and with a lisp: "Your buthineth, gentlemen?"

"We want to see Mr. Blanship," said Sackler. "And I fail to see any reason for this highhanded treatment. I have a very good mind to thrash you. I—"

Considering the gun was in my stomach, Sackler's courage

was notable. I told him to shut up, forcefully, and turned my politest smile on the lisping blond.

"We're representing the Foundation for Anthropological Research," I told him. "We'd like to see Mr. Blanship on business."

"I'm Mr. Blanship's secretary," said the blond. "My name is Hadderman. One of my duties is to see that Mr. Blanship is not bothered by dangerous characters."

His left hand moved gracefully into my coat. He withdrew my gun like a pickpocket. He took his automatic from my stomach and aimed it at Sackler. Sackler's indignation at this highhanded treatment evanesced.

"I am unarmed," he said hastily. "I never carry a gun. Never."

The blond ran a caressing hand over Sackler's coat and hip pockets. Then he stood aside and said, "Come in."

He left us alone in the hall for a few moments, then returned and led us upstairs. He flung open a door at the stair head and announced, "Mr. Blanship."

Blanship sat in a leather chair in a book-lined room. He looked older than the theory of romantic love. His face was yellow, rather resembling a Hallowe'en pumpkin stuck on the top of an emaciated broomstick. His eyes were sunken, and it seemed to me there was fear and suspicion in them.

Hadderman slammed the door behind us. I did not hear his footsteps recede down the hall and assumed he was eavesdropping outside with the automatic in his pocket just in case we proved to be dangerous characters after all. I hoped Sackler had remarked it, too. With a thousand dollar fee in the offing he might well attempt threat and bullying on the old man.

Blanship put on a pair of glasses and peered at us like a guy peeping through a chink in a tomb.

"So," he said, and there was unpleasantness and mockery in his tone, "you're from the Foundation, eh? You wouldn't be here to try to talk me into changing my will, would you?"

Sackler took a deep breath and turned on the charm. His eloquence filled the room. He pointed out the splendid work the Foundation performed, which, considering he knew absolutely nothing about it, was something of a feat. He spoke of all the better-known benefactors of humanity. He urged Blanship to inscribe his own name on the immortal list. He talked incessantly, rather in the manner of the women I seem to meet.

Bored, my gaze wandered about the room. The most striking item in it was a huge canvas hanging on the west wall. It was an oil painting of a young girl. She had a classic face from which shone a sort of somber beauty. Her eyes were deep, dark and tender. They were compelling eyes. I found myself wondering if I could dig up a date for tonight.

Then Sackler's long speech ended on a high interrogative note. He beamed on Blanship like an unctuous undertaker and said: "So you see my point, Mr. Blanship? I'm sure you'll agree the Foundation can make the best use of your wealth."

Blanship stared coldly through his glasses. A mirthless smile flickered across his thin lips.

"No," he said. "I know why you're here. Do you think I'm such a fool as to listen to you? Get out, you blundering idiot, get out!"

HIS VOICE ROSE to a shrill scream. Sackler paled, not so much at the vehemence, I knew, as at the contemplation of a disappearing fee. He cleared his throat preparatory to disgorging some more oil. But before he could speak Blanship lifted his voice again.

"Hadderman! Hadderman, get these fools out of here. Never let them in again!"

Hadderman proved he had never left the other side of the door, by entering the room immediately. The automatic was still in his hand. Its barrel was aimed in Sackler's general direction. He rose hastily.

Hadderman escorted us down the stairs. He returned my gun silently as we stepped out on the portico. He slammed the door behind us. Sackler walked toward the car with the gait of a pallbearer. I followed, drinking in the spring sunshine, with an ineffable happiness in my heart.

"Well," I said heartily as I drove back to town, "you've lost a thousand dollar fee."

"Joey," he said, shaking his head mournfully, "you are a vulture whose spirits fatten on the misfortune of others."

I didn't answer him, but on the way back to the office, as I contemplated his loss, I am bound to admit that my spirits waxed fatter and fatter.

Less than two hours later I developed a fine case of spiritual rickets. Since our return Sackler had sat at his desk, head bowed and soul darkened. He was brooding, reflecting, doubtless, on the injustice of a Deity who could so ruthlessly snatch a certified check from him—Rex Sackler. I, considering the same thing, was quite prepared to believe in the complete equity of all Natural Law.

The telephone rang and reversed our positions. Sackler snatched it up and answered. I watched his face as the remote voice trickled into his ear and saw a beatific expression crawl over it. He said, "Thank you very much," in breathless accents and hung up.

"Joey," he said, turning to me, "I am now about to thrust a corkscrew into your vicious little soul and twist it."

"I bare my breast," I told him, still unworried. "Strike."

"Call up Beresford at his home. Tell him Blanship is going to change his will in favor of the Foundation. He's doing it tonight. His lawyer is going out to the house."

I was so stunned I permitted him to steal a cigarette from my package without protest.

"It can't be," I said weakly. "The old guy was positive this afternoon. How could he change his mind so swiftly?"

"Mine not to reason why," murmured Sackler happily. "That was Hadderman on the wire. He gave me the message. Said the old guy told him to let me know. Now call Beresford, give him the news and tell him to send the check."

I picked up the receiver as eagerly as a poker player about to call his wife. I delivered the message, hung up, and said bitterly: "You're shot with luck. It's a wonder you don't play roulette for a living."

Sackler shuddered. "Good God, Joey, with a percentage of 458 plus working for the house? Am I mad, Joey?"

I didn't answer him. If from a fiscal point of view he was mad, the National City Bank was completely crazy.

FOUR DAYS LATER, at ten o'clock, in the morning, Inspector Wolfe of Homicide burst into the office followed by a dapper, blue-suited gentleman with the eyes of a lynx and the officious air of a lawyer. Sackler looked up from his desk, recognized Wolfe and the fact that there was no fee here, sighed, and returned to the morning paper. I went back to the daily true story in the Gazette and wondered how in the hell authors sold such tripe.

Wolfe sat down in front of Sackler's desk, indicated the dapper man with a thick thumb and said: "Rex, this is George Bloch. He's a lawyer. He's this guy Beresford's lawyer."

Sackler looked up and nodded distantly.

"He's got a check for you," Wolfe added.

Sackler came to the point like a bird dog. He blinked once, repeated the words, "A check?" and shook hands affably with Bloch.

"Yeah," said Wolfe excitedly. "We got this Beresford in the can for the Blanship murder. But he says that you—"

Sackler held up a hand. I put down the daily true story and cocked an ear.

"What's it all about?" said Sackler. "I didn't even know Blanship was dead. Begin at the beginning."

"Happened last night," said Wolfe. "This guy Blanship was killed in his study. Shot. Beresford gets all his dough. Logical suspect. No alibi. Says he was at a movie. Alone. But if what he says is true it's going to be hard to hold him."

Sackler ran a thin hand through his black hair. There was a gleam in his eye. "What does he say?"

"He says we've got him wrong. That he couldn't have killed the old guy because he didn't want the dough. That he'd already given a written promise to some Foundation that they'd get it if he ever got it. That, furthermore, he'd retained you to try to get Blanship to switch the dough from him to the Foundation—that you'd told him the will was changed four days before the killing."

Sackler frowned, then nodded. "I did," he said. "Why don't you check on it?"

"I have," said Wolfe. "The will wasn't changed at all. Hasn't been touched for over a year. Got that from Blanship's lawyer this morning."

Sackler thought that over for a long moment, then he came back to what lay nearest his heart.

"What was this about a check?" he asked. Rex Sackler wasn't going to put a brain cell to functioning without knowing who was paying him how much for it.

"It's from Beresford," said Bloch. "He wants me to offer you a check for twenty-five hundred dollars if you clear him on this. He believes your evidence would turn the trick. But he believes you should be compensated for any trouble you may take on the case."

"You see," said Wolfe, "if what Beresford told us about the dough, about your telling him the will was changed, is true, it knocks hell out of our motive."

"Then it knocks hell out of your motive," said Sackler. "It's true. Hadderman, Blanship's secretary, called me, told me the old guy was changing the will."

"Now, listen," said Bloch, "my client is willing to pay you twenty-five hundred dollars, Mr. Sackler, if you can clear him. What you have said here wipes out the motive the police hold against Beresford. But he wants to be cleared absolutely. He wants you to work along with the police to solve this case. If you do and clear him, he'll pay. Is that satisfactory?"

Was it satisfactory? Old Midas Sackler sat there glowing like a neon sign.

"Wait a minute," said Wolfe. "You're sure of all this, Rex? We'll have to spring the guy if what you say is true."

"It's true," said Sackler. "I told you this guy Hadderman called me about the will change."

"But the will wasn't changed," said Wolfe. "How do you explain that?"

"I don't," said Sackler, "yet. But give me time. First, were there any other heirs under the terms of the will?"

"Four," said Bloch. "All small bequests. Two women, second cousins, down for five thousand apiece. Arthur Wiley, a nephew, down for ten thousand, and Hadderman, the secretary, who, I understand, gets twenty grand. That's absolutely all. The rest goes to Beresford who, of course, isn't going to accept it. It's to be turned over at once to that Foundation."

SACKLER SIGHED AND put the bite on Wolfe for a cigarette. "What about these small heirs?" he asked. "Do you know anything of them?"

"Not much about the two women," said Bloch. "However, I'm Wiley's lawyer. He's a hotel man. Runs the Clarendon downtown."

"The Clarendon," said Sackler thoughtfully, pretending it meant something. He impressed me not at all. "All right, Bloch, I'll take your proposition. I'll work on this until the police are willing to exculpate your client completely. The fee is twenty-five hundred."

"Right," said Bloch, "and thank you. Now, Inspector, considering Mr. Sackler's testimony about the will, considering the promise to the Foundation, I think you will have to release my client."

Wolfe stood up unhappily. He didn't like to release murder suspects under any circumstances. He glanced at Sackler as if he held him personally responsible.

"Rex," he said, "you're not pulling a fast one on us just to add to your bank account, are you?"

Sackler registered horrified indignation. He did not deign to answer. Wolfe sighed and walked to the door.

"All right," he said to Bloch, "I guess we'll have to let him go. But I don't like it. I don't like it at all."

When they had gone, Sackler buried his chin in his hand and registered deep thought. I thumbed through the paper. We had remained immersed in our respective tasks for an hour or so when the telephone rang. I picked it up. I listened gleefully to Wolfe's profane voice, then hung up to see Sackler gazing at me inquiringly.

"Wolfe," I said. "He wants to know if you're an accessory to murder. He wants to know if you lied to Beresford about the will being changed in order to swindle him out of the fee he offered you. He wants to know—"

"Joey, what the devil are you talking about?"

"Hadderman. He's just denied ever calling you, telling you that Blanship was going to change his will."

Sackler stared at me. "But that's ridiculous, Joey. I recognized his voice. I'd have known that lisp of his anywhere."

I shrugged my shoulders. "Maybe you made it all up. Maybe you just invented it to get the dough."

"Joey! You know he called. You were here when the call came in."

"I didn't hear what was said on the other end of the wire. I'm inclined to agree with Wolfe."

He glared at me and his hand closed around the ashtray on his desk. Then, doubtless, recalling it had cost forty cents, he did not throw it.

Why we called on Beresford that night, I didn't know. Personally, I wasn't in favor of it as I got no time and a half for overtime. Moreover, I had lost the toss for the dinner check. Sackler, however, had something on his mind. He was still brooding when we rang the bell of Beresford's detached suburban home in Bayside.

A maid admitted us into a room that was empty of people yet filled with argument. The voices came from behind a curtained dining-room to the south of the parlor where we stood. A whining, indignant, half hysterical feminine tone was dominant.

"No," it said. "I won't give it to you. I won't throw it away. It's part of my life. My blood is in it. It's a living memory. You won't force me to, either, or it'll be bad for you. It's mine and I'll keep it. I—"

By this time the maid had announced our presence and the voice stopped. Beresford, red of face and embarrassed, appeared. He greeted us cordially and a moment later his wife entered.

She was a tiny woman, compact and giving the impression of a ball of nervous tension. At the moment her eyes were red and her lips tremulous. She acknowledged Beresford's introduction and sat down.

The longer we remained at Beresford's the less I knew what Sackler was driving at. He asked a number of desultory questions, at least one of them so utterly pointless I noted it.

"Tell me," he said to Beresford, "does your wife paint, or perhaps write? She strikes me as one with some creative talent."

I blinked at that one. So Sackler was now reading character. Mrs. Beresford registered pleasure as Beresford denied she was either Michelangelo, Mozart or Milton. Beresford rose, announced he would mix us a drink and went off into the kitchen. Sackler addressed himself to the wife. She answered him with an almost hysterical garrulity. He drew her out like a man who enjoys boredom.

She babbled on about her four children until I thought my ears would flap. Then, when she was out of breath, Sackler managed an interruption.

"Four children, Mrs. Beresford? I understood Mr. Beresford to say you had three."

Mrs. Beresford wiped her eyes. "One has passed on," she said lugubriously. She took a deep choking breath, and a sob broke from behind her handkerchief. "Passed away," she said hysterically. "Buried in unconsecrat—"

Beresford returned to the room bearing a cocktail shaker. He put the drinks down hastily and put a tender arm about his wife.

"You're upset, my dear," he said. "Will you excuse us, please?"

Sackler and I drained our glasses, bade hasty adieus and left. Outside I was about to ask him exactly what he was doing. However he was still putting on his heavy thinking act so I shut up and went home.

"YOU WILL DO two things," said Sackler to me the following morning. "Remember that guy Marsden?"

"If I've forgotten," I said bitterly, "this worthless check in my pocket will remind you."

Sackler grinned. "Good. Look up that address he gave us. The place where his sister is supposed to live. Then leap up to the Bronx and see if she actually lives there."

He opened a brown paper package on his desk and withdrew a ten cent pair of rubber gloves. These he thrust into his pocket.

"What are you doing?" I asked him. "Are those to save your lovely lily-white hands while you count your money?"

He ignored that. "Tonight, about ten, Joey, you'll call on the Beresfords. Ask them questions for about an hour. You needn't report to me until tomorrow."

"Questions? What sort of questions?"

"Anything that comes into your empty mind. The point is that you keep asking questions of both of them for an hour."

"I've got to ask questions of the wife?"

"Yes."

"My God, she'll answer them at great and boring length."

"Joey," he said reproachfully, "you've got to earn your salary somehow. But now, to the Bronx."

"To the Bronx!" I echoed heroically, like the character in a minor poem.

3

Leave It to Me

I REPORTED THE next morning that there was no such address as the one Marsden I had given us. Sackler didn't seem surprised. I reported further that I had gathered enough information from Beresford and particularly his wife to engage him with for at least six hours. Sackler declined to hear it.

"Call Wolfe," he said. "Tell him to get hold of Beresford, that guy Hadderman, too. Tell them to meet me at the Clarendon hotel. In Arthur Wiley's office. I'd like to see that guy. Two sharp, this afternoon. Tell Wolfe I'll give him the Blanship killer."

I stared at him. "You mean you've broken the case with all this fooling around you've been doing for the past few days?"

"I've broken it," said Sackler sadly.

"You're rather melancholy about it."

"Joey," he said, "little do you know what goes on inside me. Sometimes I think I am cursed."

"Only by me," I told him, going to the phone. "Heaven showers you with luck."

We took a taxicab downtown to the Hotel Clarendon. Sackler stared morosely through the window. His sigh sounded heavily like a wet wind soughing through an ancient tree. I assumed that at least one reason he looked so disgruntled was the fact that it had been necessary to return Beresford's thousand dollar check, when it was revealed that the will had not been changed after all. Once he ran a despairing hand through his hair, turned his head until his melancholy eye met mine. He sighed again, this time with such marked depression that I said brightly: "What's the matter? Is the great Sackler brain completely baffled this time? Or is it that the vast Sackler bank account doesn't stand to gain a sou? Is the trouble egotistical or economic?"

"Joey," he said bitterly, "you are a fool. The case is a crystal ball to me."

I lifted my eyebrows. I had been pretty close to him ever since the first time Beresford had walked into the office. If he'd made any progress on the mystery of Blanship's death it certainly wasn't apparent to the naked eye. I said as much.

He ignored my remark. He said: "I'm damned if I enjoy doing the work of an incompetent police department, Joey."

The cab pulled up at a marquee which once had been covered with brave gilt paint. That, obviously, was some time ago. Sackler, afflicted with melancholia or no, was still alert. He flung open the cab door and strode swiftly into the hotel lobby, leaving the meter to me. An item I would put on my expense account, to no avail whatever, for the next six months.

I followed Sackler into the hotel to find him waiting for me in front of a door bearing the legend: *Arthur Wiley—Manager.* Sackler turned the knob, brought a third sigh up out of his four dollar shoes and entered. I tagged along behind.

I entered the office and gasped. For the sad gentleman sitting behind the desk presumably belonging to Arthur Wiley was my financial nemesis, Tony Marsden. Sackler did not seem surprised. On a sofa beside the desk sat Hadderman who blinked nervously as we entered. Beresford bowed formally to Sackler and myself. Wolfe, leaning against the mantelpiece said: "How's old Shylock Sackler?"

Sackler ignored Wolfe's greeting. He walked the full length of the room and came to a guardsman's halt at the edge of Wiley's, or Marsden's, desk. He fixed the manager with fishy eyes and said coldly: "Passing a bad check signed with a phoney name, Mr. Wiley, is a forgery rap in this state."

Wiley smiled blandly. "I'm afraid you haven't much of a case," he said. "That check was given you on condition you perform a certain task. You didn't fulfill your contract. I owe you nothing."

Wolfe cocked his bloodhound ears and stepped forward. "What's this?" he snapped. "A bum check?"

Wiley lit a cigarette. "I gave Sackler a bad check," he said. "But since he did not work for it, I owed him nothing. A bad check given as a reward or an outright gift is not criminal, neither is it recoverable civilly."

Wolfe nodded. He glanced at Sackler and grinned. "He's right, Rex," he said. His grin grew broader. "How much did he stick you for?"

"That doesn't matter," said Sackler righteously. "The point is that I don't like sharp practice."

Wolfe's laughter rocked the room.

Since I had the check in my own wallet I didn't think it quite so funny. Wiley jammed his cigarette out in a hammered silver ashtray. He opened the top drawer of his desk.

"Don't take a bouncing check so seriously, Mr. Sackler," he said sadly. "In my business you get hundreds of them. Look."

He pointed downward toward the open drawer. Sackler glanced inside. I peered over his shoulder. There were at least fifty checks scattered in the drawer.

"The gleanings of the past two years," said Wiley. "All cashed, sent to my bank and returned for a variety of reasons. We expect bad checks in the hotel business, Mr. Sackler."

But Sackler wasn't listening now. His strange worried air had settled on him once again. His brow was corrugated and there was genuine concern in his black eyes. Again he sighed heavily like a steam engine suffering from unrequited love.

I REMAINED BAFFLED. It couldn't be the memory of Wiley's bad check. After all, he himself had admitted he'd done no work for that—he considered himself even. He had announced quite confidently that he knew the answer to the Blanship murder, and for that answer he had been promised a juicy fee from Beresford. What was on his mind I couldn't imagine, but judging from the lugubrious expression he wore, the load was heavy.

"Well," said Wolfe, taking the shredded cigar from his mouth, "what's all this loose talk about your having the answer to the Blanship killing?"

"It's not loose talk," said Sackler glumly, as if he were announcing the demise of his favorite and intestate grandmother.

"Then let's have the murderer's name."

Sackler regarded him distastefully. "You needn't be so damned dictatorial," he snapped. "I'm tired of doing the work for which the police department is amply paid."

Wolfe snorted at that. "You invariably get paid a damned sight better than the commissioner," he said. "What are you squawking about?"

Sackler shook his head and looked very much as if he were about to shed a tear. "I am not happy," he announced.

"I'm not interested in your spiritual condition," said Wolfe with phoney politeness. "Would you mind letting me have the name of the man who killed old man Blanship?"

"All right," said Sackler. He looked around the room. First at Beresford who met his gaze confidently, next at Wiley who still smiled blandly, then at Hadderman whose pursed-up lips gave the impression that he was lisping even though he was silent.

"Hadderman," said Sackler. He ran his hand through his hair again and stared out the window as if he were completely uninterested.

The rest of us looked over at the secretary who lifted his head and said: "Yeth, Mr. Thackler. You want me?"

Sackler turned his head and looked at his as if seeing him for the first time in his life.

"You?" he said. "What would I want you for?"

"Damn it all," snapped Wolfe impatiently, "you called him. You spoke his name."

"Oh that," said Sackler. "That was in answer to your request for the name of the guy who knocked off old man Blanship."

There was utter silence in the room. Once again we all stared at Hadderman. A slow flush crawled into his pale face. His breathing sounded stertorous. Then he suddenly beat his chest with a delicate fist and his voice rose crescendo like an insane violin.

"*Me?* You mean *me?*"

Sackler dabbed his brow with a ten cent cotton handkerchief. He looked over at me and shook his head. "Joey," he said, "I'm worried."

"*You're* worried!" screamed Hadderman. "You accuse me of murder and you're worried! Good God!"

I observed that Wiley was frowning across the room in Hadderman's direction. Beresford beamed benignly upon Sackler. Wolfe stepped forward and, as always when dealing with Sackler, spoke in the tone of a man whose patience is sorely tried.

"Look, Rex, you're worried. I'm very, very sorry. If you want an aspirin I'll be glad to offer you one. But in the meantime you've accused Hadderman of murder. Have you any evidence?"

"Evidence?" said Sackler. "A plethora."

Wolfe pretended he knew what that meant and said: "Then let's have it."

"All right," said Sackler most unhappily, "I suppose I have to."

HE SAT DOWN enveloped in an aura of misery. I still couldn't figure it. The only thing I had ever known him to worry about was money. Now, apparently, he had nailed his murderer and opposite him sat Beresford a contented client with the will and wherewithal to pay.

"The case," began Sackler, "is simple enough. The killer is Hadderman and I've enough witnesses to burn him."

"Motive?" asked Wolfe professionally.

"The usual one. Money."

"A lie," shrieked Hadderman "I'm being framed. I—"

Wolfe pushed him back in his chair and told him to shut up with the customary finesse of the police department.

"This Hadderman," said Sackler, "bets on horses. He—"

Hadderman was out of his chair again. "I never bet in my life," he yelled. "I—"

"Will you shut up in a conscious condition?" asked Wolfe pushing him in the seat again, "or—"

With an effort Hadderman shut up.

"Now," said Sackler, "you all know Wentworth the book-maker. You know, moreover, that he's a very tough character. He's a Shylock on the side and he maintains a stable of strong-armed boys to make sure that no one ever welshes on him."

"So?" said Wolfe.

"So," said Sackler, "Hadderman is gambling on the horses with Wentworth. He goes on the cuff for a few grand. Wentworth wants his money. Hadderman stalls. Wentworth threatens. And he's not a guy who threatens lightly. Hadderman becomes panicky. He knows he's down for a juicy slice of dough in Blanship's will. He knocks him off in order to get the money to pay Wentworth, and save his own skin from Wentworth's gorillas. The motive is simple."

Hadderman opened his mouth. Wolfe's hamlike hand covered it swiftly, adequately. "How," said Wolfe, "do we prove this?"

"Wentworth. I got the story from him. He'll testify willingly. I did him a favor once."

The last remark was true. Sackler had Wentworth in his pocket.

"All right," said Wolfe. "What else? How do we tie the murder on him?"

"The gun," said Sackler. "I found the gun hidden in the rock garden. Your ballistics expert has checked the fact that the bullets came from it. The Repeating Firearms Company reports that they sold that gun to Hadderman eighteen months ago."

Hadderman burbled something behind Wolfe's hand. Wolfe removed it for a moment and looked at him questioningly.

"That couldn't have been my gun. My gun was—"

"So," snapped Wolfe, "you admit buying a gun from the Repeating people, eh?"

"I bought a gun, yes, but it isn't the murder gun. It couldn't be. He's framing me. It's a dirty frame. He can't prove it."

"It may be a frame," said Wolfe slowly. "But I'm damned certain he can prove it. Sackler's not risking his reputation going into a Grand Jury room with nothing. Frame or no frame he'd odds on to get a conviction. And a conviction's what I'm principally interested in."

With his mouth, at the moment free of Wolfe's hand, Hadderman lifted his voice to high heaven. He heaped a pile of lovely lisped curses on the respective heads of Sackler and his immediate forebears. Beresford nodded approvingly in Sackler's direction.

"Very nice work," he said.

Arthur Wiley wore a dark frown. He glanced from Sackler to Hadderman, sighed and scratched his head. Sackler's face still looked as if he had just opened Pandora's box which, considering he had just earned twenty-five hundred bucks, was a collector's item.

"O.K.," said Wolfe jauntily. "If that's your case, Rex, I'll take him in. Will you see the D.A. in the morning about the witnesses?"

"Sure," said Sackler. "And perhaps it would clinch it for you if you had a confession."

"A confession?" said Wolfe.

"A confession?" howled Hadderman. "You couldn't get a confession out of me with a rubber hose. I had nothing to do with it. I'm not guilty. I won't sign anything."

"Perhaps," said Sackler, "you will."

He took a piece of paper from his pocket. It was filled with single-spaced typewriting. I glanced over his shoulder at it, but he carefully folded it over so that I couldn't read it. For the first time since he had charged Hadderman with murder he spoke to him direct.

"You've heard my case. I assure you I have my witnesses—witnesses that can very easily send you to the chair. I want you to read this paper very carefully. I'll give you five minutes to think it over. Then you can sign it or not as you please. Here."

He handed Hadderman the sheet of paper. Hadderman's eyes stared at the typewriting. Wolfe shrugged his shoulders.

"It's silly, Rex," he said. "After all, we've got a case. You can't just ask a guy to sign his life away."

"Ridiculous," said Wiley. "Why the devil should he sign a confession? Is he crazy?"

Beresford came in with his contribution. "It *does* seem unnecessary. Inspector Wolfe has the evidence. There's no point in Hadderman's signing from his angle."

SACKLER SAID NOTHING. He glowered at the scuffed tips of his shoes. The dark cloud still hovered over him. Hadderman was reading the typewritten script as intently as a virgin poring over Fanny Hill. Then suddenly he drew a deep breath and lifted his eyes from the paper. He stared thoughtfully at Sackler for a long silent moment.

He was, I assumed, searching his vocabulary for the perfect phrase to damn Sackler to hell. It's bad enough to have a murder rap pinned on you, without adding insult to injury by casually asking for a confession. Then Hadderman drew his breath in sibilantly. He uttered four words that stunned us all.

"Give me," he said slowly, "a pen."

Sackler handed him a fountain pen without looking up from the dour contemplation of his shoes. He seemed absolutely without interest in the entire matter. The fact that a killer was signing a confession of his own free will, sans duress—the fact that a guy was calmly writing his way into the death cell—left Sackler unmoved. Whatever it was he was worried about it certainly was not Hadderman.

Hadderman handed the signed paper back to Sackler who folded it up and returned it to his pocket. Wolfe glanced across the room at me, spread his palms in a gesture of bewilderment, and shrugged.

"All right," he said. "It's rather beyond me. But apparently we've cleaned up a murder case. I'll take Hadderman along. I'd thank you, Rex, but I think you'll get more satisfaction out of Beresford's check."

Sackler winced visibly. He stood up abruptly and groaned. He held his head and paced the floor. Puzzled, we regarded him.

Wolfe said to me in a loud aside: "What's wrong with him? Postal Savings cut a point off the interest rate?" Louder, he added: "Well, come along, Hadderman. I'll have the D.A. get in touch with you, Rex."

Sackler's head jerked up quickly. "Wait," he said. "Don't take Hadderman yet. I've something else to tell you—if only I could—if only I could figure—" He broke off, snapped his fingers suddenly and the cloud went from his eyes.

He spun around on his heel and approached Wiley's desk. "Those checks," he said abruptly. "Those bum checks in your drawer. You figure they're uncollectible?"

"Sure," said Wiley. "They're all dead losses. Why?"

"Will you sell them?"

Wiley blinked. Wolfe's jaw dropped and I held on to the mantelpiece for support. The idea of Sackler buying a mess of worthless checks was something my mentality couldn't quite encompass.

"Sell them?" said Wiley. "Willingly."

"Will you sell me, say, three thousand dollars worth for a hundred bucks?"

"Cash?"

"Cash," said Sackler.

Wiley opened the drawer hastily as if afraid Sackler would regain his senses before the transaction was complete. He sorted out a mess of checks and handed them to Sackler.

"Those add up to something just under twenty-nine hundred. Will that do?"

Sackler grabbed the checks. I noted that there was a febrile tremble in his hand. He examined a couple of them, said "Done," sunk them in his pocket and produced his wallet. He counted out, apparently with little reluctance, one hundred dollars. He laid the bills on Wiley's desk, turned to the rest of us and said: "You're all witnesses to this transaction."

Wolfe clapped a hand to his forehead. "I never thought I'd live to see it," he said. "Rex Sackler handing over cash for a fistful of rubber checks! Reason reels. Well, anyway I'll get Hadderman out of here."

"No," said Sackler. "Wait a little while."

He paced up and down the room like a German general. His strut had returned and the aura of misery had dropped from him. The gleam was back in his eye, and he appeared very pleased with himself. Personally I was as bewildered as a cretin trying to read Virgil on a merry-go-round.

"Wait?" said Wolfe. "Wait for what?"

"You want to know who killed Blanship, don't you?"

"You've already told me. Hadderman."

"I am a liar," said Sackler with vast amiability. "I am a dirty, low, blackhearted liar. Hadderman didn't kill Blanship."

"Then for the love of God," I said, "who did?"

"Let's all sit down and relax," said Sackler affably. "I'll tell you all about it."

4

Where There's a Will—

WOLFE, WHO ALWAYS suspected Sackler was making a fool of him, glowered. Wiley and Beresford registered complete bewilderment. I maintained a dead pan, though actually I was as much at sea as a derelict freighter. The calmest guy in the room, I noted, was our little friend Hadderman.

"Look here," said Wolfe, "are you trying to make a monkey out of me?"

Sackler refrained from the obvious reply. He drew a deep contented breath and spoke slowly.

"A few days ago Beresford came into my office and made a statement which stunned me. He said he didn't want any part of three million dollars."

"So," snapped Wolfe, "We all know that by now. We even know *why* he didn't want it."

Sackler's eyebrows moved toward the ceiling. "Do we?" he asked. "Perhaps I'm an uncultured materialist. Perhaps I haven't the beautiful gossamer soul of a professional copper, but when I hear of a guy refusing free money, I come immediately to one of two conclusions."

He paused and looked at me. I took my cue and came in as straight man.

"Which are?" I asked.

"Either he's screwy or he has an angle. Beresford is not screwy."

"But you told me you thoroughly understood Beresford's motive. You tossed beautiful thoughts about the finer things of life all over the office. You mean you were lying?"

"Of course," said Sackler. "I'll always agree with a client if there's an honest penny to be earned. Frankly, I nearly vomited while mouthing those sickening platitudes."

Wolfe chewed his cigar savagely as if he were feasting upon Sackler's liver.

"Damn you," he said, "you tell me you know who killed Blanship. You name Hadderman as the murderer. You present what purports to be a cast-iron case. Then you say he didn't do it. Now will you tell me what the hell it's all about?"

"In my own sweet and lucid way," said Sackler. "Now let's get back to the very interesting case of the guy who didn't want three million slugs."

Wiley glanced from Hadderman to Beresford. He licked his lips and expelled his breath with a little hissing sound. Sackler, completely divested of his worried air, continued.

"Being, as I remarked, a very skeptical guy when money is refused, I began to wonder why Beresford wanted the will changed. Later, when Blanship was killed I figured it out. The point is that if a guy is heir to three million bucks and the guy who's leaving it to him is knocked off, the heir is a natural suspect at once."

"You mean," asked Wolfe, "that Beresford wanted to kill Blanship but didn't do it because the will would point at him. Then later, he tried to have the will changed so he wouldn't be suspected."

"That's the general tenor of the theory."

"But it's nuts. Because if the will is changed, if Beresford intends to give the dough away there isn't any motive for the murder."

"Not to your astigmatic eye," said Sackler. "Get this: Beresford says Blanship is grateful to him for saving his life several years ago. That's the reason he's leaving him the dough. Yet the will wasn't changed until a year ago. Why? Why should Blanship suddenly become grateful after all those years?"

"What does it matter why?" I asked. "It's a fact, isn't it? The money was left to Beresford. And the will was changed a year ago. You can't go behind the facts."

"I can go behind the phoney," said Sackler, "and reach the facts. I overheard a conversation in Beresford's house between his wife and himself. Paraphrasing freely, his wife said: 'I won't throw it away. It's a part of me. My life is in it. I've put everything I have into it and I won't destroy it no matter what you say.'"

"Well, that's terrific," said Wolfe ironically. "That, of course, solves the whole case."

"Indeed it does," said Sackler blandly. "I didn't think you'd see it so quickly."

Wolfe who, along with me, saw nothing but pitch darkness, chewed his cigar, glowered and said nothing.

"All right," said Sackler, "when Blanship was killed I thought of Beresford immediately. The murder furnished the angle for his wanting to avoid that money. If the dough wasn't left to him he had no *apparent* motive for the murder. That's why he was so damned generous about the will."

"Why?" said Wolfe. "Couldn't he have fixed himself an alibi? Couldn't he have hired his killing done for him?"

"I thought of that, too," said Sackler. "The only reason I could figure that he didn't do these things is that the murder was a very personal matter. Beresford wanted to do it himself, with his own hand."

Wolfe's frown, at the moment, was of a larger per cent puzzlement than wrath. "But," he objected, "the will *wasn't* changed."

"Of course not," said Sackler, "and Beresford knew it wouldn't be. Understand this: Beresford has planned, for personal reasons, to kill Blanship for many years. At last, about a year ago, he catches up with him. Blanship is panicky. He knows Beresford intends to kill. He knows why as well. He cooks up a stunt to circumvent his own murder. He changes his will, switching his money from that Foundation to Beresford. It is his measure of protection. If Beresford murders him, he is, as heir, immediately suspected."

BERESFORD LIT A cigar. He said with cold dignity: "Do I understand that you're accusing me of murder?"

Sackler didn't reply. He looked, instead, at Wiley, and there was an odd expression in his eyes. By this time I had less idea of what was going on than Wolfe. Sackler reminded me of a juggler who has six balls in the air at the same time. I rather hoped he'd drop one.

"That doesn't make any sense," said Wolfe. "If Blanship willed the dough to Beresford in order to protect his own life, it's a cinch he'd never change the will. Moreover, it's a cinch that Beresford knew he wouldn't. So why should he offer you a fee to try to get Blanship to give the money back to the Foundation?"

"The obvious question," said Sackler sounding like Sherlock Holmes putting Dr. Watson severely in his place. "The answer is equally obvious to a functioning mind. Beresford had doubtless spent some time figuring out how to get that will changed. He couldn't do it. So he figures another mastermind. Something just as good. First he gives a document to the Foundation promising them the money if, as and when he gets it. Second, he comes to me, offers me a fee to work on Blanship to make the change."

Wolfe still didn't quite get it but by now I did.

"You mean," I said, "that the fact of the promise to the Foundation, coupled with evidence that he'd retained you, removed effectively the money motive for the killing. If Beresford was accused, he could say he had no intention of keeping the money. Besides he's even hired you to see that he never got it."

"Right. The obvious motive for the killing is then gone. Beresford really didn't want the money. He preferred to kill Blanship and beat the rap. The Foundation and myself are two first-rate defense witnesses for him."

Wolfe scratched his head. "Maybe," he admitted reluctantly. "But now you've got to have another motive."

"I have it," said Sackler. "There had to be one so I looked for it. Good fortune and intelligence found it for me."

"Will you stop bowing long enough," said Wolfe savagely, "to tell me about it."

"In Blanship's study," said Sackler, "there was an oil painting. An oil painting of a young girl. It was a good painting, a striking painting and I noted it well. Later when I met Beresford's wife, I observed a resemblance between the eyes of the girl in the portrait and Mrs. Beresford. They were quite similar. Did you see it, Joey?"

Now he mentioned it, I remembered my sensation of having seen Beresford's wife somewhere before. I nodded.

"All right," continued Sackler. "Now let's get back to those odd remarks of Mrs. Beresford to her husband. She said: 'I won't throw it away. It contains part of my life. I've put my own blood into it.' Now, Inspector, considering that Mrs. Beresford is not an artist, not a writer, what on earth could she possibly have been talking about?"

"How am I supposed to know?"

Sackler shrugged his shoulders. "That, of course, I can't answer. I, however, came to a definite conclusion. It could have been nothing but a diary. What else would contain part of her life? She was certainly engaged in no creative work. As a matter of fact, I asked Beresford about that."

Something clicked in my mind. "So," I said, "that was why you had me call on the Beresfords and ask all those dumb questions. So that you could sneak in the back way and ransack Mrs. Beresford's room for that diary?"

Sackler nodded. Beresford's face was pale. Wiley, for some obscure reason looked as smug as a Louisiana Democrat reading the election returns.

"Since," resumed Sackler, "I was looking for an obscure motive for a murder, I reasoned it was quite probably written in a diary that Beresford wanted his wife to throw away. It was.

"Beresford had a daughter, Irma. She's dead now. Died some years back. The records state she died of heart disease. I doubted that, when Mrs. Beresford, a devout woman, bemoaned the fact that her daughter had not been buried in consecrated ground. Why hadn't she? There's a reasonable and patent answer for that. Irma was a suicide."

"You're still talking Sanskrit," said Wolfe. "Guys don't go around knocking off other guys because their daughters committed suicide."

"Indeed they do," said Sackler. "Don't they, Beresford?"

Beresford didn't answer. He watched Sackler closely through narrowed eyes that looked as if the smoke from his cigar was seeping into them.

"Several years ago," went on Sackler, "Beresford's daughter met Blanship in West Virginia while Beresford was opening one of Blanship's mines. Blanship lavished promises on her and ran away with her. She expected marriage. She didn't get it because at that time Blanship was already married although not living with his wife. As I figure it, Blanship was genuinely fond of her. But the girl, brought up by an extremely religious mother, felt the shame keenly. Keenly is a soft word. As a matter of fact she killed herself."

"You mean," shouted Wolfe, now pretty sure of his case, "that all these facts are contained in that diary?"

"All of them," said Sackler. "And the diary is in my office. Beresford swore to kill Blanship. Blanship, panicky, kept out of his way, hiding behind his money and his influence, traveling all over the world with his conscience loaded and his heart filled with fear. Finally, wanting to settle down in his old age, he took that estate on the Hudson, armed his secretary and left Beresford three million dollars to prevent his own death. He failed."

BERESFORD TOOK HIS cigar from his mouth. His voice, as he spoke, was icy and defiant. "Can you prove any of this?"

Sackler looked at him for a moment, then turned his gaze upon Wiley. "Now," he said, "let's get to our friend here who passes bad checks."

"What's he got to do with it?" demanded Wolfe. "Beresford's the murderer, isn't he?"

"Wiley isn't clean, either," said Sackler.

Wolfe accomplished a gesture of wrath and exasperation. "My God," he said. "First you pin the murder on Hadderman. Then you calmly announce that Beresford did it. Don't tell me you're going to switch to Wiley now?"

"A few hours before I ever laid eyes on Beresford," said Sackler, "Wiley walked into my office. He said his name was Marsden. He gave me a bouncing check for two hundred dollars to travel to the Bronx and ascertain if his sister had been injured by her husband. Not realizing that I'm quite a hard-bitten character where cash is concerned, he figured I'd go to the Bronx long before I knew that the check hadn't cleared. He, of course, was wrong."

I glared at Wiley, remembering my own wrongs. He was the first client I'd ever had a piece of and the check burned a hole in my pocket. Particularly, since Wolfe and Sackler were agreed the check was uncollectible because Sackler hadn't fulfilled his end of the contract.

"Further," went on Sackler, "I made a fast telephone check and discovered that Wiley or Marsden had no sister at the address he gave me. That started me to thinking. Why should he want to send me on a fool's errand up to the north end of town? The only answer I arrived at was that he wanted to get Joey and me out of the office."

"Why?" said Wolfe. "Burglary? You don't keep a penny stamp in your safe, Rex. Everyone in town knows that."

"No," said Sackler. "Not burglary. Wiley wanted two things. First, to keep his identity secret from me. Hence the Marsden name and the phoney check. Second, to get me out of the office before Beresford arrived."

Beresford blinked and seemed oblivious to the fact that his cigar had gone out. I said, "Why?"

"He knew Beresford was coming to me to ask me to try to get Blanship to change his will. He knew, moreover, that Blanship wouldn't change the will under any circumstances. But he wanted Beresford to believe the will *had* been changed."

"Then why should he try to get you out of the office?" asked Wolfe.

"So that he could put a stooge there in my place. He intended to have someone impersonate me. Collect Beresford's fee and agree to try to get the will changed. The stooge would, of course, do nothing. But later in the day he would call Beresford and tell him that Blanship had agreed to switch the bequest."

I said, "Why?" again.

"Because, my little lunkhead," said Sackler, "Wiley knew that if Beresford believed the will had been switched, he would kill Blanship which is exactly what Wiley wanted. He did not, however, want the will changed at all. He simply wanted Beresford to believe that it had been."

I opened my mouth and closed it again as Sackler waved me to silence. "Don't bother asking me, Joey. I'll tell you. If the will is unchanged and Beresford kills Blanship, he burns for it. He never inherits the money. There's a law about that in this state. A killer is not permitted to benefit financially by his crime. It will then go to the next of kin, namely, viz. and to wit: Arthur Wiley,"

Something glimmered in my brain.

"And on the other hand," I said, "if the will *were* changed—if the dough actually went to the institute—Wiley, of course, would never get a whack at it."

"A Daniel come to judgment!" said Sackler and his voice was thick with irony. "What Wiley did *not* know was that Beresford realized quite well Blanship would *never* change his will under any circumstances. Beresford, as I've already told you, figured his interview with me, his arrangement with the Foundation would do as well as changing the will. Wiley didn't know that."

"But," said Wolfe, "Wiley wasn't successful in getting you out of your office in order to have someone impersonate you."

"He wasn't," agreed Sackler. "That's where Hadderman and his second mastermind comes in. Wiley was still set on convincing Beresford the will was changed to insure Blanship's murder. Hadderman knew my interview with the old man was ineffectual. He informed Wiley. Wiley put the pressure on Hadderman, promised him a cut of the estate if he'd phone me telling me that Blanship had changed his mind—that the will was to be changed. He knew I'd pass that information on to Beresford to collect my fee."

"And then," I asked, "Wiley intended to sit back while Beresford killed Blanship, wait for the cops to pick him up on the money motive and collect himself?"

"Exactly," said Sackler. "Wiley was stunned when he found out that Beresford had the money motive covered anyway. Then he played his last card. He brought pressure on Hadderman to say that he had seen Beresford enter Blanship's house that night. Probably Hadderman had. But he wasn't playing any more. He'd done his bit. Since he had knowledge that the killing was going to be committed prior to the act, he would have been an accessory. He flatly refused to play along with Wiley any further. Besides, it's quite likely that in the back of his little head he had the bright idea of blackmailing Beresford later."

IT WAS CLEARING up somewhat in my head. Yet there were a couple of things I still wanted to know. I voiced them.

"How did you know Wiley was Marsden?" I asked. "Moreover how did Wiley know that Beresford planned to visit you that day about the will?"

"That worried me for a while," said Sackler, "until I discovered that Beresford and Wiley retained the same lawyer. Undoubtedly it was the lawyer who recommended me, who tipped off Beresford, either inadvertently or deliberately, because he knew the setup and wasn't averse to holding on to Wiley's business after he collected a fortune from the old man."

"But what about Wiley being Marsden? You seemed pretty certain of that."

"It fitted in well with my theory," said Sackler, "and I had one small clue to work on. You remember that day Wiley was in the office? You remember how he looked at that hotel key with the Carlton's name on it? You remember the remark he made about the service in the place, how it had gone broke in '33? Such informed cracks indicated he was interested in hotels. When I discovered that Wiley, the next of kin, was a hotel man, I simply added it up."

Wiley's lugubrious expression looked more like the inside of a crypt than ever before. Beresford chewed savagely on the end of his cigar and glared at Sackler. Hadderman registered a sort of defiant calm.

"Wait a minute," said Beresford. "As conjecture Sackler's theory is most ingenious. It won't hold water in a courtroom."

Wolfe looked worried. He said: "Will it, Rex?"

Sackler took the folded paper from his pocket—the paper which Hadderman had signed.

"With this it will," he said. "You have a state's witness."

Beresford lifted his eyebrows and fear flashed in his eyes. "What's that?"

"It's everything I've just told you," said Sackler. "It's the complete story from alpha to the end. Hadderman signed it, attesting its truth under pressure of the frame I had on him."

Wolfe looked up from the paper. "That frame," he said thoughtfully. "Was it pure bluff, Rex?"

"What do you think?" said Sackler. "I've got Wentworth in my hip pocket. Your ballistics guy wanted a conviction. He could easily have lost the actual bullets and furnished photographs of a couple we'd fired from Hadderman's gun. Maybe I was bluffing, maybe I wasn't. Hadderman didn't call it anyway."

"It seems to me," said Wolfe, "that I drag the whole three of them in. Beresford for murder, Wiley and Hadderman at least as material witnesses."

"That," said Sackler, getting up and yawning, "is how it seems to me." He moved toward the door. "Come along, Joey."

A THOUGHT STRUCK me as we entered the taxicab and I laughed aloud. As the motor started, a second thought hit me and I frowned. Sackler glanced at me, his face smug as a Methodist sermon.

"Something on your mind, Joey?"

"Yeah," I said. "It occurs to me that since you sent Beresford so neatly to the death house, he isn't going to be particularly enthusiastic about paying your fee. As a matter of fact I'm certain he won't pay it at all. That, I am sure, is why you seemed so damned miserable for the first half-hour in Wiley's office. But why are you beaming now?"

He smiled at me. "Well, Joey," he said, with all the false modesty of a striptease artist, "after all, I don't like to work for nothing. It's true I *was* worried about that fee. But my acute brain carried me through. I shall be paid, Joey—though not by Beresford."

"Who's the sucker."

Sackler frowned. "Sucker, Joey? The word is ill chosen. It is fitting and just that I be paid by Wiley. After all, he passed off a phoney check on me."

On you, I thought? But I didn't say it. Instead, I asked: "How can you stick Wiley? You said he was clean on that two hundred dollar check?"

"He is. He isn't, however, clean on the others."

"You mean those phonies you bought from him?"

"Right."

I screwed up my brow. "It isn't possible that you've gone nuts, is it? Why did you give him good cash for that mess of rubber? Hell, you can't go around and find all the guys who signed those checks. Even if you did you'd probably never collect."

Sackler smiled sweetly like a man dreaming of something luscious and blond.

"I'll collect," he said. "From Arthur Wiley."

"From Wiley? How?"

Sackler sighed. He slipped into his role of the Ph.D. addressing his stooging moron.

"Those checks, twenty-nine hundred dollars of them, have Arthur Wiley's endorsement on their backs."

"So?"

"So, they're collectible. From Wiley. He's guaranteed them with his signature. They have the same standing civilly as notes. Wiley's got a business. He's certainly got property worth twenty-nine hundred dollars. I've a clear case. Four hundred bucks to the lawyer, twenty-five hundred for me. That's my fee, Joey."

He leaned back against the leather cushion beaming like Santa Claus. I glared at him disgruntled. If Britain has a faculty for invariably winning the last battle, Sackler always came through on the final payment. I lit a cigarette unhappily and decided my day was ruined.

Then dazzling sunshine shone through my brain.

"You mean," I asked cagily, "that the last endorser on any check is responsible for its payment."

"Indeed I do," said Sackler. "It's fragments of information like that stored away in my prodigious memory that have so often stood me in good stead."

"Me too," I said, diving for my wallet.

Sackler stared at the piece of blue paper I brandished under his aquiline nose. "Wha-what's that?" he said weakly.

"A check," I said, "a check signed by Tony Marsden made out to me, and endorsed by Rex Sackler. For two hundred slugs. Do you pay quietly or do I drag you through the courts?"

He looked at me like a gourmet at a fried worm. There was desperation and horror in his voice as he spoke.

"Joey! Do you know the meaning of the word ethics? You actually mean you'd sue me?"

I grinned happily. "Up to the Supreme Court," I told him.

He shuddered perceptibly. "All right," he said in a tone of consummate resignation. "I'll pay you." He lifted his head to heaven and cursed himself. "Why did I tell you? I'm a loud-mouthed talkative fool. I deserve no mercy."

His chin sank on his chest. He stared broodingly at the taxi-cab floor. I cut a notch in my memory. After six years I had reduced Rex Sackler to silence. I recalled that my great-grand-father on the distaff side had been a gentleman. I did not gloat.

Made in the USA
Monee, IL
18 October 2020

45326374R00225